F

At First Spite

"Olivia Dade shows once again why she's a favorite. Charming, witty, and heartfelt, *At First Spite* is not to be missed!"
—Kylie Scott, *New York Times* bestselling author

"Olivia Dade gives us another remarkable, essential addition to the modern romance canon. A slow burn that delivers in spades."
—Rosie Danan, author of *The Roommate*

"Olivia Dade never fails to make me laugh, blush, and feel like I'm being wrapped in a warm blanket. Cannot recommend enough!"
—Katee Robert, *New York Times* and *USA Today* bestselling author

"Wielding a devilishly wicked sense of wit . . . Dade deftly demonstrates her mastery of love and laughter."
—*Booklist* (starred review)

"This swoony contemporary romance is well-written and paced, but what really makes it shine are the intricate characters that Dade has brought to life. Readers will connect emotionally with Athena and Matthew, laughing at their witty banter and tearing up when they're vulnerable. Buy multiple copies of this title, because it won't stay on the shelf."
—*Library Journal* (starred review)

Ship Wrecked

"[A] smart, stellar contemporary. . . . A banger of a finish, and an absolute joy."

—*New York Times Book Review*

"[A] superbly entertaining, boldly sensual love story. . . . Combine this with wit-infused writing and some love scenes hot enough to keep any Viking couple warm during those cold winter nights, and the result is another impactful romantic triumph from Dade."

—*Booklist*

"A sexy, funny, heartwarming enemies-to-friends-to-lovers romance. . . . The story pulls readers in with well-developed, likable characters, and an unputdownable plot."

—*Library Journal* (starred review)

"We need more representation like this. . . . Filled with banter and tons of pining . . . this emotional romance will fill readers with hope for their own happily ever after."

—*The Nerd Daily*

"Dade challenges love story norms in *Ship Wrecked* with a wonderfully complex relationship that's years in the making. Sexy and delicious from page one!"

—Nisha Sharma, author of *Dating Dr. Dil*

All the Feels

"[W]eaves in sharp wit and dry humor even as it tugs at the reader's heartstrings. . . . A consistently entertaining and often insightful romance."

—*Kirkus Reviews* (starred review)

"[A] charming, sexy contemporary . . . friends-to-lovers, opposites-attract romance. The writing is excellent, with witty, banter-filled dialogue."

—*Library Journal* (starred review)

"After wowing readers with *Spoiler Alert*, Dade returns with another stunning contemporary romance that brilliantly celebrates the redemptive power of love. With a deliciously acerbic sense of humor and endless measures of grace and insight, Dade . . . skillfully develops both the sweet emotional connection and the searingly sensual attraction."

—*Booklist* (starred review)

"An absolutely witty, swoon-worthy behind-the-scenes romp! Delightful from beginning to end!"

—Julie Murphy, #1 *New York Times* bestselling author of *Dumplin'*

"Joyful, clever, and full of heart, with two irresistible characters whose connection is both gorgeously sweet and wildly hot. Mixing riotous humor and aching tenderness, *All the Feels* is all the things I love about romance. Olivia Dade has jumped to the top of my auto-buy list!"

—Rachel Lynn Solomon, national bestselling author of *The Ex Talk*

Spoiler Alert

Second Chance Romance

Also by Olivia Dade

HARLOT'S BAY SERIES
At First Spite

SPOILER ALERT SERIES
Spoiler Alert
All the Feels
Ship Wrecked

SUPERNATURAL ENTANGLEMENTS SERIES
Zomromcom

LOVE UNSCRIPTED SERIES
Desire and the Deep Blue Sea
Tiny House, Big Love

THERE'S SOMETHING ABOUT MARYSBURG SERIES
Teach Me
40-Love
Sweetest in the Gale: A Marysburg Story Collection

Second Chance Romance

A Harlot's Bay Novel

OLIVIA DADE

AVON

An Imprint of HarperCollins*Publishers*

SECOND CHANCE ROMANCE. Copyright © 2025 by Olivia Dade. All rights reserved. Printed in the United States of America. No part of this book may be used or reproduced in any manner whatsoever without written permission except in the case of brief quotations embodied in critical articles and reviews. For information, address HarperCollins Publishers, 195 Broadway, New York, NY 10007.

HarperCollins books may be purchased for educational, business, or sales promotional use. For information, please email the Special Markets Department at SPsales@harpercollins.com.

Avon, Avon & logo, and Avon Books & logo are registered trademarks of HarperCollins Publishers in the United States of America and other countries.

FIRST EDITION

Designed by Diahann Sturge-Campbell

Library of Congress Cataloging-in-Publication Data has been applied for.

ISBN 978-0-06-321597-9

$PrintCode

For everyone who's put their faith in the wrong place and their heart in the wrong hands. May you find love that rewards your trust with joy. ♥

Prologue

Twenty-two years ago

I mean, look at him." Molly tipped her head toward the other side of Principal Evers's office, where Karl Dean was mutter-shouting an obscenity-filled rant to his tired-looking father. "He's not slick enough to try cheating. He can't even whisper at a normal volume."

Her dad pressed his lips together, a telltale sign of his amusement, while her mother kicked Molly under the table.

An hour earlier, Karl, Molly, and a whiny blond kid named Ned had been handed referrals by their chemistry teacher and sent to the principal's office. Ned, for cribbing answers from Karl's test. Karl, for theoretically cooperating with said cribbing.

Her, for insubordination.

She'd seen no evidence that Karl had noticed Ned's cheating efforts, much less encouraged them. When she'd informed their teacher of that fact, then protested the unfairness of Karl's referral, she'd promptly received her own.

By all rights, the four letters spelling out Mr. Miller's genetic code shouldn't be A, C, G, and T. They should be D-I-C-K.

He didn't like anyone, but he especially detested Karl. Maybe because the teacher prized neatness, precision, and absolute obedience above all else in the classroom, and Karl's very being—his refusal to participate, his inattention to homework, and his oversized personality and physical presence—offended Mr. Miller. Or maybe he was just pissed that Karl could answer every single question correctly in class, no matter how hard the teacher tried to catch his student off guard.

Either way, when he'd noticed Ned cheating off of Karl's test, he hadn't been inclined to give Karl the benefit of the doubt. Even after Molly's ill-fated intervention.

Since Principal Evers had asked the three students for their side of the story instead of simply echoing Mr. Miller's accusations, she was hoping he'd prove more impartial. Ned had already offered his unconvincing tale of innocence and woe. Now it was Molly's turn.

The principal—impeccably suited, as always—raised a single brow at her. "Go on."

She met his eyes. "You've talked to Karl before. You know him."

He inclined his head in acknowledgment.

Karl had been sent to the office at least four separate times before today. She'd counted.

It wasn't that she truly cared about him or his disciplinary woes. She'd moved to Maryland and enrolled in Harlot's Bay High School only a week before the start of the school year, so she didn't much care about *anyone* here. She probably never would, since her mom and dad would transfer to new defense contractor jobs and another new town soon enough.

Still, she enjoyed studying him.

Because he was a sophomore too and they'd been assigned essentially the same classes, they sat next to each other anytime the teacher seated students in alphabetical order. But even if they'd freely chosen their seats, she couldn't have missed him.

His scruff sprang thick and lush from a pugnacious jaw and was the color of a penny, several shades brighter than the reddish brown of his hair. With that beard and his sturdy frame, he kind of looked like he could be everyone else's uncle, especially when he scowled. Which he did continually, at least when he wasn't glowering or glaring or frowning in a vaguely homicidal manner.

So he stood out that way. Also, she'd never met another human being so laughably bad at whispering or so attached to the word *fuck* in all its useful forms.

Molly had already spent a significant amount of time memorizing his mannerisms and intonations and the jut of his chin, then practicing them in private and learning to mimic them, as she did whenever she encountered someone especially expressive or memorable. In all her scrutiny, she hadn't yet caught Karl out in a lie. He didn't seem to be an actual dick either. Just cranky and fond of obscenities. So she'd stood up for him in class that day, even though Karl had immediately told her to sit down, keep her mouth shut, and stay out of trouble.

She hadn't listened.

"Stubborn as a mule," her mom called her. "Committed," her dad always countered.

Molly continued, "As far as I can tell, Karl has one real friend."

"Matthew Vine." The principal sounded sure of that.

"Exactly." She raised a finger in emphasis. "Why would he risk punishment for Ned, who isn't even his friend? And why would Ned choose to ally himself with someone entirely incapable of subtlety and discretion?"

As if to punctuate her statement, Karl chose that moment to fling his substantial arms in the air and mutter-shout to his father in outrage, "I didn't *do* anything! Why should I fucking *apologize?*"

Everyone else in the room swiveled to face him, and Principal Evers raised *both* brows and waited. Karl's flush reappeared, creeping over his cheeks and up to his ear tips.

"Sorry." The apology was brusque, but it sounded sincere. "I'll . . . sorry."

To draw the principal's attention away from her hapless class-mate, Molly drummed her fingernails on the wooden table. When Evers turned her way, she made her final statement.

"Mr. Miller doesn't like Karl. That's been clear from the first day," she said, and met Karl's eyes. "Which is odd, considering Dean's famous charm and friendliness toward everyone he meets."

Despite the narrow-eyed glare Karl sent her, his lips twitched faintly in the middle of that thick, coppery beard. "Doesn't like you much either now," he told her.

"From him?" She flicked her wrist in dismissal. "That's a com-pliment."

"Please stay on topic, Ms. Dearborn," Principal Evers advised, and she obliged.

"It's true that I was insubordinate and Ned cheated. Probably because he could use a tutor, and the school should make sure he gets the extra help he needs." When Principal Evers frowned and scrawled "Chem tutor => Daniels?" on his notepad, she moved him further up her list of favorite administrators. "But Karl shouldn't be disciplined, and he should be allowed to retake the quiz. He did nothing wrong except sit beside Ned."

Poor, confused Ned. Last week, he'd defined an electron as "one of those machines that reads Scantron tests."

Ned's mom turned to him, her expression softening. "Neddy, if you need a tutor, we'll get you one. Why didn't you tell me you were having a hard time in class?"

"I . . ." His voice cracked, and he stopped and took a shudder-ing breath. Then he nodded, his eyes too bright, before dropping his chin to his chest and staring at the tile floor. "I'm sorry. I won't cheat again."

Looking thoughtful, Principal Evers tapped his pen against his notepad. "And Karl had nothing to do with it?"

They watched the top of Ned's blond head shake a silent no.

In the end, the principal apologized to Karl for the false accusation of cheating, thanked Molly for telling the truth under difficult circumstances, and shuffled both families out of the conference room so he could meet privately with Ned and his mom before the final bell rang.

Outside Principal Evers's office, Karl scratched at his beard and considered her.

"Shouldn't've done that," he finally said. "But thank you."

"No biggie." She shrugged. "Merely performing my civic duty."

He rolled his eyes. "Nerd."

"You know it," she said cheerfully.

After that incident, she and Karl became friends of a sort. She sat with him and Matthew in the cafeteria. In the summer, when she began working at Ice Queen—the local ice cream parlor—on the weekends, he often walked to the store, bought a kiddie cone, and spent an hour or two reading his latest sci-fi paperback from the library at a table near the cash register, although he didn't say much.

That same summer, her parents decided they'd remain in Maryland until she graduated, which was fine by her. There would be no new group dynamics to decipher. No unfamiliar warrens of hallways to navigate. No more goodbyes, at least for the next two years. With that knowledge, she allowed a few fragile roots to grow and anchor her in place at Harlot's Bay High.

Karl was the hardiest of those roots. Strange but true.

Junior year was more of the same, although they had fewer classes together. College wasn't in the cards for him. The Deans were struggling financially, and as soon as he graduated, he intended to contribute a full-time paycheck to the family coffers. So he hadn't bothered with—as he inimitably put it—"AP Whatever the Fuck or Honors Blah Blah Blah." Especially since passing those classes without doing homework would be next to impossible. But they still saw each other at lunch every day and at the ice cream parlor on Sundays.

They didn't share secrets. Didn't call each other. Didn't talk about their feelings. But he was still the closest friend she'd had in years. If she sometimes wanted more than that, no big deal. At umpteen different schools, she'd watched relationships crash and burn over and over again. She wouldn't risk whatever they had in pursuit of something that would only end in disaster. And after so many years of studying everyone from a detached distance, she wasn't even entirely certain how to pop the invisible bubble that surrounded her. Only her dad and her grandparents seemed to step through the barrier without any trouble.

So nothing really changed between her and Karl until senior year, when he started dating.

Someone else. Not Molly.

* * *

Twenty years ago

At first, senior year fucking *ruled*.

Because of all his yard work clients and his part-time job washing dishes at the bakery, Karl was able to buy his Chevy Nova and the parts it needed to run. And after three summers of watching him mow her parents' lawn, Becky Waller unexpectedly asked him out. Which was a goddamn miracle, because she was a thousand miles out of his league.

He might be better at tests, but she was better at *life*. Hardworking. Easygoing. Cute as hell. Soft and warm against him when he pulled her close. Like the quilt on his bed, the one his mom pieced together before he was born.

The only real problem? She didn't much like Dearborn. Hadn't from the start, and he had no clue why not. The first time he'd suggested going to Ice Queen and visiting Dearborn there, even an oblivious asshole like him could see Becky's blatant discomfort.

"How did you and Molly become friends anyway?" she'd asked, her hand stiff in his.

He shrugged. "Year before last, Mr. Miller was a dick. Accused me of cheating. She defended me and got in trouble."

"Oh." Becky's stare burned into the side of his face, until curls of smoke should've been rising from his damn beard. "That was nice of her."

Dearborn wasn't nice. But she *was* kind. He couldn't explain the difference to himself, and he definitely wasn't going to try to explain it to his girlfriend. Who was, in fact, *nice*.

He liked that about her. Right?

In the end, they went to the movies instead of Ice Queen. And after a few weeks of dating, he rarely saw Dearborn anymore.

They'd been assigned different lunchtimes. No classes together either. Only homeroom. Her rusty Mercury Sable appeared in the school lot in September, so shared rides were out. And she didn't seem to actively avoid him, but somehow, even in homeroom, she was never close to him and always busy.

Not because she was dating too. If his girlfriend was out of his league, Dearborn didn't even *have* a league. She wasn't playing. Didn't want to play. Was friendly but distant with everyone. If Becky was a quilt, Dearborn was the moon, and you didn't cuddle with the fucking moon.

Besides, she was too smart for everyone in their school, including him. If he'd have asked, she'd have said no, and he wouldn't have blamed her. But her rejection would have *obliterated* him. Not worth the risk.

He cared way too damn much about Molly Dearborn. Which meant her sudden aloofness blew. Then Karl's mom got laid off from one of her jobs a couple weeks after Thanksgiving. He had to pick up more hours at the bakery, stopped getting enough sleep, and felt more zombie than human most days. Becky didn't complain often about how little time they had together, but he wasn't stupid. Her unhappiness wasn't exactly subtle.

But talking about things like that? Didn't come easy to him.

His parents had been working their asses off ever since he could remember. Sure, Mom and Dad loved him, but they were fucking *exhausted*. Didn't need to hear about his *emotions* or some stupid shit that didn't matter in their fleeting, errand-packed time off. And dealing with his younger siblings' problems was his damn job. Wasn't theirs to deal with his crap.

No one outside his family wanted to hear about some grumpy bastard's feelings either. He'd found that out real damn young, once a few of his dickwad classmates—the Whitley brothers, mostly—made fun of the husky kid who teared up and whined whenever they chose him last for kickball or square dancing or whatever.

It'd only taken a few shitty gym classes and recesses for him to learn. He might've been big and cranky from birth, but he wasn't slow. He'd stopped playing kickball, or any team sport. Toughened the hell up. Concentrated on helping his family instead of worrying about what random assholes thought. Instead of showing them he was worried, anyway.

So, yeah. He didn't know how to deal with emotions. Not his own. Not other people's.

Exhibit fucking A: When he told Becky he loved her, she didn't say it back. He had no fucking clue why not, and her silence stung like hell, but he never said word one about it. Was too goddamn cowardly to ask for an explanation or even tell her she'd hurt him.

And now, he had no idea how to handle her pissiness about his schedule either. Didn't know what to say, or how to raise the subject himself. So he didn't do or say anything. Let her handle things however she wanted.

She broke up with him, then came back a week later. Broke up with him a second time. Came back two months later. On-again, off-again, ad fucking nauseam, all senior year.

In March, during one of those awful off-again periods, his homeroom teacher assigned the senior project to everyone. At first, he didn't pay much attention. Too busy trying to look at Molly without getting caught.

She was sitting across the room, her head bent over the tattered paperback in her hands.

Shit, he missed her. Had no idea why. Not like they'd been that close, right?

"—pairings for the project," Mrs. Beanly was saying. "Wade Adams and Adrienne Bronnell. Karl Dean and Molly Dearborn. Serena Frank and—"

Wait. Had the two of them been assigned together for their senior project?

He whispered to his neighbor, asking for clarification, and Ellen winced and rubbed at her ear before confirming that yes, he and Molly would be working as a team.

Alphabetization for the damn win!

He sat back in his too-small goddamn chair. Gloried in the first taste of victory he'd experienced in months. And a *group project* was giving him that taste. Oh, the fucking irony.

Apparently, the senior project was due right before prom in late May. Before then, they'd need to volunteer somewhere for a set number of hours and create a written and videotaped presentation about their experiences. Which was going to be a huge pain in the ass, and he probably wouldn't sleep much for the next two months, but whatever. He was *psyched*.

He didn't give a crap what he and Molly did for their project, as long as they did it together.

She was friendly but distant when they talked about the assignment. Exactly like she was with everyone else, but had never really been with him. It fucking *stung*. But maybe this stupid project, this mandated time spent together, could change things. Bring them back to what they'd once been.

At Molly's suggestion, they wound up volunteering at Historic Harlot's Bay, and the next month and a half was *painful*. Borrowing a camcorder from Matthew's family for the express purpose of getting recorded while he hit a hoop with a stick in fucking *breeches* almost killed him. Using *other* sticks to stir linen shirts and shifts in a boiling-hot copper kettle over a goddamn fire sucked ass too. Every hour he spent with Dearborn at Historic Harlot's Bay either subtracted from his paycheck or added to his growing sleep deficit.

But somehow, Dearborn's company made everything fine. The

itchy, starched stiffness of his linen shirts. The mocking comments from the junior interpreters as they whipped his butt at Mancala time after fucking time. The distinct *thunks* as Dearborn's aggravatingly accurate pitches smacked his own lawn bowls farther away from the stupid jack.

As the weeks went by, she relaxed in his company. Talked to him. Even touched him.

Every time he complained about some petty shit, she patted his arm in the most patronizing possible way and told him sweetly, "These cares are but fleeting moments of discomfort. Pray do not get your breeches in a bunch, good sir." Which was obnoxious, but also pretty damn funny.

"Why not panties?" he asked her one day as they walked back to their cars.

She shot him a puzzled look. "What?"

"Why not say, 'Pray do not get your panties in a bunch, good sir?'"

After a moment of thought, she raised her forefinger. "Well, first of all, I doubt the phrase *panties in a bunch* dates back to the eighteenth century, although I could check the etymology."

"Jesus Christ." Such incredible nerdiness. She was a marvel.

Two fingers. "Second of all, I don't want the junior interpreters repeating that phrase."

"I'm a bad fucking influence," he agreed.

Three fingers, which she wiggled in emphasis. "And third of all, colonial people didn't wear panties or any real undergarments. My shift would be my underwear, and your shirt would be yours. Don't you remember our training session?"

He stopped abruptly on the path through the Mayor's Mansion gardens. "Do you mean those colonial motherfuckers were just free-balling it? All the goddamn time?"

At that, her eyes flicked down to the fall of his breeches for a long, breath-choking moment. When she looked up again, those rosy cheeks of hers had turned a deeper shade of pink.

She was looking at his crotch and blushing.

Cool-as-a-damn-cucumber Molly fucking Dearborn was *blushing*. Over *him*.

So yeah. Everything was great. Those giggling preteens in their floppy-ass bonnets could make fun of him all they liked. He wasn't the one who'd be demonstrating how a fucking box iron worked in the broiling sun all summer.

Then, late one sunny Saturday afternoon, he panicked. Realized he was running out of guaranteed time with Molly. It was their last day of volunteering. The project was due next Friday, they were graduating soon, and Dearborn was going to college in goddamn Cali. If he wanted to make sure their friendship didn't die again, he needed to figure out how.

And if he wanted more than friendship from her—and he did, always had—it was time to man up. Now or fucking never. Whether he was good at relationship shit or not.

He made his move at the end of their final shift.

On their way to the Mayor's Mansion parking lot, they passed through a long, leafy arbor, where beech trees on either side had been trained to arch and meet overhead. The setting was kinda romantic, although Karl understood fuck-all about those sorts of things.

When he snuck a glance over at her, he pictured Molly at prom. With him.

He didn't give a shit what she wore. If she showed up in the petticoat, buckled shoes, and big straw hat she was wearing right now, fine. Full set of armor? Great. One of her usual flannels and ripped jeans? He'd be fucking thrilled.

Men's-style clothing looked hot on her. Always had.

He should ask her. He *would* ask her.

When he abruptly stopped walking, Dearborn—who'd been rummaging through the basket hanging from her forearm—stumbled over the oyster shells carpeting the garden paths. She didn't fall, but the keys she'd just located went flying. They both squatted down and bent forward to pick her keys up at the same moment, and their foreheads thunked painfully.

Fucking hell. This was a disaster.

Muttering to himself, he grabbed the stupid keys and chucked them in her basket, then tossed her basket aside entirely. It landed with a thump on the oyster-shell path, and Dearborn side-eyed him hard.

"What?" he demanded, frowning.

"I brought an eighteenth-century tea caddy to show the junior interpreters today. A family heirloom. It's in my basket, which you just flung on the ground like an old bag of clothes on its way to the dump."

Mother*fucker*.

"Uh . . ." Swallowing hurt. "Really?"

"Nope," she said cheerfully, and grinned at him. "But it could've been true. Stop tossing around vessels full of unknown items, Dean. This is a public service announcement on behalf of your future companions." Her widespread hand swept an arc high in the air. "The more you know."

He stared at her incredulously as she stood again.

Unlike Becky, she was not nice. Not nice at all. In fact, Molly Dearborn was kind of a bitch. So why was he fighting a grin?

"You're a piece of work, Dearborn." He shook his head. "Next time I take you home, I'm stuffing you in the trunk."

Her eyes rolled heavenward. "Please be realistic, Dean. Basic geometry will inform you that someone of my size won't fit in your tiny car's even tinier trunk."

A bitch *and* a pedant. She was a goddamn wonder.

"I'll make you fucking fit," he told her. "Watch me."

Her lips twitched, but she clicked her tongue in disapproval. "Threats of violence are beneath you, Dean."

After getting to his feet too, he leaned in and ran his fingertips lightly over the pink spot near the part of her hair, where their foreheads had collided. No bump yet. He'd have to check again later.

Her breath hitched at his touch, and as soon as he confirmed the lack of swelling, he met her stare directly. From only two inches away.

That pale blue wasn't icy. It was the center of a flame. The hottest part.

Without conscious thought, he leaned in. A quarter-inch. More.

She didn't move away. Her soft lips parted, and he let his fingers slide down over her temple, along her silky hairline, until he could cup her warm cheek. He waited a beat more, making sure this was okay with her, and—

The entire pack of junior interpreters skipped into the arbor, giggling and shrieking, before coming to an abrupt halt.

He was going to fucking drop-kick those kids, and no court in this fucking land would convict him.

The moment was gone. He turned to Molly, about to suggest they find a private spot near the canal, but she was already greeting the girls. Next thing he knew, they were walking as a group to the parking lot.

Didn't matter. He'd call and ask her to prom that night.

But before he could, Becky called *him*. Convinced him things would be different. And yeah, he still wanted to date Molly, but she'd probably say no anyway. Girl like that—strong, confident, take-no-shit—might not want to date anyone. If she did, she'd choose someone who didn't fucking *headbutt* her while trying to ask her out. Definitely someone who could express himself better than he did.

He couldn't even figure out how to make his first-ever girlfriend love him, and she was already way the hell out of his natural reach, so . . .

He and Becky were back on.

And once the senior project was turned in, Molly disappeared on him again. They didn't talk, hardly saw each other. Until the week after prom, when she tugged him aside in homeroom to tell him it was her last day at Harlot's Bay High. She was leaving. For good. Moving to California with her mom months before she'd planned for reasons she didn't explain.

"There's not much schoolwork left. I'll do it in California and mail it here." Those pale blue eyes were red-rimmed but dry. Oddly blank too. "And I can graduate without walking across the stage. They'll send the diploma to me."

He couldn't say a word. Not without shouting or—no. He wouldn't cry. *Refused* to fucking cry. So he just glared at her as she tore off a piece of lined paper and wrote her family email address on it.

"Write if you want," she said, and didn't bother waiting for a response.

She didn't say goodbye. Didn't hug him. Didn't do anything but press the slip of paper into his palm and walk away.

The right words didn't filter into his stupid damn brain until much, much too late.

What the hell happened? Are you okay? Will you miss Harlot's Bay? Will you miss me?

I'll miss you. Doesn't matter if we haven't talked in fucking weeks.

He didn't have the fucking nerve to call and say that before she left, though. Didn't even have the guts to write it in one of the brief emails he started sending her. Instead, whenever he saw the for-sale sign in front of her home, he got out of the car and kicked it. Then put it back upright again, because he wasn't a total asshole.

Becky left for Johns Hopkins in late August. Broke up with him the first time she came back home for a visit. Told him she was going somewhere, literally and figuratively, and he wasn't. She needed a different kind of boyfriend. Someone *more* than him.

He got it. Fucking gutted him, but he definitely got it.

In his occasional emails to Molly, he didn't tell her. Too humiliated. Too unsure whether the breakup would stick that go-round.

It did, though. He didn't hear from Becky after that. Meant he had a clean shot at things with Dearborn again.

So he began to email more often. Began to hint at his interest in a closer relationship and subtly feel out whether she might be interested too. Because maybe she lived across the country now, but who knew what'd happen after she graduated from UCLA?

He still didn't say he'd been dumped. No need to sound pathetic. Once he knew she wanted him too, he'd tell her what happened.

Without warning, she stopped writing him back. Sent one last, terse message—"This doesn't feel right. I'm sorry"—and that was it. His messages started bouncing back to him.

He was a dumbass, but not oblivious. He knew what he'd done

wrong.

He should've told her he was single. Might've made a difference. Or maybe she just wasn't interested in him that way. He'd never fucking know now, would he?

She'd probably gotten a new email address at the university. He didn't have it. No one else in Harlot's Bay did either. He had no way to contact her. Even if he did, he couldn't override what she'd told and shown him she wanted—and what she wanted wasn't his sorry ass.

It was distance *from* his sorry ass.

Somehow, he'd managed to lose her without ever really *having* her.

His regret—his longing for the one person who'd seemed to understand him from the very beginning, without his even needing to try—never fully disappeared over the years. He thought of Molly every time one of the junior interpreters came by the bakery for brownies. He thought of her whenever a flame burned hot enough to turn that same gorgeous shade of pale blue. To his shame, he sometimes thought of her while he was in bed with other women, although he tried like hell not to.

Just like with Becky, none of those women ever said they loved him. Including the girlfriends he'd dated for months. His best guesses as to why? His long hours at the bakery didn't give him enough time to deepen casual relationships. He wasn't especially lovable as a boyfriend. And maybe, on some level, his partners sensed that a small corner of his heart wasn't theirs, even during sex. Couldn't be, because he'd given it away long ago to a girl who'd left him far, far behind.

He told himself that was why he'd stopped declaring his own love. Because he didn't have a whole heart to offer any girlfriend.

Not because he was scared of the silence that might follow his declaration.

After all, he should be used to silence—and not just from Becky. After Molly's last email, he hadn't heard from her. Hadn't seen her. Didn't expect to do either, ever again.

But one random afternoon, eighteen years after graduation, he left the bakery as a customer was eating a sandwich and listening to an audiobook in her car with her windows open. Some story about a guy who could turn into a guppy, which was beyond bizarre. Especially since the fishy asshole was apparently ripped and had weird fin things on his dick.

He shook his head. Kept walking.

Then the narrator's voice registered, and he stopped dead in his tracks.

Velvety. Calm yet expressive. Subtly wry.

He knew that fucking voice. Had loved that fucking voice.

His knock on the hood startled the hell out of his customer, who was clearly caught up in the story, and he felt bad about that. Not bad enough to mind his own business, though.

"What are you listening to?" He'd meant for that to sound like a casual question, not a demand, but . . . whatever.

The woman flushed. "I'm sorry. I can roll up my—"

"It's fine. Keep 'em down. I don't give a shit." He thrust his finger toward the dashboard, where he assumed her audio controls were located. "I just want to know who that is."

"The author?" The customer's thin brows drew together. "Sadie Brazen."

He gathered every crumb of his patience. After eighteen goddamn years, there was barely enough left for a starving ant. "Not the author. The narrator."

"Oh. I don't know. Let me . . ." She fumbled for her phone and tapped at the screen a few times. "Her name is Molly Cressley."

Molly. It was her. Had to be.

The *Cressley* meant she was probably married, but that didn't matter much, did it? She was long gone from his life. He would never see her again.

But now he could *hear* her again. Finally.

"Thanks," he rumbled, slapped the hood in farewell, and went back into his bakery. Back into his office. Back onto his computer. Where he promptly bought and downloaded *Desire, Unfiltered* by Sadie Brazen, as narrated by Molly Cressley.

He listened to the entire bizarro story in one sitting. Told himself that was enough.

The next day, he listened to it again. Called himself a fucking idiot the entire time.

The day after that, he proceeded to obliterate his monthly budget by buying every goddamn audiobook Molly Cressley had ever narrated.

From what he could tell, they were mostly books about women fucking weird-ass creatures. Like guppy-men. Or shadow-guys. Or . . . the Loch Ness Monster?

Didn't matter. He'd take what he could get.

Before the bakery opened in the mornings, he began listening to the stories she narrated as he egg-washed, baked off, and iced the pastries he'd shaped and refrigerated before leaving work the previous day. As he baked off breads, rolls, scones, and muffins too. As he fed his sourdough starter. As he fried umpteen million doughnuts.

He used earbuds at first, but then he burned all his English muffin bread one morning when he didn't hear the damn timer. Which was when he got permission from Bez, Charlotte, and everyone else who worked the early shift to play the audiobooks out loud.

And for the next two years, her voice was all he had of her.

Then, twenty years after graduation, Molly returned to Harlot's Bay.

Unfortunately, she came for his fucking *funeral*.

1

"Fucking flu," Karl muttered as he carved up the turkey breast he'd roasted for that day's sandwiches. "What kind of shitty-ass flu spreads in early *September*?"

His doctor had done the test to confirm it. Influenza goddamn A.

Even with the antiviral meds, it'd kicked his butt for an entire week, and he'd been forced to close Grounds and Grains for the first time ever during normal business hours. He'd still paid his staff but brought in zero income, so it was a major hit to his bottom line. And he might be feeling way better now, but he had a crap ton of catching up to do.

This Friday was going to blow.

Bez—who was currently out front, slinging coffees and lattes and patiently telling customers to hold their goddamn horses until lunchtime for food, only with less swearing—had been nagging him to get an assistant baker for years, and she was right. He could afford one, and an assistant baker would've filled in for him. Would allow him to take more time off even when he was feeling fine. But that would mean the presence of someone else in the back room with him for hours at a time, so nope.

In general, owning his own business was a hassle. But it did mean he could be a misanthropic asshole in blessed fucking solitude, and that made up for a lot.

The cowbell attached to the entrance door jingled again, and the identity of the new arrival became clear immediately.

"Where is everyone? Why aren't there pastries?" a high, quavering voice demanded to know. "Why was the shop closed all week?"

Sylvia Plude. Eighty if she was a damn day, her ebony-skinned face wrinkled like crumpled parchment. Still the only reporter for their town's tiny-ass weekly newspaper, the *Harlot's Herald*. Relentless in search of a good story. And now a true crime fan, due to Athena—Matthew's pain-in-the-ass wife; also Karl's former employee and current friend—who'd recommended the grisly books to Sylvia. Which meant Sylvia had become *even more* suspicious of any oddities she noticed and *even more* of a snoop. Which was saying something.

With a glance, he checked the swinging door to the front. Cracked open two inches at most. No way to see him back there. No risk of her cornering and haranguing him instead of his employee.

Bet Bez was wishing she hadn't sent Charlotte off on a break only five minutes ago. By the time Charlotte returned from her morning walk, Sylvia would've been grilling Bez for almost a half hour. And since the week's story deadline was closing in, the older woman wouldn't relent until she had *something* to report about for tomorrow's paper.

A better man would rescue his morning clerk. A real shame for Bez that Karl was her boss instead. Silently whistling, he wrapped up the last sandwich in waxed paper, labeled it with a sell-by date and stored it alongside the others in the refrigerator, put his cutting board in the sink, removed his gloves, and washed his hands as he listened to Sylvia interrogating his employee at top volume—woman needed a hearing aid, not that she'd ever admit it—over the sounds of soft jazz.

"—sick, but he's feeling better now," Bez was explaining. "We'll be back to normal hours next week. And in just an hour or so, we'll have some of our usual lunchtime—"

"If he was feeling better, he'd be here," Sylvia declared. "And if he were here, there would be pastries. And muffins. And some of those little cookies with autumn leaves piped on them, which I'd intended to bring to bingo on Sunday, but I can't, because he's not here, which means *he's not better.*"

"But he is, Sylvia. In fact, right now—"

Karl paused. She'd better fucking *not.*

As if she'd sensed his glare through the wall, Bez cut herself off. Her sigh was audible. "Would you like your usual?"

Every week, right before Sylvia's deadline, she ordered—

"A large hazelnut latte." The sound of drumming fingers against glass. "Soy milk this time, Bez. My youngest grandson's riding my ass about my cholesterol again."

And that was why he put up with Sylvia's nosiness, even on the rare occasions when she caught him out in the open. There was no pretense to the elderly woman. No surface politeness masking something entirely different. Her bluntness was kinda refreshing.

The familiar sounds of a latte-to-be drifted to his ears, and he began working on the dough for Sylvia's leaf cookies, because he was a sap.

Another jangle of the cowbell. "Hey, Bez! Hi, Sylvia!"

Athena. Fuck. His. Life.

He liked her, yeah, but the woman was chatty as hell, irritatingly interesting, and a major distraction during her frequent

visits. Between her and Sylvia, he wasn't leaving this kitchen for
anything. Not even if it started raining dollar bills outside. He had
work to do, goddammit.

Thank Christ the rest of his equally chatty, way-too-big family was driving across the continent and visiting fifteen billion national parks. Dealing with their nightly calls was a damn hassle,
but at least they hadn't been able to descend on him for nursing
purposes.

They'd invited him on the trip, obviously. He'd told them he
couldn't spare that much time away from the bakery. Wasn't re-
tired, like his parents. Couldn't work remotely, like his siblings.
The honest truth. But his family also couldn't have paid him
enough to ride in their cramped fucking rental RV for two entire
goddamn months, much less wear the custom-designed "Dean
Clan Trip of a Lifetime!" tee with the huge smiley face on it.

His youngest sister, Emily, swore they hadn't put it there to
taunt him, but he knew better. His family was a bunch of smart-
asses, through and through.

Shaking his head, he bent back over the cookie dough.

After a couple minutes of conversation with his clerk about random shit, Athena got to the point. "What's going on, Bez? The
bakery's been closed for days, and Karl hasn't answered my texts
all week. And yeah, Special K is a crusty, homicidal hermit, so his
unresponsiveness isn't exactly an unprecedented occurrence, but
the shop being closed *is*. Is he okay?"

Torn between irritation and reluctant warmth, Karl shook his
head.

He hated that nickname. Had made the mistake of telling her so.
Now he couldn't escape it. Even the other women in that bizarro
Nasty Wenches book club had started calling him Special K, de-

spite his most fulminating glares in response.

Still, he should've checked his texts. It was sweet of her to check on him, and she might be a major pain in his ass, but she was a good friend too and a good partner for Matthew. Karl hadn't heard that solemn bastard laugh so much in . . . ever. Never seen him so loose and happy.

"Well, if you really want to know . . ." Bez's voice turned low and conspiratorial, and Karl turned down the music a notch to hear more clearly. If she gave away his presence in the back room— "Karl's archenemy finally caught up with him, Athena."

Fine. She could spout all the bullshit she wanted, as long as she let him do his job undisturbed. Not like Athena would believe her anyway. That too-serious tone was a dead giveaway that Bez was joking.

Athena fake-gasped. "Was he camping?"

As if he'd ever go *camping*. A bear might shit in the woods, but Karl? Nope.

"You know it," Bez confirmed.

"So he was attacked in the desolate, unsanitary wilderness before he had a chance to strike his fatal blow against his nemesis?"

Silence. Karl imagined his clerk nodding in fake solemnity, her teal-tipped ponytail bouncing.

"Heavens to Betsy. Such tragedy," Athena said after a few moments, her words hushed and heavy with exaggerated horror. "Are you certain there's no way to save him?"

"It's too late." Bez heaved a dramatic sigh. "I hate to tell you this, but . . . he's already part of this afternoon's featured daily muffin. The lumps aren't just dried cherries this time. They're dried cherries *and* Karl."

Athena paused. "Are you saying today's muffin flavor is Special

K . . . with red berries?"

At that, the two women began snickering. Glass clicked against the marble counter out front.

"Hey, Sylvia, your—" The bell jangled, and Bez cut herself off. "Where is that woman going without her latte?"

Athena sounded unconcerned. "Maybe she saw someone she wanted to talk to. I'm sure she'll be back. Anyway, in all seriousness, Bez, is Karl all right?"

"He's been sick with the flu, but he's doing better. He's even been working in the back this morning, although he, uh . . ." Bez thought for a moment. "He must have stepped out just before you arrived."

"Sure he did." Athena raised her voice to a shout. "I know you're back there, Special K! If you don't want to talk to me, fine, but answer Matthew's texts! He's worried about you! And fair warning: Once you're back to a hundred percent, there'll be no escaping me and my Endless Chatter of Doom!"

His lips twitched.

"Hag," he called in the direction of the door.

"Curmudgeon!"

Another jangle of the bell and she was gone too, leaving him to his thoughts. Thank Christ. As he cranked on the industrial stand mixer to cream the butter and sugar, he considered the audiobook he'd begun playing before the shop opened that day.

A new release by Sadie Brazen: *My Kangaroo, My Kidnapper: A Dark Shifter Romance*. Which was an inexplicable title, since the main woman in the story, Riley, had gotten kidnapped in the sunshine in fucking *Australia*, so how dark could it be?

Molly had been in rare form, though, before he'd reluctantly switched over to jazz that morning. Breathless and convincingly terrified—with just the *slightest* hint of horny—as the kickboxer-kangaroo asshole shoved Riley in his pouch and hopped off.

Molly's Australian accent was spot-on too. No surprise there. But was that marsupial motherfucker meant to be the hero? Because . . . no. Hell, no. Didn't matter what special features the prick's prick had. Dude was into *abduction*.

That Sadie Brazen had a wild goddamn imagination.

Must be why people read so many novels, he guessed. Because real life was so predictable. Few kangaroo kidnappings. Fewer guppy-men with fins on their dicks.

Besides a September flu outbreak, nothing unexpected ever happened in Harlot's Bay. Especially not to a cranky, solitary bastard like him. And halle-fucking-lujah for that, right?

* * *

Two days later, sitting at the kitchen table of her small LA bungalow, Molly pushed the power button on her laptop and waited for the endless updates to finish loading.

Her shoulders hurt, and she rolled them. Rotated her stiff neck. Drank her tea with honey, doing her best to stay present in the moment. Be mindful. Get hygge with it.

Any minute now, the relaxation would begin.

Any . . . minute . . . now.

She'd slept an hour longer than usual, as befitted the first morning of a four-week vacation. Since workers would be arriving tomorrow to address the roof and plumbing issues—guided by a casual friend of hers who happened to be a contractor—best to take advantage of the last peaceful day she'd have for a while.

Those upcoming home renos were, of course, the entire reason she was taking such a lengthy vacation in the first place. An audiobook narrator needed *quiet* above all else, and even the best in-home recording studio couldn't entirely eliminate the sounds of hammering and power tools buzzing and whirring and squealing through metal and wood.

She'd put off the repairs too long. They'd become urgent and overwhelming and freaking expensive, and she wanted to get them done in one fell swoop so she could ignore the entire issue of renovations again for another decade or two afterward.

Something else would probably go wrong the week after the workers left, though. Houses built an entire century ago needed continual upkeep to stay functional. Too bad she loved hers so much. The location at the foot of the Hollywood Hills—well, more like the shin; getting to her home required surmounting a brief but steep incline—was convenient and gorgeous, and even the constant traffic wasn't particularly bothersome for someone whose commute was approximately twelve feet from her bedroom.

Moving would require disassembling and rebuilding her studio elsewhere. And wherever she went wouldn't contain the memories this home did. Her beloved grandparents had lived here for over fifty years, her one geographical constant in a rootless life. They hadn't left until a decade ago, when they'd sold the home to her for far below market value and moved to a much cheaper, equally sunny town in Arizona.

Blasting her from this place would require . . .

She didn't know what would suffice. Nothing had done the trick so far. Not the upkeep costs. Not the bitter memories of her failed marriage contained within these walls. Not even her doctor's warning that she needed to eliminate sources of tension however she could, because the insomnia was getting worse, her blood pressure kept creeping up, and her headaches had turned increasingly vicious.

"Think about moving somewhere with less upkeep," Dr. Janus had urged at Molly's last checkup. "And if you won't do that, at least go outside more. Have a picnic in Griffith Park. Walk along Venice Beach. Sit in your backyard and try to whistle with a blade of grass. Whatever it takes to lower your stress level."

Only mountain goats would find her backyard a comfortable seating location. Besides— "Are you telling me to literally touch grass?"

"I suppose I am." Looking pleased with herself, the doctor straightened her shoulders. "It's all very Gen Z of me. My daughter would be proud."

"No, she wouldn't." Molly could safely say that, having met the preteen at Vons when the young woman was reluctantly accompanying her mother on a grocery run.

"No, she wouldn't," Dr. Janus agreed. "But I'll tell her anyway. I enjoy making her roll her eyes and call me *cringe*."

"That's fair," Molly conceded, and the appointment had ended without an actual, definite plans for stress reduction. Which hadn't dismayed her in the least.

As it turned out, the thought of planning for stress reduction caused stress too. Irony!

Hopefully she wouldn't even need a plan, since a heady, vacation-induced rush of relaxation should be arriving and flushing away all the cortisol in her system. Any minute now.

Another sip of tea didn't do it, sadly. Neither did a few more rotations of her neck.

Conceding defeat, she glanced down at her laptop. There. Finally. The updates were complete, and she could check her email.

There shouldn't be any urgent messages, given her empty September calendar. But maybe a publisher would write to book one of her two remaining free slots in December, or—

Hmmm.

She frowned, eyeing a message sent earlier that morning from Lise Utendorf. Aka Sadie Brazen, a good friend and one of Molly's most prolific authors.

The email's subject: *Bad news from Harlot's Bay.*

After leaving Maryland two decades ago, Molly hadn't bothered writing or calling anyone there. With one exception. But her closest friendship in Harlot's Bay had disintegrated before her first week at UCLA, and then she was too busy with school and work to keep up with casual acquaintances.

Even after she'd begun narrating Lise's books, she hadn't known the identity of the woman behind Sadie Brazen. Until one day when they'd hopped on a Zoom call to discuss a particularly challenging scene and . . . there she was. Lise Utendorf. The shy, sweet girl Molly had worked with on the literary magazine back at Harlot's Bay High.

Small world. Big coincidence.

Lise had become a good friend, but they hadn't talked much about their shared past, probably because Molly didn't welcome reminders of that period of her life. Harlot's Bay had been the one place she'd semi-attempted to make a real home, find a real community, as a kid. And that home had been ripped from her under unpleasant circumstances, even before her fraught friendship with Karl had cracked irretrievably. Remembering all of that didn't precisely spark joy.

So Molly avoided discussing Harlot's Bay, and Lise had respected that unspoken boundary. If she now felt obligated to share news from there, whatever happened must've been big—and not simply bad. *Terrible.*

With trepidation tightening her neck muscles once more, she opened the message.

Molly, I wasn't sure whether to write you about this. As far as I know, you're not in contact with anyone from Harlot's Bay but me, so maybe you won't care. But I thought you should hear it from me, just in case. If only because you two were close for a while.

Karl Dean was murdered. His obituary ran in yesterday's Harlot's Herald.

Molly gasped in horror and curled in on herself, covering her mouth with one shaking hand. Her eyes instantly grew wet, and the words blurred in front of her.

The obit said he was killed by a mysterious enemy while camping—

Even through her tears and shock, that struck her as odd. Nature had inconvenienced and infuriated Karl, to the point where she'd once seen him address an offending tulip as "you purple-petaled motherfucker." His hatred of Mother Nature was the entire reason he'd enjoyed mowing. To him, it was a sort of ritual homicide.

Back then, infeasible threats had been Karl's raison d'être, and explaining their impracticality to him had been hers. And many of those threats had been issued against flora and fauna, so . . . yeah. Karl "if that fucking branch snags my fucking sleeve one more fucking time, I will personally throttle that fucking tree with my bare fucking hands until its rings become a solid fucking *line*" Dean wouldn't camp. Not under any circumstances.

Although maybe he'd changed over the last two decades. Or maybe a wife or girlfriend or boyfriend or whoever had dragged him outdoors, because he might not be a natural camper, but he *was* a secret softie. When she'd known him, he'd mowed his elderly neighbors' lawns without asking for money, even though his family was large and not especially wealthy. And when he'd seen her tutoring Ned in chemistry during homeroom, he'd grumpily helped, even though the other kid had once cheated off of him.

Karl was gone. She couldn't believe it.

Her chest ached. Her head throbbed. Her eyes burned.

Her heart hurt.

—and even more bizarrely, there was speculation about possible cannibalism. Involving muffins. That part was a bit unclear, apart from the Soylent Green references.

What. The. Hell.

Lise had sent a link to the obituary. After clicking, Molly tried her best to comprehend the words, but reading through tears wasn't easy. Dimly, she registered the too-brief account of his life. The bakery he'd bought and turned into a cornerstone of his community. The list of his surviving family, which didn't mention a spouse or children.

After the standard obituary elements, the reporter delved into the mysterious and violent circumstances of his death before offering an assurance to her readers:

The *Harlot's Herald* will continue to investigate threats made and received by Dean, as well as the identity of any possible enemies in the greater Harlot's Bay region and the possibility of a coverup by local authorities, who stubbornly deny that a heinous crime even occurred in our community. We will also verify the ingredients contained within muffins originating from Grounds and Grains. If anyone knows more about Dean's murder and/or the possible involvement of criminal gangs attempting to sell the

newest street drug, Special K, to our youths, please contact the paper without delay.

Molly checked the reporter's byline.

Sylvia Plude. Even back in Molly's high school days, that woman
had been—to put it politely—somewhat seasoned in years. Maybe
she'd become hard of hearing and somehow misunderstood the
situation?

Because Karl couldn't truly be gone. Not so soon. Not like that.

Quickly, her unsteady fingers fumbling over her smartphone's
screen, she texted Lise. *Are you certain the obit is plausible? Because
it sounds utterly bizarre.*

Less than a minute later, Molly's cell dinged.

*Been holed up on deadline, so I'm not sure about all the details, but
I do know his bakery was closed for a week. No warning or explanation.
First time that's ever happened. Sorry, Molly. Wish I could give you
better news.* ♥♥♥

In other words: The announcement of Karl's death was probably correct, no matter whether Sylvia had misunderstood the specific circumstances.

No matter how fervently Molly wished it was wrong.

The reporter hadn't mentioned the timing of a memorial service, but surely it would happen within the next several days. Unless Karl had changed significantly, he might not have many close
friends at that service. Acquaintances, yes. People he'd known his
whole life, people he'd helped without ever allowing them to acknowledge his efforts . . . sure. Lots of those. Not friends.

Once upon a time, though, she'd been as close to him as their
situations and mutual defenses would allow. The nature and extent
of that closeness—her feelings for him, and his increasingly obvi-

ous interest in more than friendship—had begun to trouble her after she'd left, so she'd cut things off. Even knowing she should talk to him about the issue directly.

Two things could be true at once: He shouldn't have written like that to her while he had a girlfriend, and she should've handled the situation better.

But before then, they'd been friends. Truly. Maybe, if she hadn't ghosted him, they could have worked things out, reconciled, and become friends again.

Either way, she could be a friend for him now. One last time.

Using her knuckles to dash away her tears, she sat at her kitchen table. Studied September's empty calendar. Glanced at the furniture shoved into corners, stacked into untidy mountains, and covered with drop cloths, all in preparation for the imminent renovations. Spotted, on the other side of the table, yet another letter from her ex-husband, no doubt written in yet another attempt to convince her to sell her house to him and his fiancée.

Allowed herself to remember.

Let herself be rash and spontaneous and unwise, for once in her life.

And less than twenty-four hours later, she was back in Harlot's Bay.

2

Los Angeles and Harlot's Bay might as well have existed on different planets.

In Molly's haze of exhaustion after a red-eye flight from LAX to BWI, a long line at the car rental kiosk, and two hours of driving, what surrounded her seemed like a hallucination.

Green. Green everywhere. Green grass in front yards. Green stretches of woods whipping by her rental car on both sides as she drove along the wide two-lane road leading into town. Green-stemmed black-eyed Susans planted in Strumpet Square, the center of downtown Harlot's Bay.

And what made all that green possible? Water. A breathtaking abundance of water in the air—wow, she'd forgotten about the humidity—and all around, none of it turquoise or crashing onto rocks and sand. The brown river water reflected the blue of the sunny sky, and it lapped at the shore in gentle ripples or flowed in a quiet rush toward the Chesapeake Bay.

Those ripples sparkled on the horizon as she turned into the small gravel lot beside the Battleaxe B&B, where she'd be staying the next few days. However long it took to pay her respects and attend Karl's . . .

She bit her lip, braking a little too hard once she'd pulled into a free spot.

However long it took to attend Karl's funeral.

Checking in early and dropping off her bag for safekeeping until her room was ready took five minutes, max. When Molly stepped back outside into the blinding sunshine and near-choking humidity, her cell's display indicated that it wasn't even ten in the morning yet.

There was no point putting it off, was there? She should go to Grounds and Grains, and if it was open despite Karl's absence, ask someone for specifics about whatever arrangements had been made. Her overtired brain had even retained a vague memory of the bakery's location just off Strumpet Square, so she had no excuse for waiting. Other than her unwillingness to confirm the reality of a loss she felt much more keenly than she should.

She took the walk at a leisurely pace, comparing what she saw to her memories. Most buildings in the center of town dated back at least a century, so the basic layout looked pretty much the same as she recalled from two decades ago. That said, she spotted new-to-her window boxes in full bloom, fresh coats of paint on shutters and signs, and different businesses than she remembered.

Somehow, Harlot's Bay had managed to keep most national chains out of town. In their absence, locally owned restaurants and stores had proliferated in the last two decades. There was a fussy-but-pretty tearoom. An old-school diner with red vinyl booths. A peacock-hued Indian restaurant advertising its extensive lunch buffet across the street from a dark-wooded Swiss place only open for dinner. Lawyers' and doctors' and dentists' offices. An architecture firm. A yarn store. A gallery displaying the work of regional artists and craftspeople.

Ladywright College, Historic Harlot's Bay, and nearby military bases must be bringing visitors, residents, and tax dollars into the town. There was no other way a community of this size could support so many specialized businesses, almost all of them successful-looking.

Her steps slowed and slowed again as she drew closer to her destination, but the downtown area was only so large. The deep green sign for Grounds and Grains loomed just ahead, with its un-fussy illustrations of a plump baguette and a steaming coffee mug painted a muted gold.

Molly gave herself a minute or two to study the place.

Behind the spotless glass windows, people stood waiting in front of a long counter and chose items from treat-packed display shelves. They sat around several small café tables and across from one another in the bakery's three booths. They doctored their cof-fees with cream and sugar at a side table and deposited their trash in a discreet receptable.

She didn't see a memorial, a sign informing customers about Karl's loss, or even a perfunctory black ribbon anywhere. His shop's running seemed remarkably unaffected by his death. Which was both impressive—he must have managed his business incred-ibly well if it could keep functioning this smoothly without him—and unbearably sad. No matter how crotchety he might have remained as he neared middle age, no matter whether an assistant baker could take over for him with ease, shouldn't he be mourned? Shouldn't his absence—his *murder*—at least be *acknowledged* by the business he'd spent his entire adult life serving?

Tragedy upon tragedy. Her throat ached with the tears she wouldn't let herself shed.

Sucking in a deep, hitching breath, she swung open the heavy entry door. A cowbell attached to the push bar inside jangled loudly, its sound incongruously cheerful.

Two clerks stood behind the counter, clad in white aprons. A Latina with golden skin and a ponytail, her hair dyed a deep blue-green at the ends, and a younger Asian guy with a messy man bun. They were each helping someone at the moment, but she'd be next in line.

Lifting her feet to walk toward them felt like dragging lead weights.

As she neared the counter, the heavenly smell of the shop almost dizzied her. The place was a pastry lover's fever dream, its glass-front display cases crowded with buns and Danishes and doughnuts and scones, most of them glistening with various glazes and drizzles. The door behind the clerks and to the left was cracked open an inch or two, and the roar of a powerful engine—a mixer?—drifted into the public area, competing with the soft jazz playing over the bakery's speakers.

Should she go ahead and ask the question without preamble? Or would it be more polite to order something first? Her stomach churned with nausea, and she wasn't the slightest bit hungry, but . . .

"May I help you?" The ponytailed woman—Bez, according to her name tag—sounded patient but a tad concerned, as if she'd already asked that question more than once.

"Sorry," Molly said, just as the clamor from the back ceased. Oh, crap, she hadn't even looked at the menu yet. "Um . . . I'd like one of the lemon-glazed blueberry cake doughnuts, please. And . . . uh . . . a butterscotch latte with whipped cream?"

Sugar and caffeine. The breakfast of champions, assuming the sport in question was competitive feelings-consumption.

Bez grabbed a sheet of waxed paper. "For here or to go?"

"Here." Because how could she claim she'd paid her respects if she breezed in and out of Karl's workplace for the past two decades in less than five minutes?

"Sure." Bez relayed the coffee order to Mr. Man Bun. Using a sheet of waxed paper, she transferred the doughnut onto a small white plate and set it on the counter. "Anything else?"

A quick glance behind her confirmed that no one else was waiting to be served. "Yeah. I . . . I just wanted to say . . ." Molly's inhalation shook, but she forced herself to keep speaking. "I'm so sorry to hear the news. About, uh . . . Karl. Do—do you have any idea when the funeral might be?"

There. She'd made his loss real by speaking it aloud.

Even rapid blinking was no longer doing the job. Shit.

To her shock, the tired-looking clerk with the man bun started laughing. Bez smacked him on the arm, but he was still grinning as he began working on the latte.

The door to the back room opened wider then, but Molly barely noticed through her haze of fury. She no longer had to fight tears. Instead, she had to fight the urge to vault over the countertop separating her from that bunned bastard and beat him bloody with a mug.

"I can't believe you're *laughing*." Shaking with rage, she narrowed her eyes at the asshole and marched toward his station. Leaning over the countertop and jabbing her finger an inch from his chest, she hissed, "How *dare* you?"

The clerk—Johnathan, his name tag informed her—raised his hands, palms out. "Sorry. Sorry, ma'am. I just—we've been hearing the same thing all morning, and it's all so ridiculous."

Ridiculous? A good man's murder was *ridiculous*?

At first, Molly couldn't hear Bez through the blood pounding in her ears.

"—*not dead*," the clerk was saying emphatically, waving an arm to draw Molly's attention away from her coworker. "Karl's *not dead*. I promise. It was a misunderstanding. The reporter, Sylvia, didn't realize we were joking, and . . . yeah. Things got weird. But he's in the back right now, working on our daily sandwich specials. Please don't. . . . I'm so sorry. Are you okay?"

Molly's knees had gone floppy, and she slapped her hands onto the cool marble countertop to brace herself. "He's not . . . he's alive?"

"Yes. Very alive. He had the flu, but now he's simply"—Bez raised her voice significantly—"a cranky grouch unwilling to come out front and deal with someone mourning him, even though he's perfectly fine. Instead, he's leaving it to his clerks, who aren't paid nearly enough to serve as grief counselors."

There was no response from the back, although the light pouring through the cracked door leading to the work area seemed to darken.

Was that—

"I don't recognize you." Bez's ponytail swayed as she tipped her head to the side. "Are you local? How do you know Karl?"

Still woozy with relief, Molly scrubbed her hands over her face and bought herself a moment to recover. Braced herself against the possibility of seeing her former friend for the first time in two decades, blessedly alive and awkwardly *right here*.

If she'd known that was even a faint, miraculous possibility, she'd probably have combed her hair before coming to the bakery.

"I don't live in Harlot's Bay now, but I did. Back in high school." When she finally lowered her hands and answered Bez, Molly's voice sounded calm, and she was freaking proud of that. "Karl and I used to be—"

"Friends," said a rough, familiar voice, and the door to the back room opened entirely, revealing . . . Karl. Broad and big-bellied.

Not especially tall, but still a towering presence. Wearing a tee, jeans, and a flour-flecked apron, his brown eyes devouring her from beneath the brim of his baseball cap. "Good friends. Till I fucked it all up."

She wanted to weep at the sight of him, hale and whole. She wanted to laugh, since he was wearing some sort of stretchy white net over his thick, coppery beard, and it was kind of hilarious-looking. She wanted to scream, because all that sorrow and regret had been for *nothing*, and what kind of jerk would let her think he was dead for *an entire day* if he wasn't, even if they weren't in touch anymore and hadn't been for two decades?

She also wanted to sit the hell down, because these last twenty-four hours had been *a lot*.

"You screwed things up with someone you care about?" Bez shook her head, her brow scrunched in feigned disbelief. "Wow. That seems so unlike you."

Johnathan snorted.

Karl ignored his employees and everyone else watching the tableau in rapt silence.

"Dearborn." He crooked a finger. "Get over here."

"I don't take orders from you, Dean," she reminded him. "Never have. Never will."

But when Johnathan flipped up a hinged section of the countertop for her, she squeezed through the narrow gap. She edged around a rolling cart full of cooling bread on silver trays.

And when Karl opened his arms, she walked straight into them.

3

*M*olly fucking Dearborn had come back to him.

To Harlot's Bay, anyway. But she'd come back *for* him. She'd only come because she'd thought he was dead, because the most bizarre series of events imaginable had happened, but none of that shit mattered.

She'd cared enough to revisit a place she hadn't been in twenty years. She was in Karl's arms, cheeks still damp with tears for him. And she was clutching him like she'd never let him go, which suited him just fine. In fact, it damn well *delighted* him.

Karl wasn't sure he'd experienced delight since senior year. Felt *great*.

But then she pulled away, and he had to let her go. After dashing away the remaining wetness from her rosy cheeks with the heels of her hands, she breathed deeply several times, until her hitching inhalations turned even and silent. Straightened the cuffs and smoothed the front of her rumpled men's-style button-down. Arranged a serene expression on her pretty face.

It was like watching a cracked egg fuse itself back together, until it lay on the worktable dry and pale and untouched again.

Back in high school, she was the most controlled person he'd ever met. In flawless command of every gesture and expression. Apparently that hadn't changed.

It was impressive. Always had been. But goddamn inconvenient too. After two endless decades, this was his chance to make things right, and he wasn't a fucking telepath. He needed to be able to read her reactions.

A throat cleared near him. Loudly. He jerked so hard, his head almost whacked the doorframe, and even Molly twitched a little.

"Um . . ." Bez tilted her head toward the other side of the counter and raised her brows.

Which was when he saw the cluster of nosy-as-shit customers watching him. Some of them with their phones out and aimed his way. *Molly's* way.

"Karl," she asked quietly, expression inscrutable, "why are people filming us?"

He directed a scowl at the crowd. "Because this town is full of busybodies who need to mind their own damn beeswax."

"I see." Her voice remained entirely neutral. "Your mere emergence from the back room appears to have enthralled said busybodies. In much the same way a Bigfoot sighting might."

Ignoring that, he raised his voice, so the entire shop could hear him. "Listen up, assholes. If you don't stop recording, I'll get my cleaver. Take your phones. Chop them into pieces so tiny, even a goddamn *ant* wouldn't bother eating them. And then I'll personally *shove* those pieces *down your throats*."

A few people hurriedly tapped their screens and shoved their phones into their pockets and purses. Others—the ones who'd grown up with him—just grinned and kept recording.

When he glared at his kindergarten teacher, Mrs. Dix waved cheerfully back at him, then squinted to adjust a camera setting on her cell.

"Ants don't consume electronics, Dean." Molly sounded unperturbed. "And as far as the logistics of shoving cell phone shards down your customers' throats—"

"Logistics can go fuck themselves."

"That's technically impossible." Molly raised her forefinger. "Anyway, as I was saying, there are three main problems with your plan. Shards that tiny would be hard to gather and probably quite sharp." A second finger joined the first. "Your fist wouldn't fit down your customers' throats."

"I'd make it fucking fit," he muttered.

"And most importantly," she continued, lifting a third finger, "force-feeding customers the crushed remains of their own electronics wouldn't be good for business."

Her face might be a serene mask, but those pale blue eyes were sparkling.

She was enjoying this. So was he.

"Pedant," he accused.

Her steady gaze held his. "Misanthrope."

"Whatever." His aggrieved harrumph hid a smile. "Come on, Dearborn."

Taking her elbow, he hustled her into his work area and closed the door firmly behind them. As soon as it clicked shut, the muffled roar of excited chatter drowned out the soft jazz playing over the speaker system.

Within five minutes, everyone in Harlot's Bay would know about the reunion. He didn't give a shit. Molly was *here*. They were face-to-face and alone, at long last, and—

And something about having privacy had changed things. Not in a good way.

She stepped back from him and looked around herself. "Impressive operation, Dean." Without moving another inch, she withdrew further, her tone turning formal. "Clearly, I caught you in the middle of doing something important. Sorry to have bothered you. Now that I know you're fine, I'll head back to—"

No. She wasn't going to disappear on him again. Not until he said what he needed to say.

The words weren't hard to find. He'd been rehearsing them for twenty long years.

"We'd broken up," he interrupted hurriedly. "Becky and me. Called it quits soon after she left for university. I was a dumb kid and didn't tell you. Too embarrassed. So I know what you must've thought, and I get why you disappeared on me. But it wasn't true. Before I started dropping my stupid hints, Becky'd dumped me. For good."

There. He'd told her. Fucking *finally*.

"I see." Her eyes met his again, and she leaned a hip against his stainless-steel work table, arms loosely crossed over her chest. Still guarded, but willing to linger.

"That's what happened, right? Why you cut me off?"

She nodded. "You're not the world's subtlest man, Karl. Those weren't exactly *hints* you dropped. In that last email, I believe you inquired as to whether I found"—her forefingers and middle fingers formed air quotes—"'big motherfuckers' hot or not, before soliciting my opinion on dating"—her fingers scrunched again—"'assholes with red beards and high school diplomas whose homemade eclairs would make your taste buds detonate in sheer goddamn joy.'"

Yeah. Sounded familiar.

She added, lips faintly curved, "Which, it must be noted, is not physiologically possible."

All these years later, the woman still liked yanking his chain. And all these years later, she still hadn't answered the crucial question. "Would you have said yes to a date with me? If you'd known

Becky and I were through?"

She nodded again.

The shitty verdict was in: Eighteen-year-old Karl had been *incredibly* stupid. But there was no going back, so he'd have to do better now. Better enough to make her stay. In his bakery, short-term.

Assuming she was single? In Harlot's Bay, long-term.

He heaved a gusty sigh. "Showing my interest before explaining the breakup? Dumb move on my part. I get that. Even back then, I got it."

A timer went off, and he silenced it. Didn't even glance toward the oven. Every fucking pie in there could burn, as long as he kept her here.

"Wish you'd have trusted me, though. At least enough to *ask*." He thrust a finger in her direction. "Not a cheater then. Not a cheater now. Not a cheater *ever*."

That point deserved some damn *emphasis*.

Her mouth pursed. "The issue of cheating was . . . um . . . *sensitive* for me, and since you didn't say anything, I figured you and Becky were still together. I had no way to know that wasn't true. But for what it's worth, I'm sorry I didn't ask for an explanation before just cutting you off."

Dearborn looked genuinely guilty—which gave him an idea. The greatest fucking idea ever. He could *use* that guilt. Use his wronged-party status to keep her in Harlot's Bay and earn her trust.

Timing wasn't right, though. He needed to work up to telling her about his burst of genius. Make her more comfortable with him and more likely to say yes.

"Uh." *Buy time, asshole.* "How've things been, Dearborn?"

"Good," she said with a polite smile. "I live in LA still. I'm doing some home renovations at the moment, so it was a good time to visit Harlot's Bay."

Generic question, generic answer. Should've known.

Fine. He'd do better. "Couple years ago, heard a customer's audiobook out in the parking lot. Sounded like you."

Her brows rose. "You recognized my voice? Almost two decades after I left?"

"Evidently. If it was you." It was definitely her. He'd bet his goddamn bakery on it.

"I narrate audiobooks for a living, so . . ." She shook her head. "Wow. You've listened to my work. I'd never have guessed that."

Countless fucking hours of it. Not that she needed to know.

Her head tipped. "Which book was it, out of curiosity?"

"Guppy-dude with weird-ass dick-fins."

Desire, Unfiltered. Athena's favorite Sadie Brazen story, for some godforsaken reason.

She nodded. "Ah. One of my Molly Cressley books."

Wait. Did that mean—

"I have a couple of pseudonyms. Different ones for different genres." She turned to lean her ass against the worktable, settling herself more comfortably. "Molly Cressley for erotic romance, Molly Biddenwell for literary fiction."

Molly Biddenwell? Never heard of her.

Well, there went another month's profits. Audiobooks on CD—he didn't trust purely digital files when it came to something so important—weren't cheap, and he now had more to buy.

But more importantly—"Thought Molly Cressley might be your married name."

"No." Her shoulders had visibly stiffened. "I was married. But I didn't take his name. Cressley's just my nom de narrator."

No verb tense had ever made him so damn happy before. "*Was* married?"

"Rob and I got divorced two years ago," she said flatly.

She didn't elaborate. He didn't ask. Not the right time.

"I'm sorry," he told her, and part of him meant it. The other part was dancing a fucking jig. "Know how painful that can be. Emily, my youngest sister, got divorced last year. Still not back to herself. Bastard broke her trust."

Karl wanted to break something too. Like the asshole's nose. Probably good Emily's ex lived in Baltimore.

"It's fine." Molly exhaled slowly, and her knuckles jutted as she gripped the edge of the stainless-steel table. "You're right, though. It's hard to trust anyone anymore. Even . . ."

Her soft mouth clamped into a tight line. He waited for her to continue, with the patience of a damn saint, but she didn't say more.

Good enough. He knew she was unmarried. Now to work with the opening she'd given him. "Weren't all that trusting twenty years ago either, Dearborn."

She winced. Renewed guilt creased her forehood, even as she skewered him with an unimpressed glare. "I already apologized for that, Dean, and you admitted that you should have——"

Abruptly, she paused and sniffed. Her forehead crinkled even more as she scanned the work space. "Something's burning."

"*Motherfucker.*"

Grabbing a dry folded dishcloth, he swung the oven door open and set the pies on a nearby sheet tray, one by one. Some of the crumb topping on the Dutch caramel apple had gone too far, the color turning from a deep gold to scorched sienna. In his preoccupation with her, he hadn't even noticed the telltale smell.

So much for making a good impression. Muttering to himself, he flicked away the overly browned bits with his knife, then frowned down at the pies and made his decision: salvageable. With a satisfied grunt, he lifted the heavy sheet tray and slid it into a free slot on his tiered rolling rack to cool.

"Thanks," he said, turning back to Molly. Only she wasn't there anymore.

While he'd been dealing with pie shit, she'd evidently wandered across the workroom. Right now, she was poking her head into his cramped, messy office, a few strands of her coppery brown hair falling forward, off her shoulders. Still center-parted and stick-straight. Still shiny. And after all this time, the woman hadn't lost her love for men's-style button-down shirts and—what had Emily called that loose, cuffed fit again? Oh, yeah. Boyfriend jeans.

She wore sneakers instead of boots now. Otherwise, her style hadn't changed much over the years, and it didn't need to. Looked great on her then. Looked great on her now.

With her bent over like that, he couldn't tear his stare from the lush curves of her ass. That ass was even rounder than it used to be. *All* of her was rounder, and all of it was sexy as hell. The swell of her belly. The rise of her breasts. Her long, strong, thick thighs.

Helplessly, he stepped closer.

When she straightened and turned her head, the overwhelming *familiarity* of her profile struck him hard, the same way it had when he'd first spotted her through the cracked workroom door. If it weren't for those fine lines across her forehead and at the corners of her pale blue eyes, she could've been a memory made flesh. Could've been one of thousands of fantasies he'd had over two goddamn decades.

Her curious gaze scanned his sinks. His refrigerators. His ovens.

Then she swiveled on her heel and faced him again.

He stilled, arrested once more by the sight of Molly Dearborn—Molly fucking *Dearborn*—in his bakery, only half a room away from him, after all that time. He didn't move. Didn't exhale. Didn't even blink, in case she might disappear.

"Karl," she said slowly. "Please explain something to me."

"Yeah?" Sounded like he'd run a microplane grater over his vocal cords, but that was the best he could do right now.

"After almost twenty years with no contact, how did you recognize my voice?"

Before he found an answer that wouldn't incriminate him, another timer went off. Pineapple upside-down cakes. If those went too long, the caramel mixture at the bottom of the pans would turn dark and bitter.

No choice about it. He'd have to walk away from this conversation. So sad.

"Oh, no, you don't," Molly said, dogging his heels all the way to the oven. "Your name isn't Mark-Paul Gosselaar. The bell isn't going to save you, Dean."

"Watch out," he warned her, then braced for a gust of heat from the oven as he opened its door. "These pans are hot."

After he'd deposited them on another sheet tray and shoved that tray into the cooling rack, he checked out the cherry pies. Not quite ready yet. Lattice was still too pale. With his towel-covered fist, he bumped the oven door closed once more.

When he turned around, she was right. Fucking. There. A hand's breadth in front of him, max.

Crossing his arms across his chest, he glowered at her. "Move it or lose it, Dearborn."

"Answer my question," she said without budging an inch, "and I'll get out of your way."

"I repeat: Move that sweet ass of yours, Dearborn."

Her brows shot skyward, and he barely bit back a frustrated groan. Yeah. If she hadn't realized before then why he'd recognized her voice in an instant, even when she was narrating a weird-ass story about that billionaire guppy-asshole—

"Go ahead, Dean." She slowly smiled. Leaned even closer, until her cool breath wafted across his chin as she spoke. "Make me."

4

Make me.

Did Molly realize what a dangerous game she was playing? Because Karl would gladly *make her*, if she wanted that. He would take any excuse to get his hands on her miracle of a body and put her exactly where he wanted.

Right now, out of his path.

Eventually, under him.

"Make you," he repeated, a low rumble of warning.

"Make. Me." Her cheeks flushed and shiny from the heat of the ovens, she tipped her chin high. "What? No obscenities? No threats that aren't logically possible? I'm disappointed, Karl."

Not so serene anymore, his Molly. She was breathing faster now, blue eyes flame-hot and lit with challenge, lips parted and wet from a swipe of that pink, pink tongue.

Watching for the slightest flinch or uneasiness in her expression, he lifted his hand and—

Dammit. No. If they fucked now, she'd come and *go.* He knew it already.

Sex wouldn't keep her here. So he dropped his hand and took his shot. "You owe me, Dearborn."

"Huh?" Her eyes were hazy and hooded. "I don't . . . what?"

There it was. Unflappable, sharp-as-a-blade Molly Dearborn, off-balance from their near kiss. Good fucking sign. *Best* fucking sign.

Time to sell his idea. Hard. "We were friends. Good ones. You cut me off with no warning and no explanation. Didn't even bother to ask if I was still dating Becky. Just assumed I was cheating."

"That was *two decades ago*," she protested, fists now on her hips, but he didn't relent.

"Three years as friends." He echoed her stance. Lifted a brow. "I do anything dishonest? Anything to make you think I'd cheat?"

"Well, no, but—"

"Deserved better from you," he concluded, pinning her with his stare.

She sighed. "Yes. But *you* should've told me you'd broken up with Becky, as we established mere minutes ago. The fault isn't entirely on my side."

Yeah. He was ignoring that.

"You owe me," he repeated. "How soon you need to be back in LA?"

Her forehead crinkled again. "About four weeks from now. Karl . . ."

"Twenty-year reunion's the first weekend in October." He'd been dreading the stupid event, but now? Hooray for all that school spirit shit. "Less than four weeks."

She checked the calendar on her phone. "Barely."

"You said it's hard for you to trust anyone." He sucked in a breath. Gathered his courage. "Give me from now until then to prove you can trust *me*."

His family would be gone during her whole visit, unable to interfere. Best timing *ever*.

Her mouth opened. Closed. Opened again.

"If I trust you or don't trust you, what difference does that make?" she finally asked, sounding confused. "Yes, we were friends at one time, but we haven't spoken since we were teenagers, and I live across the country. Maybe my opinion of you mattered then, but surely it doesn't matter now."

He crossed his arms over his chest. "It matters to me."

"We've already established that you weren't trying to cheat on Becky. Your official record is hereby"—with a distinct slap, she brushed her palms back and forth, as if knocking off dirt—"clean."

"Give me from now until the reunion," he repeated, unswayed. "I'll prove myself to you."

She eyed him closely, then nodded to herself. Like she'd figured something out.

"Let me be blunt, Dean. We clearly have some unfinished business." She stepped into him, nudging his arms to his sides, and he bit off a rough sound at the heat of her, the softness of her belly and breasts. "But taking care of that business doesn't require trust. Just chemistry. And until I leave on Friday, I'm happy to use that chemistry and run some experiments. Enough to make Mr. Miller write us a lifetime's worth of referrals."

Oh, Jesus. Her body pressed against his? Best thing he'd felt in his damn *life*.

His thoughts slowed. Turned syrupy, like the wildflower honey he used in his iced tea.

Dimly, though, in the recesses of his Molly-addled mind, an alarm began ringing. His plan for her wasn't about sex. Right? Or . . . not *just* about sex. But if he stayed this close to her, it'd become that, and . . .

Yeah. He knew himself. Knew how it'd feel to have her, then watch her leave again.

If she'd haunted his bed before? She'd be a goddamn *poltergeist* after they finally fucked. So if she was going, better not to fuck at all. No matter what his stupid damn dick was telling him.

Getting off and getting ditched didn't give him what he'd wanted—what he'd *needed*—for two shitty decades. A chance to make things right. A chance to make things *real*.

For him to have that chance, she needed to stay in Harlot's Bay. For her to stay, he needed her trust. And to earn that trust, he needed the rest of September. Not a few quick orgasms until Friday came and she went.

His plan. He had to remember his damn plan.

He paced back a step, until he lost physical contact with her. She swayed forward, and her little noise of protest nearly broke his resolve, but he kept his shit together.

After a moment, his brain rebooted itself. He planted his feet and made his stand.

"Fucking someone who doesn't trust me . . ." He shook his head. "No. Doesn't feel right."

Not a total lie. Also not the actual reason he'd refused her proposition.

Her brows had formed a straight, dark line across her forehead. "You're telling me we can't have sex until I trust you?"

"Yep."

"And you want me to stay in Harlot's Bay for almost an entire month, because I ostensibly *owe* you that time to prove yourself and earn my trust?"

"Yep."

"And if you *do* earn my trust while I'm still here, *then* we can fuck."

"Yep."

"That's . . . wow." She laughed then, bracing herself with a hand on his worktable. "I have to applaud you, Dean. That demand took some serious nerve. I mean, *four weeks?* All to make up for having misjudged you two freaking *decades* ago? With the prospect of sex as extra enticement to agree, even apart from the guilt trip you're laying on me?"

Didn't sound like a yes. Dammit.

She shook her head. "I'm sorry, but——"

"Listen, Dearborn," he interrupted, desperate, "don't——"

"Wait!" Charlotte surged into the back room, hot on the heels of her two toddlers, and reached for the nearest one, planting him on a hip before snatching for the second kid. "Brooklyn, stop right there. Karl, sweetheart, you know you're not supposed to put that into your mouth——"

Karl—the adult, not the toddler, although he was feeling equally sulky at the moment—pressed his own lips together, trying his damnedest not to show his aggravation at the interruption.

Charlotte had begun working at the bakery as a dishwasher at just seventeen. Four years later, she was a smart, hardworking single mom, one of his morning-shift clerks, and the closest thing to a daughter he'd ever have. Right now, she was bustling around the backroom, busily attempting to get her flock in order. And yeah, he loved those kids, but he currently wanted to send them to the wilds of Australia. Accompanied by their mother, whom he also loved, but who also belonged on a slow boat across the goddamn Pacific.

Molly's gaze swung to him. Frowning in confusion, she studied his mouth, then turned back to the kids. After a few more seconds of study, her expression smoothed into neutrality. Without another word, she moved out of his way. Far out of his way. Across the room.

His brows snapped together.

What? he mouthed, as Charlotte continued to inspect whatever Karl's namesake had shoved into his piehole this time. But Molly wasn't paying attention to him anymore. Instead, she was offering Brooklyn a polite smile as the toddler stared at her and started babbling about turtles.

"Honey, plastic isn't food. I've told you that a million times. Please remember that the next time you see a Duplo block, okay? Anyway, I wanted to talk to—oh." Charlotte's stream of words came to an abrupt halt, and she directed an apologetic wince toward both him and Molly. "I'm so sorry. I wanted to talk to you about the new quiche flavor I think we should try, Karl, but that can wait. I didn't realize you had company."

"It's fine, Charlotte," he told her, with as much patience as he could muster.

It wasn't fine. But she was too fragile, too sweet, for his usual bitching.

From her perch on her mom's hip, Brooklyn reached out both arms, hazel eyes wide and pleading. With a gusty sigh, Karl moved farther away from the ovens, gathered the child up, tossed her over one shoulder, and spun in a circle with his hand on the giggling kid's padded butt, keeping her in place and safe.

Charlotte shifted her weight, glancing back and forth between him and Molly. "Listen. Maybe I should just grab Brooklyn and go back—"

"No, no." Molly raised a hand. "You stay. I should head out now anyway."

"But—" Charlotte and Karl began in unison.

Molly didn't let either of them finish. "Karl and I are old schoolmates, and I hadn't seen him in a few years, so I just stopped by to say a quick hello. Lovely to meet you, Charlotte. Your kiddos are adorable, as I'm sure you already know. You make a beautiful family."

Truth. Whenever Charlotte, Brooklyn, and Junior managed to take a family picture, it looked like a fucking stock photo.

"Thank you?" Charlotte sounded uncertain, and he had no idea why.

Only . . . Karl abruptly stopped spinning. Did Molly think—

"Brooklyn and Karl aren't my kids, Dearborn. Charlotte's like a daughter to me." He shoved an accusing finger in Molly's direction. "You just thought the worst of me again. Not two decades ago. *Now*."

Brooklyn made an odd sound, jerked, and vomited down the back of Karl's tee.

"I've told you not to spin her like that, no matter how much she loves it," Charlotte muttered, already digging for wipes. "Last time you babysat, the same thing happened."

Cuddling Brooklyn to his chest and rubbing the poor kid's back, Karl shut his eyes in disgust. At the foul-smelling wetness seeping through his shirt. At the entire goddamn situation. "*Motherfucker*."

"I'm so sorry about the mess, but . . ." Charlotte sighed and took back her daughter. "Language, Karl. Please."

"Lang-wedge," Brooklyn echoed.

"Lang-wedge," he agreed through gritted teeth. "Don't worry, Charlotte. Easy cleanup."

Molly shifted on her feet. Looked guilty as hell. "How can I help? Do you need a towel, or—"

"You can stop assuming I'm an a—" He looked down at Brooklyn. Rephrased. "A not-good person, for f—for *heaven's* sake. You can *stay*."

Silence, other than muffled soft jazz and little Karl's Duplodeprived whimpers of complaint.

"We'll go." Charlotte finished cleaning her daughter's face, threw out the used wipes, and washed her own hands. "You two should finish your conversation in privacy."

Within seconds, she'd hustled the kids out and shut the door firmly behind her.

After glowering at Molly, he stalked to his office. Whipped off his apron and shirt, somehow without dirtying his hands or hair. Carefully balled up the soiled clothing and shoved it in a plastic bag. Good enough for now.

One fresh tee remaining in his desk drawer. He needed to restock his supply. Between cooking and kids, things at the bakery got messy on the regular.

In a perfect world, he'd ask Dearborn to wash his back. But this world was frequently shitty, and that'd be too intimate. No time to stop home either, so he'd have to scrub extra hard tonight. Probably feel itchy in the meantime. Ugh.

He tugged the tee over his head. When he could see again, Molly was in his doorway, cheeks flushed. Eyes downcast. Penitent.

"I apologize, Karl," she told him, lifting her chin to meet his stare. "When I told you I didn't trust anyone anymore, I meant it. But you deserved the benefit of the doubt, especially after I'd misjudged you already. I should have asked before assuming things. Even though Charlotte is gorgeous and clearly very close to you. As are her kids. One of whom is named Karl. As in, *Karl Junior.*"

"No shit you should have asked, Dearborn." He edged past her, avoiding dangerous body-to-body contact, and scrubbed his hands vigorously at the nearest sink. "You owed me before. You owe me double now."

"Yeah." When he turned around, she was rubbing her forehead

with her fingertips. Her voice sounded tired. "I do. And I have to admit, seeing you with your surrogate daughter and grandchildren was . . . oddly appealing. But . . ."

She dropped her hand, and he noticed it then. Exhaustion. Dark smudges beneath red-rimmed eyes. Stiff tension girding that elegant posture.

"Four weeks is too high a price to pay for the mistakes I've made, and there's no point getting close to a man who lives across the country." She spread her hands, a gesture of regret. "Once this break is over, I won't have the time or energy to try anything long-distance."

Didn't she have anyone in her life who'd make her rest when she needed it? Who'd tell her when she pushed herself too hard?

Before he'd gotten the flu, he'd assumed his own answer to those questions would be a firm, repeated *fuck, no*. For better or worse, cranky-ass hermits didn't get well-meaning interference from concerned friends.

Only . . . Bez and Johnathan had browbeaten him into seeing a doctor when his fever first spiked. Charlotte had come by his house several times to drop off medicine and check on him. Matthew and Athena had texted him way too goddamn often. After that bizarre obit had run, the Nasty Wenches book club had descended on him too, using every means of communication short of carrier pigeon.

He'd resisted getting close to all those people at first. Even Matthew, way back when. But his resistance had been futile. And now this cranky-ass hermit was still cranky. Still an ass. Maybe not such a hermit anymore, though.

He got the sense Molly couldn't say the same. And a cheerful hermit was still a hermit.

Jesus, she looked as tired as she sounded.

He cleared his throat. "Dearborn . . ."

"Please don't make my life harder right now," she said simply, holding his gaze. "I can't give you what you want, Karl."

How could he argue with that? The last thing he wanted was to make things *worse* for her after all this time. Dammit.

It took everything in him—every ounce of will and reason— not to keep pushing. When he spoke next, he could barely hear it over the howl of refusal echoing in his brain. But he did it. He let her go.

For her good. Not his.

"Will I see you before Friday?" he grated out hoarsely, gripping the edge of the worktable in front of him for dear life.

Even as he asked, he already knew the answer.

"Since you want more than just a quick fling . . ." Blue eyes sad, she shook her head. "That's probably not a great idea. You're potent temptation, Dean, and I don't want to hurt either of us."

Flattering. Still a blow to his stupid, aching heart.

He couldn't do more than grunt in response, like a goddamn caveman.

"I can't tell you how glad I am that you're alive and well. I'm sorry for misjudging you, and I'm sorry for not saying yes to your plan." Her chest rose and fell on a deep sigh. "I'm wishing you all the happiness in the world, Karl. Please take care of yourself."

And before he could muster even a single word in reply, she was gone. Again.

The door slowly closed behind her. He watched, his vision blurry, until it shut entirely.

Then he got back to fucking work.

5

The next evening, Molly waited for Lise outside the Historic Harlot's Bay ticket office, where her friend would meet her after leading the night's final Ghosts and Legends tour.

As she waited, her mind drifted toward Karl. Magnetic, broadchested, mouthwatering Karl. Whom she'd now seen shirtless and ogled as discreetly as possible. Her long-ago cranky crush, who'd turned down her offer of casual sex and urged her to stay in Harlot's Bay for almost four entire weeks instead. Which she obviously couldn't do, so . . .

Yeah. So much for fucking him out of her system after two long decades.

The whole situation kept intruding on her thoughts. Kept disturbing and confusing her, because . . . maybe her inability to stay wasn't *that* obvious.

She did owe him amends for thinking the worst of him . . . twice . . . without asking for an explanation, and she already had the time off from work. Her comfortable home had become a temporary construction zone. And because she hadn't known when his funeral service would be, she'd booked a ticket with no flight-change penalties.

Still, four weeks at a hotel would put a real dent in her savings. More importantly, she hadn't lied to Karl about the vast temptation he posed, and the last thing she needed was to become emotionally attached to a man who lived an entire continent away from her.

Her instincts were screaming at her to stay, but her instincts had also let her marry Rob, so she couldn't rely on them. As little as she trusted everyone else, she trusted her own judgment—at least when it came to men—even less.

So there would be no lemon-glazed blueberry doughnuts or butterscotch lattes for Molly. No one-off sex with the long-lost friend she'd never quite been able to forget. No more visits to Harlot's Bay.

In less than seventy-two hours, her plane back to LA would take off. As it lifted from the runway, Molly would give thanks for Karl Dean's continued survival . . . and the miles she was putting between them.

"Hey!" someone exclaimed loudly, right next to Molly. "I know you! Molly Dearborn, right?"

With a gasp, Molly leaped backward, away from the unexpected voice, and clapped a hand over her galloping heart. Holy Moses. Apparently a costumed interpreter had come up to her while she was lost in thought, a Black woman in a cap and one of those corset-like things over her shift. That woman now looked extremely apologetic, both her hands lifted to show her utter harmlessness as she helpfully angled herself into the light streaming from the ticket booth's window.

Historic Harlot's Bay should really train their employees not to approach tourists in the dark without ample warning. That said, Molly did in fact recognize the smiling, petticoat-clad woman.

"Hi." Molly offered her a polite smile. "We attended Harlot's Bay High together, didn't we? Lovely to meet you again."

Jane? Janet? Jan? Something like that. They'd been in world history together, and maybe gym class?

"Yep. We graduated the same year." Raising her arms in an

overhead vee, Jan-something waved invisible pompoms and raised her voice. "Goooooo, Fighting Floozies!"

Molly had almost forgotten about the school mascot, whose very existence perhaps helped to explain how Lise had become Sadie Brazen. That said, Lise had also lived her entire life in a town called Harlot's freaking Bay. Maybe it was inevitable that *someone* in the community would wind up writing about sexually voracious, ethically dubious kangaroo-men.

Well . . . maybe not. That particular story seemed very specific to Lise, honestly.

Jan-something was looking at her with expectant cheer, and Molly still hadn't come up with her exact name. "I'm so sorry, but I can't quite—"

"Janel Altman." Lise had appeared at Molly's side from somewhere in the shadows, again without warning. This time, Molly managed not to jump, but it was a close thing. "Class vice president, former cheerleader—"

Well, that explained the invisible pompoms, as well as the startling energy and enthusiasm that radiated from Janel's beaming, elfin face.

"—devoted wife, mother of three adorable urchins, and current night programs supervisor for Historic Harlot's Bay. Also the main organizer of our class's twenty-year reunion, which she somehow convinced me to attend, even though I get nauseated every time I think about it. The prospect of making small talk in a crowd for hours at a time . . ."

She shuddered, and the reaction was only a tiny bit exaggerated. Although Lise wrote erotic literature about guppy-men with ripped abs, the "Brazen" in her pen name was more aspirational than descriptive of her actual personality.

"You lead tours full of strangers, babe. Suck it up," advised Janel.

Lise flicked her coworker's upper arm. "It's not the same thing, and you know it."

As she'd explained to Molly last year, leading tours at night worked for her because she remained in control of the situation, knew exactly what was expected of her, and had years of experience doing it. Mingling with swarms of former classmates, though, without a clear script or conversational goal? She'd find the prospect terrifying.

Casual socializing didn't scare Molly the same way. But she'd already sent her regrets to the reunion organizer—Janel, evidently—months ago. Making idle chitchat with people she hadn't seen in twenty years and would probably never see again was pointless. If she'd wanted to stay in touch with them, she would have.

Not even Karl's urgings could make her stay for the blessed event.

Though she'd been tempted by those urgings. *Very* tempted.

"Hmmm." Janel eyed Molly consideringly. "Lise, perhaps you'd feel better if you went with a friend. More specifically, a friend who won't be running around, frantically putting out various fires during the event like I will." Her brow puckered in a momentary frown. "Hopefully not literal fires, given that we're doing a cookout for one of our activities. My husband Dave was always a bit of a pyro."

Lise snorted.

"Anyway." Janel's expression cleared, and she bounced a bit on her toes. "The reunion's in early October, during Homecoming weekend, and I would really love for you to be there, Molly. I know a lot of people who'd be excited to catch up with you and find out what you've been doing all these years. Including me. If I didn't have to get home for my kids' bedtime, I'd be dragging you to the Doxy Diner to talk about it tonight."

The diner's signature tuna melt and loaded fries were calling Molly's name, and she wouldn't have minded chatting with Janel over dinner. Not about Molly's possible reunion attendance, though. That wasn't happening, for any number of very pressing and legitimate reasons that didn't involve romantic cowardice.

"Sadly"—*fortunately*—"I fly out on Friday, so I can't make it. But thank you, Janel."

"You're absolutely certain?"

"I'm certain."

Janel's smile turned wry. "Well, you can't blame a girl for trying. Safe travels back home, Molly, and I hope you come back to us much sooner this time."

Molly returned her smile and made zero promises.

After a few more standard farewells, Janel hugged them both, then hustled toward the nearest employee parking lot. Lise and Molly turned right instead and headed down She-Devil Street, the historic area's central thoroughfare, at a leisurely pace.

"Does she know about Sadie?" Molly quietly asked after a minute.

Lise's basket swung from her arm with every step, and their footsteps tapped against the cobblestone sidewalk. "Nope."

The answer didn't surprise Molly. Her friend kept knowledge of her pen name limited to as few people as possible.

After another half block of comfortable silence, Lise spoke again. "You're still good with having dinner at Termagant Tavern? Colonial Karaoke Night is fun, but it can get loud. If you have a headache, we can go somewhere else."

Why did Lise think she had a headache?

"I'm fine. Unless . . ." She paused. "Do you expect me to sing?"

She enjoyed performing for crowds, but karaoke wasn't something she'd ever done before, and she'd have to know more about how it worked and have a song in mind before she committed herself.

"*No*." Lise's shoulders curved inward. "Hell, no. I've never participated, and I never intend to, so I certainly wouldn't pressure you to do it. But the whole event is hilarious to watch, and the drinks are half price all night."

Molly lifted a hand. "Say no more. You had me at cheap booze."

A laughing group of tourists came toward them on the sidewalk, their souvenir tricorne and straw hats still on and tipped at a jaunty angle, despite the late hour.

"Perfect." Lise stepped to the side for them, then slanted an alert glance at Molly. "So you don't have a headache. What else is wrong, then?"

If her friend could read it on her face, Molly must be more conflicted about that encounter with Karl than she'd even realized. Schooling her expression into placidity, she shook her head. "I'm good, Lise. Stop worrying about me, and start worrying about whether your coworkers will drag you up on stage for an eighteenth-century version of 'Sweet Caroline.'"

It was only a playful attempt to distract her too-observant friend, but Lise immediately recoiled and executed a full-body cringe. "Don't even joke about that song."

"Your colleagues actually *do* perform a colonial version of 'Sweet Caroline,'" Molly concluded. "Wow."

There were nerds, and then there were freaking *nerds*. Historic Harlot's Bay apparently abounded with the latter, and good for them.

Lise shuddered slightly. "They call it 'Queen Caroline.'"

"Of course they do," Molly said blandly, then hooked her elbow through Lise's before her friend could change her mind and sprint away from the imminent social outing. And together, they wandered off into the historic night, arm in arm.

* * *

TWO HOURS LATER, tipsy from entirely too many delicious eighteenth-century-inspired drinks—the Termagant Tavern's rhubarb shrub cocktail was tart, sweet, addictive, and absolutely loaded with alcohol—Molly leaned across the sticky wooden table and raised her voice to be heard over the musical cacophony created by drunk, suspiciously young-looking members of the fife and drum corps, a talented harpsichordist with an askew bonnet, the helplessly giggling viola player, and a trio of twerking women in petticoats singing at full, enthusiastic volume about whores.

"This one sounds familiar!" Under normal circumstances, she wouldn't shout like this, since babying her throat meant she could narrate two books a week instead of one. But since she was off for the entire month, who gave a shit? "Is that—no, don't tell me—"

"'WAP.'" Lise had been drinking the tavern's famous ginger ale all night, probably so she could stay alert enough to ward off any attempts to haul her onstage. After another sip from her brown glass bottle, she grinned at Molly. "'Weird-Ass Pianoforte.'"

"Because it's a harpsichord!" Molly snickered. "Ha!"

Even close to midnight, the tavern was packed with people. Mostly interpreters still in costume, but also a few obvious tourists, who were equally soused and loud and cheerful. So far, there appeared to be an endless stream of willing volunteers for the stage from both groups.

Lise shook her head, watching her coworkers belt out their song. "Couldn't pay me enough to get up there."

"Which reminds me." When Molly slapped the table for emphasis, her palm stung. "Why the *heck* did you agree to attend the reunion if you don't want to go?"

"Janel's my supervisor, Mol. I don't have any travel planned, and she knows it. I couldn't think of a good reason to refuse, other than my intense desire to avoid socializing among near strangers for hours at a time while they silently evaluate how gracefully I have or haven't aged and whether my accomplishments are sufficient to indicate two decades well spent." Lise sighed. "Even though I can't actually tell anyone what I do for a living."

Molly blinked. "That seems like a good enough reason to me."

"Well, it's not." As Lise picked at her bottle label's edge with her thumbnail, the paper began peeling off. "At least not for Janel, who is the sweetest, most enthusiastic steamroller who ever donned a pair of buckled shoes and an apron. I swear to goodness, if that woman had chosen a different career path, she'd be in charge of all of us by now. America's benevolent dictator, complete with presidential pompoms. And we'd probably be glad for it."

Ah, peer pressure. Very effective at all ages, despite what public service announcements during her teen years had implied. "So you're going."

"I'm definitely going." Lise lurched forward in her chair, and it creaked in protest. "And you should definitely come with me."

Speaking of Molly's long-ago youth: As if.

"Hahahaha. No."

If she stayed, she'd get entirely too attached to the town's hottest and most cantankerous baker, whose shirtless chest had nearly poleaxed her the previous day. And the hotel bills! She shouldn't forget the hotel bills! Which she might be able to afford, but . . .

She shouldn't stay. She really shouldn't.

Her elbows planted on the table, Lise propped her chin on her clasped hands and batted her eyelashes. "What can I do to convince you to go?"

"Nothing." Even though Lise's dark eyelashes were, in fact, quite pretty, and she'd clearly perfected that expression of guileless, wide-eyed entreaty at some point in her life.

Didn't matter. No way Molly was attending that freaking reunion, peer pressure be damned. If Karl's entreaties hadn't swayed her sufficiently, nothing could.

Although he'd come surprisingly close.

"I'll do anything, Molly. Please." Lise's mouth twisted. "It'll be so terrible without you."

That pleading, woebegone face would have softened even the hardest heart. And despite Molly's attempts to make hers impervious, it hadn't yet turned to stone.

Shit.

Fine. *Fine*. To assuage her drunken guilt, she'd say yes—but make her agreement conditional upon Lise completing a task she'd absolutely hate and refuse to do. Thus relieving Molly of the necessity of either spending another month in Harlot's Bay or flying out from California a second time for the stupid freaking reunion— and removing her from the walking, talking, grumping temptation named Karl Andrew Dean.

Congratulating herself on her cleverness, she laid down her terms. "The entire time we were slurping down peanut soup and munching on hoecakes, you were complaining about how long a dry spell you've had, how you don't like most singles' events and hate all dating apps, and how you wouldn't even know how to go about seducing someone. So I'll say yes to attending to the reunion—"

"Yay! Thank you so—"

"—on one condition."

"—much." Lise frowned. "Wait. What condition? Why are you putting conditions on the sacred bonds of friendship?"

"Because *you* want to get laid," Molly said, pointing at her. "Which means *I* want you to get laid, and apparently you need a more powerful motivator than potential orgasms. So here it is: For me to attend the reunion with you, you'll have to seduce someone before Friday. A man, a woman, whoever. Just get them into bed and into your vagina before I head to the airport, and I'll stay until the reunion."

In a way, she was leaving her future plans up to fate, which wasn't like her. But she'd also stacked the deck heavily in her favor, which very much was.

"But—"

"No buts." Molly paused. "Although, now that I'm considering the matter, butts are fine too. So are mouths. I didn't mean to be so vagina-centric."

Lise cast a gimlet eye upon her. "Very generous of you, Dearborn."

"And a bed doesn't need to be involved either." Molly spread her hands, a benefactor demonstrating the impressive breadth of her compassion and munificence. "I'm fine with a couch, or the back seat of a car, or wherever you decide to get busy. The world is your slutty oyster, my friend."

There. That should do it. Problem solved. No way Lise was

finding some rando and dragging him into bed, especially not in the next three days.

Lise slumped forward, propping her chin on her folded arms. "Unfair, Mol. You know my seduction skills are rusty at best, nonexistent at worst."

"Perhaps. But that's my condition for staying." Molly grinned at her. "And if your seduction skills are rusty, consider this your opportunity to hone them again."

Satisfied, she tossed back the last of her cocktail, thunked the glass onto the table, and waited for Lise to concede defeat.

And waited.

And waited.

On the tavern's small stage, some dude in breeches was doing his best Pat Benatar impression, accusing his significant other of being a harp-breaker, mess-maker, string-taker, before warning against further injury to his collection of musical instruments.

Once he got past the shaky opening, he wasn't half bad. Feeling loose and warm, Molly clapped along and whistled appreciatively at the next chorus.

Meanwhile, Lise's mouth worked as she glared across the table and considered the offer. Her fingertips tapped the glass of her ginger ale bottle.

"Fine," she finally muttered. "I'll do it."

It was loud. Molly had obviously misheard her. "Excuse me?"

"I agree to your condition." This time, she enunciated each syllable in a clear, loud voice.

But there'd been some misunderstanding, clearly. Because Lise wouldn't ever say yes to such a—

"I'll seduce a guy before Friday," she continued, much to Molly's shock and dismay, "and you'll have to stay here until October and attend the reunion with me."

She didn't sound happy about it. But she did sound determined.

When Lise extended a hand across the table to seal their agreement, Molly shook it, because she was a woman of her word. Then, instead of ordering another half-priced drink, she signaled their server for the check.

That rhubarb shrub concoction was the cocktail of Satan, and it had tricked her. Beguiled her senses until she'd willingly entered into a devil's bargain. Nay, proposed the bargain herself!

If Lise actually did sleep with someone before Friday, where the hell was Molly going to stay for the next month? Could she even risk remaining so close to Karl for all that time, or would she need to fly back home and return right before the cursed reunion?

Her head was spinning, and not in a good way anymore.

After paying the bill, she massaged her aching temples. "The next time I have to explain why socializing is almost always a terrible idea, I'm referring to this outing as Exhibit A."

"Amen, sister," Lise said, with feeling.

* * *

Two days later, Molly was sitting in a diner booth and finishing her tuna melt when she received a one-word text from Lise: *DONE.* Which obviously couldn't indicate what it seemed to indicate, so she put down her sandwich, wiped her hands, and wrote back immediately.

What's done?

My assignment.

Molly blinked at her cell. *You seduced someone? Already?*

A beep heralded Lise's reply. *Yup. We did it like they do on the*

Discovery Channel, as the kids say.

There were obviously more important matters in play, but . . .

The kids haven't said that since the turn of the century, Lise.

Shut up. I'm old. And so are you, my good bitch. A pause, during which Molly handed her credit card to the hovering server. *Need proof of my exploits?*

No. I trust you.

An automatic response, but Molly meant it. Which was an odd feeling, because she could have sworn she didn't trust anyone. Hadn't she said as much to Karl on Monday, repeatedly?

She couldn't quite pinpoint the moment when Lise had turned from a work acquaintance into . . . whatever they were now. Friends, obviously. Close enough friends that she couldn't help probing for more information, both out of interest and to ease her sudden concern.

If her stupid bargain had gotten Lise hurt . . . *Are you okay?*

Yes.

No hesitation. Whew.

The uber-efficient server had already returned. After adding a substantial tip to the total and signing her receipt, Molly stood to go.

Was it good? she texted as she exited the diner.

Yes. Dots came and went on the screen. *Yes.*

Brows drawn in thought, Molly paused in the shade cast by the building's brick exterior and stared blankly at the empty street in front of her.

Lise's second yes could mean two things. Either she was unsure about the first yes and trying to convince herself—and Molly—that the sex truly had been decent, or . . .

Was it VERY good?

More dots.

Perhaps. Before Molly could press further, Lise texted again. *So you're coming to the reunion with me. Hooray!*

Fine. As someone who guarded her own privacy, she'd respect Lise's too.

I suppose I am. And for some reason, that admission didn't aggravate her nearly as much as she'd have expected. Molly leaned her shoulder against the brick wall, allowing it to support her weight. *How in the world did you find someone so quickly?*

An amendment, in the interest of greater accuracy: She'd *mostly* respect Lise's privacy.

There was another lengthy pause, replete with yet more blinking dots.

Long story, Lise eventually wrote. *Anyway, I had an idea just now. Why don't you ask Karl to be your date? If you invited him, I bet he'd say yes, and we could hang out as an antisocial trio.*

It can't be THAT long a story, since it transpired in the last twenty-four hours, Molly felt obligated to note before reading the rest of her friend's message. Whereupon she sighed heavily, because . . . was Lise *matchmaking?* And why was everyone and everything—including her own traitorous thoughts—seemingly conspiring to keep her in Harlot's Bay and Karl's vicinity?

A mosquito hovered near her face, and she absently shooed it away.

You'd be surprised, Lise texted. *Anyway, what do think about inviting Karl to the reunion?*

Okay. Texting wasn't sufficient for this conversation anymore.

"Why is the entire universe pushing me toward Karl freaking Dean?" she demanded, as soon as Lise answered her phone.

"What?" Her friend sounded befuddled.

"First he ends up with an obituary while *still alive*, under entirely bizarre circumstances. Then I somehow get word of the obit despite living over two thousand miles away. *Then*——"

"I mean, you did used to live here," Lise pointed out. "So that part's not as far-fetched. Just saying."

"——he tells me I *wronged* him when I cut him off *twenty fucking years ago*, Lise, and thus owe him four weeks in Harlot's Bay so he can earn my trust, which is *bizarre*. I live across the damn country from him, so why the hell does he care?"

"Maybe he——"

"It isn't as if I wouldn't sleep with him anyway, trust or no trust," Molly said, ignoring her friend's attempted interruption. "But when I told him that, he turned me down, Lise. Even though he had a visible erection. Like, what the actual fuck? And sure, I misjudged him a second time and thought Charlotte was his partner and had borne him two adorable kids, but that doesn't mean I have to——"

"Those are definitely not Karl's kids. He's one hundred percent single and evidently ready to mingle. With you, anyway. Although not sexually, from what you're telling me. Which, I agree, is kind of inexplicable." Lise paused. "And apparently he also took possession of your vocabulary sometime over the past minute. Holy crap, Molly. I've never heard you this flustered before."

It'd been a long time she'd *felt* so off-kilter. Even longer since she'd let someone *else* see or hear it.

When her husband had completed his residency—the last major step toward becoming a doctor, after her work had paid for his medical school—and almost immediately announced that he was leaving her after seventeen years together, she hadn't yelled. Hadn't cried. Not when he'd explained that he now wanted children, as well as a younger woman to bear those children, although they'd agreed to remain a family of two more than a decade ago. Not even when she'd asked why he didn't say so much sooner, and he'd told her she was cold and uncommunicative and difficult to talk to.

"Kind of a bitch, Molly, although you know I hate to use that word," he'd said.

Ever since they'd met at UCLA, he'd shaken his head at her cynicism. Told her she needed to think the best of people. Told her she could trust him, rely on him, that he'd never disappoint her the way others had.

It had taken nine years before she'd believed him, before she'd agreed to marry him.

And he'd used her to finance his future, then shaken her off like a fleck of lint.

But she hadn't cried then. Hadn't even flinched. She'd simply thrown his ass out of their home. *Her* home. When his car had disappeared around a bend in the road, that was when she'd let herself break and rage and weep. Not a moment before.

So why couldn't she seem to feign serenity now? Had the news of Karl's death and his subsequent resurrection unsettled her that much? Was there something in the air here at Harlot's Bay, the last place she'd even half-heartedly tried to find a real community? Because none of this was like her. Not the spontaneous travel. Not the uncontrollable emotions.

Grief. Joy. Guilt. Anger. And now—anticipation? Fear?

"He . . ." A saline-scented breeze blew a strand of hair into her mouth, and she moved it aside with a hooked finger. "He was really caring and patient with Charlotte and her kids, Lise."

Lise's calm, matter-of-fact tone was a balm for all that raw emotion. "She's been working at the bakery since she was a teenager, and the father of her kids has addiction issues. And she's sweet as pie, so over the years, she's sort of become Karl's surrogate daughter. He helps her out however he can. I think he even babysits on a regular basis."

"Oh." Her suede loafers were going to start pilling if she kept scuffing them against the sidewalk. "So naming her son after Karl—"

"Was a tribute to a man she loves like a father."

The sun overhead shone brightly enough to dazzle her, and she squinted as she gazed down the street. "Quit interrupting me, Lise."

"Make me, Mol."

After a moment of companionable silence, Molly confessed, "The whole Charlotte-Karl thing is . . . really endearing. And maybe . . ." She cleared her throat. "Maybe part of me does want to agree to his stupid plan. But if I stayed . . . ."

Her friend allowed the silence to stretch, then broke it. "If you stayed . . . what?"

"I might get too attached." Her mouth worked. "I mean, we live across the country from each other. I don't have the bandwidth right now to do a long-distance thing, Lise."

"Hmmm." Lise sounded skeptical. "Is that the only reason you're hesitant to stay?"

Molly did her best to feign confusion. "What do you mean?"

Her thespian abilities and training had entirely abandoned her, though. Only a fool could fail to recognize the attempted dodge, and Lise was far from slow.

"Molly. You know what I mean."

Sure enough. "Yeah. I know what you mean."

"Then you might as well say it."

Dammit. She really needed to pick less perceptive friends.

With a sigh, she closed her overly dry eyes against the glare from the diner's windows and admitted everything. The whole ugly truth.

"I've loved two men in my entire life. Both of them turned out to be duds." In different ways, but each way had ended in a failed marriage. Her mother's. Her own. "It hurts, Lise. More than I like to admit. I don't want to . . ." She swallowed hard. "No, I *can't* hurt like that again."

Lise made a humming noise. "And you think you could love Karl too, given enough time together."

"I think part of me *did* love Karl, twenty years ago." Her temples were beginning to ache again, and she rubbed at them with her free hand. "So . . . yeah. He's dangerous."

Her overdramatic reaction to that damn obituary—after two full decades apart!—had made that much clear.

"Because you don't trust him not to betray you somehow."

"Because if he's the kind of man who *would* betray me, I wouldn't see the red flags, no matter how closely I paid attention. Because if he *did* betray me, I wouldn't realize until far too late, and I might . . ." Her chin dipped to her chest, and she exhaled shakily. "I might not ever be able to put myself back together afterward."

If someone else she cared about left her, betrayed her, disappointed her, she'd probably make herself a blanketed burrow inside her recording booth and never leave again.

Lise's voice had turned gentle. "So you're scared."

"Yes." She hated admitting that. Always had.

"I get it. I really do. But . . ." Lise was silent for a moment. "Hey, Molly?"

"Still here." In fact, her feet currently felt glued to the sidewalk.

"What if you *can* trust Karl? What if he *wouldn't* lie to you or betray you? Even if you don't owe him, don't you owe *yourself* a chance to find out what could happen between you?" Lise hesitated. "Because you're very alone in LA, Mol. I worry about you."

Frowning, Molly opened her eyes. "I don't want you to worry about me."

Sure, she was kind of isolated back home. But that wasn't necessarily a *bad* thing. Right?

"I know. But I worry anyway, because I love you. Consider it a free gift with purchase."

Molly might not be able to see her friend's smile, but she could hear its warmth. Hear the honesty Lise was offering her.

Was this what it felt like to have a best friend?

If so, it would be the first time she'd truly had one. Ever. At thirty-nine years old.

"I love you too," Molly whispered, and dry eyes suddenly weren't a problem anymore. "Lise . . . you really think it could work? Karl and I, together?"

Rather than offering an immediate response, her friend considered the question for a while. "I don't know," she finally said. "But I think it's worth a shot. And if things go wrong, I'll help you pick up the pieces. You won't be alone, Mol, I swear. If I need to, I'll take some time off and fly to Los Angeles and become a glamorous Hollywood superstar for a while. As long as superstardom doesn't involve socializing with strangers, which is a definite no-go."

Molly believed it. Lise would, in fact, get on a plane and help piece her back together, as needed.

"Okay." One deep, bracing breath. Another. "Okay."

She blotted her eyes with her sleeve, mentally preparing for the next step.

    After a minute, Lise spoke again. "What are you going to do?"

    Molly pushed off the wall. "I think it's time for a short stroll."

    "To Grounds and Grains?"

    "To Grounds and Grains," she confirmed, and began walking.

6

Karl . . ." Charlotte lingered in the doorway leading to his work area. "Are you okay?"

No. He really wasn't.

A man who wanted to seriously consider his legacy in the world would grunt less and talk more. But after reading his own weirdo obituary, after being shunted aside by the woman of his dreams a second time . . . yeah, he had things to think about.

And those things were really fucking problematic.

All the people in Harlot's Bay who'd genuinely mourned him had basically forced themselves into his life. Did he even know how to form human connections himself? Without someone else doing all the hard work?

Even worse: Would things have been different with Dearborn—two decades ago *and* two days ago—if he'd learned what the hell to say to people? How to tell them important shit? How to be brave and talk about his fucking *feelings*?

If it'd make her stay, he should find her. Should try his damnedest to express himself. Should leave the bakery right now and take his shot.

But . . . he wasn't a stalker. He wouldn't chase her down if she didn't want to see him. And if he forced a confrontation, explained himself, and got rejected anyway? It'd probably kill him. For real this time. That'd be bad for business, so he wasn't doing it.

Screw emotional bravery. Sublimation through pastry was way

fucking easier.

"Karl?" Charlotte was watching him, blond brows scrunched in concern. Waiting for an answer to a question he'd nearly forgotten.

"I'm fine," he grunted, slamming his bagel dough onto the worktable for the umpteenth time.

"You usually use the stand mixer for that dough. And if you do knead by hand, the whole process is normally a bit less . . . uh, aggressive." She bit her lip. "Also, you're muttering obscenities loudly enough that we've gotten complaints out front. Junessa's four-year-old apparently just demanded 'some motherfucking Cheerios,' and she's livid."

Shit. He'd thought he was swearing under his breath.

In his mind, a teenage Dearborn declared, *He can't even whisper at a normal volume.*

She was right. Except when it came to trusting him, she was always right.

He paused in his kneading. "Who's livid? Junessa or her daughter?"

"Junessa didn't have any Cheerios in her purse, so . . . both of them, actually."

Bracing himself on the table's edge, he bowed his head and looked down at his overworked dough. It was basically impossible to knead bagels too much, but he'd done it.

"I think this is the first time in two years you haven't listened to a Sadie Brazen audiobook before opening." Her expression so soft it actually hurt, Charlotte moved farther into the workroom and closed the door behind her. "It's her, isn't it? The narrator of those stories? I'm almost sure I recognized her voice."

Dearborn used a pen name. Probably had a good reason for

that.

His bench scraper easily transferred the ruined dough to the waiting trash can. Avoiding Charlotte's eyes, he began prepping another batch. "Can't say."

He kept expecting her to leave. She lingered instead. One minute. Two.

"Karl?" she finally asked again, her voice tentative.

He forced himself not to snap at her. "What?"

"Do you . . ." Her fingers laced together. Wrung. "Maybe I could help you back here sometimes? You work such long hours, and I'd really like to—"

"I'm *fine*," he repeated, with emphasis. "Don't worry."

The last two things Charlotte needed? A boss dumping his problems on her and more work. The kid's plate was already full. Overflowing.

Her shoulders bowed. "Oh. Okay."

A knock on the door. Which was a fucking indictment, because his employees shouldn't hesitate to enter the back area, where they had their break room. He must've been a real prick the last couple days. Would have to make it up to everyone somehow.

Still: Thank fuck for the interruption. He'd rather eat gravel than deflect Charlotte's misguided pity a second time or—even worse—continue discussing the one who got away, then returned and did it a-fucking-gain.

"Come in," he called. "Don't need to knock."

Johnathan poked his head inside. "Boss? You have a visitor."

Then Molly Dearborn walked through the door with the composure of a damn queen, all calm confidence and cool serenity. Unless you looked in those pale blue eyes. Saw the uncertainty there.

Briefly closing his own eyes in relief, Karl tipped his head back and exhaled hard.

Holy shit. She'd come back to him. Again.

Karl couldn't muster a single word. Didn't even try to speak. In the silence, Charlotte and Johnathan disappeared out front, shutting the door with a quiet *snick*.

"You can have your four weeks for trust building, if you still want them," Molly said without preamble. "I lost a bet with Lise Utendorf, so I'll be in town through the reunion anyway."

Seemed too good to be true. Maybe he'd misheard.

"You're staying?" he forced out.

"Yes."

Thank fucking Christ. "Gonna let me prove myself?"

"As best you can." Her lips quirked faintly. "It helps that the boy I knew twenty years ago wasn't ever a liar. A grump, yes. An issuer of illogical threats, definitely. A careless dumper of potentially fragile belongings—"

He waved that aside. "Get to the damn point, Dearborn."

"But you were always honest. Possibly because you're congenitally incapable of subterfuge or subtlety, but the fact remains: You weren't a sneak or a cheat. It was one of the things I liked best about you." Uncharacteristically restless, she fiddled with the strap of her cross-body messenger bag. "If you'd been a liar then, there's no way I'd have agreed to this cockamamie plan now."

"Got a head start, then." At her look of confusion, he clarified. "Convincing you to trust me."

She hesitated. "I suppose."

The wariness in her voice? The tense lines across her forehead? Not optimal.

Even back in high school, she'd been guarded as hell. The past two decades had only made her more so. But she was in his bakery now, seemingly agreeing to spend the next four weeks with him. He was getting his chance, at *last*, and he'd show her she'd made the right decision.

They had plans to make. He had trust to earn.

But before they began, he needed to be sure. Needed to hear the words one more time. "So you're definitely in, Dearborn? Willing and prepared to spend the rest of September with me?"

Doubt still clouded her blue eyes but didn't color her voice.

"I'm in," she said calmly, firmly, and for the first time in his entire damn life, he understood why people jumped for joy.

Setting aside his new bagel ingredients, he marched to the nearest sink and washed his hands. Beneath the cap, his hair would look like shit, so that had to stay. But he stripped off his beard net before turning around and walking back to her, because a man had his pride.

Five feet between them now. She'd have to close the rest of the distance.

He needed that gesture from her. Suspected *she* needed a sense of control. Like a wary cat, she'd come to him when she was ready.

They stood like gunslingers. Face-to-face. Wide stance. Fists on hips. Direct eye contact. He hoped like hell he was quick enough, smart enough, to win this battle.

Her piercing gaze pinned him in place. "I have two questions for you, Dean."

He dipped his chin in silent invitation, braced and ready.

"First question: Can you forgive me for assuming the worst of you? Both times?"

An easy one. "If you can forgive me. I screwed up twenty years ago. Should've told you Becky and I were through."

"Done." Her rosy lips curved slightly. "Second question: Would you go with me to the reunion? As my date?"

Hold the fuck on. That wasn't a challenge. Wasn't another hit to Karl's stupid heart.

It was . . . an *invitation*?

"Unless you've changed dramatically in the past two decades, I know you'd rather eat your apron than attend a social event," she added. "But like I said, I lost a bet to—"

"Was already going." Which weren't the right words, but at least they were *something*.

"Sure you were." She huffed out a laugh, then abruptly sobered. "Wait. Do you have a date lined up? If so, no problem. I can just—"

"No date. Except you now." Awkwardly, he adjusted the brim of his cap. "Remember Janel Altman?"

"As a matter of fact, I ran into her Tuesday night." Molly's smile had returned, and it rounded her rosy cheeks. Jesus, why was she so fucking *pretty*? "She's organizing the reunion, right?"

"Right." He heaved a heartfelt sigh. "Few weeks back, I put in a bid to cater her tenth anniversary party. Already have as much work as I can handle, but I've got employees looking for extra hours." Johnathan, mostly. If the kid didn't find more money soon, he'd have to drop out of college. "Janel, that diabolical busybody mastermind, agreed to hire us—but only if I came to the reunion."

You need to get out more, Karl, she'd informed him, patting him on the arm like he was a senile goddamn grandpa. *You have a whole community of people waiting to be your friend, if you'd just let them.*

Sounded like a nightmare to him. Between work and family, he was busy enough as it was, thank you very much. And he *had* friends, as that bizarro obit had showed him. Matthew. Athena.

Bez. Johnathan. Even all those harpies in their weird-ass erotic-romance-reading book club.

Bethany in particular was sweet. Fifty-something. Quiet. Fluttery. Very enthusiastic about his muffins—and also gargoyle dicks, for some fucking reason.

He wished to Christ he didn't know that, but here he was. Knowing that.

"So you agreed to go for the sake of your staff," Molly summed up.

That blue gaze lingered on him like a stroke of her palm. Soft. Warm.

Her stance had relaxed. She was leaning her round ass against the nearest countertop now, arms loose at her sides. Smiling at him, beautiful as a fucking painting.

Every time he looked at her, he had to catch his damn breath. Same as always.

Cautiously, he propped his hip against the sink edge and relaxed a bit too. "Yeah. Even though that's the weirdest hiring condition I've ever heard, and I'd rather gargle knives than go to a goddamn class reunion."

When she laughed again, her coppery hair *shimmered*. He wanted to bury his hands, his face, in that gorgeous hair. Wrap it around his fists as she moaned into his mouth. Feel it drag slowly along his skin as she crawled over him.

Swallowing hard, he wrenched his mind back to reality.

"Might've gone even without Janel bullying me," he admitted. "The Nasty Wenches have been badgering me for an entire year about the reunion. They—"

She raised a palm. "Hold up. The Nasty Wenches?"

"Local book club. They read smut."

Soft jazz. No other sound. He could've heard a mouse fart. Not that the bakery had mice, or the health department would be on his ass like a boil.

Her response came slowly. "And you're . . . part of this book club?"

"Yeah. I guess." He shrugged. "If I miss a meeting, they bitch for weeks. Easier just to read some sexy shit and show up."

Even though he still didn't understand what an *Omegaverse* was. Something about knots and glands and people who sniffed a whole lot?

Also, those assholes sprayed body fluids absolutely fucking everywhere. County health department wouldn't let a single one of 'em anywhere near a food-preparation facility. They were walking, talking, sniffing, constantly fucking sanitation hazards.

Dearborn's head tipped to one side as she studied him. "Interesting."

"Speaking of our book club, you narrated *Alpha Krampus's Knotty List*." He pointed an accusing finger her way. "So tell me, what the hell is that alpha/beta/omega shit?"

She flicked a hand. "The whole thing is a literary conceit. Not based on actual wolfpack behavior in the wild. Or at least that's what Sadie told me. She said to just go with it, so I did." Her gaze sharpened to a pale-blue scalpel as she continued to scrutinize him. "Out of curiosity, Karl . . . just how many of my books have you listened to?"

Way more than he'd admit to. A shame, since he really wanted to ask her what the fuck was up with *My Kangaroo, My Kidnapper* too. If that pouched prick actually had sex with his victim, Karl didn't want to keep listening.

So far, "dark romance" month blew, even though a few Wenches were into it. Good for them. Not him. Consent issues squicked him the hell out.

"Not sure." Technically true. He'd lost count after about twenty audiobooks. "Meant to ask—the bet you lost to Lise. What was it?"

Mentally, he thumped himself on the back in congratulations. Subtle subject change: accomplished.

She shook her head immediately. "I can't tell you. I'm bound by friendship confidentiality rules. My lips are sealed."

The two women still being in contact? Close enough to share secrets? Hell of a surprise. He hadn't thought they were friends in high school. But it wasn't like he knew Lise that well, and no one had accused him of being the most perceptive man in existence, so whatever.

"Proving yourself completely trustworthy will require close contact, I think." She drummed her fingers against her thigh and thought for a moment. "How would you feel about my coming to your bakery in the mornings and hanging out with you while you work?"

Almost anyone else, he'd respond: "Like murdering you and using your lifeless carcass in my daily soup special."

With Dearborn, he had to tamp down his goddamn glee instead. "That'd be good. And on weekends, when I'm closed, we can still meet here. For our official trust-building activities."

She looked amused. "That's . . . surprisingly formal of you, Dean. Did you have any particular exercises in mind?"

"Uh . . ." He had research to do. Tonight. Because only one thing came to mind, and it wasn't great. "Trust falls? You drop, I catch you?"

Read about those in the dentist's waiting room before his last cleaning. Some glossy business magazine with a suited, white-toothed asshole on the cover. Shit sounded ridiculous, but Dearborn had put him on the spot, so she got what she got.

She stared meaningfully down at herself, then directed a flat stare his way. "Really?"

Well . . . crap. She had a point.

The woman was a perfect, ample armful. He could handle her—was practically salivating at the mere fucking *thought* of handling her—when she was standing. Sitting. Lying flat on her back. Kneeling over his face. Arching on all fours.

Probably not landing on him like a sack of goddamn potatoes, though.

"Got till Saturday." He shrugged. "I'll come up with something."

Molly looked skeptical. "Sure."

He would, though. It'd be part two of his Official Plan to Keep Molly Dearborn in Harlot's Bay. He'd basically be making shit up, but that wouldn't stop him.

As various stupid bastards said right before they parkoured to their goddamn deaths: YOLO, motherfuckers.

7

—no idea why you won't stay at my house," Karl was grumbling as he swirled peanut butter icing over a tray of brownies. "Got an extra bedroom, and it'd be free."

A generous offer, but Molly couldn't impose on him that way. Besides, if he wanted to delay sex, actually living together for an entire month would screw that up. Literally. After a week, she'd probably just tackle him, lion-gazelle style, and start *feasting*.

"I don't feel comfortable with that, but thank you," she told him for the second time, and ignored his low growl of discontent. "I'll figure something out."

"Still stubborn as hell," he muttered, slanting her a scowl.

"Thank you so much."

Another aggravated rumble.

"Is your stomach upset? Your digestive system . . ." She shuddered delicately. "It keeps making these *awful* sounds."

With one hand, he kept icing. With the other, he offered her an upraised middle finger.

It was impressive, how his irritation didn't slow down his work. No doubt he was used to laboring through crankiness, since even Oscar the Grouch could boast a cheerier baseline temperament than Karl Dean.

The shop's lone baker had far too much on both his literal and figurative plates for a grumpiness break, as she'd quickly discovered that afternoon. Mere seconds after they'd agreed on the parameters of his half-baked—ha!—trust-building scheme, he'd told her she needed to put on gloves if she intended to touch anything that wouldn't go in the oven afterward, ordered her to sling her hair back into a ponytail, and handed her a clean baseball cap to wear while in his kitchen.

The cap matched his, which definitely didn't give her a certain warm glow of satisfaction, because that would be foolish.

Anyway, once she'd put on the non-warm-glow-inducing cap, he'd donned another beard net and begun making up for time lost during their earlier conversation. After throwing together a quick bagel dough and kneading it in his stand mixer, he'd set it aside to proof and begun working on umpteen other tasks. Making pastries to be refrigerated and baked off the following morning. Mixing up various glazes and icings. Measuring out ingredients for a batch of cakes. Cooking homemade jams as scone toppings and cake fillings.

Other than a quick pause to answer his mom's and sister's texts, he hadn't taken even a minute's break.

"Coffee break soon," he told her now, never looking up from his work. "Whatever you want, Johnathan'll make. Sandwiches too, if you're hungry."

He'd almost finished icing his brownies, even as oven timers continued to sound at regular intervals. And somehow, amidst all that controlled chaos, he'd still considered her needs and how he could satisfy them.

If anyone had asked her yesterday whether watching a man multitask in a beard net and green, flour-dusted Crocs could be sexy, she'd have laughed and given the wrong answer.

Because oh, yes, it could be sexy. Especially if she considered other arenas where competent multitasking, attention to her needs, and strong, agile hands could prove helpful.

Their time apart definitely hadn't lessened his appeal for her. She'd always liked men who appeared poised to find a cave somewhere and take a long winter's nap. Tough but cuddly, with strong shoulders and arms and a solid belly. Karl's wavy russet hair hadn't thinned yet, his reddish beard had grown even more lush over the years, and together they only added to the overall ursine effect.

His faded graphic tee clung to those wide shoulders and his round stomach, and when he turned away from her, his equally faded jeans outlined nicely thick thighs and the subtle arc of his butt. Her palms itched to shape themselves to that tempting ass. Her fingers twitched as she imagined dragging her nails over tough muscle and soft flesh and hot skin.

His style hadn't changed over the years. His body had only gotten better.

Looking up from his last tray of brownies, he caught her staring. "What?"

"Crocs, huh?" Once they'd slept together, she'd admit to ogling him. Not yet.

He shrugged. "Easy to clean. Back hurts less when I wear 'em."

His job entailed leaning over his worktable all day, and neither of them was young anymore. No wonder his back hurt. Could he use one of those gel mats on the floor?

As she considered the matter, he remained stuck on her lodging situation.

"A month at Battleaxe would cost a damn fortune, but where else . . ." The swirl of his offset spatula suddenly halted, and he raised his head. "Got an idea. Hold on."

Laying down the spatula, he stripped off his gloves and washed his hands, then disappeared into his back office.

By the time she followed him and leaned a hip against his door-frame, he already had his phone in hand and was texting some-one. When he didn't receive an immediate answer, he aggressively swiped and tapped a few times, then set the cell on his desk.

The sound of a ringing phone emerged from the speaker.

"Who—" she began, but he stabbed his finger in the air in a request for silence.

A faint click. "Karl. Is something the matter? Because I was in the middle of a conversation with—"

"Spite House still for sale?"

Her eyebrows rose. He was calling someone about the town's infamous Spite House? Because she'd rambled down that street yesterday, and there was a real estate agent's sign—Fawn Something-or-other—planted in the home's tiny patch of front yard.

The place looked a lot less abandoned than when she'd left Harlot's Bay, with pretty curtains and a flower box at every win-dow. The brick row house was still as ridiculously narrow as ever, though. Ten feet wide, at most.

"Hold on a minute." The other man sounded resigned to the in-terruption. "I'm sorry, Hector, but could we possibly postpone—"

The line went silent, presumably as Karl's mysterious contact muted his phone.

Matthew, Karl's screen informed her. And while that was hardly the world's most uncommon name, she suspected she knew exactly who was making his excuses on the other end of the call.

She pointed to the display. "You're still friends with Matthew Vine?"

Karl and his closest high school companion been an odd duo in certain ways. Matthew had been very reserved for a teenager, but also polite and kind. Karl had been simultaneously uncommunicative and loud, his own kindness hidden by cranky bluster.

But neither boy socialized much, and both were fundamentally good kids who worked hard for their families. She'd understood how the two of them could have become close, and apparently they'd stayed that way for two decades. Which said good things about both men's steadfastness and reliability.

Karl dipped his chin in confirmation just as Matthew came back on the line.

"Okay." He sounded breathless. "The Spite House is more a curiosity than a viable residence for most people, so yes, it's still for sale. Athena got an offer last week, but it was insultingly low, so she turned it d—"

"She open to a month's rental?" Karl interrupted. Again.

Let him finish a sentence, Molly mouthed, ignoring his scowl.

In a testament to Matthew's good nature and tolerance, his response was amused rather than irritated. "I'd be happy to check with her and tell you, assuming you let me finish a sentence in the near future."

She arched a single eyebrow and directed a pointed look at Karl.

"If you'd get to the goddamn point more quickly, I wouldn't—" As her stare became an incredulous glare, Karl shifted his weight and directed his own gaze to the floor. "Sorry, man. Running behind on my bakes and prep. Not an excuse. Just a reason."

"It's fine." Matthew's voice remained warm and sincere. "Before I call her, why don't you tell me what's going on? If you don't have time for that now, we can talk later."

Karl hunched forward over the phone, his meaty fists on the desk supporting his weight. "Molly needs a place to stay."

A moment's silence. "Has something else happened since you

texted me yesterday? Because last I heard, you were upset that she—"

"You're on speaker, dude. Molly's right here." His nostrils flared as he exhaled heavily. "Interrupted again, I know, but that's on her. One hundred percent her fault."

She sighed. "Really, Karl?"

"Um . . . hi, Molly." Matthew's tone had become significantly more cautious, although he still sounded friendly enough. "Welcome back to Harlot's Bay. I'm sorry you returned under such unusual circumstances, but I hope you've had a good visit thus far."

Unusual circumstances was a considerable understatement. Sometime soon, she really needed to hear the full story of how that mistaken obituary had even happened.

"Hey, Matthew. Luckily, the reports of Karl's death were greatly exaggerated, so this trip has been much better than I'd anticipated. I hope you're doing well?"

"I'm fantastic. Thank you for asking," he told her, sounding firm and sure and happy. "Since Karl is most likely on the verge of spontaneous human combustion—"

"Not a real thing," she said under her breath, and Karl screwed up his face in exaggerated shock and dismay at her near-silent interruption.

Rude, he mouthed, and shook a reproving finger at her. She wanted to bite it.

"—due to acute impatience, I'll cut to the chase. I got married not long ago, and my wife Athena owns the Spite House. She's leading a tour right now at Historic Harlot's Bay, but she should be on break soon, so if you tell me what you need, I can ask her about it almost immediately."

A woman's faint voice filtered through the speaker, growing

louder by the word. "Speak of the devil, and she appears." After a quiet rustle came the faint smack of an abbreviated kiss. "Tour got canceled. I'm done for the day, so I thought I'd come see the best husband ever, on this or any other planet."

Karl snorted. "Then why are you at Matthew's office?"

"Shut up, Special K."

Special K? Karl must loathe that nickname.

As Molly quietly snickered to herself, Karl rolled his eyes. "Told you not to call me that, Greydon. Do it again, I'll throw you in a vat of pastry cream and hold you under till you're a human fucking eclair."

"You did tell me that"—the other woman paused meaningfully—"Special K." Ignoring Karl's sputters of inarticulate, overdramatic outrage, she breezily continued, "Anyway, someone had a question for me?"

Matthew came back on the line. "Yes. Sorry. Molly Dearborn, please meet Athena Greydon. Molly is a former high school classmate of ours. Athena is the owner of the Spite House, an amazing historical interpreter at Historic Harlot's Bay, and . . . my wife."

As he spoke about Athena, pride and pleasure suffused his words, virtually dripping from every syllable.

"Lovely to meet you, Molly," his wife said, then added, "By the way, Matthew, I consulted Professor Google about spontaneous human combustion a couple of years ago, back when you could still get decent search results, and scientists are almost entirely certain it doesn't exist."

Molly liked her already. "I was just thinking that."

"Any relevant incidents are probably due to the wick effect," Athena explained. "Basically, someone catches fire due to an external ignition source, like a cigarette or spark. And then the victim's melted fat soaks their clothing and acts like a wick in a candle, so their body smolders for a long time and burns to ashes without damaging their surroundings. If there's no evidence left as to the actual cause of the fire, it looks like the body burned entirely on its own."

"Thus the seemingly logical but ultimately false explanation of spontaneous human combustion," Molly concluded.

"Exactly."

"That's fascinating."

It was the honest truth. As much as she enjoyed Sadie's work, murder mysteries and pop science books were her favorites. This whole conversation might as well have been labeled "Molly catnip."

"I know, right?" Athena's voice somehow brightened even more. "We should get together while you're in town and discuss Special K. I have *so much* to tell you. When are you free?"

"My schedule on weekday evenings is pretty open right n—"

"*No.*" Karl snatched the phone from the table and angled away from Molly. "Not happening, Greydon. You two? Together? Goddamn disaster in the making."

For all his bluster, when Molly promptly retrieved the cell from his fist, he didn't fight her for it. "I'll get your number, Athena, and we'll find a time to compare notes about Karl. Also, please ignore his previous pastry cream threat. As I'm sure you already know, he would never actually do anything like that."

"Nope. He's a secret softie. Aren't you, Special K? Yes, you are. Yes, you are," Athena cooed, as if soothing a frazzled cat or a fussy baby. "Molly, is he looking especially murderous right now?"

"He is indeed." His chest had swelled in indignation, and the homicidal fury in his glare would have terrified Molly—if he weren't, in fact, a secret softie. Which he totally was. "Rest assured: If spontaneous human combustion were possible, the searing heat of his fiery rage would have already rendered him—"

Athena laughed. "Literally."

"—a greasy spot and a heap of ashes on his tiled workroom floor." Molly smiled. "It's very entertaining to watch. Thank you."

Karl was muttering to himself again. The phrase *two harpy peas in a fucking harpy pod* stood out, although Molly couldn't decipher everything.

"My pleasure. Trust me on that." Athena's tone turned brisk, albeit still friendly. "Okay, as delightful as this conversation has been, Matthew needs to see a patient soon, and I need to make out with him before he does. So whatever question you have, let's hear it, and if we don't have enough time to nail down everything now, we can talk again later."

Molly kept things brief. "I'm looking for somewhere to stay until the high school reunion in early October. Karl apparently thinks your former home might be a good option, even though I'm concerned it may be too narrow for someone of my size."

"I know *that* feeling." A faint hum, as Athena considered the matter. "Why don't you come tour the place tonight? If it seems doable for you, we'll work out a fair rental price. Friends and family discount. Speaking of which—why haven't I heard about you before now? Special K, why have you been holding out on me, despite our deep and abiding friendship?"

Karl made a very rude gagging noise, while Molly snickered.

Even over a cell phone speaker, Athena's personality sparkled. She had charm to spare and an open demeanor, matched with obvious intelligence. If Molly were staying in Harlot's Bay permanently, Athena Greydon would be someone she'd—

It didn't matter. In a month, Molly's plane would haul her back to California.

"That's my fault," she told the other woman. "After I left town at the end of senior year, I didn't really stay in contact with anyone."

"Gotcha." Athena conducted a brief, muffled conversation with Matthew. "Okay, making-out time is upon us, so have Special K send your number to me, and we'll text to work out all the details for tonight."

A few hurried goodbyes—and one loud grumble from Karl—later, the call ended.

"Greydon's a damn menace." When his timer went off, a stab of his finger silenced it. "Speaks to me like a fucking toddler sometimes."

Molly lifted a shoulder. "If the onesie fits . . ."

Middle fingers aloft, he turned his back to her and stomped out into his work area, but not before she spotted the grin splitting his ruddy beard. She followed him, something long-knotted in her chest fraying at the edges. Loosening. Unraveling.

Rob had bemoaned her missing sense of humor so many times, she'd finally believed him. But in the past several days, she'd made both Lise and Athena laugh. Broken through Karl's fake grumpiness until he couldn't hide his amusement any longer. Felt truly likable and *connected* for the first time in years.

Why hadn't she seen it sooner?

In her marriage, in too many of her abortive would-be friendships, she'd been sending out messages in bottles that kept bumping against the wrong shores, landing in the hands of people who couldn't read what she'd written. And after years of silence in return, she'd mostly given up. Stopped launching her bottles, stopped believing her offerings could be deciphered by anyone but herself and maybe Lise.

But one of her last remaining missives had finally bobbed ashore at the right place.

Her messages could in fact be decrypted by someone. Possibly several someones. And those messages were worth reading. They were worth returning. Which meant they were still worth sending.

She didn't trust easily. She might harbor more than her fair share of cynicism. That didn't mean she had to burrow beneath her shell and give up on companionship forever. Lise was a dear friend, as Molly had only just realized. Possibly even a best friend. She could make other friends too, if she made the effort.

And she had Karl's nonexistent death to thank for that revelation about her life.

Suffused by warmth that had nothing to do with the kitchen's balmy temperature, she propped her butt against his office doorway and watched him multitask like a freaking sex god. Not graceful in the traditional sense of the word, but sure in every action, with no wasted gestures or energy. Strong. Fierce. Eminently capable.

Complaining all the while, beard net and gloves back in place, he removed several heavenly smelling baking sheets from his two large ovens, slid the hot pans onto a rack, and wheeled the rack out front, then returned to shove yet more trays of unbaked treats into the ovens and set several timers.

Under his age-thinned tee, his triceps flexed with each heft of a loaded pan, each shove of his rack. His thighs tensed and released. His thick shoulders rose and fell. His sharp eyes narrowed beneath the brim of his cap as he focused on his creations, and starbursts of tiny lines appeared at their corners. The tendons in his hands shifted beneath those tight blue gloves, delineating his tiny adjustments to temperature and placement and timing, tweaks whose purpose she couldn't begin to fathom.

Then he was evidently done. After removing his gloves with twin snaps of nitrile, he whipped off his apron and beard net and turned on his Croc-clad heel.

His stare locked her in place.

When he stalked toward Molly, her pulse thudded faster. Harder. So fast she could feel the tick at her throat. So hard she could no longer hear soft jazz or the murmur of customers or anything but her heartbeat and the faint rasp of her quickened breathing.

Her words sounded muffled to her own ears. "Do Matthew or Athena know about my alter ego?"

He halted only inches from her, and she didn't know whether to be outraged or relieved.

His brows thudded together, creasing the pale skin between. "'Course not."

"Why didn't you tell them?"

"You use a different name. Figured there must've been a reason, and I won't share information you want kept secret." His jaw ticked. "Could have an abusive ex. Stalker. Other privacy issues. No way for me to know."

Another knot of tension and uncertainty unwound in her chest. "You were protecting me."

He nodded, then bridged that final gap between them, stepping into her space fully. Shadowing her against the glare of the fluorescent overhead fixtures, pressing belly to belly, the denim of his jeans brushing hers. She bit her lip against a gasp, and her knees weakened beneath her, melting like ice beneath a blowtorch.

"After my coffee break, I've got a follow-up with my doctor," he rasped. "Means the rest of the day is fucked. Don't know how much attention I'll be able to give you when I get back, Dearborn. Not enough for my liking."

The man had a job to do. Honestly, he'd already devoted more time to talking with her than she'd even hoped.

He added, "Stay back here as long as you want, though. You're welcome whenever."

"It's fine. I should be heading out anyway. I have emails to answer and a flight to rebook back at my hotel." She smiled at him. "Will I see you tonight, at the Spite House tour?"

"Count on it." The man threw off enough heat to rival one of his ovens, and she did her best not to sway into that tempting warmth. "Before you go, I need your number. And one other thing."

"What?"

Levering himself away from her, he jerked his chin toward the interior of his office. Toward privacy. When he stepped away, stepped through the doorway, the rush of cooler air didn't do anything to ease the fevered flush of her cheeks, the budding warmth between her legs.

She followed him in silence. Once inside, she shut the door behind them. Locked it.

A flush darkened his cheeks and spread down his neck. He stood in front of his desk. Kicked aside the cheap office chair positioned between them. Crooked his finger.

She took her time answering his summons, because he deserved a little suffering after turning down her earlier invitation to bed.

"Five minutes, my next timer goes off." His dark stare devoured her as she drew near. "Till then, I want to kiss you. That okay with you?"

"Well, yeah." She gave a breathless laugh. "I mean, I already suggested that we fuck, so . . ."

His exhalation hitched at the word *fuck*. "You want me to stop, something doesn't feel good, you tell me so. Got it, Dearborn?"

She nodded.

Then his mouth found hers, and there were no more questions. No more concerns. Just heat and pleasure.

Just Karl.

His long fingers cradled her jaw with tense care, and the kiss began as a slow, tender slide of their lips. Gentle brushes of warmth and pressure that stole her breath and blanked her racing thoughts. Not tentative in any way—just very, very restrained.

Karl Dean might seem larger than life, but he was also a baker. He knew how to be precise.

Her mouth opened in a sharp indrawn breath at his first tongue-flick, and he nudged a little harder. Pressed a little closer. Tilted his head to seal their lips together and trace the curve of her smile with that slick, delicious, talented tongue.

He'd drizzled honey into the iced tea he kept beside him as he worked, and she could taste it in his mouth. Taste that familiar amber sweetness, the freshness of the mint leaves he'd muddled into his drink, as their tongues slipped and twined and explored.

He smelled like freshly baked bread. Felt like a sun-scorched stone monolith under her hands. Breathed like a set of bellows between endless kisses. Tunneled the fingers of his free hand into her hair and curled them into a fist with extraordinary caution, because he obviously had no desire to cause her pain, even in the pursuit of pleasure.

That gentleness—the contrast with his rough exterior and demeanor—unleashed something wild within her.

His shoulders tensed into bunched caps of muscle when she

braced herself against their strength and arched her hips to rub against him. He was hard, his cock prodding her thigh, and sturdy and reliable as an oak under her hands. Everything she'd wanted for twenty long, starved years.

He ground his erect dick against her, groaning.

Then his timer went off.

He lurched backward, panting and wild-eyed, and took a half-dozen hasty steps away from her.

"Not yet. *Not fucking yet*," he mutter-shouted, possibly under the impression she couldn't hear him.

She ambled forward again, until they were belly to belly, and disabused him of that notion. "You sure? Because I'm more than willing to—"

"Go." His voice was strangled. "Have some goddamn mercy, Molly, and please *go*."

So she gathered her bag, tucked away the paper-wrapped roast beef, cheddar, and chutney sandwich he pressed wordlessly into her hands, and left Grounds and Grains with a satisfied smile on her face.

Karl might want to wait for sex. But that first kiss between them had been even better—even hotter—than she'd imagined as a horny, naïve teenager two decades ago. And they were seeing each other again in a few hours. At night. In a non-workplace location.

To borrow his vocabulary: Karl Dean was fucking *toast*.

8

*D*earborn's kisses were dangerous.

Incentive for her to stay, as Karl had intended. Hot as Hades. Also temptation he sure as shit didn't need.

Made no difference how long he stared at his bakery office's laptop. Made no difference that he hadn't seen her in over two days. He still couldn't focus on his dairy supplier's bare-bones website or his order-in-progress. His stupid brain didn't give that first shit about stock inventory or budgets. Too busy remembering the slide of her soft breasts against his chest, the pressure of her plush thigh against his prick. The cinnamon-spiced taste of her tongue and woodsy scent of her shampoo or soap or deodorant or whatever the hell made her smell so *amazing*.

Wasn't like he didn't already think about sex whenever he saw her. But now that he'd had a taste of how it'd be between them, he was hungrier than ever to wolf down the whole meal.

Even after twenty years apart, though, he *knew* Molly Dearborn. If they fucked now, she'd dismiss what they had. Call it hormones and chemistry and history. Not—

Didn't matter what it was. Didn't even matter what it could be. He needed to get his act together. Trust building started today, and she'd be arriving soon.

Couple more clicks, and the order was in. Time to make the most bougie sandwich in his arsenal. Charlotte had suggested the flavor combination a few months ago, and the first time he'd sold a batch as a daily special, customers had lost their damn minds, so it'd stayed on the regular menu.

With a bread knife, he split two fresh croissants from the batch he'd shaped and refrigerated yesterday, then proofed and baked off that morning. Stuffed both of 'em with goat cheese, thinly sliced pickled pear, arugula, salt-roasted almonds, and a drizzle of his usual wildflower honey.

As a rule, taste trumped presentation for him. But yeah, a few years back, he'd bought a pair of those big, fancy tweezers for special occasions, so he could place everything just so. He dug them out of a drawer. Used them. Put truffle potato chips on the plates too, the brand Athena pimped like it was her fucking job. Made a butterscotch latte and set out a bottle opener for the Italian blood-orange soda he'd gotten from the gourmet food shop in town.

Class all the way. Perfect for Dearborn.

Fifteen minutes to go. He stripped off his gloves, cap, and beard net, then washed his hands and snatched fresh clothes from his Subaru before hustling into the staff bathroom.

After brushing his teeth, he inspected himself in the mirror. The cap had flattened his hair. Looked like shit. Tossing aside his flour-streaked shirt, he splashed water over his head and kind of patted and pushed and combed until things up top kind of looked better? Maybe?

A brisk knock at the back door. She was early, because *of course* she was.

Swearing, he pulled his new tee over his head, then heaved open the door just as she began to knock again.

"Ten minutes early, Dearborn." Grumbling to cover his nervousness, he waved her inside. "Serve you right if I fed you expired deli meat for lunch."

"Ah, threats of listeria. The classic first step in trust building." Amusement curved her lush mouth as she strode inside. "Sorry I'm early, Dean. Did I catch you bathing in your dish sink?"

She reached up and flicked away a few drops of water from his cowlick. A moment's glancing contact, not even skin to skin. But his heart still stuttered in his chest, his head tingled, and his whole body heated in an instant. Those drops should've become *steam*.

Unable to make a sound, he kind of grunted in response as he closed the door behind her.

Again: The woman was dangerous as hell.

He'd only seen her once since their first kisses had burned him down. Later that same night, when she'd taken a quick tour of the local Spite House while he tried to keep at least an arm's length from her at all times. For a while, she'd kept edging closer and eyeing him with those fiery blue eyes, like he was her fully clothed, big-bellied personal Chippendale. Best feeling in his goddamn life, but yeah. No good for his resolve.

Those lustful looks stopped after Athena and Matthew warned her they could see inside most windows in the Spite House—and mentioned they'd removed the main bedroom's curtains for cleaning the day before. The drapes would return soon, but since that bed was the only place where two people of their size could comfortably have sex—especially for the first time—he could almost see Molly's plans for him go up in smoke.

Goddammit. But also: thank fuck.

Athena wasn't charging much for a month's stay. Which meant he and Matthew spent ten minutes cooling their damn heels while Molly actually bargained the rent upward. *For fairness*, she explained. But the two women eventually compromised, and Athena—after making sure it was okay with Molly—tackled her new tenant in a hug. Molly had blinked a few times before cautiously closing her arms around Matthew's wife, smiling, and squeezing back.

Something about seeing that smile, watching all that fucking bonhomie, had made his chest go warm and squishy. Would've suspected a heart attack, but cardiac events weren't supposed to feel *good*, right?

One more long, hot look in his direction—and no actual physical contact—later, she'd left for her last night at the B&B. And over the next two days, she'd moved in and gotten herself supplied for the month, with Lise's and Athena's help.

Meanwhile, the bakery had occupied all his non-sleeping hours.

Pretty often, weekdays didn't give him enough time to get everything done. Coming in on weekends for brief stints, when the bakery was officially closed, to tackle the shit he hadn't managed to do Monday through Friday—that was normal. What he'd done since Thursday wasn't. Instead of heading home at his usual time, he'd spent Friday evening in the workroom. All day yesterday too, from dawn until bedtime. This morning, the sun hadn't risen yet when he'd unlocked his store and suited up in his apron, cap, and beard net.

The time he intended to spend with Molly had to come from somewhere, which meant lots of prep. His freezers and refrigerators should've been bulging by now. To make things even harder, Janel's anniversary party had been Saturday—yesterday—so there'd been extra work to do already. Canapés and other shit to bake, put together, and pack into Johnathan's rusty hatchback, for the kid to arrange and serve at the party.

Karl was tired as hell. But one look at Dearborn—still in Harlot's Bay, against all odds—and he could have hefted a damn semi.

"You ready to begin our agreement?"

"As promised." She scanned his workroom curiously, her gaze lingering on the sandwiches. "What trust-building exercise did you have in mind?"

Frankly, he didn't want to say. The whole thing sounded asinine.

He scratched his beard, shifting his weight. "Lunch first. Then we'll talk about plans."

Grabbing both of their plates, he led the way to his office. Before today, the surface of his desk hadn't seen daylight in years, but he'd put away or shoved aside all the usual crap. The scratched wood now gleamed. So did the silverware he'd set out for them, the glass mug containing her butterscotch latte, and the condensation on her blood-orange soda bottle and his own glass of iced tea.

Looked great, if he did say so himself.

She took the seat he'd placed in front of the desk. Shook out the napkin he'd carefully folded an hour ago and laid it in her lap. Watched him while he arranged both plates and plopped down into his office chair.

"Thank you for all this, Karl. It looks incredible." Posture straight as a queen's, she neatly cut a bite-sized chunk of the croissant. "I was surprised you wanted to meet at the bakery, though, instead of your house or even the Spite House. Don't you spend enough time at your workplace on weekdays?"

"Lunch ingredients are here," he pointed out, then held his breath as she chewed her first bite. When she smiled, sighed in pleasure, and forked up another, even larger bite, his chest actually puffed up like a rooster's, because he was a damn idiot.

Her pale throat shifted as she swallowed, and she reached for her soda. "This is absolutely delicious, Karl. Although . . ."

His chest deflated, and he glared at her. "*What?*"

"Are you *sure* that's the main reason we're meeting in the bakery? Because it's easier to make lunch here?"

Her smile had turned taunting, and his glare intensified.

That gorgeous shrew knew the main reason they weren't meeting in a home. Give the two of them time, privacy, and access to a bed, and they'd be naked faster than he could say *I ruined my fucking plans by not keeping my dick in my fucking pants.*

He didn't bother answering her question. Asked his own instead. "You legally obligated to be a pain in my ass, Dearborn?"

"No." She lifted her latte, lips still curved. "Just constitutionally inclined."

He hid his snort behind his iced tea. "Yeah, you sure as hell are."

Normally, not an issue. One of the things he liked most about her, to be honest.

But in this case—"That mean you're planning to break my resolve? Get us into bed, even though you don't trust me yet?"

When she shook her head, that coppery hair swirled around her shoulders. "I'm not going to pressure you into sex, Karl. I don't want a reluctant, conflicted lover."

An emphatic statement. Before he could exhale in heartfelt relief, though, she continued.

"But if all our close, trust-building proximity encourages you to change your mind . . ." Her glass mug clinked against her plate as she set it down. "Well . . ."

She raised her finger. A request for patience he didn't have.

Slowly, deliberately, she ate another forkful of her sandwich before speaking again. Because . . . yeah. Dearborn was *constitutionally inclined* to be his greatest temptation *and* his greatest trial.

Chew chew chew. Swallow. Pat of her napkin to her lips. Sip of soda. More patting.

With that last napkin-dab, the final dregs of his limited patience drained away.

He threw his hands in the air. "I swear to *Christ*, Dearborn, I'll reach down to your fucking vocal chords and *rip the goddamn words*—"

"As I was saying: If all that close proximity changed your mind, I wouldn't weep," she finally concluded. "Also, side note: Your hand is too big to fit down my throat."

He had to close his eyes for a moment.

No more talk about big things fitting down her throat. Jesus H. Christ.

"Even if it did fit, I wouldn't be able to speak intelligibly around the obstruction." Classic Dearborn. Calmly discussing logistics while his brain and libido both exploded. "Your threat is both impractical and self-defeating, Dean."

He didn't trust himself to say a single word. Just sat there and ate his damn food. When she figured out he wasn't going to reply, Molly did the same.

The silence wasn't weird, though. Not awkward. She clearly thought she'd won their most recent skirmish. Smiled while she ate. And he might be lust-stricken and impatient, but the woman of his fantasies was an arm's length away, happily downing food he'd prepared for her and hoping her nearness would seduce him. Under the circumstances, it was hard to feel sorry for himself. Especially when he showed her the pavlova he'd made earlier, and her pale blue eyes lit with pleasure.

Her voice was hushed when she spoke. "Holy crap, Karl."

Hard to preen without dropping a cake stand, but he damn well managed.

"Pavlova topped with shaved plums, orange-rosemary syrup, and vanilla-bean whipped cream." Another of Charlotte's ideas. Kid had a good feel for flavor and ingredient combinations. "Eat it and fucking weep, Dearborn."

He set the footed stand in front of her.

"Only you, Dean." She shook her head. "Only you could make the presentation of a gorgeous dessert sound menacing."

"You're welcome." Grumpy at the thought of what came next, he stomped around his desk and dropped back into his chair. "Now stop bitching and shove the pavlova down your piehole, woman. I'll explain our plans while we eat."

"At least my throat can actually accommodate a pavlova," she murmured. "As opposed to your hand."

He didn't even recognize the sound he made at that. Something between a growl and a groan. "Are you doing this shit on purpose, Dearborn?"

She didn't answer. Merely gazed serenely at him while he fumed. Which was answer enough, he guessed. When she gestured toward the knife, asking mutely if he wanted to serve the dessert, he offered her his own gesture. With both middle fingers.

"I'd be more than happy to, Karl, but you won't let me." She cut herself a slab of the dessert, her lips curved in that smug smile he hated but also really fucking loved. "If we aren't spending the day in bed, what *are* our plans for the afternoon? Nothing too strenuous, I hope, since I intend to eat more than my share of this pavlova. It looks *ridiculously* good."

Dearborn sparked a million different emotions in him, all at once. Always had. In this moment alone, there was pride. Frustration. Joy. Lust. Amusement.

And above all else: He felt *alive*. No one else on this godforsaken planet had *ever* made him feel more alert and electric with possibility. The sensation might agitate him, but he wouldn't lie to himself. It exhilarated him too.

He couldn't get enough of it. Couldn't get enough of her. Didn't think he ever would. But sappy declarations would have to wait until she trusted him. Which wouldn't happen until he actually got this stupid damn show on the road.

Quickly, he mowed down his pavlova—perfect; Charlotte deserved a damn raise—then pushed his plate aside.

"Here's the plan: I'm gonna blindfold you," he announced without preamble.

She choked on her mouthful of meringue. He had to sprint around his desk to thump her back. Once she could breathe easily again, he shoved her soda bottle in her hand and retreated.

Ears flaming hot, he muttered an apology and tried a second time. "Blindfolded trust walk outside. I'll stand behind you. Give you directions."

Her brows drew together. "To where?"

"You'll find out soon enough." The spot in the Mayor's Mansion gardens where he'd nearly kissed her, hopefully. He'd drive them to the historic area before blindfolding her. "Ready?"

"I don't think I am." Those sharp eyes narrowed on him. "Karl, where are you getting your trust-building ideas?"

"Dentist's office."

He'd gone back on Friday and—with the permission of the gorgon at the front desk—taken home the magazine where he'd first read about trust falls.

She blinked at him for a moment. "You asked your dentist? Or your hygienist?"

"Hell, no." Discussing his plaque levels was as intimate as he cared to get. "Waiting room magazine had an article about trust building."

"I . . . see," she said slowly.

He shook his head, remembering the piece. "The dude who wrote the article was super into blindfolds. Blindfolded walks. Blindfolded obstacle courses. Even blindfolded putt-putt, which sounds like an absolute nightmare."

Her brows drew together. "What kind of magazine was it?"

"*Corporations Today*." Though it should've been *Generationally Wealthy Old White Guys in Suits and Somewhat Younger, Also White Tech Bros Pursuing Venture Capital and Placating Shareholders at Any Cost Today* instead. "Fortune 500 companies must be kinky as hell. Blindfolds up the fucking wazoo. Had no idea before I read the article."

"So you're using a guide to corporate trust building." She sat back in her chair, lips pursed. "Not romantic or friend-oriented trust building."

"Only other guide I found was for established couples. *Cosmo*." He scratched his bearded jaw. "Lots of blindfolds there too, actually."

Fun, quick read. Although the position they'd recommended as *particularly conducive for intimacy*? He'd dislocate his damn hip.

He cleared his throat. "Not, uh . . . not stuff we can do yet. Didn't have much of a choice, really. Either corporate trust building or nothing."

She exhaled slowly and said nothing.

"Article listed lots of large-group activities. I narrowed down the suggestions. Chose things that'd work for just the two of us." He gestured to the table. "Already completed the first exercise without you even knowing. Eating together to build trust. Pretty slick, huh?"

Honestly, most things on the list? Weird and embarrassing—but also a breeze. *Of course* he'd make sure she didn't get hurt while blindfolded. *Of course* he'd keep his word to her. Catch her, guide her, feed her, whatever. That was the sort of task-oriented shit he *excelled* at. Way easier than the more personally revealing activities on the list, which he'd ignored.

Building trust should take a week, max. He was a natural.

"Karl . . ." Leaning forward again, she set her elbows on the desk. Rubbed her face for a moment before dropping her hands. "Lunch was amazing, and I appreciate all your . . . uh, in-depth corporate research. But here's the thing: I already know you won't let me trip or fall. I'm not sure what a blindfolded trust walk would actually prove or how it would help."

Her voice sounded incredibly tired. Also sincere.

Too bad he didn't understand what the hell she was telling him. If she already knew he wouldn't let her get injured on his watch and he'd guide her safely to the finish line, wasn't that trust?

Why were they even doing all this crap, then?

Unless . . .

Was the whole trust thing about honesty instead? Making sure he'd tell her the truth? Because if she wanted proof he couldn't lie for shit, the list had an exercise for that.

"Fine." He slapped his hands on the table and stood, scanning the office for blank notepads and pens. "Two Truths and a Lie, then. You done that before?"

"Of course. But . . ." The fingertips of one hand rubbed her temple. "I already know you can't lie worth a damn, Dean. Your inability to tell a convincing falsehood is right up there with your inability to whisper. Unless that's changed over the years, there's no point wasting our time to establish something I don't even question."

Well, now he was completely lost. "Then what the hell do you . . ."

Aggrieved beyond words, he glowered at her and tugged roughly at his beard.

"Okay." She laid her palms flat on the desk and met his eyes. "Here's the thing, Karl. Making sure I'm not physically injured isn't enough to make me trust you. Not lying isn't enough either. It helps, but . . ." Her huff of laughter was bitter as pith. "My ex would keep me from falling when I lost my balance. One time, when a pan on the stove overheated and caught on fire, he snatched my hands away before I got burned. And he never outright lied to me. That didn't mean he was trustworthy."

Her face was expressionless. Entirely calm.

Her eyes? Wounded and wary.

"What . . ." His hands curled into fists. "What did that bas-tard—"

"No." That was all she said. All she needed to say.

He dropped it. Wasn't going to be the asshole who forced her to discuss something she wanted to keep private. Something that obviously hurt her.

But her reticence only proved what she'd already said. She didn't trust him. Not fully. She'd shot down most of his trust-building exercises, though, so how the hell was he supposed to prove himself to her?

He flopped into his office chair again. Groaned. Ripped spread fingers through his hair. Frantically racked his stupid goddamn brain.

"Hold on." Across from him, her face brightened, and she

straightened in her own chair. "I have an idea."

The woman looked entirely too gleeful.

He eyed her suspiciously. "What?"

"I know exactly what we should do." Slowly, she smiled at him. "It'll show me what you're like in a stressful situation you didn't plan for and can't fully control. And you're going to absolutely hate it."

He groaned. He grumbled. He stomped.

But he followed her out the door anyway, because he'd follow her fucking anywhere.

9

After your introductory video ends, you'll have an hour," the escape room attendant told Molly and Karl, after they'd both signed their waivers and Molly had insisted on paying for their allotted hour. "When you're ready for one of your three hints, tap the icon on the screen. If you need to leave before the hour is up and before you manage to escape, press the emergency exit button next to the door."

Molly inclined her head. "Got it."

The young woman left, brandishing an enormous metal key, and the door shut heavily behind her. The key turned in the lock with an emphatic *clunk*. Unable to stop herself, Molly tugged at the brass door handle, testing just how locked in they really were. The handle didn't move a millimeter. There'd be no escape until they either put together all the clues, employed the emergency button, or ran out of time.

Hopefully they'd work together and communicate well under pressure, even in an environment unfamiliar to them both. Which was precisely what she hoped to find out today.

Whenever a situation turned difficult and her ex got frustrated, he either gave up or turned snarky and unpleasant. And too many times, Rob had turned his snarkiness on her. When that happened, she hadn't put up with his behavior—she'd told him to cut it out or simply walked away—but she'd always managed to excuse it afterward. She'd told herself medical school was stressful, that he hadn't gotten enough sleep, that he didn't realize how sharp and disagreeable he was being.

Turned out, Rob was just a dick. That was all. And if her long-lost high school crush could do better, even under artificial circumstances, that would be one more step toward trusting him with more than her friendship and her body.

"'The Curséd Amulet of Egypt'?" When Karl squinted at the computer touchscreen on the wall, the corners of his eyes creased in an unfairly handsome way. "That's our scenario?"

Before she could answer, the informational video started.

"In the final year of the nineteenth century, an Egyptian expedition led by a prominent British archaeologist uncovered the ancient, untouched tomb of an unknown queen." The computer screen flickered with black-and-white photos of archaeological digs, mustachioed Victorian men in suits looking extremely pleased with themselves, and the local Egyptians hired to do all the hard, dirty work. "The tomb was ruthlessly opened, and priceless artifacts of Egypt's rich historical legacy were packed away to far-away London museums—including the queen's breathtaking amulet, made of turquoise carved into a scarab shape and hung on a plaited chain of gold wire."

Karl stabbed a blunt finger at the amulet on the screen. "Are we supposed to steal the amulet from her tomb or something?"

He sounded disgruntled by the prospect. Well, even *more* disgruntled.

"I certainly hope not," she said with feeling.

He grunted in agreement. "Only an asshole takes another country's artifacts."

As she twisted her neck to smile at him, the informational video's narrator continued speaking.

"—remained tucked in a dusty drawer for over a century. Until last week, when a museum curator came across the artifact once more, cleaned it, and translated the inscription on its back, which warned of a curse placed upon whoever might despoil the queen's tomb."

Karl folded his arms across his chest, satisfied. "Of course there's a curse. Bastards should've kept their eugenics-obsessed meat hooks off a foreign country's historical legacy."

"The curse wouldn't only target the expedition's original members. It would also doom their descendants and their descendants too, unto eternity. They'd ripped away a queen's and a nation's legacy, and so their own legacies, the fruits of their loins, would—"

"Fruit down there? Basically asking for a yeast infection." Karl pursed his lips and shook his head. "Doesn't matter how hot that old-school romance scene was. Like I told all the Nasty Wenches: Raspberries don't fucking belong in vaginas."

"—rip and destroy too," the voice-over actor announced. "And so it came to pass. With the first utterance of the inscription in a dusty museum storage room, the Colonizer's Curse fell upon the expedition members' descendants. Hundreds of them transformed into zombies and rampaged throughout their communities, killing without thought or pity and creating yet more undead creatures."

The narrator paused for emphasis. "The only way to break the curse and save humanity? Steal the amulet back from the museum, survive the ravenous zombies, and overcome all the dangers of the despoiled tomb to return the artifact from whence it came."

"Like a reverse Indiana Jones?" Karl looked significantly more enthusiastic now. "Ignore my bitching and sign me the hell up."

"Your mission begins with the necklace," the narrator concluded. "Find it first, then enter the tomb. Good luck, and your time begins . . . now."

The overhead lights of the ersatz museum storage room flicked off, and only the soft glow of two vintage-looking lamps illuminated the space. The computer screen went dark too, other than its bright blue hint-dispensing icon and the timer ticking down from sixty minutes.

The wall across from them was lined with shelves. A solid wooden desk to the right boasted several drawers, a metal typewriter, an enameled ashtray, and a pile of files. To their left: the exit door with its old-fashioned lock and a safe of some sort.

She headed for the desk and those tempting files.

"Take us half an hour, max." Karl reached for the nearest shelf. "Let's fucking *do this*."

* * *

"THIS FUCKING *BLOWS*," Karl grumbled approximately fifty-seven minutes later. They were the first intelligible words he'd spoken in a good half hour.

The zombies' shrieks and howls were getting louder minute by minute. Even the dim lamps in the corners had begun flickering, in yet another sign that she and Karl were running out of time.

As if she hadn't realized that already. Three minutes left, and they hadn't even made it out of the museum storage area. They had no amulet, no key, no tomb, and no clue.

Well, they did have clues, obviously. But they couldn't seem to decipher those clues. The two of them were so bad at escaping, the room's monitor had actually given them six bonus hints, for a total of nine. Then the young woman had begun typing helpful messages to them on the screen, directing them to look under the rug;

telling them it wasn't a problem with the lock, they simply had the wrong combination; and suggesting that they compare notes about what they'd each found.

Once, she simply wrote "NO." In a startlingly large font.

About five minutes ago, the notes had changed in tone. Turned pitying and comforting, as the end drew near.

"You're doing just fine," read the latest message. "And it'll be over soon. for all three of us."

Molly sighed and chose one last tactic at random. "Why don't we try to decrypt the typewriter keys again?"

With a groan, Karl rose from a squat, where he'd been studying the locked artifact cabinets. Wordlessly, he walked to her side and leaned over to contemplate the typewriter too.

He tapped a random key. "That a fish?"

"Your guess is as good as mine."

To his credit, even a near hour of nonstop frustration hadn't made him give up and admit defeat. He hadn't said much—apart from occasional outbursts of profane crankiness—but when she'd asked questions, commented on what she'd seen, or made suggestions, he'd listened to her and followed her lead. And while he was definitely pissy, he wasn't pissy toward *her*. More the nature of human existence in general and escape rooms in particular.

Her sole responsibility for suggesting the activity had gone entirely unmentioned.

Was he the best possible escape partner she could have had? No. Clearly not. If he were, they'd probably have found the amulet before now. But he could say the exact same thing about her. More importantly: In this sort of situation, Rob would've been livid, all blame and cutting remarks. Well before the allotted deadline, he'd have been smacking the emergency exit button and stomping out of the room without checking whether she intended to join him.

Sure, Karl had barely spoken an unprompted word, and they were going to be ripped apart by zombies at any moment, but at least they'd be ripped apart *together*. She supposed that was a victory of sorts.

While he continued poking at various mechanical components, she tugged futilely at the metal lock securing the lowest desk drawer and began turning the dials to choose digits at random. They needed five numbers, which seemed simple enough—but those five numbers encompassed a hundred thousand possible combinations, and there was nothing in the room that actually narrowed down their options or outright supplied the code.

"This is the most impossible escape room ever." Giving up, she sat back on her heels. "Why in the world would they require a five-digit number for this drawer without giving us clues to determine that number?"

Karl stilled. "A five-digit number? Thought you needed four."

"The locked storage cabinet has a four-digit code," she corrected. "The drawer is five."

"That, uh . . ." He scratched his chin, and his Crocs shuffled a bit on the floor beside her. "That museum worker's name badge I found a while back? Under the rug? Employee number below the picture has, um . . . five digits."

Slowly, she tipped back her chin to stare up at him in utter disbelief. "And you didn't consider *sharing* that information with me?"

"Thought you knew. Used it to type the employee's name and number on the typewriter, although that didn't do shit." He winced. "If I'd realized you needed a five-digit number for the lock—"

She'd seen the engraved badge, but had assumed he'd let her

know if it contained anything worth mentioning. "Hand it over."

When she wiggled her fingers, he gave her the palm-sized metal oval. Whose identification number, yes, opened the desk drawer, which in turn contained a puzzle of some sort. The puzzle appeared to have subtle, hidden numbers, so that would probably help open the storage cabinet compartment, where the amulet might—

A beam in the ceiling above shook and semi-collapsed—in a theatrical, clearly predetermined way—as the lamps went dark. The howls became deafening, and the door began rattling in its frame. *Thud. Scrabble. Shake. Thud-thud.*

"Holy *shit*." Karl grabbed her and shoved her behind him, brandishing a file folder in his fist. "If those assholes—"

A key clicked in the door, which swung open noiselessly, revealing . . .

Not zombies, obviously.

Their room monitor walked into the room and raised the lights by tapping on her tablet, wearing a look of resigned tolerance. Exhaling harshly, Karl lowered his arm, stepped to the side, and allowed Molly to move forward again.

"At this point, I usually go through what needed to happen for you to complete your mission, but that might take some time for you guys. Like, *a lot* of time." The young woman tucked the tablet under her arm. "Would you rather just leave?"

"Oh, no. Definitely not." Molly leaned a hip against the damn desk, folding her arms across her chest. "I want to know *exactly* what we could have accomplished . . . *if* I'd been told the number on the employee badge much, much sooner."

Karl's face creased in a wince, but he didn't protest.

Ten minutes later, the room monitor was still talking.

"—and then you'd place the amulet back inside the tomb and

close the sarcophagus lid, thus causing the zombies to collapse in place before they could quite reach you," she concluded, sounding weary. "The hidden door would swing open, and you'd have escaped successfully."

Silence.

"Wow," Molly finally said. "So there were different spaces to explore, including a boobytrapped tomb and its treasure room. We could have met the holographic reincarnation of an Egyptian queen and slain a zombified, phrenology-obsessed Victorian archaeologist. And yet we spent our entire hour in a museum's ten-by-ten back room storage area."

She raised her brow at Karl.

"No way in h—" He caught himself, then turned to the employee. "No way anyone actually gets all that sh—stuff done before the hour is up. This room's gotta be the hardest one you have, right?"

She directed a flat stare his way. "Our record for this room is fourteen minutes. Set by a trio of eighth-graders during a slumber party."

His shoulders sagged.

"Within those fourteen minutes, they also created and exchanged friendship bracelets—"

Karl grunted. "Fu—freaking Swifties. Should've known."

"—and began coding a Snapchat filter that made them look like talking butts."

"Damn overachieving tweens," he muttered under his breath.

Half amused, half annoyed, Molly followed the room monitor through the now-opened door, down the hall, and to the exit, where the young woman shooed them outside with an audible sigh of relief.

After the air-conditioned chill of the escape room, the humid warmth of the late September afternoon felt like a benediction. She turned her face up to the sun, let her eyelids slip shut, and basked in the heat for a moment. When she blinked her eyes open again, Karl was staring down at her, his intent, tight-lipped expression spangled in her sun-dazzled vision.

His voice had turned to sandpaper. "You ready to go?"

She nodded. In unspoken mutual agreement, they began to walk in the direction of both the Spite House and his bakery. Neither said anything for a long time.

He didn't touch her either. Didn't take her hand or bump hips or sling a heavy arm around her shoulders. Just scowled down at the brick sidewalk and stomped as best he could in his Crocs. In other words: not very effectively.

"Figure that clusterfuck didn't help me prove myself." As he finally spoke, his fingers tunneled through his hair and tugged agitatedly. "Sorry, Dearborn. Waste of time and money."

"Well . . ." The waterfront glinted blue over the horizon, and she squinted at it while they walked. "The premise of the room was fun. And now I know you don't get mean under pressure, insist on making all the decisions, or simply quit. Those are all necessary qualities for me to trust someone."

Honestly, the more ways Karl differentiated himself from her ex, the better.

"But?" His tone was resigned.

The obvious unhappiness in his voice almost silenced her, but . . . he'd always encouraged her bluntness in the past. And if he wanted her to trust him, he needed to understand how he was making that task more difficult on them both, right?

She exhaled slowly. "I can't say I'd be eager to rely on you in any situation requiring teamwork and clear, consistent communication."

He didn't reply with words. Just grunted again, which seemed apropos.

While helping Molly move in on Friday, Athena had explained the whole bizarre story behind the mistaken obituary. And yes, the reporter's desperation for a story, her hearing problems, and her true crime habit caused the whole uproar. But so did Karl's unwillingness to text his closest friends or even crack the door to his workroom and wave at the woman when she asked about him.

Poor communication. Again. Just like today.

A relationship with a man who didn't see the point in sharing crucial information would be an exercise in frustration. Hell, even casual sex with a man who couldn't talk through what they both wanted and what was or wasn't working for them didn't sound great. Chemistry and good instincts could take a lover pretty far, but not as far as she'd prefer.

Their footsteps crunching against the sidewalk were the only sound for a while. When her phone rang, it was a welcome distraction. She ducked her head to dig for it in her bag, and when she halted at the sidewalk's edge, next to the brick exterior of a bank, he stopped beside her.

"Sorry," she murmured. "Just want to make sure there's no problem with the renos."

When she unearthed her cell, though, it wasn't her contractor friend on the line.

She really should've followed her initial post-divorce instincts and assigned Rob his own special ring tone. "Armor" by Sara Bareilles, maybe. Or if she wanted to go old school, Carly Simon's "You're So Vain" might've worked too. Either way, she'd know when to ignore her phone when it rang.

After seventeen years together and only two years since the divorce, too many aspects of their financial lives still involved each other. Complete avoidance wasn't an option right now, but someday—some sweet, sweet day—she'd be able to block him entirely.

For today, she'd just pretend he hadn't called.

Hands steady and cold as stone, she tucked her phone away again. When it dinged repeatedly with incoming text messages only seconds later, she didn't flinch, and she didn't check the screen again.

She raised her head. Karl was frowning down at her.

She frowned right back. "What? What's wrong?"

"About to ask you the same thing." Eyes narrowed, he studied her closely. "You look stressed, Dearborn."

Did something about Harlot's Bay make her especially easy to read? Or did Lise and Karl simply know her better and pay her closer attention than anyone else ever had?

She smiled, doing her best to radiate unruffled serenity. "I'm fine."

His frown deepened into a glower.

"Uncommunicative pot, meet uncommunicative fucking kettle," he muttered in what he undoubtedly—but incorrectly—believed to be a quiet voice.

Her occasional wary reserve wasn't at all the same thing as his overall inability or unwillingness to communicate. But since she had no desire to discuss any subject even tangentially related to her ex-husband, she bit her tongue and resumed walking toward the Spite House.

Karl's Crocs slapped the sidewalk in an agitated rhythm. Whenever people waved or greeted him, he simply nodded or grunted in response. And every time she glanced over at him, the lines in his forehead had deepened, and his lips had clamped into a thinner, tighter line.

"Listen, Dearborn." Only half a block away from the Spite House, he abruptly halted. "Today's exercise went off the rails. We both know it."

As soon as she stopped beside him, he adjusted his position to block the late afternoon sun from her eyes. Because, for all his grumbling and terseness, Karl Dean paid attention. He cared. He always *tried*, even if he didn't always speak.

"Kind of." She laid a consoling hand on his sun-heated forearm, and all the remaining chill in her bones melted away. "But it started out really well."

Today's delicious lunch had confirmed just how much thought and effort he was willing to devote to something he considered important. *Someone* he considered important.

Back in high school, she'd wanted to be his important someone. Maybe she still did.

"Didn't end that way," he countered, and she couldn't argue with that. "You going to back out of our agreement, Dearborn?"

The pink-gold light haloed his head and turned his hair to copper. With her free hand, she smoothed a section ruffled by the waterside breeze, and the softness of the strands slipping through her fingers surprised her.

His breath hitched at her touch, and she smiled. This time, for real.

"No." Her arm dropped to her side, and she waited for him to touch her in return. "I'm a woman of my word."

His shoulders dropped a fraction, and the hard muscles under her palm relaxed. "Good. Second activity will be better. Promise."

She certainly hoped so. "Do you still want me to hang out at the bakery tomorrow?"

"Whenever you want." His brown eyes bored into hers, and he spoke slowly to emphasize each word. "Long as you want. Always."

Fumbling a bit, he lifted her hand from his forearm and pressed a kiss to her palm, and she had to suck in a deep, steadying breath as her knees went wobbly beneath her.

How such an awkward gesture could pierce her heart so deeply, she'd never know. But to her dismay, she couldn't move. Couldn't speak. Could only stare up at him, speechless.

Shaking his head, seemingly at himself, he lowered her arm to her side, let her go, and backed away a step. And with every inch between them, her thoughts cleared. Enough that she could muster a bit of shaky sass.

She spread her hands in feigned confusion. "What, no goodbye kiss on the lips?"

"Hell, no." His voice was a low, gravelly rumble, his gaze hot on her mouth.

"I see." Tempting him with proximity, she leaned closer. So close the fine hairs on her body stood on end, electrified by his nearness. So close she could taste the mint of his breath with every rise and fall of that broad chest. "Not even one little peck?"

"No." Firm. Immediate.

Her lips curved in a taunting smile. "Too dangerous?"

"Too undeserved." His fingertip carefully smoothed a stray strand of hair off her cheek and tucked it behind her ear. In a lingering, featherlight caress, he traced the sensitive rim of that ear and watched as she shivered beneath his touch. "Next kiss from you? I'll fucking *earn* it."

The pad of his finger lightly rubbed her earlobe and trailed slowly down her neck. A bolt of electric heat raced down her spine and gathered between her legs, and her lips parted in a silent gasp. But all oxygen had abruptly left the universe, so there was no air to be found.

That slow, smug grin of his should've been illegal. "See you soon, Dearborn."

By the time she could breathe normally again, he was already stomping down the street toward his bakery, hands in his pockets, ruddy hair aflame in the late afternoon sun.

Whistling.

"You're a jerk!" she called after him. "A stupid, sexy jerk!"

Also a clit-tease, but she wasn't going to holler that down a street.

His laughter was loud enough to echo off the nearby buildings and joyful enough that she couldn't feel as aggrieved as she probably should.

"I'll fucking take it," he shouted back, and disappeared around a corner before she could either whack him with her bag or climb him like a truly aggravating yet seductive tree.

So much for her vaunted reserve and legendary calm.

"Freaking Harlot's Bay," she complained out loud, then stomped into her ten-foot-wide house and slammed the door. And despite her best efforts?

She was grinning the whole time.

10

$\mathcal{F}$our days later, Molly set aside her latest failed attempt to decorate a cookie—the autumnal leaf looked like it was bleeding; how was that even possible?—and finally let herself ask the obvious question.

"Why haven't you asked Charlotte to help you back here?" Stripping off her gloves, she watched him bend over the other side of his favorite stainless-steel worktable and begin decorating a custom-ordered two-layer round cake. "From what you've told me, her instinct for flavor combinations is impeccable. She's reliable. You enjoy her company. So why not make her your assistant, if she's willing?"

With an offset spatula, he liberally applied the almond cake's apricot buttercream, velvety in texture and tinted a gorgeous, pale shade of peach. "Not happening."

She frowned at him, befuddled by his immediate rejection of the idea.

Over the course of the week, she'd spent almost all her daylight hours at the bakery—and by Tuesday, she'd already begun to comprehend the scope of his staggering workload and the neverending nature of his tasks. It all seemed very Sisyphean, frankly.

When she finished narrating an audiobook, it was done. As eternal as anything digital could be. Rarely revisited by her. But when Karl finished making brownies, people ate them. He then had to make more, which would also be consumed promptly. So he was never truly finished. He could always do more prep for the days ahead, and each morning he'd confront the same beast he'd slain the day before. The same boulder to be rolled up the same hill, ad nauseam.

But hopefully not *literal* nauseam, or else his sanitation grade might drop.

An assistant could ease his workload. Why he didn't have one already, she couldn't quite understand. Unless . . . "Is the bakery not profitable enough to support an apprentice baker?"

At that, he ceased spinning the cake turntable in front of him, set down his spatula, and directed a withering glower her way. "Of course it is. What the hell made you think it wasn't, Dearborn?"

"Because if it's not a money issue, I don't understand why you wouldn't ask her to help."

He was a ridiculously busy man, with half-moon shadows under his eyes that darkened day by day. And he wasn't in his teens anymore. Sooner rather than later, the constant abuse on his body would take its toll. From the way he sometimes stretched his back, groaned, and mutter-shouted a heartfelt *motherfucker*, she figured at least some of that bill had already come due.

A few more hours of rest would do him good. Simple as that.

"Got enough on her plate already. Asking her to work my shitty hours and spend all day with an asshole like me. . . ." He shook his head and returned his attention to the cake. With a steady hand, he carefully placed a delicate bone-white rose on top of the now-smooth apricot frosting. "It'd be cruel. Taking advantage of her kindness."

The layers for all of today's cakes had apparently been baked in large batches over the weekend, then frozen until the appropriate day. Now they sat on the counter, fully defrosted and ready to be . . . well, frosted. Also decorated with the flowers he'd created and set aside on little squares of wax paper.

The entire flower-piping process had fascinated her. The equipment, with various lovely colors of frosting contained within a dozen cone-shaped plastic bags, each punctuated by a differently shaped metal tip. The precision and artistry, as he rotated what he called a piping nail—essentially a long steel spike with a round, flat top maybe two inches in diameter—between his gloved thumb and forefinger, squeezed a frosting bag with his other hand, and produced each fragile, gorgeous petal, one by one, gradually creating a bloom on the square of parchment topping the nail. The easy confidence and speed with which he created those lush roses, bold poppies, and ruffled, blush-pink peonies.

He was so very talented. Also so very dense, on occasion.

"Yes, having her become your assistant would help you. But it might help her as well." When she echoed his posture, bending over the table to study his work, her own back immediately twinged. "Have you asked her what she wants to do for the rest of her life? Maybe she'd like to be a baker too."

His answer didn't include words. Just a discouraging grunt.

Stifling a sigh, she tried again. "How about someone else, then? Wasn't Johnathan looking for extra hours? Could he come in to help before class?"

Another discontented-sounding grunt.

Fine. She'd let it go.

Excluding Lise, the people of Harlot's Bay were still basically strangers to her. In a little over two weeks, she was leaving them, without any definite plans to return. Their decisions, however misguided, shouldn't concern her this much.

Even when it came to Karl.

Hanging out with him had been fun, and she appreciated his ill-fated trust-building efforts. He was a good man, one whose grumpiness didn't fully hide how deeply he cared about others. But she wouldn't consider moving across the continent or risking her fragile heart for someone who couldn't—or wouldn't—discuss important issues with her. Issues that, if she and Karl ever tried to make a real relationship work, would become her concerns too.

If they were a real couple, she'd actually want to spend time with him outside the bakery. Especially since her own post-vacation projects wouldn't allow her to hang out at his workplace all day. With his current schedule, they'd barely see each other except on weekends. And if he wasn't willing to even *consider* getting help— help he could apparently afford—so he could change that schedule . . . well, that told her something, didn't it?

If he didn't want to fundamentally change his existence for someone else, fair enough. But seventeen years of shaping her life around someone else's needs, preferences, and professional obligations had left her exhausted and utterly unwilling to repeat the experience.

Because she worked for herself, Rob had always expected her to accommodate his demanding doctor-to-be schedule. Tiptoe around the house whenever he slept and make herself available whenever he was awake and at home. Scrimp and save and deny herself travel, conference fees, and upgraded recording equipment so they could afford medical school.

More precisely: so *she* could afford *his* medical school.

She'd gone along with it all, because each individual sacrifice had seemed reasonable. Because they were a team. Because she prided herself on being Unflappable Molly Dearborn, able to sail through the choppiest of seas without undue fuss. Because, as he kept reminding her, he'd be the one paying their bills soon enough.

Because she loved him. Because he supposedly loved her too.

Then he'd left her high and dry, and she was done twisting herself into knots for someone else's plans. Any sort of accommodation on her part now would require an enormous amount of trust, and Karl hadn't earned that trust yet. Couldn't earn it, unless he chose to share more of himself with her. Which was an outcome that seemed increasingly unlikely, given his heartfelt love of grunts and general avoidance of complete sentences.

"I'm going to grab a latte out front." *And also impose some necessary distance between us*, she silently added. "Can I get you anything?"

When she straightened, her spine audibly popped in a disconcerting manner, but a quick stretch didn't hurt. Reassured, she walked to the interior door and paused, waiting for his answer.

"Hold your goddamn horses, Dearborn." After he finished placing the remaining roses on top of his cake, he began piping decorative swirls around its base. "I'll make your latte myself. Give me two minutes."

Another pastry bag lay beside him on the worktable, its buttercream contents a slightly deeper shade of peach due to judicious application of gel food coloring. He laid down his swirl bag and picked up the darker color. His movements deft but careful, he piped out the first letter of the cake's message in a lovely, flowing script.

She couldn't look away, despite her better judgment. Something about the contrast—a gruff, burly man crafting such delicate beauty, his nonchalance matched by his meticulousness—melted her knees and tangled her tongue. Made her lean harder against the doorframe as her cheeks flamed.

Only . . . wasn't he starting the lettering too far up? "Happy Birthday" didn't require that much vertical space, and the cake was a full twelve inches in diameter.

Pushing off the door, she drifted closer again.

Oh. He wasn't piping out a birthday greeting after all. In fact . . .

"Dildos, Vibrators, and Clamps, Oh My: YOU SUCK," he spelled out in creditable calligraphy, before adding a star-shaped asterisk at the end. Below that, he piped out another asterisk, then a clarifying addendum in smaller, swooping letters: "And Not in a Fun Way."

Brow furrowed, he glanced over the order sheet again. Then he nodded a little, grabbed a box Molly had folded and taped into place earlier, and cautiously slid the cake inside, making sure not to damage any of his decorative elements.

She fought herself. Lost.

"I have to ask, Karl. Who exactly buys a twelve-inch cake in a custom flavor combination, asks for that cake to be beautifully decorated"—because she'd also read the order sheet just now, and the delicate colors and roses had been special requests; moreover, whoever placed the order had inspired an underlined note reading, "Please make it pretty!"—"and then specifies a message like that?"

"Rival sex shops." He wrote "SLATTERNS 'R' US" on the side of the box with a Sharpie, then taped the order form to the top. "Across the street from each other. Owners need to have sex already and get that shit over with."

"You . . ." Processing that information took her a minute. "You're telling me a town this size supports not one, but *two* adult stores?"

His thick shoulders lifted in a shrug. "Harlot's Bay, Dearborn.

Thirstiest motherfuckers on the planet."

Dumbfounded, she watched him heft the heavy box with ease and carefully slide it beside the others on the custom-order rack located just inside the door. "And the owners of those adult stores sublimate their sexual frustration through insults written on beautiful custom cakes?"

"Yep. Probably get a retaliatory order tomorrow. Has to be eating into their profits by now." Another shrug. "Helping mine, though."

Another pair of gloves landed in the trash, as did his latest beard net. After washing his hands, he took a moment to study her attempted cookie artistry.

"Nice blood spatter." He indicated a stray red splotch. "Never would've thought of decapitating a maple leaf. Creative."

He sounded entirely sincere, bizarrely enough.

Instead of basking in the warmth of his gruff approval, she forced herself to scowl at him. "That's not a headless leaf. It's a seasonal swirl of autumnal wind."

"Looks like murdered foliage to me, Dearborn. I like it." He leaned in closer. "Not as much as yesterday's weird dick-cone, though. Should market that design to Dildos, Vibrators, and Clamps, Oh My. Resembled one of their toys."

She gasped in outrage. "It was a cornucopia!"

"Sure," he said, then straightened and nudged her through the doorway to the bakery's public area. "Whatever you say, Dearborn."

* * *

FIFTEEN MINUTES LATER, she was sitting across from Lise in one of the bakery's three booths and sipping on Karl's latest creation: a lavender–white chocolate latte, with a small, pristine cornucopia on top. Which, yes, looked significantly less like a penis than yesterday's sacrificial cookie, not that she'd ever tell him so.

Apparently he and Charlotte had collaborated on the custom flavor, although the art was all his. Both were utterly glorious and utterly confounding. Karl had spent the entire week making fun of her "bougie-as-hell, sugary-ass" drink orders, and yet he kept coming up with new recipes especially suited to her preferences and making ever-more-elaborate art on top of his beverage offerings. The man was a riddle wrapped in a mystery inside a beard net.

And what his agile hands could accomplish with only some foam and a toothpick didn't bear thinking about. Give him different tools—something from Dildos, Vibrators, and Clamps, Oh My, for example—and heaven only knew what he could do. To her. Or to himself while she watched. At this point, she wasn't picky.

"What sandwich is that?" Lise poked at the bread, and Molly smacked her hand away. "I've eaten everything on this place's menu, and I don't remember anything with watercress."

"It's not a menu item." Each day that week, around lunchtime—without her asking for anything or even hinting—Karl had presented her with a one-of-a-kind sandwich to go with her one-of-a-kind latte, grumbling the entire time. And as the days went by and he learned what she most liked, his creations had only gotten more and more incredible. "Roast-beef panini, on marble rye with a horseradish-Dijon mayo, horseradish-chive Havarti, red onion slivers, and watercress."

After a few minutes in the bakery's panini press, the bread turned thin and crispy, the cheese had begun oozing deliciously out the sides, and she would have married that enormous damn sandwich if given the opportunity.

She wasn't sure whether all Karl's time and effort and thoughtfulness had made her trust him more, but it was definitely making her want to bang him more. Turned out, she was kind of a slut for personalized sandwiches and lattes.

Molly's friend sighed. "It looks amazing. I love rare roast beef."

Lise—all huge dark eyes and pleading eyelash flutters—gazed at the sandwich like a long-lost lover. Molly wasn't a monster, so she deposited half of it on her companion's plate.

Lise clapped her hands together in glee. "Thank you!"

As her friend dove face first into the newly acquired half sandwich, Molly took a moment to survey the lunchtime crowd packed into the modestly sized bakery. There appeared to be even more customers than the day before, which was something of a trend—and also not a coincidence. According to both Lise and Athena, Harlot's Bay residents were coming by to confirm wild rumors of Karl Dean voluntarily letting someone who wasn't a Grounds and Grains employee into his backroom. Nay, *encouraging* that civilian to enter the sanctified, profanity-packed domain, his Fortress of Furious Fucking Solitude.

Zoo animals could probably relate to the sort of endless, delighted scrutiny she was receiving. And if she was a panda chewing on her chosen stalk of bamboo for curious, benevolent crowds, Karl was definitely the cryptid in their midst. Rarely spotted. Potentially dangerous. Able to communicate only in grunts and guttural brevity. Best observed from a respectful, cautious distance. A creature of mystery, whose strange ways fascinated other denizens of his native habitat.

He was basically a Sadie Brazen hero, albeit one with only a single penis. She assumed.

"Maybe Hector finally worked up his nerve," Lise murmured, her gaze directed at the cash register, where Charlotte was ringing up a familiar customer. "Cross your fingers."

Hector, if Molly remembered correctly, was one of Matthew's nurse practitioners. A twentysomething Black man with short twists in his hair, round, wire-rimmed glasses, and a startlingly sweet, shy smile he'd directed at Charlotte every day that week.

If today's lunch resembled the others, he'd buy a muffin of some sort from Charlotte. Then he'd sit down at a table by himself and eat that muffin alongside his takeout poke bowl—all while his phone rested in his free hand, screen lit and open to whatever book he was reading. Before leaving, he'd find a less busy moment to come up to the counter again, place a tip in the jar, and awkwardly strike up another conversation.

Molly recognized a nerd when she saw one. She also recognized a man smitten. "Does she like him back?"

"I think so, but it's hard to know. Given her history, Charlotte's more cautious than most." In the brief silence, both she and Molly studied the couple as they bent toward each other on opposite sides of the counter. "If the town scuttlebutt is true, her kids absolutely love Hector. Supposedly, they insist on seeing him every time they visit the doctor's office."

The couple was too far away and too quiet for eavesdropping purposes. But when Hector paused after putting away his wallet and spoke to Charlotte, her lips parted in seeming surprise. Then she smiled back at him and responded. His own smile widened, and he ducked his head.

Once another customer approached the register, the young man moved away with an awkward wave, his heart in his eyes. And as soon as he turned his back, Swinging-Teal-Ponytail Bez grinned, elbowed her pink-cheeked colleague, and—if Molly's lipreading could be trusted—said something like, "Told you so."

Something inside Molly's chest warmed. Twisted. Ached. Maybe the tiny, tiny portion of her heart that cynicism and painful experience hadn't hardened to flint.

She wasn't sure she still believed in happy endings. But she was wishing one for those two, cynicism be damned.

"Look at you." With a swipe of her napkin, Lise cleaned a few stray crumbs from her mouth. "Molly Dearborn, being nosy. Just like a local."

Molly couldn't even deny it. "You're a bad influence, Utendorf."

Lise's round, pretty face bloomed in a pleased smile. "That's the nicest compliment I've gotten in ages. Thanks, Mol."

Molly shook her head and opened her mouth to respond, only to pause when the shouting began.

Karl was the source of the shouting, of course. When she looked toward the espresso machine, he appeared to be arguing with a youngish, muscular guy in too-tight track pants. One sporting what she'd guess was an ironic handlebar mustache, twisted to sharp, gleaming points against either cheek.

"Gotta go," she told Lise, then scooted out of the booth and approached the combatants.

"C'mon, man," she heard the customer complaining as she got closer. "Don't be a latte-withholding grouch. I heard about the miso-caramel matcha version you made yesterday, and I *need* one."

That flavor combination had been conceived by Charlotte, concocted by Karl, and given to Molly in latte form. And it was freaking *incredible*. She couldn't really blame the guy for wanting a taste, but—

"Like I tell you every week: Read the sign, asshole." Karl stabbed a finger at a small slate propped on the counter, where someone had written a message in bright blue chalk: NO OFF-MENU ORDERS DURING THE LUNCH RUSH. THANK YOU FOR YOUR UNDER-STANDING!

There was a smiley face at the end too, so . . . Karl had probably inspired that directive, but he definitely hadn't written it.

Mr. Track Pants's tone turned wheedling. "I'll double the usual price. No, I'll *triple* it."

"No." There was no hesitation in Karl's answer. No give.

A wiser man would have retreated at that point. Instead, the customer crossed his arms across his chest, thick biceps bulging, and stood his ground. "I thought the customer was always right."

Uh-oh. That *gotcha* tone was obnoxious enough that even she kind of wanted to punch the guy. Karl was going to lose his shit, guaranteed.

Swiftly, she rounded the sales counter and trotted toward the impending explosion. By the time she arrived, Karl had already thrust one of his glass latte mugs between him and the other man and was shaking it so hard she half expected it to rattle.

"—take this mug, break it into pieces, and use a shard to slice off your precious goddamn mustache." The heat of Karl's glower, if directed at the mug, should have melted the glass then and there. "Then I'll rip out each individual hair follicle, so those mother-fuckers *never* grow again. And *then*—"

"Hey, Karl?" Molly said in her calmest voice.

Karl stopped mid-profanity, swung his head her way, and—did mustache guy actually look *disappointed* by the interruption?

She carried on anyway. "Just FYI: Using a broken shard of glass as a cutting implement is dangerous."

"Yes." Karl narrowed his eyes at the customer. "To this prick's mustache."

"Well, yes, but also to you. You could seriously injure yourself during the barbering process." Nudging her arm against his, she tried to draw his full attention. "Also, as anyone who's ever gotten waxed realizes—"

He snorted. "We both know you've never waxed even a square inch of that gorgeous body, Dearborn."

"—ripping hair out by the roots might make it grow back more slowly, but it *will* grow back. For more permanent removal, you probably want to consider professional electrolysis."

It was, as he'd guessed, purely theoretical knowledge. But she'd read enough women's magazines in her own dentist's waiting room to feel confident in her information.

The pugnacious jut of Karl's bearded jaw had softened a fraction. "What the hell is electrolysis?"

Out of the corner of her eye, she could see Johnathan urging Mr. Track Pants toward the door. Good. Soon enough, the entire encounter would be—

"This week's Yelp review for your bakery is going to be *scathing*," the customer called out, wriggling away from Johnathan and approaching the counter once more. "One star for customer service, one star for—"

Molly gave up and left the man to his deserved fate. RIP, fancy mustache.

Before finishing her lunch, she needed to pee. Besides, the man and his facial hair weren't truly in danger. Karl wasn't violent. Just very fond of impractical verbal threats.

With a nod at Bez and Charlotte—the former appeared amused by the ongoing confrontation, the latter resigned—Molly ducked into the work area again. By the time she emerged from the bathroom, all the shouting had stopped, and Charlotte was standing by one of the stainless-steel worktables, shifting from foot to foot.

Her hands twisted near her waist, and she met Molly's gaze with pained blue eyes.

Why in the world did the young woman seem so nervous and unhappy? Unless—

"Did Karl actually assault that guy?" Holy shit. She'd never, ever have predicted that. "Let me get my bag, and I can cover bail or find a lawyer. Where should I—"

"No. Of course not." The younger woman's entire body had stiffened in affront at the very suggestion. "Karl would never hurt anyone."

Whew. Well, thank goodness.

"That was what I assumed, but when I saw your expression . . ." Molly stepped toward Charlotte. "Are you okay?"

Charlotte's pixie cut only emphasized the delicacy of her narrow features, and she wore no makeup. In her tee and jeans, she looked like the teenager she must've been not that long ago, vulnerable and heartbreakingly young.

"I don't . . ." She paused. Seemed to gather her courage before continuing. "I don't mean to interfere. I'm sorry if I offend you, but . . ."

Utterly perplexed, Molly waited for her to gather the right words.

"Karl would never hurt anyone," she eventually repeated, and met Molly's eyes directly. "Please don't hurt him."

Why in the world would Charlotte worry about that?

Molly shook her head decisively. "I won't. I couldn't."

"You could," Charlotte insisted, her voice firmer this time. Even though she was entirely wrong, for very obvious reasons.

Molly had seen the man maybe a half-dozen times in two decades, all within the past few days. Yes, he wanted her. Yes, he cared about her good opinion—enough not to act on that wanting until and unless she trusted him. But she couldn't truly hurt someone who barely knew her. More importantly, she couldn't truly hurt someone who wouldn't open himself up enough to *be* hurt. All that distance he kept between himself and the world, the buffer reinforced by his gruff, vaguely homicidal manner, surely protected him from emotional damage. From her. From anyone.

Unless . . . that was why he'd donned his armor to start with. Because he was so easily injured. Because he had a heart too big, too fragile, to keep exposed to the world.

Maybe . . . maybe she'd misjudged him.

She'd concluded that he wouldn't be willing to change his life in fundamental ways, even for the people he cared about. But wasn't Charlotte evidence to the contrary?

Her little family could barge into his workspace in the middle of the day, no matter how busy he might be, without worrying about his reaction. A child could vomit down his back, and he'd only sigh in response and rub the kid's back to comfort her. Even with his horrifying schedule, he made time to babysit Charlotte's children. In short, he'd changed his life enough that she'd felt it fitting to name her son after him.

Sure, Karl hadn't been willing to discuss certain important subjects with Molly, but again—they'd only met a handful of times in twenty years. Perhaps, despite his insistence that she trust him, he hadn't had enough time to trust *her*.

And if she'd misjudged him, a single question could set her straight.

Molly swallowed hard over a dry throat. "Does Karl talk to you, Charlotte? About personal things? Important things?"

Because if he did, if he shared himself with his surrogate daughter—with *anyone*—that changed things.

"Well . . ." Charlotte's eyes dropped, and her clasped hands started twisting again. "Yes. He'll talk about my personal, important things. If I bring them up."

Molly wanted to be absolutely clear about this. "But not his own concerns?"

Silently, the younger woman shook her head.

Ah. So he cared deeply about Charlotte and her family. Probably even loved them. But not enough to share himself.

"Good to know." She forced herself to smile. "I appreciate your concern for him, but please don't worry. I'll be leaving soon, and he knows it. He won't let himself get hurt."

Suddenly exhausted, she flicked a glance at the door and wondered whether she should head back to the Spite House after lunch. Take a nap or read for a while, in blessed solitude. Regain her emotional equilibrium.

"Wait." Charlotte's hands flew up, palms out. "I shouldn't have—"

The bakery's backroom phone jangled. Normally, someone out front would pick up the call—since Karl did not want to chat with customers over the phone, heaven forbid—but this time, the receiver kept ringing.

Brows drawn together in a pained expression, Charlotte answered the phone. "Grounds and Grains Bakery. Charlotte speaking. May I help you?" She paused, her eyebrows lifting. "So . . . you want a twelve-inch round cake reading, 'You blow, Slatterns "R" Us,' then an asterisk, followed by 'Also not in a fun way'?"

Another pause. "Okay. Hold on. Let me get my pen and an order form, and we'll nail down all the details."

Distracted from her weird sense of deflation, Molly squinted at the custom-order rack. Sure enough, the earlier cake had disappeared. Must've been picked up while she was eating with Lise. And from the sound of this call, it had already been delivered to its intended recipient.

She kind of wished she was staying in Harlot's Bay long enough to watch the entire rival-adult-stores saga play out. Not to mention the Charlotte-and-Hector saga, and . . . yeah. A lot of other things too.

Her fondness for the community shouldn't surprise her. Harlot's Bay was the one place where she'd tried to put down roots as a teenager, the one place she'd missed after leaving it behind, and there was good reason for that.

Honestly? She could very easily love this town. Just like she could very easily love Karl, if she weren't careful.

Without trust, though . . . love alone wouldn't be enough to keep her. Not this time.

She waved at Charlotte before leaving the back room, then at Karl—who was still helping out front, his expression highly aggrieved—before saying goodbye to Lise. She left the remains of her lunch to her friend.

As she exited the bakery, she thought she heard Karl shout something. To her, to a customer, to the universe at large—hard to say which.

Didn't matter, really. She was already gone.

And she made very, very sure not to look back.

11

*U*nlike every other goddamn thing he'd tried with Dearborn, food was working for Karl.

Escape room last Sunday? Utter failure. Still embarrassed about that disaster. Thursday, she'd fled the bakery during his latest pointless argument with Jerry, the bakery's most annoying customer. She'd returned yesterday, spending most of her Friday with him, but seemed distant for some reason he didn't understand and didn't have time to question her about, given his current weekday schedule.

Yep. Definitely a matter of appropriate timing. Not cowardice on his part.

Coward or not, by the time she'd packed up to leave yesterday afternoon, he'd been in a near panic. Desperate for uninterrupted time together, even apart from their trust-building session scheduled for today. Anxious to erase her new reserve. Willing to propose anything and everything that might convince her to give him—and Harlot's Bay—a real shot.

So, against his better judgment, he'd invited her to the Nasty Wenches meeting tomorrow. September's bizarro theme? Sexy Satans. Luckily, he knew for a fact she'd narrated Sadie Brazen's *Bedded by Beelzebub*, where the horned asshole hero had a prehensile tail and a super-long forked tongue, because of course he fucking did.

Invitation seemed like a no-brainer to him. Not to her, though.

She'd claimed she didn't want to impose. When he'd told her she'd like the Wenches—they were a bunch of weirdos, but good people—she'd said there was no point getting attached, since she was leaving soon.

Kick to the goddamn gut.

She'd bang him—that was clear—but not stay long-term. Didn't seem to trust him more than before either.

So yeah, things looked pretty bleak. But lunch last weekend was great, until everything went sideways in that stupid escape room. And all this week, even an oblivious bastard like him could see how she softened each time he fixed her something special. One of her sweet-as-hell lattes, or those bougie sandwiches.

Desperate—a man fighting for his life—he'd used actual *microgreens* yesterday. Total fucking travesty. But it'd *worked*. He'd plunked her plate down in front of her at that booth where she liked to eat with Lise—now reserved for them during lunch hours, though she didn't know that shit—and watched her lips curve in a wide, sweet smile, her eyes brighten as they held his, and her body sway in his direction.

She'd told him she liked a good banh mi. He'd listened. That meant something to her.

Sexual chemistry between the two of them came easy. But her reaction to his food wasn't about lust. Well, it kinda was, but that lust was mainly sandwich-directed. The emotion aimed his way? Only a hint of desire. Mostly pleased surprise. Warmth. Connection.

Everything he needed from her. Everything he wanted to nurture.

To encourage that reaction, that softness in her expression? He'd do whatever was necessary. If food did the trick, good enough.

This Saturday's trust-building activity hadn't been chosen at random. He was leaning hard on the lone area where he'd felt some give. Pushing at the spot with everything he had.

And he was beyond terrified.

Unlike last weekend, he made sure he was fully dressed and clean before she arrived at the bakery. When she knocked at the back door, coolly composed and gorgeous as ever, he immediately waved her inside while his heartbeat echoed in his damn ears.

Then he shoved his hands inside his jeans pockets before she could see them tremble with nervousness. Thrust his chin toward the relevant worktable instead of speaking, so his voice couldn't waver.

"Hi again," she said, and he grunted in response.

Not a good start. She already had doubts about his communication skills. Silence and caveman sounds would only confirm them.

He'd do better the rest of the day. He had to. No choice.

Before he managed to grasp the right words, though, she was already speaking. Already moving toward today's setup, the thighs of her own jeans swishing together with each step. Only to slow to a halt once she saw the only uncovered item on the table.

"A blindfold, huh?" She turned on her sneakered heel to face him. "Are we mini-golfing today? Or did you decide to take *Cosmo*'s suggestions this go-round?"

He replied without thinking. Immediately regretted it.

"If I'd listened to *Cosmo*, there'd be a bed," he told her, then inwardly groaned.

Shit. Now he was thinking about Dearborn naked in bed. Even more than usual, and that was damn well saying something.

"I'm sure not all their suggestions involved beds. There are always walls. Chairs." Her head tipped toward his setup, and her eyes met his boldly. "Tables."

Holy crap.

He sucked in a hard breath. Made himself think about work-place sanitation guidelines. The health inspector's last visit. How he'd be unable to escape memories of fucking Molly every time he came to work if they did it here.

"Like you'd know." Deep breathing wasn't doing the trick. Neither was impending middle age. Something about Dearborn made his dick stand up and take notice. Always had. Probably al-ways would. "Lay good money you've never read a goddamn issue of *Cosmo* in your life."

"Then you'd lose that money." When he raised a skeptical brow, she rolled her eyes. "I've had dentist appointments of my own, Dean. Occasionally, my choice was either *Cosmo* or *People*, and I was freaking tired of hearing about some minor celeb's"—she crooked her fingers—"'weight loss journey.' But reading about blowjobs always made the time pass more quickly."

He choked on thin air. Began coughing violently.

Moving to his side, she thumped his back helpfully. Even though she knew exactly what she was doing to him, and why he couldn't accept her implicit offer.

When he caught his breath, he stared at her balefully. "You're a piece of fucking work, Dearborn."

Her lips quirked in a self-satisfied smile. "Well, some of those waiting-room articles were also about how to"—crook, crook—"'drive your man crazy.' I just chose to take that concept in a slightly different, more literal direction."

"You sure as hell did." He shook his head at her, then pointed to the table where the blindfold and multiple amorphous lumps cov-ered with clean dishcloths rested. "Sit."

"Woof-woof," she said, but plunked that fine ass down on one of the two stools he'd placed beside the table. She looked up at him expectantly, and Jesus H. Christ, he wanted to kiss her so goddamn much.

He jutted his chin toward the silk band and all the lumps. "Blindfolded taste test. Another *Corporations Today* suggestion."

Her dark brows rose. "Really? That sounds more like *Cosmo* material." She paused, idly drumming her fingers on the table as she considered things. "Also like potential ground for lawsuits and sexual harassment claims. All those CEOs and middle managers are surely old enough to have visited a Blockbuster. Did no one ever rent *9½ Weeks*? Or at least secretly watch it on late-night Skinemax while their parents were out of town?"

"Told you." He crossed his arms over his chest. "Managerial types? Kinky as hell."

Her big blue eyes blinked up at him. "*You're* a manager."

Yeah, he guessed he was. Wouldn't necessarily call his preferences kinky, but . . . wait. "Quit causing trouble, Dearborn. Less sex talk, more trust building."

Her hands raised in surrender. "Fine, fine. Just making light conversation."

"Bullshit." He produced his reminder list from his jeans pocket. It crinkled as he unfolded it. "Okay. Here we go. You're blindfolded. I feed you crap. You——"

"Not literal crap, I presume?"

He offered her a withering stare. "You guess what it is. You get it right, great. You don't, I ask questions. Give hints. Talk to you about what you're tasting."

In short: He'd *communicate*. Express himself so eloquently her damn eardrums would *weep* in ecstasy. Hopefully.

"You okay with that?" Because, yeah, this plan involved some trust on her part. Or maybe she'd had bad experiences with blindfolds. How the hell would he know? "If not, no problem. Got a Plan B."

Blindfolds could go. Simply closing her eyes would work instead. Or if she wanted more information about the foods before they started—

"It's . . ." Her forehead had crinkled. "It's . . . fine."

Not very convincing.

"Got food allergies?" he guessed.

That question was his next list item anyway, since she wouldn't know ahead of time what she was consuming. Yeah, he had an EpiPen nearby, but zero desire to use it.

She shook her head immediately. "No."

He waited. Nothing else. Not one complaint or concern. But he had eyes, didn't he? Saw her pinched lips. Ramrod-straight posture. Stiff shoulders.

Dammit. Something was wrong, and he was total shit at guessing games. "Talk to me, Dearborn. Either we fix whatever's worrying you, or we scrap the whole thing. If you're uncomfortable, this isn't happening."

She sighed. Set her elbows on the table and rubbed her face with her palms for a second.

"Just . . ." Her head lifted, and she met his eyes. "Don't smash food in my face. Please."

He scowled at her, offended. "Why the hell would I do that?"

More face-scrubbing. Very un-Dearborn-like, but he was too incensed and hurt to pay much heed.

He crossed his arms over his chest. "You think I'm that kind of man? Asshole who'd make you vulnerable, then take advantage of you?"

"No. Not really. It's only . . ." Another sigh, and her shoulders slumped. "Look, Karl. When my ex and I got married, he wanted a big wedding. I didn't, so we hired a planner, and I let him be the go-between. I had two main demands."

She held up a finger, tired lines bracketing her mouth. "First, no heels. Flats, boots, sneakers, or bare feet. Those were my acceptable options." Her middle finger joined her forefinger. "Second: When we cut the cake at the reception, I didn't want to do the whole feeding-each-other thing, but if they insisted, Rob would give me a small, manageable bite. I had no intention of getting crumbs all over the most expensive outfit of my life or choking on a huge chunk of dark chocolate fudge cake in front of a crowd."

"You don't even like dark chocolate." Might be fancier than milk chocolate, but not sweet enough for her. He'd learned that much within a day of their reunion.

She smiled faintly. "No, I don't."

"Guessing that prick fed you a huge goddamn bite of cake," Karl ground out, his irritation now aimed at an entirely different target. "After saying he wouldn't."

Her laugh was brittle. A broken shard of sugar left too long on the heat, until it turned bitter. "Oh, he didn't feed it to me. He basically shoved the entire piece in my face. As a practical joke, he said. Wedding shenanigans."

All his remaining hurt had vanished, replaced by outrage. Also a rising urge to find this Rob bastard and smash his teeth in.

"Only a practical joke if both sides think it's funny. Otherwise? Bullying." A lesson he'd taught each and every one of his younger siblings, because it was damn important.

She fiddled with a strand of her hair, twisting it into a rope and releasing it, again and again, gaze pointed downward. "He told me I was only angry because I had no sense of humor."

Total gaslighting bullshit. "And you didn't knee him in his balls, shove the entire cake down his throat, and dump that motherfucker on the spot?"

The girl he'd known, the woman she'd become—both held power in every goddamn inch of their strong, sure bodies. Confidence too. Pride. So why the hell had she stayed married to that asswipe until two years ago?

Her fingernail flicked the blunt ends of her hair, and her buttondown tightened against her breasts as her chest rose in a silent sigh.

"I should have," she finally said, her voice quiet and raw. "I should've left right then and there, even if it meant starting divorce proceedings less than an hour after our wedding ceremony, because I knew better. I could see all the red flags flying, clear as day, but . . ."

Her pale blue eyes rose to meet his, and he hated that tentative expression. The silent plea for understanding, when she didn't have to justify herself to him. Ever.

"Molly . . ." Rounding the table, he reached for her hand. "Baby, you don't need to—"

"We'd been together for nine years by that point. We were newly married." Her fingers were stiff against his. Cold. "I told myself I was overreacting. He eventually said he was sorry I didn't enjoy his joke, and I allowed myself to take that as a real apology instead of the responsibility-dodging asshole statement it was. So . . . I stayed."

With that explanation, some of her trust issues—with men, with herself, with everyone—became clearer.

"Not gonna feed you anything I know or suspect you won't like.

Won't try to trick you." A simple vow. Least of what she deserved, but he meant it with every ounce of his goddamn being. "Definitely not going to shove food in your face or make you choke. Most things, you can put in your own mouth."

She nodded, looking down at their joined hands.

Gradually, her fingers curled around his. Warmed in his grip.

"You know . . ." she began, her words stronger. Louder.

"What?"

Her chin tipped high, and her expression had turned serene once more. "We had a five-tiered cake that fed well over three hundred guests. Volume-wise, it would never have fit down Rob's throat. No matter how hard I shoved."

Ah, there she was. His pedantic girl, back in nitpicking action.

"There's a fucking will, there's a fucking way." With his free hand, he scratched his bristly chin in thought. "Could've pureed it."

"I appreciate your creativity in the revenge-based arts, Dean. You're a real pro." A final squeeze, and she let him go and picked up the blindfold. "I assume you're feeding me lunch after this?"

"Yep." Inspired by his flavor-combo chats with Charlotte, he'd gotten his hands on a truffle and planned to shave that expensive-ass shit over a Brie-and-prosciutto grilled cheese.

"Then let's get going." She stretched the silk blindfold over her head. Settled it over her eyes. "The sooner we start, the sooner I feast."

"Let's do this," he agreed, and uncovered the first mystery food.

12

Karl started easy, with foods Molly identified without much trouble. A strip of fresh mango speared on a fork, which he handed to her. A shard of crisp bacon on her plate, which she could easily locate and deliver to her waiting mouth. A generous spoonful of Nutella, unmistakable in flavor and texture, sweet enough for her tastes. He gave her the handle, and she did the rest.

When things got harder, though, he had to start talking.

A cube of marinated goat cheese stumped her first. "Is this . . . a savory cheesecake? With garlic and herbs?"

"No. Close, though." When she struggled to find a different guess, he put a new cube on her spoon, pressed the handle into her palm, and let her register the flavor and texture. Then he asked, "What are you tasting, other than the herbs and garlic? Are there other notes?"

"There's a tang." She thought for a moment. "A bit of a citrusy taste."

"Okay." He could work with that. "You were partially right with your first guess. It's a type of cheese. And what type of cheese can be soft and often has that kind of tang?"

Turned out, talking about food was way easier than most other subjects. Fucking handy.

"*Can* be soft," she repeated. "So not cream cheese, which is pretty much always soft. Is it . . . is this goat cheese? The most delicious goat cheese I've ever put in my mouth?"

He grinned, pleased with them both. "Yep."

"I want the name of that brand before I leave here today." She was smiling too. "Good job with the hints, Dean."

His chest expanded, and his grin grew.

Karl fucking Dean, his brain announced. *The best fucking communicator in the fucking universe!*

He cleared his throat. Played it cool. "Good job figuring out my hints, Dearborn."

After that, the sugar-dusted lemon drop only required one clue—"That sourness you're tasting, where do you think it might come from? Vinegar, fruit, alcohol?"—and the thin slice of orange-caramel crunch scone didn't take her more than five seconds. Turned out, she'd bought one last week. Did it on the downlow, because he wouldn't've let her pay, and she knew it.

A single food left. This particular item, he should probably feed to her.

"Last one. Okay if I handle the spoon this time, Dearborn?" He twisted open the glass jar. Watched her expression for doubts. "Worried it's gonna drip on you otherwise."

"Sure."

Her lack of hesitation made him feel a thousand feet tall. A million.

He carefully dug out a small spoonful. It wasn't as liquid as he'd imagined when he'd seen it at Costco yesterday. More crystallized, less pourable.

"Spoon's coming your way." No surprises for Molly. If she was trusting him, he'd fucking earn it.

He touched her lower lip with the utensil's end, the contact light as cotton candy. Her mouth parted. He slowly slipped the spoon inside, doing his best not to picture anything else sliding over that pink, slick tongue of hers.

Her mouth closed around the half-full bowl of the spoon, and he guided her fingers to the silver handle. Gave her back control. Tried to ignore how his whole body clenched at even that glancing contact.

"Honey," she said immediately, then ran her tongue slowly over her plump, shining lower lip. "But something tastes . . . different."

One more swipe of that tongue, and he'd kiss her. Either that or explode into flames. Science and Athena's goddamn wick effect could go fuck themselves, because spontaneous human combustion was a definite possibility for him right now.

"In what way?" he choked out.

"It's not just sweet and syrupy. It's *thick*, and the flavor is more complex than what I usually get at the store." Meditatively, she sucked the remaining honey smears off her spoon, and his dick ached. Swelled behind his jeans zipper. "I can't quite . . ."

When she didn't finish her thought, he forced out another question. "Apart from sweetness, what notes are you getting?"

"Maybe it's a tiny bit . . . floral?" Her brows drew together in thought. "Is this the wildflower honey you used in your goat cheese croissant?"

"Nope. But you're getting close." As close as he was to breaking his private vow. Because it'd be okay to sleep together, right? Even if she didn't fully trust him yet?

The blindfold had rumpled her hair, which gleamed copper in the stray sunbeam streaming through the back room's lone half window, placed high on the outside wall. Her posture had relaxed. She was slumping comfortably now, elbows on the table. Soft. Warm. Face bright with interest and pleasure.

If she trusted him, she'd look like that in bed. After he'd made her come once and started working on the next one.

Her head turned in his direction. "Another spoonful, please? I need to taste it again."

"Want to take care of it yourself?" Because he needed not to watch. One more tongue swipe? His resolve would incinerate. "Could hand you the jar, now that you know it's honey."

She didn't reach for the glass container. "I'll let you do the honors."

Dammit. Great sign of trust. Horrible strain on his control.

Muffling his pained groan, he got a fresh spoon to avoid contaminating the jar. Scooped up more honey. Brushed the bowl's edge over her lip again.

"One more hint." His voice was a rasp. "The honey originally came from France. It . . ."

He trailed off. Because this time, she put her warm hand over his as he guided the spoon inside her mouth, onto her tongue. Kept their fingers tangled while she slowly began sucking the honey off the bowl.

Electrified, shaky with lust and anticipation, he overbalanced while leaning forward. Fumbled to recover, trying his best not to knock the metal utensil painfully against her teeth.

In the hubbub, the spoon slipped from her mouth, and thick, viscous honey spread everywhere. It smeared over one of her hands, then the other, as she blindly grasped for the spoon and tried to steady herself and him. Stuck two of his fingers together. Left a sticky trail on the table as the utensil clattered on the steel surface, then got knocked aside by an elbow.

He began swearing and apologizing. She began laughing. And from somewhere in the depths of her bag, her cell began ringing.

Through adorable little snorts, she pointed one honey-dappled finger in her bag's general direction. "I'm"—a brief pause, while she snickered again—"I'm expecting a call from Lise. She needs to know my schedule for tonight. Are your hands still clean?"

He inspected them with a scowl. "One of 'em."

"Can you grab the phone, then? I don't want to get honey all over my bag or take off my blindfold and ruin the game."

Grumbling, he snatched up her bag and hurriedly hunted for the device. She gave him her code, another sign of trust his disgruntlement stopped him from appreciating fully, and told him to accept the call and put the phone on speaker.

Must've happened a millisecond before Lise hung up or the call went to voicemail, but he managed to answer in time. He plunked the cell on the table in front of her. "You're on."

"Hey, Lise," Molly said, still smiling.

Only it wasn't Lise. At the caller's first words, Dearborn's shoulders squared. Her posture went ramrod. Her expression smoothed into that marble mask of hers.

Instead of washing his hands, Karl planted his feet and stayed right where he was.

"Molly?" The asshole sounded impatient. "I thought you'd never pick up. Where are you? And who just answered the phone?"

Her own sticky hands now folded serenely on the table before her, she paused before responding. Maybe to gather her thoughts. Maybe to screw with the guy on the phone, since he was in such a goddamn hurry.

"I'm not sure why that matters, Rob," she eventually said, sardonic as hell.

Instead of seizing the phone and telling her ex-husband to leave her the hell alone, so Karl never had to watch her happiness curdle into sour cynicism during the space of a single damn sentence again, he carefully used his clean hand to remove her blindfold.

She blinked, squinting in the sudden light. But as soon as it looked like she could see again, he pointed to himself, then the door to the front, and raised his brows in question.

He wanted to stay. Support her. Defend her.

But Dearborn was private. Always had been. That wedding cake story? First specifics she'd ever shared about her ex. Karl's presence during this call, overhearing every damn word, would make her uncomfortable.

To his shock, though, she spread her hands in a gesture of resignation, then pointed to the stool across from her.

So he stayed. Listened. Tried not to take the stainless-steel table in his fists and snap it in half as he listened to her asshole ex wheedle and browbeat and—eventually—insult her.

"Is there some reason I shouldn't know where you are?" The bastard just wasn't giving up. "It's a simple question, Molly. I thought we were trying to be adults about all this."

"It may be a simple question, but it's one you have no good reason to ask." Her jaw flexed. "If it'll end this pointless conversation more quickly, though, fine. I'm in Harlot's Bay. Now, why are you calling? Is there some problem with the bank?"

"Really? Harlot's Bay?" His tone was thoughtful. "That place in Maryland where you lived way back when?"

"Why are you calling?" she repeated, with extra emphasis.

He finally got to the point. "I saw Derek yesterday at the gym. He said the upkeep on our house was getting to be too much for you"—bastard sounded happy about that—"and you might be thinking about listing it."

Her eyes closed, and her nostrils flared as she inhaled sharply.

When she eventually spoke, her voice was calm. Even. "When

I asked Derek for home-renos advice, I didn't expect him to run tattling to you. But let me be clear: He has no idea how I feel about my house. And it's not *our* house, Rob. It's mine."

Couldn't take this battle for her. Didn't know the weapons each side had. Didn't even understand the stakes. But he needed to do *something*.

His stool scraped the floor as he lurched to his feet. Dearborn didn't startle, because the woman was damn near unflappable. Kept her eyes shut as he stomped to the sink, washed up, and wet a couple of soft, clean dishtowels.

When he carefully took her hand in his, though, and began cleaning the smears of honey from her fingers with the damp cloths, her eyelashes fluttered. She looked up at him. Leaned her shoulder infinitesimally to the side, until it just barely bumped his chest.

She let him support her, if only the tiniest, tiniest amount.

He made sure not to move an inch. Didn't react. Just rooted himself in place and kept wiping off the stickiness.

"It's yours for now, but maybe not for much longer." Her ex's voice brimmed with confidence. "Alexis and I want to buy it from you before it officially goes on the market. I figure the current value would be around . . ."

He named a price that literally dizzied Karl. Jesus H. Christ, was that how much houses cost in LA? Or did Dearborn own a goddamn *mansion*?

"I don't even know what to say anymore, Rob." With another of those brittle, bitter laughs, she leaned a little harder against him. "I currently have no plans to sell the house. If that changes, I'll let you know. Which is something I've told you at least a half-dozen times already."

"If the house isn't on the market, it should be." Disapproval dripped from every word, and Karl wanted to reach through the phone and throttle the prick. "We both know it's too much work for you, and your health is suffering for it. All that stress isn't good, Mol. I'll bet your blood pressure—"

"My health, much like my home, is no longer your concern," she interrupted, the words as steely as the table before her.

Karl frowned, his honey-removal efforts pausing. Because what was up with Molly's blood pressure? And her health in general?

"I care about you, and I'm a physician, Molly. Of course it's my concern."

Fantastic. Her ex was a damn doctor. With a medical degree, not just a high school diploma. With money to burn, no doubt, and shiny leather shoes instead of Crocs.

That said, he was clearly a dick. Also, Crocs were fucking comfortable, so his loss.

"Listen, I know firsthand how little you paid for that house." The bastard was still talking. Still trying to badger Molly into doing what he wanted. "I was there when your grandparents sold it to you, remember? With the extremely generous price I offered, you'd be making an enormous profit at my literal expense. Taking care of your health too, so—"

"My health is fine, and you can easily afford that price. Which *I know firsthand*"—she emphasized that phrase, her voice like acid—"since you used my earnings and savings to get through med school with zero debt."

Holy shit. She'd paid for his entire medical degree? How much money had *that* taken?

Defensiveness stiffened his response. "That was a joint decision, if you'll remember."

"Sadly, you're correct. Which is why I'm taking my time with this one and ensuring I get it right." Her eyes had narrowed with anger. "Again: I'll contact you if and when I put my house for sale. In the meantime, stop contacting me."

"Turning down that kind of offer . . ." A puff of air, as the other man blew out a breath. "It's just incredibly foolish, Molly. I never expected you to be so *irrational*."

A wave of heat engulfed Karl. Pure, undiluted rage. If her asshole ex were here, spouting that bullshit? He'd get two extra-wide Crocs up his—

"Goodbye, Rob." She extracted one hand from Karl's grasp. Tapped her screen with her now-clean finger. Ended the call while that prick was still talking, talking, talking.

When her cell immediately rang again, she swiped at the screen a few more times. Blocked her ex's number. Then set down the phone again, exhaling slowly.

All stickiness was long gone from her hands. Cleanup efforts had become a massage a while back, and Karl kept at it. Rubbed the hand he still held. Waited.

Yeah, he needed to know more about her asshole ex. But a smart man—a man who cared—would let her come to him. Let her share what she wanted, when she wanted, because Molly shouldn't be pushed into anything she didn't choose to do.

"I suppose you could use some context for that conversation," she eventually said, rewarding his exemplary goddamn patience.

He grunted noncommittally. Kept massaging. Kept her in control of the discussion.

"We met in college and moved in together after graduation." Her spine was straight enough to use as a goddamn level. "It took him nine years to convince me to marry him, because I had doubts.

Almost from the very beginning, actually. But I blamed those doubts on my own emotional damage, rather than paying attention to them. So we got married."

Karl scowled down at her pinky, which he was squeezing and lightly tugging. "And that fucker shoved cake in your face."

"Yes. But I stayed anyway." Her silent sigh lifted and lowered her shoulders. "At first, we both did voice-over work and audiobook narration. After a while, though, he decided he wanted to go to med school instead."

He scowled harder. Switched to her ring finger. "You paid for it."

"I thought it was what a good partner would do. And in practical terms, it seemed to make sense. He said to consider it an investment in our future, since he'd be outearning me once he joined a practice. I'd pay now, he'd pay later."

Her laugh contained zero joy. "It's such a cliché. I'd even read a newspaper article about it years before."

"About what?" He started massaging her middle finger. Aka the digit he wished she'd flipped her ex at their wedding ceremony, right before noping the hell out of there.

"How frequently men rely on their wives' or partners' income while they're in med school and doing their residencies, then immediately leave after they're earning an independent income of their own." Her lips thinned. "And that's exactly what he did. He finished his residency, joined a practice, started making good money, and then asked me for a divorce. There was no warning. No sign of anything seriously wrong until he was packing his bags and heading for the door."

Took some real effort not to squeeze her finger too hard. Not to rant and shout and swear at the sheer injustice. But it wasn't about him, his feelings, his outrage. Also? More he said, less *she'd* say.

"When I pressed him on why he was leaving, he said there were two main reasons. First, he wanted children and I didn't. The issue was a deal-breaker for him." Clear exhaustion weighted each word, and she shook her head. "I couldn't understand why he hadn't told me that from the very beginning, or at least before we got married, because he knew I didn't want kids. I *never* wanted kids."

That bit, Karl could kinda understand. "He change his mind over the years?"

"That was my best guess too, but no." Her jaw turned to stone. "Instead, he told me he hadn't said anything because I was so difficult to talk to. So cold. And my coldness was his second reason for leaving."

Okay, screw staying quiet. "I'll show that bastard *cold*. Cart his ass to Antarctica in winter, shove his face in some goddamn dry ice, and—"

"I wouldn't recommend that plan of action, Dean," she said with a small smile, and offered him her thumb to rub. "First of all, flights and cruises to Antarctica are prohibitively expensive and would require more time off from the bakery than you can spare. Second, once you already had him in mid-winter Antarctica, wouldn't dry ice be literal overkill? Third, and most importantly: I didn't believe what he said, even the moment he said it. After being with the man for almost two decades, I recognized what was happening. Rob knew he hadn't behaved well, so he was getting defensive and trying to relieve his guilt by blaming everything on me."

He grunted, unappeased. "Still hurt, I'll bet."

Dearborn made a noncommittal noise.

Fine. He wouldn't push her on that point. Especially since he had another nosy-as-hell question he needed to ask.

"Just how big is your damn house?" He rested her left hand on the table. Grabbed her right. Started massaging her palm. "At that price, I'm assuming you live in a goddamn palace, with diamond-crusted potholders and gilded chip clips."

"Not that big." A little shrug. "Two bedrooms, one bath. About twelve hundred square feet. Zero potholders decorated with precious gemstones or golden snack-oriented accessories, sadly."

He gaped at her. Only two bedrooms? For that amount of money?

"Los Angeles housing prices are famously prohibitive, especially when you're talking about the more in-demand areas." Her back arched in a stretch that made his mouth dry and thoroughly distracted him from his sticker shock. "My grandparents love me, they had plenty of retirement savings, and the condo they found in Nevada wasn't nearly as expensive, so they gave me a significant discount on the sale. Otherwise, I never could have afforded their home."

That explained a few things, but— "If your ex wants kids, why not buy a bigger house?"

Maybe the prick was a minimalist or some shit. But wouldn't an LA doctor with that kind of selfish audacity demand something more grandiose?

"Good question. Rob's obsession with the house confuses me, given its size. With kids, things would get very cramped, very quickly. My guess? He and his fiancée—she's a doctor too—have big home-reno dreams." She paused. "That was a genuinely good offer he made. If I were smart, I'd probably take it. Use the profits to move someplace cheaper. Buy a place that's easier to maintain."

Her phrasing bothered the fuck out of him. "You *are* smart."

"Not always." Her faint grimace wrinkled her nose.

"Always," he countered stubbornly. "Whatever you choose? It'll be the right call."

Exhaling slowly, she extended one leg in front of her. Flexed her sneakered foot. Pointed her toes. Switched legs. "It's lavender honey, by the way."

Seemed they were done talking about her house and her ex. Changing gears took him a minute, though. Especially since he kept eyeing her long, thick thighs and wondering how they'd feel as a necklace.

"You saw the damn jar," he finally managed to reply. "Cheating."

"I figured it out before I looked at the label. I promise." She held up her left hand, as if swearing an oath. "Your hints were just that good, Dean. As soon as you mentioned France, I knew."

Clearly, he'd *nailed* that communication crap.

If he were a rooster? He'd be strutting around the barnyard, feathered chest puffed out in pride, crowing loudly enough to deafen all other nearby cocks.

"Teamwork," he told her, relieved as hell this plan hadn't gone to shit, unlike the stupid escape room. "Progress."

She snorted. "Verbs. Missing."

"Quit busting my chops, Dearborn," he complained with zero sincerity.

"I would, if it weren't such fun." As he began working on her thumb, her smile lingered. "Listen, I have an idea for our next activity."

When she didn't elaborate, he looked up. Met her eyes.

They were the fiery blue of an oven's pilot light. He couldn't look away. Couldn't move. Her scrutiny, blatant and hot, surveyed him top to Croc, lingering on his shoulders, his chest, his own thighs. Her pink tongue darted out and wet her lips.

His throat promptly went dry as overbaked scones.

"I was thinking . . ." Her mouth glistened, and the sight of it was a taunt. "May I touch you?"

His thoughts had gone real goddamn fuzzy. All he could do was nod, then nod again for no good reason, as all his mental warning sirens abruptly went silent.

Her legs stretched out, hooked the backs of his knees, and hauled him closer, until his half-hard dick pressed against the heat-soaked seam of her jeans. Both of them exhaled hard at the contact, and her lids went half-lidded, but she didn't blink. Didn't release him from that tractor-beam gaze.

If he kissed her, she'd taste like honey, rich and melting and subtly floral. Sticky on her lips, sweet on her tongue. Sweet on his tongue too, as he sucked the tip of hers.

He gripped her hand for dear life. Because if he let go, he'd seize her by the hips. Hold her in place and grind his erection against her until they both came.

The constriction of his jeans, the friction against hers, the soft give of her inner thighs— they were agonizing. He wanted to plant his feet and *rut*.

"I suggest a staring contest." Her velvety voice stroked over him, and if his cock had gone stone-hard, his knees suddenly had the structural integrity of an underbaked meringue. "Sixty seconds without blinking, close up. I've heard that's a really effective trust-building exercise."

He shook his head, trying to clear it. Because, yeah, his article in *Corporations Today* had listed a staring contest, but . . . weren't they kind of doing that shit already? Even if someone offered him the amount of money her house was worth to look away from her, he couldn't do it. Not for a single second. Not right now.

When she shifted on the stool, his dick rubbed against the scorching inner seam of her jeans. He stifled his own groan, but a little noise escaped her throat, and her cheeks flushed.

Yeah, he was stroking in just the right place. Friction through the fabric, cock against clit, just as he'd suspected.

Those blue, blue eyes burned hotter than his butane torch. Hot enough to char his damn bones where he stood.

Off-balance in every possible way, he dropped her hand and braced his palms on either side of her, gripping the table hard enough that his fingers ached and the stainless steel should've bent under the pressure. Tried his best not to move. Tried not to roll his hips, grind hard, and find out just how much they could do through two layers of denim.

His guess? A whole lot. Even more if they stripped off those jeans.

And if he didn't wrench himself away, right now, he'd also find out how much disinfectant he'd need after taking Molly right here on his worktable.

He wanted her so goddamn much. But . . . he *needed* more. Needed *everything*.

"Motherfucker," he ground out.

With effort, he broke eye contact. Broke the loose hold of her legs and stepped way the hell back. Kept retreating until he hit the cool cinder-block wall beside his sink. Ignored the temptation of her seemingly involuntary sway toward him and her small sound of protest.

"You . . ." He ripped a hand through his hair, every nerve howling in agitation and thwarted horniness. "You know how a real staring contest would end, Molly."

She subtly pressed her thighs together, then blew out a shaky breath. "With us sleeping together, you mean?"

"Yeah."

Another fifteen seconds of that up-close eye-fucking and cock-to-clit contact? He'd jump her, if she didn't jump him first. Even though he'd planned to wait until he knew she trusted him, knew she wouldn't leave his ass behind yet again.

She shrugged. "I know."

Her voice was cool and calm as a breezeless lake. If he hadn't nearly incinerated himself in the heat between her thighs, couldn't see her fingers trembling as she laced them neatly in her lap, he'd be completely convinced. Think she was unaffected.

Great acting. Not good enough to fool him anymore, though.

In another infinitesimal movement, she squirmed a bit on that stool. Shifted her legs, even as her cheeks continued to burn.

He watched. Considered.

He couldn't have her yet. Didn't matter how much he wanted to.

But if she needed to take the edge off? Could use a demonstration of what he could do for her, do *to* her, if given the chance?

Well . . .

In that case, he was at her service. Which he'd be happy to show her.

Right goddamn now.

13

Somewhere around the time Molly had let Karl listen to that awful conversation with Rob and physically support her while she sparred with her ex-husband, her iron-clad independence had cracked, with predictable consequences. All her self-discipline had drained out, then promptly evaporated in the towering heat that kept rising between the two of them in his silent back room.

In its place, lust filled her to drowning.

Mere moments ago, Karl had stood between her legs, solid and strong and sheltering, eyes locked to hers, his cock pressed tightly against the spot where she ached most, and she could barely see, hardly breathe. All her most atavistic instincts had urged her to arch her back, cinch her legs to yank Karl tighter against her needy clit, and make herself come.

God, she wanted to come *so much*.

The only thing she wanted more? An orgasm that *wasn't* self-induced, because the last several years hadn't offered her many of those. Preferably, one coaxed out of her by the strong, sure, capable hands of the man she'd wanted for two entire decades. Or, alternatively, dragged from her very willing body by that man's filthy mouth and talented tongue. Or even deep-dicked into glorious, climactic life by him, because she wasn't freaking picky at this point.

Nevertheless, she'd let him go when he pulled free, because she wouldn't force him into sexual intimacy or beg for what she wanted—and now the poor man was cowering against the wall. Apparently her excessive levels of horniness terrified even Karl fucking Dean, which she should probably consider a troubling revelation.

She closed her eyes. Gave herself a few seconds to steady her breathing and regain her vaunted self-mastery.

Karl didn't say anything as she struggled, because of course he didn't. But that was fine, because she didn't feel like talking either. Just banging. Or, alternatively, doing some light shopping at key Harlot's Bay businesses.

Several excellent vibrators—along with other useful items— resided in her bedside table back home. Because she'd come for Karl's funeral, though, she hadn't planned for coming in another, more pleasurable sense, and all her toys remained in California.

Good thing this town contained not one, but two adult stores. After her near miss just now, she intended to burn through some double-As tonight.

"Come here, Dearborn."

That was Karl's rumbly growl. Karl's hard hands on her hips hauling her off the stool as her eyes flew open. Karl keeping her upright when she stumbled, Karl rotating them until he was walking her backward, away from the table.

He crowded her up against the cool concrete-block wall. Her body jolted at the slight impact, even as his hand cradled the back of her head, protecting her from injury.

She braced herself against his chest and regained her balance. Tipped her chin to stare up at him, befuddled and aroused and besieged by a million different emotions. Far too many to process in speech.

"What . . ." The word was barely audible, but it was the best she could currently do. "Karl, what are you . . ."

Then he kicked her legs apart, and her thoughts promptly disintegrated.

He pushed his thigh between hers and leaned into her. Propped himself against the wall with his free arm, his elbow near her shoulder, his right palm flat against the concrete.

"Want to make you come." His open mouth, his prickly beard, dragged over her flushed cheek, and he licked the rim of her ear as her lips opened on a startled, needy gasp. "You good with that?"

He might as well have asked a woman wandering alone and delirious through Death Valley whether she was good with an icy bottle of sparkling lemonade.

"Oh, god, yes," she breathed, and that was all he needed.

He pressed his thigh up and in and observed her reaction, her hitched breath, with a stare sharp and dark as volcanic rock. Readjusting his weight, he lowered his right arm from the wall and unfastened her jeans with quick, confident movements.

His grip on the zipper stilled. "Anything doesn't feel good, anything you need I'm not giving you, you tell me. Got it?"

He waited for her nod. Then his fingers tangled with hers as they both shoved her jeans down over her ass. He simply watched, his own breathing labored, as she did the same to her soft cotton boy shorts—or as best she could with his thigh in the way.

They'd created a tangled, lumpy mess of fabric just below her hips, and the wall was hard and cold against her bare butt, and she didn't give a shit. Didn't try to slow things down or make anything about the moment more practical.

She gripped two handfuls of his tee for balance. Her half-lowered clothing bit into her legs as she tried—unsuccessfully—to spread them farther in invitation.

Within a heartbeat, his hard, broad hand wedged between her thighs and cupped her there. Squeezed carefully but firmly, until her head tipped back in pleasure, pressing tighter against his other palm.

Her eyes closed, and she relaxed into the wall. Let the concrete bear her weight and let the press of his body into hers keep her upright.

"That's it, Dearborn." His hot tongue swirled over her throat, his voice vibrated against her prickling flesh, and his fresh-bread smell dizzied her. "I'll take care of you. Just hold on and trust me."

Her legs were barely splayed wide enough for his hand to fit, but he managed. His warm, strong fingers slipped through her vulva, opening her to his confident touch, spreading her slickness wherever they leisurely roamed.

The pads of those agile fingers were rough from all his work, all his handwashing, and the unexpected friction against her swollen, sensitive skin sent a jolt of lightning up her spine. Her mouth opened in a silent moan, and her back arched in an attempt to shove harder against him, even though there was nowhere to go. They were already as close as two mostly clothed people could be.

His forefinger teasingly circled her entrance, then trailed to her clit. He stroked slowly around and over the spot, flicked and pressed, and she couldn't hold back a rough, raw sound of building pleasure.

"There, huh?" He sucked hard at the base of her neck, and the pressure, the sting, arrowed straight between her legs and made her jerk against the wall. "Got it."

Her brain full of nothing but light and static and need, she released one hand's trembling grip on his soft tee and groped blindly between them. Slid her arm between their soft bellies, until she could reach down to where his fingers were gliding and rubbing, pleasuring her with such sure, gorgeous skill.

She laid her hand over his. Not to urge him to go faster or even press harder. Just to feel his movements inside and out. To trace each tendon and jutting knuckle as he worked her toward the orgasm that rushed closer with every labored breath she sucked into her straining lungs. Her hips were hitching against him now, rhythmic and searching, and she was so wet even his rough fingertips couldn't gain much purchase. They slipped over her clit in easy, repeated glides, each one a sunburst behind her eyelids, sweet as honey trickling down her throat.

"Come on, baby." His words were almost too rough to decipher. "I've got you."

No. If she came, this would end, and she couldn't stand the thought.

"I don't . . ." she managed to whisper, before he gently squeezed her clit between two knuckles, and her legs nearly gave way beneath her. Her head would have thudded against concrete, but his palm cushioned the impact. "Oh. *Oh.*"

A slow rub of his thumb over and around her clit. Another light squeeze between his broad knuckles, as she arched and trembled and gasped. Then his hot breath washed over her shoulder and his teeth pinched the tender muscle there, biting just firmly enough to sing down her spine and detonate her orgasm.

She came so hard, it verged on pain. Eyes scrunched shut, her back arched violently under the impact, mouth open wide as her body clenched and released again and again, urged on by the endless glides of his fingers over her slick flesh.

She ground herself against his touch, mindless and panting.

"That's right. Take what you need." His lips rested against her temple, and he pressed a hard, fierce kiss there. "Fuck, Molly. So gorgeous when you come."

Eventually, her muscles began to release, and she sagged against the wall, against the thigh still helping to hold her upright. Her thoughts had become a vague buzz, and every inch of her body felt limp and well used. Well satisfied.

Her first semi-coherent post-orgasm thought: *Well, damn.*

Her second semi-coherent post-orgasm thought: *Apparently Karl Dean can finger a woman as capably as he pipes out a peony.*

Even in her own muzzy head, piping out a peony sounded like a euphemism for deep dicking. But she couldn't focus on that. Couldn't focus on much of anything, really.

While she was still floating in a come-drunk haze, those steady, peony-piping hands slid from behind her head and between her legs and efficiently put her clothing back in order, then zipped and fastened her jeans. Even though the soft cotton of her underwear seemed to abrade her oversensitive skin, and the way her jeans separated his skin from hers was a total outrage.

Dimly, she marveled that they were both fully dressed now, despite how naked and raw she felt. Both completely covered, down to the sneakers on her feet and the green resin foam ridiculousness on his.

Which prompted her third semi-coherent post-orgasm thought: *Does this mean the sight of Crocs is going to turn me on now? Because that would make future healthcare visits very awkward.*

Self-assigned tasks complete, he didn't hustle her out of his bakery, and he didn't speak. Not to demand orgasmic reciprocation. Not even to ask whether the experience had been good for her. Which . . . fair enough. He didn't need to ask. The answer was beyond obvious.

Instead of talking, he simply gathered her into his arms and held her. She huddled into him, letting him support a good chunk of her weight as her heartbeat gradually slowed and steadied.

For some reason, the embrace seemed more intimate than his fingers between her legs.

His bristly cheek rubbed over the top of her head, and his hard dick prodded her thigh. He was apparently ignoring that inconvenience, though, so she did too as he ran a slow palm up and down her back and urged her face against his neck.

Slowly, her thoughts began to clear.

When was the last time Rob had offered her pleasure without expecting something in return from her? Ten years before their divorce? Fifteen? She genuinely couldn't remember, it had been so damn long. When it came to orgasms, if she got one, she gave one. Because that was only fair, right? Even though she was multi-orgasmic, and he wasn't.

In retrospect, their entire marriage had been a series of carefully calibrated equivalencies, attempts to balance what they each got and gave in a practical, equitable way. And to her shame, she hadn't noticed her husband's thumb on the scale until far, far too late.

Or at least she hadn't allowed herself to acknowledge the injustice, because that would mean she'd made a terrible mistake in marrying him, even after so many years together. That would mean she'd wasted her time and energy and not valued herself highly enough.

It would also mean she'd repeated her mother's mistake of trusting the man she'd wed. Repeated her own teenage mistake too: trusting the man she'd loved most in the entire world.

Still, here she was, leaning on Karl as if she could depend on him. He was sheltering her, soothing her, and she was letting him. Which was probably a terrible mistake too, but she couldn't seem to stop herself from making it.

Untold minutes later, she finally stirred in his arms. "My legs are pudding, and it's your fault, Dean."

There. That had sounded convincingly casual. Calm and unruffled.

Mentally, she offered herself a round of admiring applause.

"My fault, huh?" His snort ruffled her hair. "Gladly plead guilty to *that* charge."

More lighthearted conversation, coming right up. "You're also facing one count of attempted cannibalism and one count of reckless hickey infliction."

The teeth marks on her shoulder would probably disappear in minutes, since he'd barely nipped her. That love bite on her neck, though? Given how hard he'd sucked, it'd take far longer to fade. If her shirt collar didn't cover it, all of Harlot's Bay was going to see it and know exactly what she and Karl had been doing. Well, *some* of what they'd been doing, anyway.

"Please know that anything you grunt in response can and will be used against you in a court of law," she added.

His hand glided up to the base of her neck and squeezed. He rubbed his thumb over the sore bit of skin there, then slid his fingertips over the place where he'd sunk his teeth so carefully into her shoulder.

He paused on that spot. "Shouldn't have marked or bitten without asking. Got carried away. I'm sorry."

His voice was gruff but sincere. And honestly, even though he really *should* have asked first, she didn't truly mind. Especially since she hadn't relaxed this thoroughly in years.

"The court accepts your explanation and is prepared to render judgment." She lifted his head to smirk at him, then nudged her leg against his unflagging erection. "I hereby sentence you to one afternoon of blue balls." After a moment's thought, she added, "Although, technically speaking, sexually disappointed testicles don't actually turn blue. Otherwise, I imagine there'd be way more Papa Smurf–related jokes made at their expense."

He waved that off, intent brown eyes searching hers. "We good, Dearborn? You forgive me?"

"Yeah." Part of his beard had gone wonky, and she smoothed it down with her finger. "We're good. Truly."

His shoulders visibly relaxed, and his palm stroked back down her spine as he tried to ease her closer once more. With regret, she resisted the gentle pressure.

"That said"—she fished her phone from her back pocket, where it had luckily remained safe and sound during all their shenanigans, and checked the display—"I'll need to take a rain check on lunch. It's later than I realized, and Lise and I should be meeting not too long from now. I want to get cleaned up before seeing her."

Her inner thighs remained uncomfortably damp, he'd worked her into a light sweat before she came, and she probably smelled like sex. As soon as she got back to the Spite House, its tiny bathtub-shower combo would have to reluctantly accommodate her once more.

Also, she needed to impose some distance between herself and Karl. Needed enough time alone to emerge from her orgasm-induced daze and get her head on straight.

Sliding free from his embrace was harder than it should have been. But she locked her shaky knees and did it, stepping back from him. One pace. Two.

He let her go without a struggle, although his stare remained uncomfortably sharp. "Today went way better than that goddamn escape room. Even before I finally got my hand inside your jeans. You agree?"

She nodded and tucked her phone back into her pocket.

While the orgasm definitely constituted the highlight of her afternoon, today's exercise had in fact convinced her of a few important things. For instance: Karl wouldn't take advantage of her vulnerability. Even blindfolded, she hadn't felt unsafe for even an instant, which wasn't such a small revelation. Also, when given the chance to talk about foodstuffs, he could in fact communicate clearly and sufficiently, and they could work as an effective team.

Those discoveries probably explained why she'd let him overhear her call with Rob. Why she'd willingly explained why and how her marriage had ended and what her ex-husband currently wanted from her. Why she'd allowed herself to accept Karl's support.

But life wasn't all blindfolds and bougie goat cheese, sadly. She wished it were. And unfortunately, she had a sinking feeling that he was about to—

"You trust me now?" he asked, his voice gruff but eager.

There it was. The question she'd hoped to avoid. The question that, if answered with total honesty, would douse the hope and anticipation gleaming in his dark eyes and erase the small, happy smile curving his slightly swollen lips.

An expression of even cautious joy didn't appear often on Karl Dean's face. The thought of wiping that joy away literally nauseated her. But . . . lying wouldn't help anyone in the long run, including—maybe even *especially*—him.

Did she trust him now?

"More than I did before," she said carefully, and watched his smile flicker and die, because he didn't get it.

Even that guarded, incomplete faith in Karl was far more than she would have predicted after their disastrous escape room attempt. More than she'd granted anyone but Lise in years. The shift constituted genuine progress, and it had real significance. It *meant* something.

Something wasn't everything, though—and Karl apparently wanted *everything*. Now.

"You trust me more than you did before," he repeated, each word precise.

She braced herself for an argument. Nodded again.

He set his fists on his hips. "Enough to stay in Harlot's Bay?"

"I . . ." Her brow crinkled in confusion. "I *am* staying in Harlot's Bay. Currently, in a ten-foot-wide house built as a fraternal middle finger."

Hadn't they already had this discussion? And hadn't a mixture of guilt and lust and her lost bet to Lise led to an entire month spent far away from home?

His eyes rolled to the drop ceiling. "Long-term, Dearborn."

Her mouth clamped tight as she processed that question and what it implied. What it revealed about what he truly wanted.

Was her moving to Harlot's Bay his real end goal here? Rather than getting her to trust him enough that he'd feel comfortable fucking her, as he'd led her to believe, or—more ambitiously—enough that she'd consider a long-distance relationship?

If so, why hadn't he told her before?

Because if he wanted her to trust him *so much* that she'd uproot her life and move across an entire continent for him, if that was the fundamental reason they were cycling through various corporate trust-building exercises, then . . . wow. When she'd thought that Karl wanted everything, she hadn't realized what *everything* truly entailed for him.

She genuinely didn't know what it would take to trust him so completely. And even if she figured out what was required, the prospect of putting that much faith in yet another man terrified her.

Once again, he'd left her with only one honest answer to a very difficult question.

"I don't think so," she told him quietly. "I'm so sorry."

Then, before he could push her even harder, she snatched up her bag and fled the bakery.

14

*W*ell, that blew.

Not the blind taste test—and *especially* not the orgasm he'd given Molly, which was amazing. Maybe the most satisfying sexual experience of Karl's goddamn life, and he hadn't even taken off his pants. Knowing that he'd pleased her, that Molly fucking Dearborn had writhed and gasped and come so hard against his hand that she hadn't been able to stand without assistance?

Karl Andrew Dean, passable small-town baker and crotchety hermit, had split his skin. Transformed into Karlzilla, towering over skyscrapers. Karl Kong, beating his chest from a mile high. Captain Harlot's Bay, strong enough to heft the world on his tireless shoulders.

Predictably, all that testosterone and self-satisfaction had made him stupid. Made him think he'd won the war when he apparently didn't even understand the rules of battle.

She trusted him more than before—but not enough. He had no idea what he was doing wrong. Time was running short.

And that part? Yeah. It totally blew.

Once Karl washed his hands thoroughly and cleaned up his worktable, grumbling to himself all the while, he reluctantly texted Matthew and Athena to ask if he could come over to their house that night to get some advice.

Athena responded by asking whether he'd been body-snatched by an alien, because of course she fucking did. Hassling him? That woman's favorite hobby. No, her goddamn raison d'être. Good thing his best friend would stick up for—

Who are you? Matthew wrote. *And what have you done with Karl "Interpersonal Communication Is Poison to Me" Dean?*

Traitorous bastard!

Karl sent them a row of middle-finger emojis.

Ah, there you are, Special K, Athena replied. *Congratulations on inhabiting your own body again! In answer to your question, I would be more than happy to impart my immense wisdom concerning any matter you have in mind. And by "any matter you have in mind," I clearly mean Molly. Because you are so incredibly gone for that woman, it's almost comical, and nothing and no one else would drive you to voluntarily exchange actual human words with us at your own behest.*

Karl contemplated tossing his cell in the garbage disposal.

Matthew added, *Come on over whenever you like, Karl. We're not going anywhere.*

I'LL BE THERE, Karl pecked out. *TO MURDER BOTH YOU DICKS.*

Athena posted a fireworks emoji. *Can't wait! BYOMW!*

Karl's brows drew together. Bring Your Own . . . Mulled Wine? Neither Athena nor Matthew was a big drinker, but maybe—

Bring Your Own Murder Weapon, Matthew helpfully supplied. *Our kitchen knives aren't particularly sharp.*

After sending four entire rows of dagger emojis interspersed with skulls, Karl ended the conversation by turning off his phone. Because even a stubborn, cranky bastard like him knew when to admit defeat.

Also because he was already feeling better.

Not that he'd ever tell those two assholes.

* * *

"Got no idea what the woman needs from me," Karl informed Matthew and Athena early that evening. "The two of us? Chemistry to burn. History. Friendship. But all that's not enough to make her trust me. Not the way I want her to, down to her bones, and I don't get why."

After more bakery prep, he'd come straight to their row house. Which had changed over the past year, since Matthew married Greydon. In a good way. Fewer heavy, dark, uncomfortable furniture pieces inherited from his useless parents. More bright colors and clutter. Felt way more like a home.

The den now had an overstuffed couch that embraced Karl like a hug when he sank into it. When the duo led him upstairs, he promptly plunked himself down there. Matthew perched on the other end of the cushy sofa in his rumpled tee and jeans, while Athena lounged on a velvet brocade fainting couch or chaise or whatever the hell you called that shit, her skirt spread around her in a semicircle, glasses slightly askew.

Made his heart lighter to see her looking so happy and confident after the rough patch she'd had. Especially since she was—as he told her each time they met—a potato-obsessed pain in the ass, and if *she'd* found love and happiness? Maybe he had a shot too.

Before he took it, though, he had to improve his goddamn aim.

"Need your help," he concluded. "You two have this relationship shit down, so—"

"Plus, we're not easily intimidated by your threats to stab us. That makes us particularly useful helpers, I think you'll agree."

"—I hoped you might be able to give me advice," he gruffly finished, ignoring Athena's interruption, then forced the next word from his resistant vocal cords. "Please."

She and Matthew exchanged glances in that irritating, wordless communication some couples had. Exactly the sort of communication that best suited Karl and that none of his past relationships had ever achieved.

Matthew nodded a little, then turned to Karl. "Tell us what you like about Molly."

Odd question. Easy one, though. Could've given a thousand-part list. Instead, he boiled the pool of reasons down to essentials.

"Never get sick of her company. Being around her, talking to her . . . it's easy. Fun. Doesn't make me feel like throttling anyone." The sun shone brighter in Molly Dearborn's presence. Simple matter of fact. "Rare for me. You know that."

Athena snorted. "The entire population of Harlot's Bay comprehends its rarity. Probably all of the Eastern seaboard too."

Matthew's lips rolled between his teeth. Trying not to smile, the wife-adoring bastard.

"So I like her," Karl continued, and he deserved a damn medal for disregarding Greydon's blatant provocation. "Admire her too. Smart, funny, capable. Sexy as hell. Willing to call me on my crap."

He loved that about her. Half the time, he made his threats ridiculous on purpose, because he wanted to hear her inevitable pedantic analysis of their feasibility.

The other half?

Well, the world could be infuriating, and he was a cranky asshole. An occasional over-the-top response to bullshit was inevitable, which Dearborn seemed to realize. Even appreciate. Or at least find amusing, which was good enough for Karl.

"Molly fucking Dearborn?" He shook his head. "Everything I've always wanted. For over half my goddamn life now."

Sure, he'd dated other women. For a few weeks or a few months, until they'd gotten tired of his baker's schedule—bed at seven, up at three—or concluded he was too *withholding*. Too cranky. Not open enough about his emotions. Other times, things just hadn't clicked quite right, and he and his partners had separated by mutual agreement.

Nothing had worked long-term. No one had loved him, even when he'd given them as much of his heart as he had available. All the parts Molly hadn't already claimed long before.

For the first time, that didn't hurt anymore.

Like he'd just told his friends, no other woman but Molly had ever left him gasping for air at the mere sight of her. No other woman had ever made him feel so comfortable and understood, so valued and *wanted*. No other woman had ever amused him, infuriated him, and excited him, all at the same time.

So if he and his previous girlfriends hadn't been willing to call what they had together *love*? No fucking wonder. Those relationships had ended for good reason. Left him with zero regrets, especially now that Molly was back in his life.

Matthew and Athena exchanged more of those annoying, significant glances.

"Okay. Those are all excellent reasons to like her." Matthew sat forward. Idly rubbed at his stubbly jaw. "Have you told her any of them?"

Lay his heart at the feet of a woman who could easily crush it underfoot? Who didn't even trust him and had no intention of staying in Harlot's Bay?

Karl laughed in Matthew's misguided face. "Hell, no."

"Ah." His best friend turned to his wife. "Athena? Do you have anything to say?"

Karl's eyeballs rolled so far back in his head, he almost lost them. "Of course she does. That woman loves three things above all else." He ticked them off on his fingers. "Tubers. Useless information. Not minding her own damn business."

"What about me?" Matthew asked, smiling slightly. "Where am I on the list?"

Karl lifted a shoulder. "Maybe you rank above tubers. Probably not, though."

That was a lie. They all knew it. Karl might frequently issue violent threats, but Athena? For all her good cheer and kindness, she'd fucking *obliterate* anyone who hurt Matthew.

"Luckily, I don't have to choose between you and potatoes, baby. Consider yourself lucky." Athena grinned at her husband, then twisted to face Karl. "Here's what I'm wondering, Special K. You say she doesn't trust easily. That she's cynical. Right?"

Did they really need to restate the entire point of this conversation?

He heaved an impatient sigh. "Yeah. That's why I'm here, Greydon. Talking. Like a fucking chump."

"Hmmm." Athena's head tipped to the side, and she eyed him contemplatively. "Do you think her lack of trust is due to something about you in particular? Or simply general wariness around others? Maybe because of bad past experiences?"

One thing Karl now knew for sure about Molly: The bastard she'd married had damaged her. Karl had guessed that already. But until earlier today, he hadn't known how deep the injury must've been. Hadn't known that hearing the full story would tempt him to track that dick of a doctor down and shove him headfirst into a shark-filled moat. Or at least into a cake, the same damn way Rob had done to Molly.

"Won't violate her privacy, but . . ." His hands ached, they were fisted so hard on his thighs. "She's got an asshole user of an ex. Divorced two years, but he's still hassling her. Wants her house."

Athena pressed her lips together. "That'd certainly give someone trust issues."

Karl wasn't Dearborn's former husband, though. Why couldn't Molly see that? For that matter, why couldn't *Athena* see it?

"Her ex—shit. Hold on." Sitting up straight on that marshmallowy couch took some real effort, but he managed to heave himself upright and start again. "Her ex is a selfish, heartless prick, yeah, but I'd lop off my dick with my cleaver before hurting her, and she damn well knows it."

Athena's brow creased, her hazel eyes warm.

"Knowing something intellectually and knowing it in your bones, in your heart . . . those are two different things, Karl." Her voice was gentle but emphatic. "And just to be clear: You wouldn't *deliberately* hurt her. But you might do it by accident, because you're both human, and people hurt each other even when they don't intend to. Even when they love someone."

She waited for him to take that in, much as he didn't want to.

"I get that Molly's distrust hurts your feelings." She held up a hand when he began to protest. "Please don't insult us both by pretending your heart isn't essentially a Cadbury Creme Egg. Hard shell. Gooey innards. Very sweet." She paused, then added under her breath, "Albeit somewhat off-putting to many and widely unavailable at most times of the year."

He glared at her. But he didn't argue. "You hungry, Greydon? Sound hungry."

Because he'd brought some potato bread for her—along with a few of Matthew's favorite orange-caramel crunch scones—despite knowing she'd hug him when he tossed her the freshly baked loaf.

Or, possibly, *because* she'd hug him. Though he'd rather rip out a toenail than admit that.

"Yep." She beamed happily at him. "And I already saw what you have in that bakery bag by your feet, so don't bother trying to escape me once this conversation is done. Resistance to my grateful embrace is futile."

He supposed the Borg were nosy and information-obsessed too, what with that hive-mind shit. Probably less fond of spuds and hugs than his former employee, though.

"Anyway, here's my point." Her bright smile softened again. Turned sympathetic. "I understand how you're feeling and why you're feeling that way. You know you're trustworthy. She's not recognizing that as quickly as you'd hoped, though, and it stings."

Even an uncommunicative bastard like him knew what came next.

"But?" he prompted.

"But . . . maybe she just needs more time, Karl," Matthew said quietly, and Karl turned his attention to his best friend of over thirty years. "She's been back in Harlot's Bay—back in your company—for less than two weeks, after twenty years apart. Also, I'm not all that certain Molly's ex is the full story here."

That last bit was clearly leading somewhere. Too bad Karl had no idea where the destination might be.

"What do you mean?" Athena asked for both of them.

"I knew Molly back in high school too. Karl was closer to her, obviously, but she and I shared a lot of classes and ate lunch together most days. Even back then, she wasn't the most . . ." He hesitated. Dragged a hand through his dark, curly hair. Seemed to search for the right words. "She wasn't the most *unguarded* person around. Friendly, sure. Kind, definitely. Open? No. I wouldn't say so."

Karl thought that over for a few seconds. "Dearborn always valued her privacy. Could be reserved sometimes. But these days, it's not just that. She seems more . . . wary. Cynical."

Or maybe . . . scared.

Was that what he kept sensing in her? In her reactions to him? Fear?

The teenage girl he'd known had been distant and cool on occasion, but seemed utterly unafraid of who she was or what others thought about her. Unworried about getting hurt, or at least confident she could recover from that hurt with ease.

"Matthew told me she left school abruptly, without much explanation, in the final weeks of senior year. He doesn't recall why." Athena's glasses slipped down her nose as she absently picked at a cuticle. "Normally, people don't move across the country at a time like that unless there's an emergency. Do you know what happened?"

Her agile brain was trying to make connections. In unlikely places, Karl could argue, but whatever. He'd play along for now, because he had no idea what the hell else to do.

"If I'm remembering it right . . ." He frowned. Tried to think back twenty years. "She went to California with her mom. Not her dad. Even though I got the sense she and her father were pretty tight back then."

Karl shrugged, unhappy he couldn't tell them more. "Guess I assumed her parents were splitting up. Didn't want to ask, though. Especially since she didn't volunteer the information."

Her parents weren't together now. He knew that much, at least.

Matthew's forehead was creased in thought. "Since she's been back, she hasn't explained what happened?"

Karl's sigh hurt his chest, it was so huge. "Nope."

Athena pushed her glasses back up to the bridge of her nose. "Has she mentioned her parents?"

"Not really."

"And you haven't asked."

"Nope." Even though her one mention of her father had been . . . weird. And he'd meant to pursue it, but had gotten distracted. Dammit.

"Huh." Squinting in thought, she absently straightened her crooked frames. "Interesting."

"So that's one part of her history you don't understand. There could be others." Matthew angled himself to meet Karl's eyes directly. "Maybe the changes you've seen in her are just the effects of passing time and the state of the world, in addition to an ugly divorce. But you won't know that for sure until you open up her black box and get all the crucial information."

"Good news, everyone." Athena snickered. "Karl was already pretty damn eager to open up her black box."

She wasn't wrong. Karl still flipped her the bird on principle.

"You've clearly spent far too much time with the Nasty Wenches." Matthew shook his head at her. "It was a metaphor, not a euphemism."

"No reason it can't be both. And I have a correction to issue, Vine." She raised her finger in emphasis. "The Wenches haven't corrupted me. If anything, *I've* corrupted *them*. Before my arrival, sure, they read about butt plugs and threesomes and even a little light nipple-clamping or two, but they hadn't once considered the erotic possibilities in getting kidnapped by a kangaroo with a luxurious pouch and an absolutely enormous—"

Her husband's face disappeared into his hands. "I don't want to know."

"But his penis has special features, Matthew." Her voice dripped with suggestion. "So *many* special features."

His palms muffled his response. "I'm sure it does."

Both of them? Entirely missing the crucial goddamn point.

"Trick dick or no trick dick, that kangaroo asshole's still a kidnapper," Karl interjected. "To me? Zero consent means zero romance. Why the group picked that book for next month's discussion, I'll never fucking know."

"You really think Sadie Brazen dabbled in dubcon?" Athena— who'd pointed out consent issues herself in countless goddamn meetings, albeit never in a Brazen story—had the gall to look disappointed in him. "Come on, Karl. You've listened to every single one of her audiobooks. You know better than that."

Wait. That meant— "There's a twist?"

"There's a twist," she confirmed.

"Riley's secretly a kangaroo too?"

"No." Her lips twitched. "Although, it must be said, kidnapping a sentient kangaroo before boning her would still constitute dubcon."

Karl thought for a minute. "Brazen pulled a Bobby Ewing switcheroo? Everything's a dream?"

Bobby Ewing, Matthew repeated silently, then extracted a small notepad from the side table's drawer and jotted down a note to himself.

"I'm not going to tell you, Special K." Athena resettled herself on her ridiculous settee. "You'll just have to find out for yourself."

He scowled at her. "Dammit, Greydon."

"I have a suggestion." Matthew's voice was drier than the strawberries currently shriveling in the bakery's dehydrator. "One that doesn't involve kangaroos, but rather the actual reason Karl came to our house tonight."

"Please excuse me, Dr. Matthew Vine the Third. I got off topic again." Athena blinked up at him through smudged lenses, all remorseful innocence. "You'll have to teach me some discipline."

Karl groaned and scrubbed both hands over his own face. Jesus H. Christ, that woman was a hellion. And now he needed to soak his brain in fucking bleach.

"To return to my suggestion . . ." Matthew's voice and expression remained calm, despite his bright-pink ears. "Let me sum up the situation, and please correct me if I've gotten something incorrect. Karl, you're confused as to why demonstrating your honesty and protectiveness toward Molly hasn't convinced her to trust you as much as you'd prefer. You haven't told her how you feel about her, however, and you don't know key parts of her history."

A decent summation, but not congratulatory enough when it came to Karl's exemplary patience and research efforts.

Nevertheless, he waved Matthew on.

"Your next activity needs to involve open communication," his best friend concluded.

No goddamn way. "Today's food-tasting exercise covered that, Vine. We've *already* communicated. Thought we'd do putt-putt next."

"Communication's not really a one-time event, Special K." Athena's tone was overly patient, like a parent explaining to her toddler why shitting his pants was problematic, and Karl did his best to murder her with his eyes. "Which I know comes as a disappointment, but it's true. Especially since your communication today involved food, not feelings. Not personal histories. Not your hopes for the future or concerns you might have."

"Did too learn some personal history," Karl muttered.

That fucking terrible cake-smushing wedding story. All the divorce shit. None of which he was being given sufficient credit for, dammit!

"Good." Athena's approval sounded genuine. "You can build on that. We can help."

Woman wasn't going to relent. He could already tell.

"Mother*fucker*." This groan came from deep in his tortured fucking soul. "Fuck. My. Fucking. Life."

"Sure, Special K." Athena beamed at him. "If you insist."

* * *

GRUMPILY, KARL LISTENED to their ideas. Took notes on his phone, because those assholes were *thorough*.

By the time he stomped downstairs and reached their front door, he knew what he needed to do—tomorrow *and* next weekend—and was way past ready for bed. Right before he left, though, Matthew drew him aside in the entryway.

"Karl, I understand why you want to prove yourself to Molly. You're hoping for a real future with her, and that can't happen if she doesn't trust you." Lines creased his forehead as he spoke quietly. "The part I still don't get is why all this needs to happen now, before she leaves Harlot's Bay. She can visit here again. You can visit her in California. There are video calls, texts, and emails, or even—and I know this is an upsetting concept for you—old-fashioned phone calls to tide you over between reunions. You can build trust over time, instead of trying to compress the entire process into four short weeks."

Karl sighed heavily. "I want her to stay, Matthew."

"I know. Eventually, you'd like her to move here, but—"

"Not eventually," Karl corrected. "Now."

"But . . ." Those lines across Matthew's brow deepened. "Karl, that's not—"

"Molly's squirrelly as hell. Give her enough distance, and she'll retreat further. If things don't happen now, got a bad feeling they won't happen at all." That feeling had been hounding him since the first moment of their reunion. Drumming in his temples. Roiling his stomach. Keeping him awake no matter how exhausted he was. "Why I asked for your help tonight. I don't have time to keep fumbling this shit. I need to know what to do."

His best friend took that in for a minute.

"Okay," he finally said. "I get it now. I might not agree completely, but I hear you." Matthew's chest rose and fell on his own silent sigh. Then he tugged Karl into a hug, squeezing tightly. "Good luck, man."

"Thanks." Karl squeezed back. "Got a feeling I'm gonna need it."

15

Against her better judgment, Molly spent her Sunday evening discussing the validity of Satan as a fictional love interest.

Up until that very morning, she'd had zero intention of attending the Nasty Wenches book club meeting. As she'd told Karl two days ago, there was no point in putting down roots that she'd only have to rip up again, sooner rather than later. And she wasn't a fool. If she went to the meeting, even her best efforts might not be able to stop the tendrils, however doomed they might be, from unfurling underground.

Athena. Matthew. Janel. All Nasty Wenches, apparently. All people she already liked. Hell, even Lise had overcome her shyness—not to mention the occasional awkwardness of discussing her own books as if she were simply a reader—and joined the group last month.

If Molly went, she'd probably enjoy herself too much. Which was a real problem.

Then there was the issue of Karl. Also a Nasty Wench, and the entire reason she'd changed her mind about attending.

When he'd called her that morning to reiterate his invitation, she'd worried about residual awkwardness from the way they'd parted yesterday. Wondered whether he'd employ all the sound and fury he typically employed to disguise his hurt feelings.

Instead, his tone had been casual, as if nothing notable had happened between them recently. And in typical Karl fashion—i.e., without much preamble—he'd told her he needed her at the meeting. Not because he wouldn't finish his chosen book and hoped she could act as a human CliffsNotes—by the time they talked, he was already halfway through his audiobook of *Bedded by Beelzebub*—but because he required a bodyguard.

"Wouldn't let the Wenches visit when I was sick. Frustrated their caretaking urges," he explained. "First time they see me again? Those smut-loving busybodies are gonna fucking *swarm* me, Dearborn. Bury me in soggy tuna casseroles and weird-ass home remedies. Few of the damn harpies might even *hug me*."

He sounded utterly appalled, that big faker. They both knew he secretly loved hugs, however reluctantly he accepted them. Probably adored tuna casseroles too, soggy or not.

"You coming?" His voice had suddenly gone tight with tension. "Need you to help fend them off, Molly. Please." A lengthy pause. "Besides, you'll like everyone there. Your type of people. Could be a ready-made community for you. If you, uh, wanted that. At some point."

In typical Karl fashion once more, he'd finally said the quiet part loud. He didn't need a freaking *bodyguard*. He wasn't inviting her to the Nasty Wenches meeting to protect him from casseroles and hugs. Not at all. Despite what she'd told him, he wanted her to put down some of her ill-fated roots, in hopes she'd decide not to rip them up after all.

Responding to him had taken a few moments of thought.

She really shouldn't encourage his dream of getting her to stay in Harlot's Bay long-term. But she was flattered that he wanted her at the meeting so darn much. Enough that he'd even employed his best manners—an actual *please!*—for the repeat invitation. And heaven knew she couldn't resist watching a dozen people fuss over the crankiest man alive.

Also, yes, maybe she *was* embarrassingly eager to see him again. Not to mention more tempted than she cared to admit by the thought of a ready-made community full of people who might make her feel valued and understood.

"Fine," she'd eventually told him. "I'll go. But I'll drive myself, in case I want to duck out early."

He'd hung up before she could change her mind. Then turned off his damn phone for the rest of the day so she couldn't cancel on him.

So now here she was, at the modest, cozy home of a fiftysomething white librarian named Bethany. Seated, improbably enough, on a floral-upholstered couch with Lise on one side and Janel on the other, listening to sweet, whispery Bethany talk about gargoyle junk.

"—and once she mounts Lucifer's stone dick and rides him to climax, he breaks free from his marble prison for the first time in countless centuries and becomes flesh and blood once more." Bethany carefully buttered one of the muffins Karl had brought especially for her. "Although his penis remains stone. Well, all three penises, to be exact."

Molly blinked. Oh, wow.

From his seat nearby, Matthew leaned over to his wife and spoke quietly. "Again, my apologies on behalf of human men, sweetheart."

"Bethany hasn't even told you what his tail can do yet." Athena sounded jazzed. "It has a suction-y tip. And it's ridged!"

Matthew groaned and bowed his head. "Of course it is."

Say what you would about the Nasty Wenches—those easily shocked should stay far, far away—but they were damned entertaining. Not to mention welcoming. From the moment Bethany had greeted her at the front door, Molly had been adopted into the group warmly and without fuss. Included in conversations. Asked for her opinions.

Yes, sometimes said opinions concerned the potential sexual sensitivity of devil horns and whether cloven hooves could ever be considered hot in a nonliteral sense, but Molly did in fact have thoughts on those matters. Thoughts the book club members had listened to, with seeming appreciation.

Upon Karl's own arrival, the poor man had dodged a swarm of concerned book club members and tried to sit next to her. Only to be shooed away by Janel, Lise, and Athena, who'd claimed Molly's proximity like a prize.

Early in the evening, he'd kept an eagle eye on her anyway, shoulders bunched in clear worry. Then, once he'd apparently satisfied himself as to her comfort in the situation, his tension had eased. He still glanced over at her often, though. Brought her cookies. Even kissed the top of her head once, which had prompted a number of whispered, excited-sounding conversations around the room.

To Molly's surprise, that kiss wasn't her only affectionate physical contact of the evening. Lise's shoulder bumped against hers every time something funny happened, in companionable nudges of mutual amusement. At regular intervals, Janel doled out Goldfish crackers and megawatt smiles to her couchmates, as well as approving pats on the arm every time Molly participated in the discussion.

It was all . . . lovely. Disconcerting and a bit overwhelming, but delightful.

A wise woman would leave the meeting now, before enjoyment

turned to longing. Molly couldn't seem to make herself go, though. If wisdom meant missing the rest of the meeting and truncating this unexpected joy, long live foolishness.

"Hey, everyone!" Janel half rose from the couch and waved her hand to catch the group's attention. "If I remember correctly, Slatterns 'R' Us actually carries a limited-edition dildo inspired by Satan's prehensile tail-dick!"

"They do," Bethany confirmed through a mouthful of muffin.

Janel grinned, pleased. "And they're having a ten-percent-off sale this week!"

To Molly's left, Lise produced a notepad from her purse and scrawled a quick note to herself. Molly chose not to read it, for plausible deniability's sake.

Across the room, in a big winged armchair with a half-dozen casserole dishes stacked near his feet, Karl mutter-shouted to the bespectacled Black woman next to him, "I get why someone might want two. But what the fuck would the third dick even *do*?"

"Vibrate," the woman—Jackie?—told him succinctly.

Molly hesitated to ask, but . . . "Wouldn't having three stone penises attached to a flesh-and-blood body be painfully heavy? If they got caught somewhere, couldn't they just . . . rip off?"

"Excellent question, Molly." Bethany swallowed her bite, then smiled at her. "They regenerate. And the third one isn't located where you might expect."

That . . . brought up new questions. Ones that would have to wait, because apparently it was time for a real snack break before the discussion resumed.

"Ten minutes!" Athena called. "Then we talk about *Bedded by Beelzebub*!"

Lise grimaced faintly. When Molly patted her leg consolingly, though, she mustered a genuine-looking smile and bumped their shoulders together again.

As soon as Janel rose from the couch and beelined for the bathroom, Karl started Molly's way—but was immediately swarmed once more by concerned Nasty Wenches bearing resealable containers and offering hugs. All of which he accepted with gruff thank-yous amidst his grumbling, his cheeks flushed pink in pleased embarrassment.

He'd tidied up for the occasion. His beard was newly trimmed, his hair still gleamed with fresh-showered dampness, his logoless tee was clean and a flattering shade of forest green, and his usual Crocs had been replaced by pristine-looking sneakers. His dark jeans also molded his ass in a very flattering fashion, which Molly had noted with appreciation multiple times.

Sadly, the crowd surrounding him had blocked that very pleasant view at the moment. Just like when she'd seen him with Charlotte's family, though, Molly couldn't help being charmed by the sight of Karl with people who clearly cared about him—and whom he clearly cared about in return. Because yes, various Nasty Wenches had presented him with casseroles, but he'd somehow found time to bake and bring along those Wenches' favorite treats in return. And yes, they were all asking him about his flu recovery. But in between their questions, he was posing his own. Prodding them for news on their parents' health. Checking on kids' grades. Demanding updates about how things were going at various jobs.

Even with his overloaded schedule, he'd listened to a book fitting this month's theme. He'd participated in the discussion. He'd—

"Hey, Molly!" Athena appeared in front of the couch, wreathed in smiles. "You doing okay?"

"I'm great." Did Molly not look like she was having fun? Because she really, really was. "Um . . . thank you for asking?"

Her befuddlement must have been clear, because Athena plopped herself down in Janel's spot and immediately explained, "I know meeting us en masse can be *a lot*."

Well, Molly couldn't really deny that. "Only in the best of ways."

"Oh, good." After a quick glance over her shoulder, toward the corner of the room where Matthew and Karl were now talking, she turned her full attention back to Molly. "So . . . tell me more about life out in LA. Is it all tacos and sunshine and glamour, like I imagine?"

Molly laughed. "Tacos and sunshine, yes. Glamour, no. Since I work from a home studio, I generally wear my pajamas all day and don't bother brushing my hair."

"Aka 'living the dream,'" Lise murmured.

Athena tilted her head, eyes bright with curiosity. "Was your studio hard to build?"

"Not especially." Putting everything together had only taken three days, even without much help from Rob. "It's modular, so it sort of snaps into place?"

"That's really cool." Athena pushed her cat-eye glasses up to the bridge of her nose. "Would it come apart easily too, if you ever needed to move it?"

"In theory, yes." According to the manufacturers, as well as the online testimonials of several other narrators. "Although I've never personally tested that claim."

"And you've been in Los Angeles since college?" When Molly nodded, Athena made a thoughtful humming noise. "I can't even imagine living in such a large city. You must have an enormous circle of friends there."

Molly's smile faded, despite her best efforts, and the couch squeaked when she shifted her weight.

Rob did in fact have a large social network. Not Molly. With the divorce, their theoretically mutual friends had all fallen his way, and thank heavens for that. At the risk of sounding very sour grapes-y, he was welcome to those self-important blowhards. She'd always kept a certain distance from them for a reason.

"I . . ." Her lips pursed, but she forced herself to tell the truth. "Not really. It's . . . it's hard when you work from home."

Lise's soft right thigh nudged Molly's left. A gesture of silent support.

"I bet." From behind her smudged lenses, Athena's warm hazel gaze studied Molly. "You know, I haven't lived in Harlot's Bay all that long. I learned one thing pretty quickly, though: If people here care about you, they don't stop caring. Even when you do your best to drop off the face of the Earth, they'll still try like hell to be there for you. In certain cases, to the point of committing illegal acts."

Her tone was fondly reminiscent, her smile sweet as she caught her husband's eye.

Molly blinked at her, befuddled once more.

"Wait." Lise leaned forward and craned her neck to see past Molly to Athena. "What's this about illegal acts?"

"Trespassing, for example. Breaking and entering too." Without elaborating further, Athena got back on topic. "Anyway, Molly, my point is this: If you ever find yourself needing a friend—in Harlot's Bay, in California, or wherever you go—all you have to do is contact one of us. We'll come running."

Something about the sincerity in the other woman's voice caused Molly's eyes to prickle.

"Thank you," she said quietly, then ducked her head and stared at the carpet for a few seconds, struggling to regain her equanimity.

"I was just thinking . . ." Lise's hand rested gently on Molly's forearm. "I bet we can even set things up so you can attend the Nasty Wenches meetings virtually, Mol, if you'd be interested in that."

Molly murmured another *thank you*, unsure what else to say.

She *shouldn't* be interested. Why the hell would anyone participate in a book club meeting from across an entire continent, after having met most of the members only once?

The problem: She *was* interested. More than interested. *Eager.*

For the first time since her divorce, her isolation out in LA no longer felt benign. She'd tried so hard to insist that she didn't need companionship, didn't need anyone other than herself, but . . . she should admit the truth, at least in the privacy of her own mind.

She was lonely.

And even once Janel returned to the couch and called the meeting back to order, Molly couldn't banish a persistent, uncomfortable thought.

She might leave Karl and Harlot's Bay. She might have excellent reasons for doing so.

But the possible future she might have had with him, in this place . . . it might not ever leave *her*.

* * *

SINCE LISE HAD a deadline fast approaching, she hugged Molly goodbye and left quickly at the end of the meeting—and as soon as Karl spied the empty couch space, he dodged his crowd of concerned Wenches and claimed the spot for himself. Tired eyes ringed by dark circles, arms folded over his barrel chest, he waited with barely leashed impatience for Janel to finish chatting.

He clearly wanted a private conversation with Molly. Janel clearly didn't give a damn.

"Have you considered getting your own espresso machine?" The other woman bounced on her cushion a little. "Because I have to tell you, it's transformative. I don't know what I'd do without mine."

Honestly? Janel owning an espresso machine explained *a lot*.

"I do like fancy lattes, as I've recently discovered," Molly admitted.

"That's what I heard!" Janel grinned, looking highly amused. "Gourmet sandwiches too, if the local gossip is correct."

"Town of damn busybodies," Karl mutter-shouted, and Molly rubbed her ringing ear.

Janel ignored him. "What's your favorite latte flavor so far?"

"Lavender white chocolate." The thought of re-creating that deliciousness at home was tempting, but . . . "My kitchen's kind of compact, unfortunately. I'm not sure I have the counter space for another appliance."

The revelation didn't dampen Janel's enthusiasm even one iota. "If you want to try out mine, you're welcome anytime. Or if you want to just hang out and catch up, that's great too. My husband's bowling league meets on Thursday nights, so—"

"I'm gonna go." Karl heaved himself to his feet with a sigh, exhaustion stamping crow's-feet at the corners of his eyes. "See you at the bakery tomorrow, Dearborn?"

"Yes. Definitely." Directing an apologetic smile at Janel, she stood too. "I'll walk him to his car, then be right back."

To her surprise, Karl raised a staying hand. "I'm good. You stay and chat."

Despite his beard, the small smile curving his mouth wasn't hard to see—or interpret. He might be impatient for her company, but he was pleased by his night's work, and for good reason. After he'd ensured her attendance, everyone in the Nasty Wenches book club had amply displayed the kind of warm, fun, and supportive in-person community she could have . . . if she left behind her entire life in California.

Her quiet, lonely life. Where no one could hurt her, because no one truly *reached* her. Where her blood pressure kept creeping upward and her headaches turned ever more vicious, both conditions likely exacerbated by her isolation.

But she could make friends out there if she really tried, obviously. Finding necessary social outlets didn't require uprooting her entire existence. Besides, if she moved to Maryland and things went bad with Karl, this ready-made community might disappear too. It was too much of a risk. Right?

Bending down, Karl pressed a quick, firm kiss to her mouth. "See you soon."

That kiss, Molly reflected as he strode away, was like everything else that evening: a taste of what could be. What she could have if she did what he wanted and stayed in Harlot's Bay long-term.

His tactics might not be subtle—but she couldn't say they weren't effective.

16

"Don't even think about it," Karl told a squirrel the following Saturday.

The fluffy-tailed little rodent kept eyeing the sandwiches.

Karl met the squirrel's inquisitive, unafraid stare. Glowered. "Swear to Christ, I'll speed up evolution and make you a flying squirrel ahead of schedule."

Molly had to laugh, even as she shook her head. "I'm not entirely certain why flying squirrels would become the dominant species, evolutionarily speaking, but—"

"They *fly*, Dearborn." Karl sounded outraged, and he turned his glare from the squirrel to her. "'Course they'll be naturally selected as squirrel kings and queens."

She lifted a finger. "Technically, they don't actually fly. They *glide*."

He rolled his eyes to the cloudless sky above. "Oh, here we go. Come on, tell me what I got wrong, even as a diseased, hairy rat without sufficient fear of humans snatches our goddamn sandwiches."

The man had a point.

"Quit befriending the local wildlife, Dean." The nearest enormous, wax paper–wrapped Brie, truffle, and prosciutto sandwich was calling her name, and she intended to answer immediately. "I'm hungry. Let's eat."

After one last longing look at their plastic container of potato chips, the squirrel scampered away. Easing his vigilance, Karl turned his attention to the enormous duffel bag that contained their carefully packaged picnic dinner and several other mysterious items, none of which he'd let her examine as they'd driven from his bakery to Historic Harlot's Bay.

At first, she'd thought he intended to guide them back to the site of their first almost-kiss as teenagers, the arbor beside the Mayor's Mansion pleasure gardens. Instead, they'd climbed down the steps leading to a colonist-made fishing pond and spread their quilt on a flat, grassy spot not too far from a picturesque wooden footbridge, under a stately old weeping willow. The arched branches surrounded them on most sides, the leaves almost brushing the grass—which offered them a bit of privacy and dappled the golden sunlight pleasantly.

In short, it was a perfect place to eat. For them, and apparently for Harlot's Bay's various fauna too.

"I can unpack the food." Karl waved aside her offer to help. "Relax for a minute."

In between calling a nearby woodpecker a "disease-ridden, asshole jackhammer" and informing a nearby wild apple tree that if any fruit dropped on their heads, he was "going full George Washington on its woody ass, because gravity was already fucking invented," he unearthed endless items from his duffel. Not just umpteen food containers, but also a bottle of sparkling cider, along with sturdy plastic flutes, cloth napkins, mini salt and pepper shakers, and actual silverware, all of which he was arranging just so on the quilt.

Bracing her hands behind her, the cotton fabric soft and smooth against her palms, Molly stretched out her legs and tipped her head back to bask in the gentle heat of the September afternoon. The breeze tugged at the grass and her hair, the insects droned, and the autumn sun soaked into her bones until they seemed to sag, heavy with warmth. Or maybe that sensation could be blamed on Karl instead, and the thoughtfulness evident in everything he'd prepared for them today.

After a full week of ceaseless, grinding work in the bakery— work she'd personally witnessed, since she'd kept him company every day—he'd somehow managed to prepare everything for this outing too. That sort of thoughtfulness and care, his prioritization of her and their time together . . . well, she'd witnessed stripteases she'd found less seductive.

"Eat up, Dearborn," he finally told her, after taking out the last bowl. "Before that damn rodent comes back with all his rat friends, takes our damn food, and gives us weird-ass squirrel diseases."

Energized by the prospect of their early dinner, she sat up straight and reached for the plate he held out to her. By the time they finished their sandwiches and chips, the mint-flecked berry-balsamic salad, and the oversized s'mores cookies in companionable silence, though, her eyelids were drooping more than she cared to admit.

"That was beyond delicious." Her jaw cracked as she stifled a yawn. "Thank you."

His brows had formed a single ruddy line. "You need a nap, Dearborn."

"It's fine." The yawn had made her eyes water, and she blotted away the stray wetness with her button-down's sleeve. "I'm used to it."

Her last good night's sleep had been . . . a decade ago, maybe? Sometime around her engagement. Once Rob had slid a ring on her finger, insomnia had crept up on her and made a restful eight hours of unconsciousness impossible. After the wedding, things had only gotten worse. And since—despite her most fervent hopes—divorce hadn't returned her sleep schedule to normal, she'd begun suspecting this was it. This was her life from now on, spent steeped in hazy exhaustion as her blood pressure rose and rose again.

"You look tired too," she told him, in a vast understatement.

Those bags beneath his eyes were huge and dark enough to resemble shiners. But when she'd suggested they skip their weekend exercise to give him time to relax, he'd refused loudly and profanely enough that one of his bakery customers had startled and dropped a cherry Danish on her preschooler's head, filling side down.

"Motherfucker," the little girl had lisped, and her mom had glared even harder at Karl.

He'd heaved a sigh, apologized gruffly to the mother—June? Junessa?—and led them back to the bathroom to get the kid cleaned up, while Bez put another cherry Danish in a bag.

Which was all very entertaining, obviously, but didn't change the fact that the man clearly needed a vacation—or at least a nap—even more than Molly had.

"If you'd like to rest instead of—" she began, already knowing his answer.

"Nope." His expression had turned intractable. "We have an activity to complete."

No point in further argument. The man was even more stubborn than he'd been twenty years ago. Instead of saying anything, then, she simply gave him a disapproving headshake. Which he blithely, irritatingly ignored as he got to his feet with a rumbling groan, shuffling away to dump their trash in a discreet barrel receptable nearby.

In his absence, she produced more sunscreen from her bag. When he sat again, she began dabbing it onto his face and exposed forearms. He remained very still under her touch, his breath hitching at the stroke of her thumbs over his cream-slick cheeks.

The sunscreen should have hissed upon contact with his hot skin. His entire body was flushed, maybe from too much sun exposure, or from discomfort at being tended to, or . . . other reasons. The same reasons she felt a bit overheated too.

Once he was protected, he nodded in thanks and turned away to dig around in his duffel again. Two small notepads appeared in his fist, alongside two ballpoint pens.

"There it is." Looking triumphant, he plucked a small plastic baggie from the duffel too. One filled with what appeared to be old-fashioned index cards, of the type she hadn't seen since she'd last crammed for college exams. "Just to be clear: This activity's not my idea. Matthew and Athena browbeat me into it."

"Ooooh-kay." Truthfully, she suspected her neighbors were better suited to brainstorming trust-building exercises than Karl. "Hopefully they didn't get their ideas from a business magazine too."

"Fuck you, Dearborn." He was glaring at her now. "My blindfolded food activity was *awesome*."

"It was," she told him soothingly. "A real triumph of corporate synergy."

He flipped her the bird. Since he was clearly fighting back a grin too, she considered that a double victory.

"*Anyway*." Maintaining meaningful eye contact, he scratched his nose with his extended middle finger. "Three games for today, starting with Winner or Loser. Instructions . . ." His attention dropped to the baggie, and he flipped through the cards. "Here they are. Read 'em and weep, Dearborn."

He handed her a neatly printed card. Matthew's handwriting, if she had to guess, in contradiction to doctor-related stereotypes.

"Winner or Loser," she read aloud. "How to play: The first person discusses an unpleasant event that happened to them, adding as much detail as they're willing to share. After they're done, the second person repeats the story, but emphasizes any positive aspects of or favorable results from the incident. Then the two participants switch tasks."

A notebook and pen plopped beside her on the quilt.

"For note-taking. If needed." Karl settled back against the weeping willow's trunk. "You good with this, Dearborn?"

Truthfully? Not really. If at all possible, she avoided discussing her hurt feelings and failures with . . . anyone. But if playing Winner or Loser meant Karl "Grunts and Illogical Threats of Violence Are My Love Language" Dean would actually tell her more about his *own* history and emotions?

Game freaking *on*.

Shoulders squared, she braced herself to dredge up unpleasant memories. "I'm good."

"Then you go first." Karl flipped open his own notebook, his meaty fist gripped his pen, and his entire attention turned to her. "Tell your story."

Like anyone, she'd had plenty of little defeats, both personal and professional, and she could easily pick any of those incidents. But if she wanted to share something meaningful—if she was actually willing to expose her heart—there were only two *unpleasant events* to choose from. Only two that truly mattered, either then or now.

Fine. She'd tell him. If everything went to shit between them, it was far too late to avoid getting hurt, right? So what did one more revelation matter?

Suddenly tired again, she fiddled with the ends of her hair. "You already heard most of it last weekend. Rob, my partner of seventeen years, used my income and savings to put himself through medical school. Then he dumped me and told me our divorce was entirely my fault, because I was such a terrible, cold wife."

Karl's jaw ticked. With uncharacteristic patience, though, he waited for her to say more.

"But I . . ." Her chest hurt, and she forced herself to inhale slowly and blow out the breath to the count of four. "I didn't tell you the very last thing he said. I didn't tell anyone."

Still no verbal response from Karl. But he stretched out his legs until they bracketed hers, his face hard as flint.

"He stood there in the kitchen of the home we shared, the home I'd offered him freely for over a decade, and informed me he wanted children. That much you know. Then he told me . . ." She fumbled for the bottle of water Karl had packed. Took a swig to moisten a throat as parched as a sun-baked desert. "Even if I were willing to get pregnant, it didn't matter, because he didn't want kids from *me*. He wanted them from someone younger. Someone more likely to bear him healthy children. Someone who'd make a warmer, better mom."

Karl was literally vibrating with anger. "That's bullshit, Molly. He—"

"I thought about it, you know," she interrupted, because if she didn't say it now, it would never get said. "When he told me he needed"—her fingers crooked—"'a real family,' I honestly considered tossing aside everything I'd always planned for myself, the future I'd always wanted, to give him what *he* wanted. To keep him with me."

The impulse probably wouldn't have survived the hour, but she'd never know for sure. In that moment, she'd been frantic. Desperate to save her marriage at any and all costs, despite her surface calm.

"Then . . ." Her laughter knifed upward from her chest, drawing blood the whole way. "Then I found out he wouldn't even *accept* that kind of sacrifice. Not from me, anyway. Problem solved, right?"

He took her hand. Squeezed it tight. "I'm so sorry, Molly. So goddamn sorry."

"All of it hurt way more than I could've imagined. His leaving. Everything he said. The eventual divorce." Her eyes were wet again. Not from yawning this time. "And now, the way he keeps endlessly *hassling* me to give him more, give him my own grandparents' freaking *home*, when I've already given him far too much—that hurts too."

His notebook pressed against one thigh, Karl jotted something to himself with his free hand in large, slashing letters. Two particular words stood out clearly: FUCKING DICK.

"Every time he calls or texts or emails, it's a reminder of how stupid I was. For trusting him. For not seeing the red flags." She blotted away unshed tears with her shirt's wrist cuff. "I knew better, Karl. I truly did. I should've seen who and what he was before we even got married. And the fact that I married him anyway, that I didn't leave him after getting a cake in the face, that I didn't divorce him long, long before he left me? It doesn't say good things about my judgment or my instincts."

Karl's fingers tightened around hers, and his note-taking halted.

Enough. Time to bring this sad story of her own foolishness to a close. "I know my lack of faith bothers you. Here's the thing, though: I may not trust other people very much these days, but I trust myself even less. Hopefully that's some consolation for you, Karl."

She exhaled shakily, then clamped her mouth shut.

Karl scrawled one last note, then tossed aside his pen. "All done?"

Her chin dipped in silent agreement.

"Then it's my turn. I'll retell that story." He looked up from his notepad at last. And to her shock, he glared at her. "With better goddamn accuracy, Dearborn."

His aggressive tone startled her so much, the urge to cry entirely vanished.

Then Karl "Never Met a Sentence Fragment He Didn't Love" Dean gave an actual speech. It was short, but it featured actual complete sentences, which included—in a stunning turn of events—actual verbs *and* pronouns.

"Based on my notes and what you told me last week . . ." After one final, fulminating scowl in Molly's direction, Karl's attention returned to his paper. "You had doubts about that asshole from the beginning. You were together a long time before he convinced you to get hitched. You almost left him before your reception even finished." He shook his head, looking disgusted. "Your instincts are fine, Dearborn. You just need to listen to them. All your divorce proves? Your ex is a dick, and you should trust yourself *more*, not less. End of fucking story."

And that, it seemed, was that. His entire response to the revelations she'd dredged from the murky depths of her repressed psyche, contained in a single aggrieved tirade aimed at *her*.

What the hell kind of exercise *was* this?

Flabbergasted, she flung her hands wide. "Why are you so angry at *me*?"

"Because you're being an asshole to yourself for no damn reason, and it makes me fucking *furious*." He flung the notepad down on the quilt, brows beetled, cheekbones streaked with livid color. "What your husband did to you was some fucked-up bullshit, but what you just told me is bullshit too, Dearborn. How *dare* you blame yourself for trusting your damn husband? For loving a man you met when you were basically still a kid? For wanting to believe the best of him? For being loyal and not giving up on your fucking *marriage*?"

The genuine outrage and absolute disbelief ringing in Karl's every overly loud syllable landed like a punch. His accusing words rang in her ears, echoed in her brain, and somehow—once she fully comprehended everything he'd semi-bellowed—cracked the defensive shell she'd kept around herself for longer than she could remember.

Maybe his sheer volume had rattled something loose inside her. Maybe she'd created an opening for him by telling him the full story of her divorce, with all the ugliest bits intact. Or maybe no one had believed in her so completely since she and her mom moved to California, and having that kind of unstinting, stout support back again—if only for a gut-wrenchingly brief time— popped her protective bubble.

Either way, his words seemed to enter her bloodstream in a heartbeat, spreading warmth through her veins. Like the world's best, angriest, most profane drug, they immediately salved the rawest edges of her hurt and neutralized some of the corrosive shame that dissolved her confidence every time she thought about Rob and her marriage.

She replayed Karl's speech in her head, and her spine straightened.

He was right. Of course he was right.

Why should she blame herself for the careless selfishness of the man who'd promised to love and honor her for an entire lifetime? Unlike Rob, she'd operated in good faith, always, and she'd already given him the fruits of almost two decades of her labor. Why the hell was she giving up her self-respect to him too, like the cherry atop a shit sundae?

Fuck that.

No, really. *Fuck* that. It was past time to stop flagellating herself.

She was Molly goddamn Dearborn. No asshole narcissist in scrubs could make her small, scared, shamed, or powerless.

And then, for the first time in a long, long while, she wasn't simply feigning calm. She *was* calm. And maybe the effects of this exercise wouldn't last longer than the day's waning sunlight, but the respite from turmoil felt really, *really* good.

At some point, she'd closed her eyes in thought. Now she opened them. Smiled at Karl. Continued listening to his rant-in-progress.

"—but if my heart's a Cadbury Egg, Dearborn, yours is a chocolate lava cake surrounded by lots of ice cream." Karl was standing now. Pacing. Blustering, pointing accusingly at her, and occasionally glowering at wildlife. "Cool on the outside. Warm and gooey inside, where no one can see. And that goo's not a fault or stupidity or whatever the hell you think it is. It's a fucking *miracle*."

She contemplated that claim while he paused for breath, then shook her head in disagreement.

"I appreciate the compliment, Karl. Back in the nineties, though, basically every chain restaurant had a chocolate lava cake," she pointed out. "If each one constituted a miracle, there'd be a lot more Applebee's cooks up for sainthood."

He halted. "Ever heard of hyperbole, Dearborn?"

"Never." Her brow crinkled in feigned confusion. "Is that an energy drink?"

He eyed her balefully. "Haha-fucking-ha. You done being a wiseass?"

"Probably not. It's one of my greatest talents." Since he'd abandoned his spot against the trunk, she claimed it for herself. "But go ahead and tell me your story for the exercise, so I can channel my artistry in a new direction."

Thank goodness for back support, the savior of the newly middle-aged. Pleased and much more comfortable, she sat cross-legged against the tree and admired how the pink-gold glow of the late afternoon light coaxed fiery glints from Karl's hair.

Slowly, his scowl faded, and his head tipped as he studied her closely. "You sound different, Dearborn. Less goddamn brittle. Look different too."

"I *feel* different," she told him honestly. "I can't say how long it'll last, but . . . yeah."

His lips curved in a pleased, irritatingly smug smile. "Shit I said got through to you?"

"At least for the moment."

"Good," he declared with feeling, and thumped back onto his butt. "Then let's get my part of this sharing crap over with. Grab your notebook and pay attention."

"You may recall my telling you this before, but . . ." She raised an eyebrow at him. "I don't take orders from you, Dean. Never have, never will."

Still, she readied her notebook and pen, because she'd always been an excellent—if occasionally disobedient—student.

"Probably be better off if you did," he grumbled, then launched into his own tale of woe.

17

*T*urned out, Matthew and Athena knew their shit when it came to communication. Or maybe it was the picnic—intrusive questions combo that worked, and Karl could take part of the credit too. Either way—speaking of miracles—Molly Dearborn had actually *opened the hell up*.

Sure, what she'd told him was beyond infuriating. Her bastard of an ex-husband should have his balls pureed in an industrial blender and poured down his throat like goddamn soup. And how Dearborn had managed to turn the entire situation around and blame it on herself, Karl would never understand. His head had nearly blown off his shoulders when he'd heard that absolute bullcrap.

But it was still progress. Halle-fucking-lujah.

He knew more of her history now. Understood her better. Best of all: voluntarily sharing a painful story like that? Required *trust*.

Too bad he'd have to do the same thing. No way Dearborn would let him get away with prodding her for an upsetting, incredibly personal story, then refusing to pony up a tale of intimate fucking woe himself.

He cleared his throat. Dragged one hand roughly through his hair. And then, before he could lose his nerve, he started talking.

"Loved Becky. Not the way I should've, but I did." Much as a dumb teenage kid could, with his dumb teenage heart already captured by another girl. "Told her. She never said it back."

Noisy-ass cardinal kept hopping around and chirping in a nearby tree. Distracting as hell. Definitely the main reason he wasn't meeting Molly's gaze.

Even from the corner of his eye, though, he spotted her wince. "Ouch."

He shrugged. "Should've realized then it wasn't going anywhere. Didn't, though. All those endless breakups, I always figured we'd get back together sooner or later. Until . . ." Dammit. The next part still sucked, even all these years later. "She left for Johns Hopkins. First time she came back to Harlot's Bay, she made some shit pretty fucking clear."

Her soft blond hair in a neat, pretty French braid, she'd laid things out for him. Not cruelly. Matter-of-factly. Like a teacher reciting information he should've already known.

"She was going somewhere with her life. Literally. Metaphorically. I wasn't. So she was done 'playing around,' as she put it." Stiffly, he raised his knees. Lowered them again, restless and slightly sweaty. "Which was when I realized she'd been *amusing* herself with me, killing time until we graduated. I wasn't her goddamn boyfriend. I was a placeholder for someone better."

After that, he'd only dated locals who didn't intend to move. Once burned, twice no-way-in-hell-that's-happening-again.

Molly would've been his lone exception. To that rule and most others too.

She still was. And he still couldn't force himself to look directly at her.

"Becky was my first girlfriend. First everything." Kiss. Lover. Heartbreak. "What she did hurt, and why she did it was humiliating. Which is why I didn't tell you we'd broken up in one of our email messages. Stupid wounded pride. Also . . ."

He sighed, then bit the damn bullet and met Molly's sympathetic blue eyes.

"I was scared you'd hear the story and agree with her." There. Now she knew the worst of it. "Tell me I wasn't good enough for you either. I'd been into you since that day in Principal Evers's office, and if you'd rejected me directly, it would've fucking *destroyed* me. So I tried to come at it sideways instead. Gauge your interest before explaining the situation. But I'm clumsy at that sort of shit, so I screwed it up."

With each word he spoke, the real driving force behind his sense of urgency—his *need* to keep Molly in Harlot's Bay and have her commit to stay here, *right now*, before she got the chance to see California again—became clearer and clearer to him.

Yeah, he was worried about her guard going back up as soon as she'd put some distance between them. But that wasn't the possibility that twisted his gut and kept him up at night, was it?

Once she was gone, part of him fully believed she'd realize she could do better. Just like Becky had.

Weird how someone he truly didn't give a single crap about anymore could warp his thoughts so badly. Even after two decades filled with nothing more intimate between him and Becky than hand waves and occasional, awkward chitchat he cut off as soon as possible.

"I'm confused." Molly's forehead had crinkled. "If you were into me since Mr. Miller's class, why didn't you ask me out? Before you started dating someone else?"

The answer to that question? Almost as embarrassing as the Becky story.

"Too chickenshit." His fingers closed on a handful of grass beside the blanket. Tugged fretfully. "Certain you'd turn me down. Then I'd have to run the hell away with my broken goddamn heart and join a cult. Or a circus. Didn't quite settle on which before Becky made the first move and asked *me* out."

The lines across her brow only deepened. "I see."

But she didn't. Not clearly. At this moment, the woman had no way of knowing just how much he'd wanted her back then and how much he still did now.

That'd change shortly, though, when they got to today's final, terrifying game. Athena and Matthew were fucking *ruthless* when it came to communication.

"Okay." Molly's pen tapped against her notepad as she thought for a moment. "From my perspective, here's the fundamental story you just told me and how I interpret it."

He braced himself. Accidentally ripped up a patch of grass in the process.

"You started dating a girl in high school," she began, her voice maddeningly neutral. "You dealt with her honestly, treated her well, and loved her as best you could, even during tough patches. She ended the relationship after a major life change, most likely because *she* was changing too, and did so in an unkind way. Knowing Becky, she maybe didn't even realize she was *being* unkind. Nevertheless, you were hurt and embarrassed and didn't want to talk about the circumstances of the breakup, which I can understand."

Somehow, it didn't sound so embarrassing when Molly explained it like that.

"But, Karl . . ." She leaned forward then. Laid a warm hand over his socked foot. "You had nothing to be ashamed of, either then or now. I hope you know that. You're"—air quotes—"'good enough' for anyone, and you always were."

He ticked off his counterarguments on his fingers. "No college degree. Barely ever left the goddamn state. Bad with words. Not exactly an athlete or supermodel."

And if who and what he was hadn't been sufficient for Becky or the other women he'd dated, how the hell could he possibly be enough for Molly fucking *Dearborn?*

Her hand left his foot, and she sat back against the tree with an audible thump.

Dramatically, she raised her own right thumb. And when she spoke again, her voice sounded less neutral and more pissed off.

"Through sheer stubborn determination and hard work, you've expanded the bakery to twice its size and made it a central business in Harlot's Bay." Her index finger went up. "You've gathered a fantastic crew of workers, whom you pay well and help however you're able." Middle finger. "You've taken a vulnerable young woman and her children under your wing, when absolutely no one asked you to do so." Ring finger. "As today showed, you can communicate effectively when desired." Pinkie. "You can always travel if and when you choose to do so. And having a passport doesn't somehow guarantee good character or a good life, Dean."

Abandoning her finger count, she threw her hands in the air. "I mean, *Rob* has a damn passport! From what I heard, he and his fiancée celebrated their engagement in St. Barts!"

Point made. "Yeah, but——"

"You're an amazingly talented baker," she declared, with zero acknowledgment of his attempted interruption. "Not to mention a successful business owner, a hardworking member of the Harlot's Bay community, a committed Nasty Wench, and a loving son and brother."

Mingled pleasure and discomfort had him flushed and shifting uncomfortably. She either didn't notice or didn't care, because she kept going.

"Plus, you're *hot*." Sounded like an accusation, which was weird, but whatever. Only a total dunce wouldn't take that compliment from a woman like her. "Like, *really* freaking hot. If a supermodel or athlete tried to get his hand inside my pants, I'd break his arm. Yours is still intact, Karl. There's a reason for that. And that reason is your undeniable hotness. I thought I'd already made said hotness clear, so start paying attention, will you?"

Her lips-pursed, disapproving headshake would've done a schoolmarm proud.

Coincidentally? He kinda felt proud too. Less inadequate. Way more confident.

"You're also really good with your hands, so I had high freaking hopes when it came to your fingering skills," she added. "Hopes that—to be clear—were *fully* realized."

At that, his dick basically stood up and saluted her. "Yeah?"

"What did you think, Dean?" Her eyes rolled to the wispy clouds above. "That I poured a gallon of lube down my jeans before going to your bakery? Then proceeded to fake coming so damn hard, my abs actually *hurt* the next day?"

He snorted, amusement battling abject horniness. "A gallon, huh?"

She raised a superior brow. "Ever heard of hyperbole?"

Using his own words against him. She was a damn delight.

"A good life—a worthwhile life—doesn't require moving somewhere else, and it doesn't require a college diploma. Becky should have realized that, and the breakup was her loss. *Not* yours." Her cheeks flushed with sun and conviction, she stabbed a finger in his direction. "There's no way she found a better man than you, no matter where in the world she roamed. And as someone who's lived in a dozen different places, I would freaking *know*."

They were in public. Five feet to the left? Two hairy, over-grown rodents with fluffy tails eyeing his duffel bag way the hell too curiously. Straight ahead? A couple of gap-toothed elementary schoolers skipping around the pond in dorky tricorn hats.

Good thing she kept lecturing him before he could jump her anyway.

"Here's the last thing I'll say: Twenty years ago, you should have *trusted me* not to be as shallow as Becky and explained the situation before asking whether I found"—the woman truly loved air quotes—"'big motherfuckers' attractive, Mr. Your-Lack-of-Trust-Is-a-Mortal-Offense." Looking triumphant, she set aside her notebook. "See the irony? Because it's *glaring*."

Another point: hereby made.

His phone beeped with a text. Grateful for the reprieve, he snatched his cell from the blanket and held it directly in front of his face.

Communicate like the wind, Special K! While he was still reading Athena's first text, another popped up. *Only with actual words instead of howls or groans! Just to clarify!*

Dammit. How did Greydon know? She invent some sort of sensor that activated whenever he got too tempted to stop talking and start sexing?

After sending a middle-finger emoji in response, he tossed his phone aside. "I get your point, Dearborn. Sorry."

"Which one?" Molly immediately asked. "Because I made *many* excellent points."

He paused a beat too long. "All of 'em?"

"Really?" Challenge lit her eyes, turning them an incandescent blue. "Name them."

Challenge damn well accepted. "Should've trusted you to be kinder than Becky."

"And?"

She was going to make him say it? Fine. *Fine.*

"Shouldn't've thought you and Becky were too good for me."

"And?"

Why the hell did her relentlessness turn him on so much? Along with every other goddamn thing about her?

"You think I'm hot."

"And?"

If she pushed him, he'd gladly push right back. "My hand between your legs makes you incredibly fucking wet."

A sly, sexy smile dawned on her gorgeous face. "It certainly does."

Those round, strong thighs of hers rubbed together as she shifted. Her hard nipples pressed against the smooth cotton of her shirt, her bold stare tractor-beamed him closer, and he gave the hell up. Surrendered to their mutual horniness. Clambered to his knees and—

His phone dinged a third time.

He froze. Groaned and scrubbed his hands over his face, then painstakingly got his shit together again.

"Better . . ." *Dammit, Greydon, you cockblocking pain in my ass.* "Better keep doing the exercise. Getting off track here."

"Not in my opinion," Molly said wryly.

"Run out of daylight before too long, and I go to bed early." Avoiding temptation, he glued his eyes to his remaining stack of index cards. "Gotta hurry with the other two activities."

Her chest rose and fell on a silent sigh. "If you want to end before sunset, we probably have time for one more game. Not two."

"Yeah. You're probably right. Second game will be quicker, so . . ." Were those goosebumps on her forearms? "We'll do Secret Exchange. Exactly what it sounds like. You tell me a secret, I tell you one."

Definitely goosebumps, dammit. He shuffled off the quilt, still on his knees, then tossed his half over her legs. Would give a month's profits to warm her himself, but no way they'd finish the game if he did that. They'd be lucky to make it to his car.

"You go first," he told her.

Because if she shared some piddling shit, he'd follow suit. But if she confessed something meaningful . . . yeah. He knew what he'd finally confess in return.

"If my secret's big enough, will that finally get you into bed with me?" Cool, composed Molly sounded impatient as hell. "Because I've been waiting for two decades now, Karl. I can see your erection through your jeans—*again*. And these past two weekends, I've been telling you a whole crapload of things no one else knows. *Please* tell me that's enough for you."

She flicked the edge of the quilt. "Also, thank you for this, but I'd rather be underneath *you*."

Jesus H. Christ. Did she want him to die from thwarted lust?

And even apart from that—what she'd just said? It implied things he didn't like. At all. Troubled, he scratched his beard. Forced himself to think through his response.

He'd never intended to use his stupid dick as *leverage*. Never intended to dangle sex in front of her to force confessions she'd rather not make. He just hadn't wanted to make it easy for her to explain away everything between them as simple sexual chemistry, then promptly peace out for good. And he'd worried about the aftermath if she fucked him and ran.

From that day on, every time he had sex with someone else, he'd have to battle his memories. Try not to compare. The task? Already hard enough. Long before her return, before they'd even kissed, she'd haunted his most intimate moments. Sleeping with her would only make things inconceivably worse when she was gone.

Only . . . that explanation wasn't the full story, was it? Wasn't the main reason he'd shied away from sex with the woman of his literal dreams.

He squeezed his eyes shut. Blew out a hard breath.

The rock-bottom truth: Deep in his Cadbury Creme heart, he hadn't just been *worried* about what might happen if they tumbled into bed together. He'd been *scared*. He *was* scared, and not only for his future sex life.

Sleeping with Molly would mean surrendering even more of his heart to her, along with his body. Which—if she left afterward— would mean even more of that stupidly fragile heart shattered. So he'd put her off. Denied himself what they both wanted.

He was doing the same thing he'd done twenty years ago. Hedging his bets. Protecting himself. Probably screwing up the same way he had twenty years ago too.

How much of his heart was still *his*, anyway? At this point, couldn't be a lot. Maybe none at all. And wasn't having Molly god-damn Dearborn—if only for a couple weeks—worth the risk, no matter what?

"Karl? Are you all right?" All the impatience had vanished from her voice, replaced with sincere concern. "I'm so sorry. I shouldn't have pressured you. It's your body. Your decision. I'm being a jerk, and I hope you can forgive me."

Huh?

Opening his eyes, he waved that off. "I fucking love that you want me, Dearborn. Makes me feel like . . ." What was the comparison he'd come up with the other day? "Like *Godzilla*."

She blinked at him. "Poised to destroy downtown Tokyo?"

At that bit of deliberate obtuseness, his middle finger made a reappearance. "Powerful. Taller than a skyscraper. Ready to beat my chest."

"Beat your . . ." Her forehead smoothed, and she shook her head at him. "You're thinking of King Kong. Who's a primate, not a lizard."

"Reptile."

"Whatever." She poked him with her quilt-covered foot. "Get to the point, Dean."

"You're the one who questioned my Godzilla comparison, woman." He captured her ankle. Tickled her toes until she squeaked. "Anyway, as I was *trying* to say before some nitpicky asshole derailed me—"

"Your train jumped the tracks long before you met me, and we both know it."

"—I don't feel pressured by you. I feel desired. Different thing entirely." He shook his head. Tickled her arch some more. "That's not the issue. Not why I was thinking for so long."

"Okay, then." She jerked her foot free. Lightly kicked him, for good measure. "What *is* the issue?"

These days, he had more damn issues than *Corporations Monthly*. But right this very second—"I'm worried you think I'm using sex to pressure *you*. I'm not, Molly. Swear to Christ, I'm not. You don't have to somehow *earn* it by telling me shit you don't want to."

This was the most ridiculous conversation of his entire life. In what universe was access to his dick something he could use as a potential *bargaining chip*? Even inadvertently?

He was a small-town baker, for fuck's sake. Not the world's crankiest gigolo.

"I know that, Karl. Don't worry. I'm just being dramatic." She considered that for a moment. "Which isn't something I do often in real life. Maybe you're rubbing off on me."

"Nope. I'd remember."

"*Figuratively* rubbing off on me." She side-eyed him while he snickered at his own joke. "Okay, then. Let's get this over with. Give me your dick, withhold your dick, do whatever you want with it. No matter what, I'm telling you my secret, so shut up and listen, Dean."

Long as she didn't feel coerced? He'd listen to whatever she wanted to tell him. Gladly.

The breeze blew hair across her cheek, and she tucked it behind her ear. Nodded to herself. Started talking, her tone blunt and matter-of-fact.

"My doctor is worried about me. Worried about my health. Mental. Physical. All of it." Her fingers plucked at the edge of the quilt, although she held his gaze. "The only other person on this planet who knows that is Rob, but he hasn't gotten any updates for years now, so he doesn't realize the full scope of the problem."

She paused. "Problems, rather. Plural. Insomnia. Rising blood pressure. Headaches."

Shit. That sounded fucking *serious*.

The phone conversation he'd overheard last weekend came back to Karl. *Your health is suffering*, the asshole had told her, then blamed everything on her house. Which was very fucking convenient, since the bastard wanted to snatch it from her.

"And it's not just my doctor," she added. "I'm worried too. Scared about what might happen if I don't get a handle on my stress level. But I can't seem to do it."

If Molly and her doctor were anxious about her health? That made three of 'em.

"What the hell's causing all your stress?" He leaned forward. Claimed her foot again, wrapping his hand around her arch and feeling its warmth, its strength. "Work? Family? Where you live?"

"I love my job. My house too, even though it needs a lot of maintenance." Her mouth twisted. "I think part of the issue is isolation, even after all so many years in LA. I didn't grow up there. My college friends are scattered all over the country. I'm divorced, I work from home, and . . . you know how I am. I tend to keep my distance from everyone."

For some stupid reason, it'd never occurred to him before: He and Dearborn both did that. In very different ways, but . . . yeah. Main difference? Karl had people who'd forcefully shoved their way into his life over a lifetime in Harlot's Bay. Not to mention—

"What about your family?" Matthew and Athena were right: He should know this already. Why hadn't he asked long before now? "You have one set of grandparents in Arizona, but where's everyone else?"

Sure, Karl lived in his parents' old house, but they hadn't moved far away. Just to a little single-story duplex on the outskirts of town, one they could easily maintain. All his siblings lived somewhere between Harlot's Bay and DC, and Emily—the youngest Dean kid—had her CPA office just down the street from Grounds and Grains and did the bakery's books.

He might not see them every day, but they were always there. Even when—frankly—he didn't want them to be. They were great. Loving, funny, smart, hardworking. But chatty as hell. And loud. So goddamn loud. The knob on his family's volume control had broken off at birth.

Couldn't say that to Molly, though, or she'd respond with some pithy bullshit about *irony*.

Normally, his parents and siblings swarmed the bakery every day or two. She'd have run into them long before now if they weren't currently driving an overcrowded RV across the damn country. Excellent timing on their part, since meeting the Zero-Sense-of-Personal-Space Dean family would make Dearborn feel even more pressured. Which, in turn, might launch her toward the nearest Cali-bound plane, so thank fuck they were gone. At least the endless nosy phone calls from Mom and Dad and the steady stream of taunting texts from his pain-in-the-ass brother and sisters didn't require Molly's active participation.

"Mom and my stepfather live in Oregon. I don't have siblings, and my other grandparents died while I was still in college. Dad and his"—her lips pressed together tightly for a moment—"family are somewhere in NorCal, last I heard. So no one's close to Los Angeles."

His family, huh? Like she didn't count?

And why the hell didn't she know where her father lived?

Another crucial issue to cover first, though. "You lonely out there?"

Would be good for his cause, but he hated the thought anyway. Wanted her happy, even if he wanted her happy with *him* even more.

"Sometimes."

Her guarded tone tipped him off. "That an understatement?"

She didn't answer the question. Just stared at him, expression cool and smooth as a polished rock. Which answered the question.

Yeah, she should definitely stay in Maryland. For his sake, obviously, but hers too.

Here in Harlot's Bay, she'd have a real community, even apart from him. He already knew his family would swallow her whole, adopt her into the Dean clan, and smother her with affection, regardless of whether she asked for any of it. And she'd gain friends and neighbors too, all of 'em ready to offer help or company whenever she wanted either. Which was something he'd tried to show her at the Nasty Wenches meeting, even before he'd understood how badly she needed that kind of in-person support.

"You ever go on vacations? To visit friends, or just relax?" Gently, he tugged at her foot until she scooted closer. Kept tugging until his spread legs bracketed her quilt-covered lower half. "Might help with the stress."

Not that he'd know from personal experience. Without an assistant baker, no time for vacations. But the rest of his family loved traveling, with or without a too-damn-small rental RV. Previous summers, they'd all spent a week plonked on a Cape May beach, kayaking in Chincoteague, or driving the Blue Ridge Parkway together. Parents even flew to Aruba once, for their fortieth anniversary. Came back with sunburns, big smiles, and a few pics that looked like the surface of the damn moon.

"I haven't taken a vacation since . . . my mid-twenties, maybe?" Molly's shoulder rose in a shrug. "Once Rob started med school, all our spare income and most of our savings went toward his education. Then there were lawyers to pay. House renos to do."

He nodded. "Got it."

All that? Almost the same exact shit he'd been dealing with the last couple decades. A relentless work schedule. Helping to pay for his siblings' education and Em's divorce lawyer fees. Pouring money into an aging house's annoying-ass repairs.

LA had to be way more glamorous than Harlot's Bay, and Molly's job made her kinda famous. Otherwise, he and Molly were apparently two of a damn kind.

Her foot flexed in his hands. "My doctor suggested a vacation too. She's the main reason I took this whole month off, instead of working at night or booking time at a recording studio until the workers were finished. But I didn't feel great about spending a bunch of money on travel, so I had no plans to go anywhere." Her lips quirked. "Until I read about your mysterious campsite murder and possible street-drug connections."

He snorted.

"Your turn, Dean. Secret time." Her warm hands lowered to her sides. Clasped his ankles over his socks. "I await your sordid confession."

The subject of her health? Nowhere near closed, as far as he was concerned. But for now, he'd drop it. Because she'd done what was asked. Shared a meaningful secret.

Now it was his turn. And if he kept protecting himself, didn't that mean she was proving her point? That he didn't entirely trust her either? Or didn't trust himself to be enough for her?

Screw it. He was doing this shit.

"Got all your Molly Cressley audiobooks." His voice was gruff, the words ripped from a resistant throat. "Every single one. Buy them on CD, because I'm old. Play them before the bakery opens. Over the store speaker system."

Silence, followed by more silence.

When she finally spoke, her eyes had gone Bambi-big. "So . . . just to clarify: You've listened to, say, *My Kangaroo, My Kidnap-*

per? At your place of work? Because . . . I'll be honest, Karl. *That* seems like a lawsuit waiting to happen."

Stripping off his clothes in public would've been less embarrassing. Pressing two fingers between his brows, he squeezed his eyes shut for a moment. Forced the sentences to keep coming, like what he'd told her wasn't damning enough. When it really, *really* was.

"Listened to you each and every morning," he ground out. Hesitated. Then met her stare and made himself finish the confession. "At work. At home. For the last two years."

Her mouth had dropped open slightly. She sucked in a huge breath as her grip on his ankles tightened in a convulsive squeeze. But before she could speak, he held up a staying hand. Asked the crucial question, while he still had the nerve.

"After you came back? Brought my collection home, so you wouldn't see." His throat hurt, it was so goddamn dry. "Want to see it now?"

"You . . ." She spoke slowly. "You know what will happen if I go home with you."

"Yeah." He held her stare, heart thudding like an overloaded stand mixer. "I do."

"Then . . ." A grin gradually dawned on that beautiful face, spreading wide and heart-piercingly bright. "As you might put it, Karl . . ."

He waited, unable to breathe.

"Let's fucking *go*," she told him, and they did.

18

*M*olly followed Karl to his white-painted split-level—clearly built at least half a century ago, but maintained well—in her rental car. They met at the sidewalk, and he grabbed for her hand and kept hold all the way up the three steps to the front porch, as if worried she might flee if given the opportunity, then immediately reclaimed his grip once he'd dealt with the door and locked it behind them again.

He should know better. The foundations of this house could crumble, and she'd simply plant herself on his cock in the dusty rubble. If aliens invaded? They'd get a live-action demonstration of human anatomy, because her eagerness had turned into outright impatience sometime over the past few days. She was done waiting.

Even apart from her uncharacteristic, lust-honed edginess, she felt . . . odd. Giddy, almost. Disoriented by a sudden, unexpected sense of . . .

She wasn't certain.

How did a circuit feel after years of failed attempts at connection, at spanning an unbridgeable gap, when the final, necessary wire slotted into place? When electricity hummed at last, powering movement and light?

And if some sort of internal circuit had been completed, she knew precisely why and how: Their intimate conversation on the quilt beneath the willow had shifted the necessary components.

Her charged lust for Karl hadn't changed, but . . . something inside her had settled into place with each revelation he'd offered. Her resistance had softened with each supportive response to her own confessions, each sign that he'd wanted and cared about her much longer and much more than she'd ever realized.

Bravo to *Corporations Monthly*. The same magazine that helped business leaders avoid fair taxation and exert undue influence on the political system could also, apparently, help two childhood never-quite-sweethearts reach an understanding, at long freaking last.

Inside the small foyer of Karl's childhood home, she dropped her bag beside the door, and the rickety console table shuddered as he flung his phone, wallet, and keys into the clay bowl on top. He tugged her deeper into the house, and the faint buzz of a refrigerator accompanied them up a short set of carpeted steps. His bedroom apparently lay at the end of the postage-stamp hall, whose walls were entirely lined with framed family photos. As he ushered her through the doorway, rosy late-afternoon light streamed through the lone, half-open window, transformed dust motes into glowing embers, and turned his ruddy hair to flame.

Neither of them had spoken a word since leaving their cars.

Still holding his hand, still silent, she looked around herself. The king-size bed, topped by rumpled gray sheets and another faded quilt, dominated the room. Apart from a battered dresser and a matching nightstand, there was no other furniture. No room for other furniture either.

Then she couldn't see anything but Karl, because his fingers were delving into her hair, his other hand was cupping her jaw with tense care, and his mouth covered hers in a fierce, hard kiss. Too needy to tease, she returned it without hesitation. Her tongue met his in a twisting, playful battle for dominance that made her blood feel carbonated, fizzy and tickling as it effervesced through her veins.

When she sucked on the tip of his agile tongue, he lurched even closer. Backed her up against the side of the bed, one big, warm hand sliding down to cup her ass. He squeezed. Molded her. Kneaded her giving flesh and hauled her tighter against him. Dizzy with excitement, she shifted her thighs for friction and rubbed against him without a single iota of shame, and his erection grew with her every movement, pressing almost painfully hard into her thigh.

He was throwing off heat like one of his ovens, melting every too-stiff bone in her body. When his teeth scored her lower lip, her knees went wobbly, and she sank down onto the soft, cool sheets, then down onto her back. He immediately stepped between her dangling legs and bent at the waist, forearm braced on the mattress as he cradled her nape and kept kissing her. She explored him with eager hands, stroking down his taut, flushed neck, over his bunched shoulders, along the thick muscles bracketing the groove of his spine.

After one last squeeze of her ass, his own hand slipped from beneath her, skimmed over her hip and the side of her belly, up to her breast, and paused. His knuckles lightly skimmed over her nipple, back and forth, for a freaking eternity. Then his loose fist uncurled, his thumb rubbed slow circles around her areola, and her breath hitched and caught.

His palm weighed her breast, and his mouth ripped free from hers. Moved lower.

"So goddamn soft," he muttered. "Knew you would be, but *shit.*"

He nudged the hard tip of her nipple with his nose. His hot

breath seeped through the thin cotton of her shirt, warming her. Then he licked her, his tongue flicking and rubbing through the barrier of fabric. And maybe the sensation wasn't as sharp as skin-on-skin contact, but she was buzzing with pleasure anyway. Arching her back. Pushing herself closer in a demand for more.

He stilled, panting, and he smelled like sunshine and grass. She turned her head to nuzzle his inner forearm and opened her mouth for a taste. Salt, atop tough muscle from backbreaking work. Velvety skin.

His flesh prickled when she followed a raised vein with the tip of her tongue.

When he spoke again, his voice was shredded. "Okay if I undress you?"

"Yes." She dropped her arms and spread them in open invitation. "*Please.*"

As he undid the row of buttons down the front, his fingers fumbling in an impatient rush, she sighed in relief. She just . . . needed them unclothed. No barriers. Only the two of them, open and honest and bare.

Her shirt landed behind the dresser, and he moved down her body, unbuttoning her jeans with a quick flick of his finger and thumb. Her zipper lowered with a hasty *vrrrrip*, and he hauled the fabric toward her feet, muttering a hoarse *thank fuck* at the garment's ease of removal. As he flung the denim and her socks over his shoulder, she squirmed out of her sports bra and let it land wherever it fell on the sheets.

Cool air washed over her nipples, battling the heat of his gaze when he stopped. Stared down at her bare breasts, ruddy hair rumpled, face flushed, attention transfixed.

She was nearly naked now. Only wearing her panties.

His rapt expression told her he loved what he saw.

Her nipples hardened to an ache, and she stopped bracketing his thighs so tightly with hers. Instead, she splayed her legs wider on the bed, her tender skin rubbing against the sheet. Another invitation.

He accepted without hesitation. Slid his hard palms slowly up her thighs and over the swell of her belly, until his fingers hooked into the waist of her soft cotton boy shorts. Instead of lowering them, though, he lightly tugged them upward. Hitched them infinitesimally tighter against her pussy. Stroked her swelling clit with subtle twitches of the fabric, side to side.

Her head fell back on the bed, and her exhalation shook.

"Yeah?" he rasped. "That good?"

"Yes." It was a hiss, as he slowly used the cotton to rub her into near delirium.

"Want these off?"

"*Yes.*"

He tugged off her panties while backing out from between her legs, and she levered herself up to sitting, then standing, following him as he retreated, because no way she was letting him get away from her this time. But when his palm raised in a silent request for her to stop, she stilled at the side of the bed.

"Want to do this right." He cautiously edged around her, like a man skirting a live bomb, and looked everywhere but at her naked body. "Let me . . ."

After shoving the quilt off the other side of the bed, he straightened the sheets with a few hasty adjustments. Ran his palms over the cotton, smoothing away wrinkles. Then he took her hand and guided her back onto the mattress, nudging her to crawl toward the spindled headboard. His steady hands stacked two of the fluffy pillows and helped her prop herself semi-upright against them, then dropped away.

When she reached out to haul him on top of her again, he edged back a step.

His eyes met hers. "Just want to look at you for a while. Okay?"

Molly was private, not shy. Nakedness with a lover had never fazed her, even in the unforgiving light of day, and Karl clearly enjoyed the sight of her body. That said . . .

"I'm not eighteen anymore," she told him. "Please remember that."

The breeze through the cracked window raised goosebumps now, as she lay there alone on the bed, bare. Arms outstretched, legs slightly parted, braced for his appraisal whenever he chose to glance downward.

He lifted a shoulder, eyes still pinned to hers. "Neither of us is."

"Whatever body you might have pictured over the past two decades? It's long gone. I hope . . ." Her fingertips twitched against the sheets, but she kept her expression neutral. "I hope that's not a problem."

He laughed then, a loud snort of mirth. Plucking her hand from the mattress, he pressed it against the fly of his jeans. "You tell me."

Even through the denim, the heat of him seared her palm. His cock was a heavy, solid bar straining against his zipper.

"Already got a good look at you wearing nothing but panties. Most beautiful thing I've ever fucking seen." He hitched his hips, grinding against her touch with a strangled groan before letting her hand drop. "This is the damn result."

Her body sank deeper into the mattress as she relaxed. And without further ado, she raised her knees and spread them wide enough to feel the stretch. "Then look all you want, Karl. Just be warned: If you don't make me come in the near future, I'll do it myself."

As soon as she gave permission, his eyes dropped immediately. Feet planted, so tense his body shook with nearly imperceptible tremors, he surveyed her splayed body in silence. His feverish stare swooped over her, lingering between her legs for several thudding heartbeats as she melted beneath its heat. His expression changed as he studied her there. Turned possessive, like her body belonged to him. Famished, like a man starved.

The chill from the window had vanished, and she was sweltering again. Flushed and aching with unslaked desire. She shifted her ass, desperate for friction, and her needy body clenched around nothing.

Ruddy color glazed his cheekbones and the bridge of his nose as he continued studying her. His nostrils flared with each harsh inhalation, and a vein at his temple throbbed rapidly.

There was no impartial judgment here. Not even a hairbreadth of cool distance. When he finally tore his eyes from her pussy, they devoured her breasts, the swell of her belly, and the dimpled softness of her thighs in voracious, lingering sweeps.

At long freaking last, he stepped closer again. Reached for her. But not in the way or in any of the places she'd anticipated.

His hand clasped hers. Lifted her arm out straight and gently rotated it until he could brush a finger over her outer elbow. "Always loved the dimples here. Thought about them for two damn decades. Pictured touching 'em."

The least practical corner of her soul swooned at that, although she'd have sworn to anyone that souls didn't actually exist.

Eager to touch him in return, she freed her hand and reached for his jeans-clad erection.

He shook his head. "Not yet. Lose control if you do that."

"Really?" Her glower was only semi-faked. "You're *still* deny-ing me your dick?"

He lifted a burly shoulder, unapologetic. "Seems like. That a problem?"

Honestly? Even though she was hungry to get her hands on him and make him feel as good as he was making *her* feel, she was enjoying this pillow princess gig too. At least for now. The utter unfamiliarity of receiving more than she gave to a man was kind of intoxicating.

With a lazy flick of her wrist, she flopped back against the pil-lows. "Go ahead and pleasure me, then. I'll just lie here and take it."

"Appreciate your cooperation, Dearborn," he told her, sound-ing amused.

His smile faded as he refocused on her body, his expression turning intent. Slowly, he skimmed his knuckles over the soft skin of her inner arm, from shoulder to wrist. Traversed the swell of her cheek with a light stroke of his thumb. Had her flex her thigh so he could admire the muscles there. Urged her onto her belly so he could rub his bristly cheek along the length of her neck, up to her hairline. Trailed a palm down her spine, then skipped her ass entirely to wrap his fingers around the sturdy curve of her calf.

"When we volunteered at HHB?" His voice was a rasp, quieter than she'd ever heard it. "You'd lift your skirt to climb over bar-riers. Saw your legs in those thick white stockings a dozen times. Wanted to get my hands on them so goddamn badly. Thought about them at night. Jerked off to them in the shower."

She turned her head toward him on the pillow. Smiled tauntingly. "I'd gladly jerk you off myself while you touched my legs, but you won't let me."

He glared at her. Then kept exploring without another word, each touch a tribute to every overlooked part of her. Only . . . those details hadn't truly been overlooked, had they? He'd noticed them. Noticed and *admired*.

Something about that made her eyes prick with tears.

By the time he finished paying homage to her shoulder blades, her ankles, her hair, she was trembling too, overwhelmed by physical need and emotional upheaval, seconds away from sliding a hand between her own legs and taking care of the need he'd stoked.

Once he had her on her back again, though, there was no mistaking the increased urgency suffusing every bit of physical contact. Without hesitation, he reached out and ran his thumbs over her nipples. Tweaked them boldly as she sucked in a sharp, pleased breath. Plucked at them until they were hard enough to ache, each little pinch echoing in her clit.

She lifted eagerly into his touch. Snapped her thighs shut and squeezed them together, because some pressure was better than nothing.

His palms cupped her breasts, and he lowered his head between them. Lightly rubbed his beard against the sensitive flesh there until she helplessly giggled and squirmed. Still bent over the side of the bed, he slid his chin higher, into the crook of her shoulder, and dragged his open, hot mouth up her neck as his right hand smoothed over her belly and down lower.

"Stop," she panted, because yes, she wanted that big hand between her legs again. But until she'd actually seen him naked too, explored his body too, given him pleasure too, she intended to wait for her next orgasm. "Time for turnabout, Dean."

The moment she slammed on the verbal brakes, he froze. Wrenched himself away from her, eyes wild with need.

She met his dark stare boldly.

"Strip." If the pillow princess intended to become the reigning queen of his dick, his clothing needed to disappear. Right now. "Slowly."

Part of her wanted to do the job herself. But she'd be touching him soon enough, and she'd undress him next time. This time, as he'd said earlier, she just . . . wanted to look for a while.

Maybe more than a while. Maybe more than a month, even.

Heaven help them both.

19

Karl set his fists on his hips, outrage drawing his brows together. "I was gonna—"

"I know." The memory of that hand-delivered orgasm in his bakery would fuel her fantasies for decades to come. "Take off your clothes instead, please."

To her satisfaction, he didn't keep arguing. Instead, cheeks reddening even more above his beard, he swallowed visibly and reached for the hem of his tee. The journey his shirt took over his head wasn't especially slow, but she wouldn't quibble. Not when she could openly admire the breadth of his bare, barrel chest at long freaking last, then compare the swell of his belly with hers— his looked harder, for whatever reason—and visually trace the central trail of hair leading inexorably downward. Not when his strong shoulders and thick arms flexed so beautifully as he tossed aside his shirt and started on the button of his jeans.

He was definitely the hottest man she'd ever seen shirtless. Bar none.

Sure, Rob was good-looking enough, but he had an endurance runner's build. Stronger legs than arms. Spare and lean. Pared down to the essentials. Given her own size and build, part of her had always worried she might snap him in half if she wasn't careful. Even during sex.

But Karl . . . she wasn't worried about breaking him. That sturdy body of his could handle hers. And she couldn't wait to feel all that heat, all that hair-roughened skin and tough muscle and ample softness, surrounding her so completely that she couldn't register anything but how he felt. Around her. On top of her. Inside her.

She let out a long, low wolf whistle—half sincere appreciation, half taunt—and he flipped her off with both hands before unzipping.

When his jeans dropped to the floor a moment later, his wide, muscular thighs were finally bared to her gaze. They were *glorious*. Between those thick thighs, the insistent swell of his erection strained the fabric of his burgundy boxer briefs, and she wanted to squeeze his hard cock with her hands. Suck it so deep, he'd swear and beg.

With a crook of her finger, she urged him closer. He toed off his socks before stomping up to the side of mattress, looking cranky. His eyes weren't quite meeting hers, and his flush had spread down his neck and over his chest. Which meant he was nervous and trying not to show it, but that wasn't a problem. A few honest words would fix everything.

She flipped onto her side, facing him more directly, then offered him a smile that contained all her genuine appreciation and desire. And when she spoke, she let those emotions inflect her voice too.

"You are so fucking sexy, Karl," she told him bluntly. "I've never wanted anyone like this. Ever."

His shoulders dropped a fraction. "Yeah?"

"Yeah." With her forefinger, she slowly traced the line of his rampant cock through his boxer briefs. "Take these off too, and I'll show you just how much."

His expression much less grumpy now, he shoved down his last remaining clothing and kicked the fabric aside, then set his hands on his hips again and let her observe him.

In her experience, the appearance of a dick didn't tell an outside observer much about its usefulness in bed. But at first glance, Karl's still seemed promising. It reminded her of his agile, strong fingers. Not abnormally long, but definitely thick—and hopefully very, very capable of bringing her pleasure.

Under her gaze, his erection twitched and grew even more. A responsive bolt of heat flashed between her legs at the sight, and her next exhalation shook.

"How . . ." She cleared her throat. "How do you like to be touched?"

"By you."

Brusque. Seemingly sincere. Not nearly informative enough.

She pressed her lips together. "That's flattering—"

"Not flattering. Honest."

"—but doesn't actually help me much. So let's get more specific. Do you want me to be gentle or firm? Slow or fast? Is there anywhere I should avoid, or anywhere that feels particularly good, apart from"—her eyes involuntarily drifted back toward his dick—"the obvious?"

"Touch me anywhere you damn well want," he said immediately.

"Anywhere? Really?"

"Yeah. But make it firm, not gentle. Fast, not slow." His chest expanded even farther in a deep breath, which he blew out slowly. "Don't tease, Dearborn. Can't take it. Not this time."

No problem. Waiting had turned from painful to unbearable somewhere around the moment his boxer briefs had dropped to the floor.

"Fair enough." She grabbed his wrist and tugged him onto the bed beside her, tumbling closer to his naked body as the mattress dipped under his weight. "Let me know if something doesn't work for you, and I'll do the same."

A single nudge of her hand turned him onto his back. She climbed half on top of him, straddling his thigh. The coarse hair dusting his chest, his legs, his arms scratched delightfully against her overheated skin, and she rubbed up against him for a moment and closed her eyes at the faint abrasion against her stiff nipples and throbbing clit. He made a low, harsh sound, one big hand clamping on her hip while the other fisted a handful of her hair.

"Too rough?" he managed to grit out.

His hold was firm. Inescapable. Not even a tiny bit painful.

"Perfect," she told him, and hardly recognized the muffled rasp as her own voice.

Without further ado, she licked her palm, claimed his berry-sweet mouth in a voracious kiss, and reached between them for his dick. She gripped it. Squeezed hard. Used the wetness at its tip to jack him in a fast rhythm as he grunted and bucked into her grasp.

His hold on her hip urged her into a rocking motion too, encouraging her to grind her clit against the tense, flexed muscle of his thigh. He pressed her down firmly, a silent demand to chase her own pleasure. She did—and promptly lost track of what she'd intended to do to him.

Lost in a haze of lavender and sunshine and need, she moaned into his mouth.

He ripped it from hers, panting. "Fucking take it, Molly. Take everything you want."

His thigh was wet now, slippery from her arousal, and she was nearing orgasm, eyes squeezed shut, her inner muscles tightening in urgent twitches around nothing as her hand slowed to a halt on his dick.

Only . . . wait. *Wait.*

No, this wasn't happening. She wasn't coming without him again.

Jerking away from his hold, she clumsily scrambled to the foot of the bed, disoriented and aching with thwarted lust. And before he could do more than grunt out an aggrieved "Get the hell back over here, Dearborn," she shuffled between his legs, pushed his knees up and out, and dove down to swallow his dick.

He shouted and arched, every muscle turning to stone, his fists white-knuckled and pressed into the mattress on either side of him. With every suck, every flick of her tongue against the underside of his pulsing cock, half-strangled sounds ripped from his throat, but he somehow wrestled himself into near stillness. Those powerful hands didn't grab her skull or urge her down farther on his dick. Didn't force her to take even a millimeter more of him into her mouth than she'd intended.

"Fuck. Fuck. *Fuck*," he grated out with each dip of her head, his own head pressed back so hard against the pillow she couldn't see his face when she glanced up, only his beard and the taut muscles and tendons in his neck.

His skin was salty and startlingly hot against her tongue, his inner thigh trembling with strain against the palm she'd braced there to keep her steady and him open to her. Her other hand gripped his base and pumped, because no way she could fit something that thick down her throat. She worked him ruthlessly, since that was what he needed. What he'd asked of her. And maybe she couldn't give him everything he wanted, but she could definitely give him this much.

When one of his hands finally uncurled and reached for her again, it shook. His head rose from the pillow, and his fingers sifted through her hair. Not to pull, but to gather the strands away from her face, so he could see her. He rubbed an unsteady thumb lightly over her cheek, even while he still gripped the sheets in his other white-knuckled fist.

"So damn pretty," he told her, his chest flushed and heaving. "Christ, you're incredible. Those eyes. That mouth of yours. I can't . . ."

He trailed off, groaning long and low when her head dropped again.

His molten brown eyes locked with hers as she sucked. The fierce possessiveness in his stare, the all-encompassing need in his tense grimace, and the tender care of his touch all gathered in a flash of electric heat between her legs. She pressed her thighs together, sucked harder, and hazily wondered whether she had a hand to spare for her own pleasure.

Then her mouth and hand were suddenly empty, and she was being hauled up the bed and pushed down onto the mattress, onto her back, a pillow beneath her hips. He palmed her knees. Lifted and spread them wide and crawled between them, just as she'd done to him moments earlier. He knelt there for a moment, breaths sawing in and out of his heaving chest, and rolled on a condom he'd produced from . . . somewhere. His bedside table, maybe.

Electrified, she licked her lips and tried to remember her plan. "I wanted—"

"You'll get what you want," he interrupted. "That's a goddamn promise."

His broad, rough fingers opened her and stroked her pussy with confident deliberation, all slow slides and swirling thumbs, and she grasped desperate handfuls of the pillow under her head, panted, and lifted to him.

"Can't wait any longer." His voice was shredded. "But I'll get my mouth on you soon. Another promise."

She believed it. He stared between her legs like an addict spotting his next hit. And if he kept touching her like that even a minute longer—

His hands stilled. "You ready?"

"Beyond." She reached out to him. "Get down here, Dean."

When he fucked her, she wanted to feel him everywhere. Wanted him on top, swamping her in his heat, his scent, his strength, and his softness.

He moved up the bed and bent over her, propped on his elbows. Belly to belly, they gazed at one another, and she sighed in relief at how he filled her entire vision, how the weight of him pressed her deeper into the mattress, how the flush of his skin warmed her everywhere they touched.

Jaw ticking, he studied her expression. If he was looking for doubts, though, he wouldn't find any. He nodded a little, then reached down to position himself at her entrance. Braced himself, both his hands clasping hers.

Then he sank inside her in one long stroke, planting himself to the root. Filled and electrified, she moaned and gripped his fingers tight enough to hurt.

"Holy *shit*." His words were a thready rasp, barely audible over her pulse drumming in her ears. "Good?"

In answer, she planted her feet flat on the mattress to push against him and take what she wanted. The movement propelled him even farther inside her for an electric, heart-stopping moment, and he groaned. The vein at his temple pulsed faster. And at long last, he began taking her in measured, hard thrusts, every grinding push punctuated by a sharp slap of skin against skin as they both grappled to get closer, to force him deeper.

Each body-to-body impact stole her breath. He rutted into her in the same unhurried, merciless rhythm, no matter how she arched and lifted beneath him, and something about her lack of control, the way he was driving her toward orgasm with or without her assistance, wound her even tighter. Excited her even more.

His half-lidded eyes bored into hers. "Yeah?"

"Harder." It was all she could gasp out. "Oh god, *harder*."

Obediently, he fucked her harder, slamming into her over and over, and helpless sounds of pleasure escaped her open mouth with each thrust. Restlessly, her legs shifted, then wrapped around his waist, and they both gasped as he sank deeper still.

One of his hands slipped from hers. Slid between them. Spread her vulva so each lunge of his hips scraped him over her clit, and holy *shit*, she'd never, ever felt like this in bed with anyone before. By the time he'd entwined their fingers again, she was already squeezing her eyes shut, already climbing toward a cataclysmic orgasm.

His cock stretched her open again and again, his hot mouth latched onto her neck and pulled hard, and she clutched at him desperately as the swelling ache between her legs built into intolerable pressure and blinding white heat.

With a powerful twist of his ass and hips, he ground into her firmly with his next stroke, and she detonated with a harsh cry, her body clamping down on his dick as she bucked futilely against his immovable mass. He kept fucking her steadily through the orgasm exploding fever-bright behind her scrunched-closed eyelids, claiming every twitch of response her body offered, raising his head to sip her moans straight from her tongue.

She didn't have to work for any of it. Didn't have to do anything but relax into it and feel. He gave her what she wanted, exactly as he'd promised, and she took it all. Wallowed in the pleasure and let it come to her, pulse by pulse, as she gasped and arched.

By the time she finally finished coming and opened her eyes again, she was already halfway to another orgasm. Above her, though, Karl's flushed face had twisted, his rhythm turning fast and choppy for the first time. He was still holding back his orgasm, and while part of her wanted to encourage that—because another couple of minutes of this would make her climax again—the rest of her wanted to watch his pleasure. Wanted him to feel as amazing as she did.

"Karl . . ." She met his gaze. Held it. Squeezed her inner muscles as tightly as she could. "Come for me. Now."

The sound rumbling from his chest could've been the earth tearing apart. Fault lines appearing and groaning into open chasms. His right hand let go of hers, then reached down and gripped her thigh, pushing it higher. He powered into her in deep, desperate lunges, and she scraped her short nails down his back and spread her legs even wider.

"Molly . . ." He groaned. "*Fuck*, Molly. You're *perfect*."

With one final, rough thrust, he shoved himself deep, froze above her, and shook, growling in agonized pleasure as he released inside her at last.

She held him tight, inside and out, while he came. And when he collapsed on her for a fleeting moment, she cushioned him gladly. Stroked a hand down his trembling upper arm, over his sweaty shoulder, as he panted and recovered.

Far too soon, he scrambled back onto his elbows with a muttered obscenity and an apology. Then he shook his head and told her, "Holy shit, woman. Never come that hard in my goddamn *life*."

She smiled at him, pleased. "That makes two of us."

"Fuckin' A." He grinned back, sounding as happy as she'd ever heard him. "Got some unfinished business, though."

Her brow crinkled, and she stared up at him in confusion.

"Think I didn't notice you squirming beneath me right before I came?" He shook his head disapprovingly. "Hold on tight, Dearborn. You're not done yet."

He eased himself out of her and heaved himself onto his side with a heartfelt, exhausted groan, took care of the condom, and then slid his hand back between her legs, where she ached. From hard use, yes, but also lingering arousal. His fingers parted her swollen vulva once more, and he rubbed his thumb over her clit. Watched her legs drop open for his touch. Rubbed again and listened to her breath stutter in her chest.

"Yeah." Smug pride radiated from every inch of his newly relaxed face, and she couldn't even blame him. "That's what I thought."

Five minutes later, she was coming for the second time that afternoon. This time, around his thick, twisting knuckles as his thumb worried and teased her clit, his stare studied every involuntary clench of her muscles, and her sharp cry rang in her own ears. Through her tear-blurred eyes, the rosy light drifting through the half-open window lit each dust mote like a firework, and she'd never experienced anything so beautiful before.

This was unlike any sex she'd ever had. In her entire freaking life.

Yet again, he'd given her more than he'd taken. As much as she could handle. Without her asking, and without asking anything in return. All while she'd lain beneath his hands, beneath his body, like a woman with complete confidence in his ability to please her and his unwillingness to take advantage of her vulnerability.

And maybe that wasn't the type of trust he seemed to want from her. But it was far from nothing—and more than enough to scare her to the marrow of her rag-limp, pleasure-soaked bones.

20

Just past dawn the next morning, repeated rings of the doorbell dragged Karl out of bed.

Normally, he was up way earlier. Normally, he wasn't fucking the woman of his goddamn dreams or cuddling with her in his bed, though. Much less lying wide awake most of the night, either basking in the glory or worrying the whole thing might be a once-in-a-lifetime event.

He'd slept four hours, max. But he knew who was at the door, so he fumbled in the shadowed bedroom for his clothing, didn't let himself look at Molly's still-resting form under his covers, and closed the door silently behind himself.

Sure enough, one glance through his peephole showed Mrs. Carter and her walker stationed on his front porch. Wincing, he swung open the door.

"Sorry, Mrs. C," he said before the sharp-tongued, bent-backed harridan could lay into him. "Planned to come by later than usual. Should've let you know."

"Yes. You certainly should have." Her crackly voice wavered, and she glared at him above her bifocals, gray curls hidden beneath her pink silk bonnet. "I was worried about you, young man."

"Sorry," he repeated, and meant it. Getting around was hard for his neighbor these days, and he didn't like that she'd climbed up his front steps alone. "I'll help you home. Then give me an hour, all right?" He pictured Molly upstairs, wrapped in nothing but his family quilt. "Maybe two. I'll be over and ready to go."

On Sunday mornings, he mowed Mrs. C's lawn early. Everyone on their block hated it, but none of them was brave enough to defy her. Neither was he. If the woman wanted her yard clipped low and tight as a golf course, all before the sunrise service at her church? Her yard would look like hole fucking eighteen before the Deemer family's damn roosters quit crowing, and no other creature on the block would utter a single peep.

The older woman harrumphed. "I suppose that's acceptable. Additional tardiness may result in decreased wages, however."

He dipped his chin in acknowledgment, then intervened before she finished rotating her walker to descend the porch steps. For once, she allowed him to take her elbow to help her stay upright and steady on her feet, and thank fuck for *that*. Another broken hip, her asshole son in New York was gonna put her in a home, and she'd be totally miserable.

By the time he got Mrs. C comfortably settled in her recliner and sorted out her morning pill and breakfast situation, Molly had apparently registered his absence. When he let himself back into his home, she was sitting on the carpeted stairs and waiting for him, legs stretched out in front of her, wearing one of his old tees.

Fit her great. Especially since it left those long legs of hers bare. Her kiss-swollen lips twitched. "Young man, huh?"

Apparently she'd heard the whole thing. Didn't even look sleepy anymore. Damn shame. He'd hoped to climb back into bed and wake her up with something more enjoyable than an overly loud doorbell.

Arms folded across his chest, he leaned against his front door and enjoyed the view. "Woman's five hundred years old. To her, I'm still a kid. Always will be."

"If I'm remembering correctly . . ." Her forehead creased in thought. "You used to mow her lawn every weekend from spring to fall and shovel her driveway and sidewalk every winter."

Teenage Molly had been paying more attention than teenage Karl realized. "Still do."

"For over twenty years now." Her face had softened, her smile turning warm and sweet. "Out of curiosity, what kind of wages are you risking with your tardiness and unrepentant hooliganism?"

"Five bucks." Same as ever. "Ten if I trim her hedges or do a bit of weeding."

Every birthday, he also received a crisp twenty in a Hallmark card featuring Snoopy. Like clockwork. And every birthday, he snuck that twenty back into her purse when she wasn't looking. Same with his yardwork income.

While he was growing up, Mrs. C had checked on him regularly. Strong-armed him over to her place whenever elementary school ended and his mom was running behind schedule. She'd bitched about his loudness, his messiness, his clothing, his terrible handwriting on his homework. She'd also planted powdery-lipstick kisses on his dirty forehead to show her approval when he aced quizzes and baked him chocolate-chip cookies from refrigerated dough.

He loved that woman. Planned to help her live forever, even if that meant doing her yardwork until the day he dropped dead himself.

Molly's fingers plucked at the shitty beige carpet on his stairs. "My dad thought about hiring you to mow our lawn too. I don't think I ever told you that."

It was the first time she'd mentioned either of her parents since returning to Harlot's Bay. Of her own volition, anyway, rather than in response to a direct question.

That had to indicate *some* level of trust, right?

"Why didn't he?" Teenage Karl would've jumped at the opportunity. The money would've been the least of it.

She frowned down at a bit of fuzz. "He enjoyed doing it himself. Said no matter how often he had to travel for work, he could still make sure his family had a nice yard."

The weird inflection in her voice? He couldn't read it. But it wasn't happy reminiscence, that was for damn sure.

If he pushed too hard or too fast, she'd pull back. The reunion was next weekend, though. Only six days from now. If he didn't ask now, maybe he'd never find another chance. And since his friends seemed to think the topic might be important . . .

"Speaking of your parents . . ." He cleared his throat, shifting uncomfortably against the paneled wooden door. "You haven't said much about them. They okay?"

"Mom's good." Her shoulder lifted in a brief shrug, and she kept squinting at the carpet. "My father, I have no idea."

Not dead, then. But not in her life. Which, knowing how undramatic a person Dearborn was, didn't bode well.

Before he could gather the nerve to keep pressing, her head rose. She looked directly at him, her jaw set with determination. "Want a bonus secret, Dean?"

Abso-fucking-lutely. But first . . . "Cuddling okay with you?"

"Uh . . ." Her brows drew together. "Yeah. I guess."

Pushing off the door, he grabbed her hand and towed her to the shadowy living room, then plopped down on the ancient couch and tugged her onto his lap. Because if she was going to share something shitty? He was going to hold her.

Briskly, trying not to elbow Molly in the face, he shook out the quilt hanging over the sofa back—his favorite of his mom's work—then swaddled Molly and himself in the fluffy, flower-scented cotton.

Way better. "Tell me."

Slowly, she relaxed into his embrace. Let herself slump against his chest. When she finally spoke again, she sounded weary to the marrow.

"Okay. So . . ." Her voice was muffled against his tee. "Mom didn't want me to say anything back then, and she'd probably want me to keep my mouth shut now too. The memories don't hurt her like they used to, but what happened still humiliates her. A lot. Even my stepfather doesn't know the full story."

Holy shit. Had her father *murdered* someone? Or—

"All right, here goes." She sucked in a deep breath. "You know when Mom and I suddenly left for California, right before graduation?"

He nodded and stroked his palm down her spine, trying like hell to remember whether anyone had ever found the Zodiac Killer. Also racking his brain for the last name of the Unabomber, which he couldn't quite—

"My father had gotten his other wife got pregnant. Again."

Karl's mind blanked. "His . . . what?"

Her chest rose and fell on a sigh. "As Mom and I found out right before prom, he had another family in NorCal. A wife named Cara, although their marriage wasn't actually legal back then. Two sons in elementary school. He visited them on all his"—her fingers crooked—"'business trips.' And once he found out Wife Number Two was having another baby, he decided his most urgent obligations were to them instead of us. Especially since I was graduating from high school and going away to college soon anyway."

"Holy fuck," he muttered, gathering her closer, and she rubbed her ear.

No wonder the woman had trust issues when it came to men. Between her ex and her father, she'd gotten up close and real damn personal with two incredibly crappy examples of the breed.

"I mean, he wasn't wrong. Young kids do need a dad more than an eighteen-year-old does." She tugged at a fold of his tee, straightening the fabric and avoiding his eyes. "But my mom was devastated and embarrassed. She needed the support of her family. So we moved."

Just her mom, huh? No one else was devastated too?

He called bullshit. "What about *your* hurt? What about *your* embarrassment?"

"I wasn't embarrassed." A stout declaration. Sounded honest. "I didn't do anything wrong, and neither did my mother." She paused. "Other than being a bit too naïve, I guess. In retrospect, Mom recognized lots of signs that something wasn't quite right, and she beat herself up for ignoring them. But she loved my dad, and he was good to us both. So when he said his work required frequent trips out of state, she believed him. We both did."

Karl hid his wince as he kept rubbing her back.

Yeah. The two most important men in Molly's life? Both those bastards had yanked the rug out from under her. Punished her for having faith in them.

Karl had no idea what that kind of bone-deep betrayal would feel like. Hoped he'd never get the chance to find out.

"You're right. No cause for anyone to be ashamed but him." Gently, he tugged at a rumpled strand of her soft hair. "Bet it still hurt like hell."

"Well . . ." Her neck bent, and she resumed smoothing his shirt.

"He was . . . he was kind of my role model growing up?"

Aw, shit. Leaning down, he pressed a hard kiss to the top of her head.

Sadness crept into her neutral tone, freighting each heavy word. "Mom and I are similar in a lot of ways. Too similar to get along well, I think. As I grew up, Dad was the glue that held all three of us together." She hesitated. "He was so warm. So outgoing and *open.*"

Well . . .

She said it before he could. "Yes, yes, I know. He wasn't *really* open. But I didn't realize that back then, and I was a total daddy's girl before . . ." With a swift circle of her wrist, a loose thread from his tee wrapped around her finger. She let it unwind, then repeated the process. "Before."

He had no idea what the hell to say. "I'm so damn sorry, Molly."

"He truly seemed to adore both of us. With all his heart." Wind. Unwind. Wind. Unwind. "After a trip, he'd swoop into the house and shout, 'Where are my best girls?' Then he'd lift us up and swing us in the air while he went on and on about how badly he'd missed us and how much we were going to love his gifts."

He stroked her hair until her fidgeting stilled and her body relaxed against his again. And when a small wet spot formed on the shoulder of his tee, he let her pretend it didn't exist.

"So yeah, it hurt." Because she was a consummate actress, there was no hint of tears in her voice. Just matter-of-fact pragmatism. "And maybe it would've hurt less if we'd stayed in contact with him. But by the time I was willing to hear what he had to say, he'd given up trying to reach out months before. I decided to just let it be. If he wanted to contact me, he would."

Karl couldn't help but wonder whether talking to the man might bring her some necessary closure, even now. Or whether having her father back in her life might feel good, if both she and her dad wanted that. But a possible reunion wasn't—would never be—Karl's decision. Molly knew herself far better than he did. She could determine the bounds of her own life, her own heart, for herself.

In his opinion, the idea of closure was often a goddamn lie anyway, the search for it an excuse to delay accepting the inevitable. And far too often, even honest answers wouldn't satisfy anyone. One more conversation, one more look, one more explanation wouldn't do anything but dredge up old grief from where it'd been laid to rest.

Or maybe that was just the self-justification of a cowardly man who avoided difficult conversations whenever possible.

She laid her head against his upper arm and finally let her red-rimmed, weary eyes meet his. "Today's your lucky day, Dean. Want another super-special double-bonus secret?"

"Always."

Whatever she'd give him, he'd take. Because this was what trust—enough to undergird their future, enough to either keep her in Harlot's Bay or bring her back here—looked like. Had to be. Right?

When he smoothed a stray lock of hair behind her ear, she tried to smile at him. "That summer after high school, I cut things off with you because I thought you had a girlfriend and were looking to cheat on her with me."

He sighed. "You thought I was a two-timing asshole. Like your father."

That was the part he hadn't understood before. The missing piece of Dearborn's confusing-as-hell puzzle.

"I also thought I was feeling far too much for a guy who'd already committed to someone else." She tapped his chest, right over his stupid besotted heart. "And yeah, that reminded me of my dad. Which is why cutting you off was such a knee-jerk reaction and why I couldn't bring myself to ask for the truth." She hesitated. "I wasn't sure I could bear to hear it, Karl. Not then."

He'd known she was attracted to him back in high school. Hadn't realized her feelings had run deep enough, even then, to scare her. Just like his own emotions had terrified him.

He pressed a fierce kiss to her palm. "Understood."

When she exhaled slowly, he cuddled her closer and rubbed her back some more. After a minute, her breathing slowed, her arms looped around his chest, and she looked more asleep than awake. But her lips were still pressed thin. Still downturned.

Finally, he shifted beneath her. "Any other secrets to share?"

"No." She snorted faintly. "Thank heavens."

"Hurt to talk about all this shit?"

Another faint sigh. "Yes."

"Help if I make you come?"

She straightened in his lap, suddenly looking way less tired. "Obviously."

Gently, he tumbled her to the side, onto the sofa cushions. By the time she regained her equilibrium, he was already tugging off her boy shorts, pushing her knees apart, and kneeling between them on the floor.

She gazed down at him, eyes bright, lips tipped in a pleased smile. "If I'd known talking about my quasi-bigamous father would earn me head, I'd have confessed twenty years ago."

"Wasn't as good at this back then."

Enthusiasm, he'd had. Experience? Not a whole hell of a lot.

Her hand flicked, a graceful gesture he could've watched a million times over. "I'd have taught you what felt good for me."

"Yeah." He lifted that strong hand. Placed it on his head, a silent demand for guidance. "You can teach me now too."

Her fingers slowly curled into a fist, and his dick twitched at the tug on his scalp. "It would be my pleasure."

Yeah. It would.

He'd make damn sure of that.

21

*T*hat twist toward the end?" Karl sat back in his kitchen chair, shaking his head. "Fucking bananas."

Molly dabbed at her mouth with a paper towel. "You should've known Sadie Brazen wouldn't dabble in dubcon, Dean. There was no way on this green Earth she'd give a happy ending to a kickboxer-kangaroo shifter who'd just shoved a human woman into his pouch and hopped off without her permission."

He threw his hands in the air, outraged. "How the hell was I supposed to know Riley and Jack were married already? And that they were re-creating key scenes from the shitty-ass movie they watched on their first date together to cure her amnesia from being kicked in the damn head by the asshole wallaby-shifter crime boss determined to force Jack to bend the knee to him?"

"The clues were all there if you paid attention." Her expression turned infuriatingly lofty. "Which you clearly didn't."

He flipped her off with both middle fingers.

Unruffled, she chewed for a while before swallowing her last bite of buttered toast. "If you can't decipher subtext, that's not my fault, Dean."

Trying his hardest not to laugh, he sneered across the table at her. "Screw you, Dearborn."

"Already did that." Appearing contemplative, she glanced down at her cotton-covered chest. "And all I got was four orgasms and this lousy yet very comfortable T-shirt."

When he broke and laughed, she did too.

Just another reason this was the best morning of Karl's life, bar fucking none.

After he'd gone down on Molly until her thighs shook and her voice was hoarse from loud moaning rather than tears, he'd texted his nosy family, mowed Mrs. C's lawn before the older woman put out a goddamn APB on him, then showered, called Charlotte to check on her and the kids, and eaten the breakfast Molly fixed for them both.

Now they were sitting at his kitchen table, sipping coffee. First cup for each. Still felt like he'd pounded a billion lattes, with all the energy pumping through his bloodstream, and his brain was working like a champ despite his lack of sleep.

Turned out, pure goddamn joy was the world's most powerful upper. Which he now knew, solely because of Molly fucking Dearborn.

Part of him had loved her for over twenty years. Now part of him had become all of him, and he could admit it to himself. Wasn't even scared anymore. Not after the past twenty-four hours of great sex and communication fucking galore.

Basically everything Matthew and Athena had wanted him to do? Hereby *done*.

He and Molly had exchanged personal histories, and after the whole audiobook-collection reveal, she clearly knew how he felt about her. If that hadn't clued her in, the way he'd touched her should've done the trick. And her opening up to him like she had, in bed and out? Told him she felt the same way about him. No declarations necessary, on either side.

For the first time, he was actually anticipating that stupid reunion. Because it wasn't marking an end for him and Molly—it was celebrating a small part of their new beginning. Also because an amazing idea had just surfaced in his super-sharp post-bedding-Molly brain.

After all those Nasty Wenches meetings and all of Sadie Brazen's crackpot plots, he knew exactly what should happen at the reunion. Sure, he wasn't an abduction-happy Australian marsupial, a cobra shifter, or a weirdo sexy Satan, but . . .

No way they were hanging out at the reunion as mere attendees, just two more chumps who'd been browbeaten or bribed by Janel into awkwardly socializing until they could make their grand goddamn escape.

He had bigger plans. *Way* bigger.

"Been thinking about the reunion," he told Molly. "Normal date isn't good enough. Over the—"

She frowned. "Good enough for what?"

"—past couple of years, I've listened to a crapload of your books—"

"Sadie Brazen's books," she corrected, because the woman couldn't help herself.

"—and also read a crapload of *other* 'spicy'"—he crooked his fingers into air quotes, because Molly ate that shit up—"romances for the book club, so I know how this whole damn situation is supposed to go."

"Do you?" She raised a single eyebrow, clearly skeptical. "Do you really, Karl?"

He pointed at her. "You're the girl who left her hometown in a hurry, returning for the reunion with something to prove." He jerked his thumb toward his chest. "I'm—"

"I have nothing to prove to anyone. Here or anywhere else."

"—the sexy bad boy who stayed in town and made good, and

now it's your chance to show everyone who teased and bullied you that you're successful and happy and banging your love interest like you're both literal fucking bunnies. The horniest bunnies on the entire damn planet."

Silence. Lots of silence.

She blinked at him for a minute, blank-faced.

"Holy wow, Dean," she finally said. "I don't think I've ever heard you say so many words at one time. Ever. And I don't understand what in the world you're talking about. No one teased me. No one bullied me."

"Doesn't matter." He waved that off. "Let's keep talking about our plan."

Her forehead puckered. "We don't have a plan, Dean. *You* have a distorted reimagining of our high school history and a cockamamie, middle-aged version of every Hollywood teen movie that's ever existed." She took a sip of her coffee. Thought for a moment. "Not to mention several Netflix original films. Amazon too. Possibly Hulu."

He ignored that. "Just imagine it, Dearborn. Walking into the gym, your fancy dress *crusted* with sparkly-ass sequins."

She raised both brows this time. Directed a pointed glance down at herself.

"Okay. Yeah." Rapidly, he edited his vision. "Imagine walking into the gym, you in your . . . sexy tuxedo? Or maybe one of those shit-hot suit jackets that opens to the waist, and you don't wear a shirt underneath?"

Her lips twitched. "Better."

Encouraged, he kept going. "And everyone's like, 'Oh, she's here alone, poor Molly, we were obviously so right to torment her all those years.' Then your love interest rolls up—"

"Just to confirm: You're that love interest?" Her voice was as dry as those shitty snickerdoodles he'd overbaked last Friday. "The aforementioned 'sexy bad boy'?"

"Stop interrupting, Dearborn." At his glare, she held up both hands in surrender.

"*Anyway*, the sexy bad boy arrives, looking incredibly dashing in his tuxedo." He frowned. "Which he should rent as soon as possible, now that he's thinking about it."

Assuming she agreed to his plan. Which was a big assumption, but whatever. He'd damn well make it happen.

"He should probably start a list. Let's title it 'Sexy Bad Boy Supplies.'" She started ticking things off on her fingers, looking highly entertained. "He'll need one tuxedo, suitably dashing. One corsage, lavish enough to show up all the nonexistent haters. One boutonniere, chosen to complement said tuxedo and coordinate with the corsage. One limo, with rose petals scattered over the seats, for when they triumphantly ride off into the night together."

Her forehead creased in thought, and her fingertips drummed against her thigh. "Preferably pink petals. Yellow's fine too. Red looks like blood, so unless I'm playing a Goth in this story or he's a sexy bad boy turned hometown hero turned vampire, I'd avoid that color."

Jesus H. Christ.

"He'll make his goddamn list later." Manfully, he ignored her snicker. "As I was *about to say*, before I was so *rudely interrupted* . . ."

She mimed zipping her mouth shut.

Eyeing her with suspicion, he continued. "The sexy bad boy arrives. Without a single word, he sweeps her into his strong arms—"

"They didn't ride to the reunion prom together? Does that

mean I have to make separate transportation arrangements for the night?"

"—and kisses the ever-loving shit out of her, then proceeds to make heart-eyes at her the rest of the night, much to the shock and jealousy of all the mean girls who made her high school life a living hell."

"Another quick question." She held up a finger. "Those mean girls: standard-issue, I assume?"

He loved her snark, but he still wasn't going to honor that with a response. "And at the end of the night, they crown you Homecoming reunion queen—"

"No such thing, Dean."

"—because despite their envy, they recognize that you're gorgeous. The most incredibly gorgeous Harlot's Bay High graduate ever. We drive away in our shiny limo, and—credits roll. It's a triumph." He pumped a fist. "The feel-good story of the fucking millennium."

"That was quite a tale." Her head tipped to the side. "Have you considered writing fiction?"

"Been there, done that. Got the clucking T-shirt." Literally. Athena had made tees with a fake book cover for *Down to Pluck* plastered on front, because she was a damn menace. "Don't bothering asking, Dearborn. I won't tell you."

If she found out he'd coauthored an erotic chicken-man romance with Matthew, she'd hassle him forever. Probably become lifetime besties with Athena on the spot, which was a terrifying prospect.

"Hmmm." A swipe of Molly's pink tongue wet her lips. Made them glisten. It was distracting as all hell. "In this scenario, I'd be incredibly gorgeous, huh?"

The way she'd hooked her arms over the back of her kitchen

chair thrust her breasts against his tee and created lines of strain in the cotton. The fabric near the hem wasn't quite wide enough, so it cupped the swells of her belly and ass. Beneath that hem there was nothing but boy shorts and her long legs, bare and beautiful.

She wasn't an hourglass. More a column, like the ones they'd seen on school field trips to DC every year. Subtly curved, thick, elegant. Strong.

Statuesque, his grandma would have called her. *Handsome*.

But to him, she was just . . . perfect. Always had been. With that body and hair, those eyes, that pretty, round face, she should wear a crown. Should've risen from a fucking scallop shell in the ocean. Molly Dearborn could strike him speechless with a single look, when she wasn't busy annoying the living hell out of him.

That was true even before he'd seen her buck-ass naked. Now that he had?

Incredibly gorgeous was the understatement of the fucking millennium.

He waved an arm, indicating the entirety of her, from head to toe. "Well, yeah."

Her lips curved, and her cheeks darkened in a pleased flush.

At the sight of her blushing in happiness because of something he'd said? His chest expanded. His spine straightened. He could've hefted a damn truck with how strong he felt in that moment.

"Good to know." Her cheeks might be warm, but her voice was as calm and cool as ever. "So you'd act over-the-top smitten. The entire night."

"Yep." Easiest thing in the world. Might as well order him to keep breathing.

She tucked a swath of hair behind one pink-tipped ear. "Ideally, we'd both have exes in attendance to torment with regret and jealousy. I won't, but maybe some of yours will be there?"

"Janel told me Becky's coming." Then she'd winked at him, like he gave a shit whether his ex from over twenty years ago showed up at the reunion. "Might be others too. Don't know, don't care."

He'd lived in Harlot's Bay his whole life. Limited pool of options. So yeah, he'd dated women in their class who'd stayed local. A few would probably show up to the reunion. If he was with Molly, though? He might not even notice 'em. Probably not the nicest thing to say, but it was the honest damn truth.

He met Molly's gaze. "Well? What do you think?"

Her mouth opened, then closed again.

"You didn't go to prom," he pointed out, in his best wheedling tone. "Time to rectify that shit the most awesome way possible."

And after such an incredible night? She'd never want to leave Harlot's Bay again, guaran-fucking-teed. Which was what turned his plan from great to genius-level, if he did say so himself, and he damn well *did*.

She gulped back the last of her coffee, then plonked her mug on the table and eyed him askance. "I already know I'm going to regret this bizarro plan."

"That mean you're gonna do it?"

She exhaled gustily, slumping in her chair. "I suppose."

"Hell, yeah!" he shouted, then got out his phone and got to work.

22

That afternoon, Karl mounted the block outside the tuxedo rental place's dressing room and modeled yet another penguin suit for Matthew and Athena.

After receiving his texted demand for reunion prep assistance, the couple had agreed to "provide extremely necessary social-event guidance to the man voted most likely to firebomb an etiquette school," as Athena had annoyingly put it. Next thing he knew, they were tearing him from Molly's side, hauling him downtown, carting endless tuxes to his dressing room, and strangling him with bow ties.

Probably what he deserved for voluntarily texting someone. Should've known better.

He scowled at them both. But when Athena gave the finger-swirl signal, he obediently made a quarter turn. She tugged at the hem of his deep-navy jacket, straightening it, then had him turn again.

"According to the last reunion update, the theme for the night is 'Under the Sea,'" Matthew volunteered. "In case that helps with your flower selection. You might want to choose something marine-life-themed."

How was that even possible? Did the florist just staple a fucking eel to the arrangement and call it a day?

Fancy-people shit mystified him. Always had, apparently always would. Which was why he'd requested backup today, despite his numerous subsequent regrets.

"Decision time, assholes." He planted his feet on the block. "This design? Or the black tux with the stupid cummerbund?"

"This design," Matthew and Athena said in unison.

"You heard 'em," he told the hovering sales assistant, and that was that. One errand down, two more to go.

After he paid and laid his plastic-covered tux in the back seat of his car, the three of them walked down the cobblestone sidewalk to Fishwife Floral. Matthew immediately claimed Athena's hand, and she jauntily swung their arms between them.

After a few steps, she slowed. "Listen, Special K, I was thinking . . ."

"Jesus H. Christ, anything but that," Karl muttered, and Matthew glared at him.

The woman herself paid him zero goddamn heed. "You and Molly should do another trust-building activity tonight." She halted entirely, then tugged both men into the shade beside Bitches & Daughters Bank and huddled close, voice pitched low for privacy. "This is basically your last free evening before the reunion, and Molly's leaving soon after you attend, right?"

A week from tomorrow, according to her damn plane ticket. He knew better, though. "Yeah, but—"

"So time's ticking down for her in Harlot's Bay. You need to build maximum trust in minimal time. We can help." Athena thought for a moment. "Why don't you and Molly come over to our house for dinner? Afterward, we can play Pictionary for communication- and trust-building purposes."

Karl shook his head. "Not necessary."

"What's not necessary?" Matthew's brows drew together. "Dinner, or—"

"More trust building." Karl shrugged. "Things are going great, thanks to your advice. Communication up the wazoo. By the time the reunion's done, she'll either trash that plane ticket or buy another one to get back here as soon as she can."

"I'm thrilled things are going so well for you, Karl. Really. But . . ." The knuckles of Matthew's free hand dug into his jaw. "Has Molly *told* you she'll stay? Or visit again in the near future? Using actual words?"

Rude goddamn question. Especially when Karl had finally been feeling more confident about all this long-distance shit.

"Not out loud." Shifting uncomfortably, he glowered at his best friend. "But I can tell."

"Have you asked?"

Karl slumped against the bank's brick exterior and continued glaring. In silence.

"So you were too scared to ask. But have you at least told her how you feel?" In response to his fulminating grumble, Athena lifted her own free hand. "Don't bother trying to stare me down. I'll repeat myself: Karl Andrew Dean, have you told her *how you feel*?"

Well . . . "No. But she knows. She *has* to know."

"How?" Matthew immediately asked. "How does she know, if you haven't told her?"

"The same way you two assholes figured it out without my saying so." Karl flung his arms wide, outraged and uneasy. "I can't hide it, okay? Every time she's close, the way I feel pours out of me like a motherfucking *fountain*, Matthew. No way she could miss it."

"I just . . ." Matthew's eyes closed for a moment. "I just think maybe you should tell her. Using audible, easily understood words, rather than counting on her ability to read you."

Athena nodded. "Seconded."

Every last corner of Karl's affronted soul rejected the suggestion, and the sheer magnitude and violence of that automatic denial overwhelmed him to the point where he couldn't even speak. Only fume.

"I know you hate that idea. Here's the problem, though." All the sincerity in Matthew's pristine goddamn soul showed in his solemn gaze. "When you asked us for advice last weekend, we were honored that you trusted us to help you. But we were also shocked you were willing to discuss something that bothered you without obfuscating the issue in eighteen separate layers of crankiness and denial. You don't tend to talk about your emotions. Not with us. Not even with your family."

Athena cut in. "You don't talk about much of anything, actually. Except what's currently annoying you. Also the creative yet practically infeasible ways you intend to murder those around you."

He flipped her off for that, but didn't argue. Couldn't argue.

Of course he didn't fucking talk about his emotions. Easier to show them. Besides——

"People can say whatever they want." Karl crossed his arms over his chest, relieved to have finally found a good rebuttal. "What they do? That shit matters more."

Karl bet Molly's ex had talked a good game. Right before he did his best to bleed her dry. Hell, her two-timing father had told Molly and his wife just how much he loved and missed them every time he got home from his secret second family. Pretty words meant *nothing*.

"True. But it's hard to get close to someone who's an emotional mystery, especially in a tight time span." Matthew bumped his shoulder against Karl's, a consoling gesture. "Which is why you need to tell her how you feel and what sort of future you want with her. Directly."

Ugh. Had to be a better way to build trust and intimacy.

Like, for example, whacking a stupid ball through a stupid mini-windmill while wearing a stupid blindfold. Karl clearly hadn't appreciated *Corporations Monthly*'s total genius enough until this very moment.

"Don't want to pressure her." Aha! Another excellent argument! "Thought holding back would make her comfortable. Give her time to trust me more. Still think that."

So—for Molly's sake—he shouldn't tell her jack shit about his goddamn *heart*.

Both Matthew and Athena side-eyed him.

His best friend shook his head. "That's not why you're holding back."

"You're protecting yourself," Athena elaborated. "Not her. You can—and should—explain your feelings without pressuring her to return them."

This time, he flipped them both the bird, because . . .

Well, just *because*. They'd earned it. They knew why.

"More importantly, I don't think holding back will get you far with Molly. Not as far as you want to go, anyway." Matthew kissed his wife's hair, then raised his head to meet Karl's eyes. "As I said, it's difficult to trust someone you don't know. And you are highly, highly reluctant to let yourself be known."

"*You* know me." Karl directed his best glower their way. "Both of you."

"That's true," Matthew conceded. "But understanding how you think and how you show what you feel took me *years*, Karl. Years you don't have with Molly, because she's leaving in eight days."

Athena leaned against her husband. "As for me . . . Matthew is kind of my Karl Cheat Sheet."

"Doesn't matter how it happened. You know me." Karl stabbed an accusing finger in their direction. "Besides, you two don't need words to communicate."

"Sometimes we don't," Matthew admitted. "But that's only because we've talked so much this past year and still talk so much now."

Karl's murderous scowl should've sent them both scurrying. Didn't, though, because fuck. His. Life. "You're good at words. I'm not."

"No shit, Special K." Athena's wrist flick dismissed that line of argument. "Were you great at making bread the first few times you did it?"

Of course not. Getting good took practice. Wouldn't admit that out loud, though, because he knew where this was going.

In short: not his way.

"Just try. Please." All the patience and affection in Matthew's voice? Would've melted the stoniest heart, much less one made of Cadbury goddamn Creme. "For your own sake, because you deserve happiness and love. But also for Molly's. Everything I know about her says she deserves a good partner too. One who respects her and treats her well."

"And who clearly adores her. Someone honest and reliable"—leaning to the side, Athena poked Karl's upper arm—"whose shoulders fill out a henley really impressively."

"It's true," Matthew said gravely. "Your shoulders are exceptional."

"Not to mention those thick thighs." Apparently Athena could wolf-whistle. Which she did, loudly, while Karl's ears burned. "Hubba-hubba."

"Okay, assholes, that's—" Karl began.

"Hubba-hubba indeed." Matthew might've been narrating a BBC documentary, his voice was so dry. "Molly couldn't have a better partner than you, Karl."

"That would be true even if your ass gave up easily. But it won't." Athena offered Karl an innocent blink-blink of the eyes. "It just won't quit."

Holy fuck. Shoulders shaking, Karl buried his face in his hands.

"All right, I think that's enough objectification of my best friend, sweetheart. He's trying to suffocate himself with his own palms." Wryly, Matthew added, "Plus, I'm getting jealous. We both know my butt isn't nearly as dutiful as Karl's."

"I love it anyway." The smack of a hard kiss was far too recognizable. "Don't worry. Your thighs may only earn a single hubba, but that hubba is heartfelt, baby."

Matthew said something in return, but Karl couldn't hear it over the sound of his soul dying.

"Fine. I'll think about your stupid suggestion," he told his hands, loudly enough for his friends to hear. "Just stop whatever obnoxious bit you've got happening, you dicks, before I shove you both in front of oncoming traffic, scrape up your remains, and make smartass pancakes tomorrow's daily goddamn special."

"Made you laugh," Athena noted, equally loudly. "Hard enough that you had to hide inside those meaty mitts."

"Wasn't laughter. More like spasms of fucking disgust." Once he could keep a straight face, he dropped his arms. "Look. I get what you're both saying."

"Excellent." Even through her smudged lenses, Athena's eyes

were sharp on him. "So you're going to tell her what she needs to know?"

"If necessary."

Matthew's shoulders drooped. "In other words, not if you can possibly help it."

Well, duh.

Expressing himself through his actions? Paying attention, caring for her, and doing his best to make her happy? No problem. Loved doing it. Considered it a privilege.

Expressing himself with his body? Fucking her like a man obsessed, then making love to her like a man who'd surrendered his heart two damn decades ago? Risky—now that he'd had her, he'd never want anyone else in his bed, no matter what happened next—but brain-meltingly pleasurable. Better yet: something he knew he could do and do damn well.

Expressing himself in words, though?

Too much risk, too little pleasure. Not enough natural skill *or* practice. If—no, *when*—he said the wrong thing, he'd drive her away. Become the roadkill under her rental car tires. Spend the rest of his godforsaken life doomed to remember the moment he lost her for good, when he should've just kept his damn trap shut.

If a conversation about his damn *feelings* wasn't necessary, it wasn't happening. Period.

"Hear what you're saying." He stepped away from the wall and nodded toward the florist. His signal that the discussion was definitely over. "Thanks."

His closest friends exchanged another of those annoying glances, then both exhaled heavily in what sounded like surrender. Halle-fucking-lujah.

Matthew's arm around Athena's shoulders, they joined Karl in the center of the cobblestone sidewalk. Together, the three of them began walking toward Fishwife Floral.

After a minute, Athena bumped her hip against Karl's. "You two coming over tonight?"

Wasn't his preference—his friends would harass him about Molly again, he knew it already—but strengthening Molly's community ties couldn't hurt. Neither could another trust-building activity. Maybe she'd even announce her decision to stay tonight, if everything went right?

"I'll ask Molly." He'd text her after ordering flowers. Which reminded him— "Listen. Before we go into the shop, I gotta know. Morbid curiosity."

The other two glanced over at him, brows raised in identical curiosity.

Karl halted in front of the florist, blocking the entrance. "What the hell is a marine-life-themed corsage?"

"The arrangements are supposed to be a surprise, so . . . ." Matthew looked down at his wife. "Sweetheart, can I cover your ears?" When Athena agreed, he cupped his hands over them like impromptu earmuffs, then turned back to Karl. "There are pearls. Tiny, decorative shells. Cream-colored mini roses and aqua accents. Some sparkling net. There was talk of a bedazzled starfish."

Athena perked right up, because apparently Matthew's palms did fuck-all for noise-canceling. "That sounds amazing! Like something straight out of *Desire, Unfiltered*!"

That woman was *way* too into Brazen's story about a guppyman with dick-fins.

"That sounds tacky as hell," Karl countered.

"It's both." Dropping his useless hands, Matthew sighed deeply. "Somehow, simultaneously, it's both."

Athena beamed. "I can't wait."

Rising up on her tiptoes, she planted a smooch on her husband's mouth. He returned the kiss with nauseating enthusiasm, drawing her closer with the arm draped over her shoulders.

"Get a room, you horned-up assholes," Karl told his friends, then stomped into the shop and directly toward the tall Black woman stationed behind the customer service counter. "Whatever weird sea-related flower shit you have left? I want it. Pick it up next Saturday afternoon." He pointed at her, narrowing his eyes in menace. "And if there's a stupid-ass starfish involved, it better sparkle like an actual damn star, Latoria. Or else."

His younger sister's bestie tossed her long red braids over her shoulder, one dark eyebrow arched. "Fuck you, bro. You'll take whatever I give you and *like* it."

Ten minutes later, the order was in. Latoria looked way too pleased with herself. His credit card should've been smoking. And as he gathered his kiss-drunk friends and steered them toward the limo rental place—owned by another sibling's still-friendly ex, so an in-person visit might mean a steep discount—he could only hope Molly liked the flowers too, along with everything else he was doing to make the reunion special. Special enough for her to stay, or at least come back ASA-goddamn-P.

No words necessary.

Please, for the love of Christ, no words necessary.

23

Despite Athena's weird homemade Pictionary clues—"Express Yourself" and "The Importance of Being Earnest" had proven particularly difficult to illustrate—Molly genuinely enjoyed the evening at Karl's friends' home. Upon receiving "Tell It to My Heart" as her next clue, though, her patience finally ran out.

Tugging Karl closer, she whispered in his ear. "Let's stay at the Spite House tonight."

"Why?" His body tensed. "Something bothering you at my house?"

He didn't sound defensive or angry. Just worried.

"Not at all. The Spite House is just considerably closer." Her lips brushed his ear as she leaned in and spoke as quietly as humanly possible. "It's also where I'm storing all the toys I purchased today."

Since the nice blouse and flowing cuffed trousers she'd intended to wear to the reunion clearly weren't sufficient for Karl's bizarre *She's All That*-inflected vision for the event, she'd set out with Lise to do a little shopping of her own that afternoon—only to find that Harlot's Bay's stores didn't stock her preferred type of formal wear. Not in her size, anyway. In the end, she and Lise had parked themselves at the Doxy Diner, eaten tuna melts while they located better outfit options online, paid for rushed shipping . . . and then found themselves with time to kill and nowhere in particular to be.

Naturally, they'd visited the rival sex shops. Molly *needed* to know what was earning the stores all that custom-cake money, all right?

Also, she'd wanted a vibrator. Make that three vibrators, because while the first shop had carried an array of gorgeous, high-end toys, the second included shapes and functionalities she'd never even imagined before. Including a dildo with strategically placed fins and another with pulsing bulb-type things, which—as Lise had confirmed—Sadie Brazen's books had directly inspired. Molly had felt obliged to pick up one of those clit-sucker toys at the first store too, because those were freaking incredible, and she deserved *choices* in her adult-toys arsenal.

"Toys?" When she nodded, Karl's brows rose. "Assume you don't mean goddamn Lego."

"Nope." This time, she lowered her voice until she could barely even hear herself. "Not unless the Lego manufacturer has begun dabbling in Sadie Brazen-inspired guppy-dick vibrators."

For a moment, he simply stared at her.

Then he grabbed her hand, hauled her up with him as he stood, and turned to Matthew and Athena. "Appreciate the food and your weird-ass busybody version of Pictionary, but we gotta go."

And that was the end of their evening with friends. She barely had time to wave goodbye before they were out the couple's door and inside her own. Once there, they stumbled up the stairs to her narrow bedroom, making out all the while. Within minutes, they were both naked and surrounded by a panoply of delightfully odd toys, and Karl was inside her.

As he would definitely put it: halle-fucking-lujah.

* * *

MOLLY WAS MAYBE ten seconds away from her third orgasm of the night—on her back at the edge of the mattress, hips propped on a pillow, feet braced high on the nearby wall as Karl stood between her legs, gripped her hips in his big hands, and fucked her hard and deep—when he paused, panting.

"You . . ." He sucked in a breath. Rubbed a thumb over the rise of her belly and stared at the spot where his dick stretched her open, his cheeks flushed a deep pink. "You keeping your clit-Roomba in place? Can change positions, if that helps."

He might not be moving anymore, but he was buried to the root inside her while the toy continued sucking away, building the pressure between her legs until sparks flew behind her eyelids. Pretty soon, it wouldn't matter whether he kept thrusting or not, because she'd come either way.

"I'm keeping it in place." With difficulty, since the impact of each penetration and her own arching and grinding had made holding the oval-shaped aperture directly over her clit tricky, but— "Keep going. I'm so close. *Please.*"

She squeezed her eyes shut and mindlessly rocked back and forth, chasing more friction.

Before she tipped over the edge, though, she had to—had to—

"A Roomba moves . . ." She was gasping in between words. "It moves without the need for immediate human guidance. This is more of a . . . a clit-Hoover. It'll stay in . . . in one spot and suck until you . . . until you move it. Just . . . just saying."

Karl's laughter echoed off the bare walls of the tiny bedroom. "Only you, Dearborn. Only you would nitpick shit while getting full-on railed."

After pressing an affectionate kiss to her inner knee, he began fucking her again. With an appreciative moan, she slapped a protective palm over the clit-Hoover still working between her legs and clutched the pillow beside her head with her free hand.

Only moments later, her orgasm lit her like the dawn. Electrified, jubilant, she cried out and let the toy coax every twitch from her tingling flesh as Karl clutched her thigh, shoved as deep inside her as he could, and came with shaking legs and a long, loud groan.

Seeing his pleasure only prolonged hers, and she clenched around him as hard as she could. His hips jerked, and his inhalation hissed through his teeth.

"Holy shit, Molly. *Yes.*" When she opened her eyes, his face was taut in teeth-gritted ecstasy, his body gleaming with sweat in the low light. "*Yes.*"

When she got too sensitive, she removed the toy from her clit, turned it off, and tossed it aside. And when he collapsed into her open arms, she wrapped them around his torso and held him close despite their mutual stickiness.

"Jesus," he eventually mutter-shouted, and brushed a kiss over the shell of her ringing ear. "Never used sex toys on anyone before. That was incredible."

"There's a reason they're called toys." She stroked a hand over his still-heaving flank. "They're fun."

As he laughed again, his face buried in the crook of her neck, the vibration prickled the skin there. "Molly fucking Dearborn. Hottest pedant on the whole damn planet."

She tickled his ribs, and he squirmed and snorted adorably. "How's your back?"

Earlier that evening, her scrutiny had detected an unfamiliar wince on his face whenever he had to twist to reach something. Even now, the muscles along his spine were far too bunched under her skimming palm, when they should be supple in post-orgasmic relaxation.

"I know you were hurting tonight," she added. "Don't bother denying it."

He made a rumbly, dismissive sound in his chest. "It'll be fine. Just standing a lot lately."

In other words, he'd been working extraordinarily long hours to make time for her. Which was his choice, but she hated that he was suffering for it.

"While you deal with the condom, I'll get the massage oil I bought today. I can give you a good rubdown." When he began to object, she cupped his skull and shoved his face harder into her neck, until his protests became indecipherable. "What, you thought you were the only one who liked taking care of your, uh . . ."—what were they, anyway?—"your lover? Wrong, Dean. One hundred percent wrong. As per usual."

Nudging him until he rolled off her and to the side, she smothered his continued bitching with a lingering kiss, then got up, put on his tee, and took care of her post-sex bathroom visit. By the time she got back with the bottle of sweet almond oil in hand, he'd disposed of the condom but not done much else.

Sprawled facedown across the bed, the poor guy looked exhausted.

Since her return to Harlot's Bay, he'd been trying so damn hard. Staying late at the bakery, so they had more hours to spend together on the weekends. Dealing with nosy customers and neighbors and friends and family and protecting her from their scrutiny. Cooking for her. Planning exercises and outings. Catering to her preferences whenever possible. Making her come at least twice as often as he did.

Somehow, even amidst all that effort, he'd still found the time and energy to listen to his family's excited chatter every night, give Charlotte and her kids a ride whenever her parents needed the family car, unofficially cater an erotic book club, and mow his elderly neighbor's lawn at the crack of dawn on Sundays.

He was such a good man, and he would make an excellent life partner. That much she now knew, despite all her hard-won cynicism.

At tonight's weird Pictionary game, each clue had felt like a neon sign pointing toward the obvious: She was a goner for Karl Andrew Dean. And because earnestness was in fact very important, she'd had to admit the anxiety-inducing truth, if only to herself: If he asked her for a long-term commitment, she trusted him—trusted *them*—enough to express herself and say yes.

Hopefully he'd give her the opportunity to tell it to his heart. Sooner rather than later, because her time in Maryland was running out far too quickly. Yesterday, an email from her usual airline had reminded her to reserve her preferred meals on her upcoming flight. She hadn't responded. Kept hoping she wouldn't need to.

Kept hoping he'd talk about a real future together.

But that was a problem for another time. Not now. After all his hard work, Karl deserved her full attention, and she'd give it to him.

Pouring her affection into each stroke of her hands, she took her time with his massage. Rubbed his shoulders and arms and back and thighs, and everywhere else he seemed tense. When he didn't object to oil in his hair, only rumbled in happy-sounding approval, she gave him a scalp rub too, alternating between gentle pressure and firm strokes. At which point he started snoring, exactly as she'd planned.

Doing her best not to jostle him, she settled more comfortably beside his sleeping form and kept kneading until her hands cramped. As soon as she lifted them, though, he woke with a snort.

"Molly? Where the hell—" His arm flailed in an arc, reaching for her, and he sounded half panicked. "There you are."

Using his hold on her forearm, he pulled her down beside him. Then he turned over with a groan that sounded less pained than before and rose up on an elbow. His brown eyes searched her face, a deep line carved between his brows.

"Sorry I fell asleep on you. Felt too good to stay awake." His hairy thigh slid between hers. "Forgive me?"

She shook her head. "I hoped you'd fall asleep. You need your rest."

"So do you." A rough thumb brushed featherlight beneath her right eye. "I see these circles, Dearborn. I kept you up most of last night, and you're tired as hell. Giving me a fucking incredible massage didn't help that shit."

Her eyelids *did* feel spectacularly heavy, but she had her priorities. "I enjoyed taking care of you."

The concern creasing his brow didn't disappear, and his gaze never wavered.

"Want me to return the favor?" His thigh nudged higher, where she was still tender and sensitive. "Or make you come again?"

Smiling, she smoothed a strand of oil-soaked hair back from his temple. "It's a sweet offer. But I think we both need sleep more than anything else right now. Why don't you shower off the oil while I change the sheets?"

"You sure?" His jaw promptly cracked in a wide yawn. "Ignore that. Wide fucking awake. More than happy to finger-blast you into goddamn oblivion."

When he immediately yawned again, she laughed at him. "I'm

sure."

"Fine." Disheveled and grumbling, he heaved himself out of bed, then bent down to kiss her forehead. "Don't change the sheets yet. I'll help you with 'em. Always easier with two."

"Okay," she agreed, then remembered a crucial point as he headed for the stairs. "Be careful! Your feet are slippery!"

He grunted in response, then disappeared down the steps.

After getting out of bed too, she tried to remember where she'd tucked the extra sheets. The tiny third-floor closet, if she wasn't mistaken, so she put on her slippers and prepared to follow him down—only to hear the ding of an incoming text message, then another in rapid succession.

Curious as to who would be texting her so late, she shuffled back over to the tiny bedside table and checked her display.

Azlan, her casual friend and house-renos contractor. Who was on California time, obviously.

Tackling the last of the plumbing issues first thing tomorrow. Anticipate being done by noon. We'll clean up, haul out the construction debris, and be out of your hair by end of day. His second text was brief, but punctuated with a smiley-face emoji. *Welcome back home, Molly!*

Staring down at her screen, she exhaled slowly.

Her heartbeat thudded inside her skull, and her stomach roiled.

The workers had finished right on time, a full week before she was due home. Which was great, right? Impressive, even, given the frequency of construction delays.

Only . . . she wished the whole concept of *home* didn't seem so nebulous to her right now, or its location so unclear. Wished she didn't feel like a hummingbird hovering in midair, ceaselessly flapping her weary wings as she waited for a place to set down and rest.

Suddenly jittery, she opened her browser. Checked her email. Since this morning, a half-dozen unread messages had appeared in her inbox, most of them regarding the literary novel she'd soon begin narrating as Molly Biddenwell.

Her in-home recording booth was excellent and expensive. It was also—as she'd told Athena—modular, specifically built to be easily taken apart, moved, and reassembled. If Karl wanted a future with her, she could get it transported cross-country with relative ease, although she might need to rent recording studio space until it arrived in Harlot's Bay.

But he hadn't asked for a future together. Hadn't even introduced her to his family during the Dean clan's nightly phone calls or their weekly, much-loathed-by-Karl video chats.

Yeah, he'd tried convincing her to stay in town, but without giving her the foundation she'd need to build a life here. Without offering her the assurance of long-term love and commitment that would allow her to leave behind her grandparents' home and her comfortable—albeit lonely—existence out in LA.

She was trying her hardest to have faith that he would, to trust that he hadn't said anything yet because he didn't want to pressure her, or because words were hard for him. Which she knew. Of *course* she knew talking about his feelings pained him. But if he couldn't bring himself to do it anyway, how could she possibly believe what they had together meant as much to him as it did to her? How could she redirect her entire life for a man who hadn't offered her his heart?

And sure, she hadn't mentioned her willingness to move to Maryland for him either. Hadn't mentioned love or lifelong devotion. She'd told him all her secrets, though. Things she'd never shared with another living soul. In every conceivable way, both physical and metaphorical, she'd let him in, and he understood how private she was. Understood how terribly she'd been hurt not all that long ago.

He had to realize what all that meant, right? How much she was already risking for him?

So she needed more from him. She needed him to meet her a few steps past halfway, one final time. She needed him to declare himself first.

And maybe that wasn't reasonable or just. But she'd spent her entire girlhood with a man who'd eventually measured her need for him, his love for her, and clearly found both less powerful than the draw of another family. Then she'd spent seventeen long years trying to be equitable with another man who'd used her remorselessly and tossed her aside the moment he no longer required her presence.

She wouldn't survive someone else who'd count the cost of loving her, of staying by her side, then leave her empty-handed or brokenhearted when she came up short.

No more scales. No more bargains. This time, she wouldn't accept anything less than a heedless, reckless love, entirely free from calculation. A love so overwhelmingly powerful Karl had to express it, even if that meant prying each word from the terrified depths of his soul with the Jaws of freaking Life.

If she got that kind of love from him, she'd move across the country for it. Uproot herself from the only long-term home she'd ever known and take her chances building a new one with a man she hadn't seen for over twenty years, until three short weeks ago.

She'd give and give and give some more. She'd break her damn back for him.

And if she didn't get that kind of love?

She was leaving, because she'd rather fracture her own heart than wait for him do it.

Again, maybe that wasn't fair. But she didn't claim to be fair anymore. Only honest.

24

"$\mathcal{H}$oly *Jesus*," Karl wheezed the following Saturday.

Sounded like someone had punched him in the gut. Felt like that too.

Mouth agape, he watched Molly come down the Spite House stairs to where he was fidgeting in his rental tux near the kitchen table. In the late afternoon sunlight slanting through the over-sink window, her pin-straight hair streamed over her shoulders in a gleaming sheet, her glossy lips shimmered, her blue eyes sparkled, and—

Shit, the rest of her should've burned out his retinas.

She'd actually *done* it. Worn one of those hot-as-hell suits with a low vee in front, no shirt or bra in sight. Her midnight-blue satin jacket and matching high-waisted pants shone from her shoulders to her wrists and ankles, demanding attention without apology. The jacket's lone button held the fabric together beneath her pale, pushed-together breasts, and the whole thing fit like a burnished second skin.

No wonder she'd visited Trollop Tailoring earlier in the week. Elderly Mrs. Bertens deserved a damn medal for her work on the outfit.

The flat soles of Molly's strappy metallic sandals slapped against the final few steps. Then she was there, right in front of him, and his thoughts leapt to middle-school social studies and its Greek mythology unit. For the first time, he wondered whether—in another universe—Medusa had killed men stone-dead like this. Not through snake-haired hideousness. Because of literally petrifying beauty.

He was too afraid to touch her. Didn't want to ruin anything so goddamn perfect.

While he stood there frozen, dry-mouthed, and so fucking in love he might actually die from it, she looked him up and down with clear approval.

"Hey, we match." The observation sounded pleased. "Nice tux, Karl. I genuinely can't believe Athena and Matthew got you into a bow tie." Her fingers skimmed his jaw. "You even trimmed your beard and put on shiny Oxfords. Wowza."

Anything for you, his dazed, dazzled brain silently informed her.

Without a word, he offered her the bouquet he'd hidden behind his back. Ivory calla lilies, bundled together with an eggplant-purple silk ribbon. Elegant. Reserved. Lovely. Just like her.

The corsage and boutonniere followed the reunion's stupid under-the-sea theme. But since she wouldn't be taking this bouquet to the dance, he'd figured he could get her some flowers that actually seemed more her style.

"Oh my goodness, I love these so much!" she exclaimed immediately, and his shoulders loosened. "They're stunning, Karl. Thank you." Smiling happily, she accepted the flowers. Cradled them in her arms and studied them carefully. Caressed a silky petal with a featherlight touch. "Hold on. Before we go, let me get the arrangement in water."

For a minute, she was bustling around the tiny kitchen, searching for a suitable vessel, then filling a glass pitcher with water and arranging the stems artfully inside. Then she turned back to him and stepped close enough to radiate heat.

He still couldn't speak. Could barely breathe.

"For a rental tux, this fits remarkably well." She smoothed a hand down his sleeve. "I'm beyond impressed. You're not just handsome in formal wear, Karl Andrew Dean. You're *dashing*."

At that, his chest strained the small, weird studs fastening his shirt. Yet another accessory the rental place had recommended and charged him for, with Athena's enthusiastic support.

"Th—" He had to clear his throat. Shake himself a little. "Thanks. You . . . that suit . . ."

The way Molly looked tonight? Woman deserved a poet to explain how gorgeous she was. Instead, she had an inarticulate asshole who spent his weekdays in Crocs and a beard net.

Wasn't fair to her. She deserved better.

But he could only do his best, right?

"People make statues of women like you," he told her, voice raw with honesty. "Armies go to war. Men like me wait their whole lives for a single glimpse of something as ridiculously fucking beautiful as you are right now."

She stilled. Stared up at him for a minute while he tried not to die of sheer embarrassment and emotional overexposure.

"Thank you," she said quietly.

Those blue eyes of hers, suddenly bright with tears, damn near slayed him. But if he held her, no way he wouldn't wrinkle her outfit or otherwise screw up all her prep work, so . . .

"Just the simple truth. Shouldn't make you cry." Gently, he tugged at a strand of her hair, trying like hell not to muss it. "Don't make me dry you off with my tuxedo jacket, Dearborn. Hefty security deposit. Plus, this is your moment of triumph, remember?"

She sniffed, then offered him a shaky smile. "Ah, yes. My long-desired opportunity to confront all those extremely stereotypical mean girls and bullies whose opinion meant so very much to me in high school."

"That's the one," he confirmed.

She blinked back the last of her tears, and his incipient panic melted away.

"I see my flowers." Her head tipped toward the pitcher. "I see the limo outside. I see my sexy-bad-boy, hometown-hero date in front of me." She laid her palm on his chest, got up on her tiptoes, and pressed a quick kiss to his mouth, then wiped away any gloss residue with the side of her thumb. "I think we're ready to go."

Even that tiny bit of contact? He'd had orgasms that didn't feel as goddamn good.

"More crap inside the limo." He hitched a thumb toward the window, which showed the fancy-ass car parked by the sidewalk, its uniformed driver patiently waiting nearby. "Everything else on our list."

She'd offered on multiple occasions to pay for half the expenses—and received only an incredulous glare in response every damn time. In the end, thank fuck, she'd dropped the subject and let him take care of everything. Including the final items, put in place only minutes ago.

Cream-colored and soft aqua rose petals were now strewn evenly across the rear limo seats. He'd seen to that himself. Then he and Matthew had rested their corsages and boutonnieres on a lacquered tray back there, ready to be fastened in place as the four of them traveled to the Harlot's Bay High gym.

"Karl . . ." She waved a hand, encompassing his tux, the calla lilies, the limousine. "This is more than enough."

Not for Molly goddamn Dearborn. Not even close. But he wasn't arguing with her when he'd rather be admiring her. Or, even better, stripping that suit off her gorgeous body and—

Nope. Not thinking about that.

Climbing into a shared limo with a hard-on? Inappropriate as hell. Plus, Greydon would never let him hear the end of it. Start calling him Honey Bunches of Cock or some shit.

"Thought we'd ride with Matthew and Athena," he told Molly. "Hope you don't mind."

"Of course not." She smiled at him, grabbed his hand, and headed for the door. "I figured that'd be the plan. And I'm glad you're not having me make my grand reunion entrance alone, despite your teen-movie aspirations."

As if he would ever willingly watch her leave him behind.

They stepped outside. And as he waited for her to fiddle with her sleek clutch purse and lock up behind them, he basked in her presence. Hungrily studied her beautiful sunlit face, something he hadn't been able to do for way the hell too long.

Since Wednesday, he'd spent almost no time with her during daylight hours. Two minutes after he'd opened the bakery that morning, Janel had called. The reunion caterer had backed out unexpectedly over the weekend, leaving her in a bind, and she'd wanted to hire him instead. For the dance, but also the Friday evening picnic on Ladywright College grounds.

He'd wanted to say no. But who else could Janel call at the last minute and be sure the caterers wouldn't screw everything up? No one. Besides, Charlotte and Johnathan had offered to help, and they could use the extra cash.

Coordinating with the two employees had gone better than he'd expected. Both of them worked hard—Jonathan on logistics and food prep, Charlotte on baking under Karl's direct guidance—and didn't complain once, despite their boss's shitty mood.

Still. Molly's final scheduled week in Harlot's Bay, and where was his pathetic ass?

Not holding her tight in bed. Not making her bougie lattes and sandwiches. Not lying on a blanket with her under the autumn sky, napping and talking. Instead, he'd spent three days bent over a stainless-steel table in his overheated, overcrowded, fluorescent-lit back room, giving directions and baking goddamn *canapés*. Like a chump.

His only consolation? Almost every evening that week, once he'd left work, he and Molly had taken a moonlit walk around Historic Harlot's Bay, hand in hand. Because if her blood pressure was getting too high, maybe going outdoors and stretching her legs might help. And yeah, Molly might've insisted on giving him a rubdown each night and refused to let him return the favor, despite his protests—but he'd bought her a crap ton of lavender-scented spa shit so she could take a long bath and relax right before bed too.

In case that didn't work, he'd also been doing his best to wear her out with orgasms. Hands, mouth, dick, toys, whatever combo it took. She said all that coming helped her sleep better. Also made him feel like a damn king, so win-fucking-win.

Last night, though, they hadn't even gotten their walk. Barely exchanged a private word. She'd spent the whole evening helping him, Charlotte, and Johnathan dole out the prepared food at the picnic while she made casual chitchat with their former classmates. By the time they'd cleaned up and made it back to his house, neither of them had the energy to do anything but collapse directly into bed. And in the morning, he hadn't wanted to disturb her restless sleep, so he'd left for the bakery in the predawn darkness as quietly as possible.

Without even a quick goodbye hand job. It was a fucking travesty.

"Hey!" Athena's cheerful voice called from the street. "You two look amazing!"

Reluctantly, he tore his gaze from Molly. Spared a nod for Athena and Matthew, who'd emerged from their home and were walking toward the limo, arm in arm.

His best friend's tux, black and classic, made him resemble James Bond—but only if double-oh-seven preferred reading medical texts and contemplating his life choices to killing international assholes and banging double agents. Athena shone like a sun against her husband's night sky, all blond hair, bright red lipstick, and an even brighter grin. Her yellow-flowered, flowing dress rippled around her ankles as she walked, revealing . . . yep. Keds.

Both of them looked great. Glowing with happiness. One glance established that much.

After that glance, his attention returned to Molly as she tucked away her keys, strolled down the alleyway, and greeted her new friends.

He didn't follow. He knew Athena pretty damn well by this point, and no one was going anywhere until outfits had been admired and gossip exchanged. Besides, appreciating Molly's tight suit in motion, her unbound breasts subtly bouncing in the deep, open vee of the jacket, her ass swaying in midnight-blue satin, wasn't something he intended to rush.

The main reason he didn't move, though? Pure indecision.

Anytime he had a free moment—which hadn't happened much this week—his mind arrowed straight to the same problem.

Two days. Two short days until Molly's flight left for LAX. And neither of them had uttered a single word about that fast-approaching deadline.

Athena and Matthew kept saying he needed to broach the subject himself. But in Karl's defense, he and Molly had *felt* like a committed couple for a while now. Even if she left on Monday, they'd sure as hell date long-distance. Right?

That had to be enough. They didn't need to talk specifics yet.

Even though not knowing what happened next was driving him goddamn *bananas*.

As Molly and Matthew gabbed about something or other, Athena caught Karl's attention with a wave, bugged out her eyes, and mouthed, *Tell. Her.*

He flipped her off but kept churning through the mental possibilities. Because . . . if he and Molly *were* going to have a totally unnecessary define-the-relationship talk? Tonight would be the time. Middle-aged prom—as Molly called it—would be the place.

For the first time in two decades, they'd be back at Harlot's Bay High, where everything started for them. And if he laid all his cards on the table?

Might be where everything ended for them too.

Or . . . where their future began.

"Fuck my fucking life," he grunted, and stomped toward the limo.

25

One step inside the crowded school gym, Karl halted abruptly. "What the hell?"

For the first time since Molly came down the stairs in that shit-hot suit, he wasn't devoting at least half his attention to her bared cleavage. Or wallowing in the gut-deep satisfaction he got every time he spotted the bizarro corsage he'd slipped on her wrist, with its crystal-studded starfish and what appeared to be tiny metallic and aqua-lacquered Pepperidge Farm Goldfish crackers nestled among the ivory mini roses. Or glancing down at his matching boutonniere and wondering how to keep his family from ever seeing him wearing that thing, because he'd never hear the end of it.

Latoria was talented, but also a goddamn menace.

Much like whoever had decorated this gym, because *Jesus H. Christ.*

Athena's sharp elbow moved him aside and out of the gym doorway, and the other three members of the party joined him inside the room. Then drifted to a stop almost immediately, as soon as they caught sight of the weird-ass shit awaiting them all.

"This is . . ." Matthew trailed off, agape, then tried again. "I don't . . ."

"Oh, wow." Eyes shining, lips parted, Athena turned in a slow circle and surveyed the dimly lit space. "This is *incredible.*"

"Yeeees," her husband said slowly. "In the sense that it's very difficult to believe someone did this."

If Karl wasn't mistaken, a song from the *Titanic* soundtrack was playing over the loudspeakers. Which would normally be romantic, but in this room? Beyond fucking macabre.

"Hey, everyone." Lise suddenly appeared at Molly's side, wearing a dark-green dress that could've come from a Ren Faire. "You're finally here!"

"Unfortunately," Matthew muttered.

Lise waved a hand at their surroundings. "Janel tells me Victor Diab and the other science nerds on the reunion committee took charge of themed decorations. Which may help to explain what you're seeing."

"I'm not sure a sufficient explanation exists for the choices made here tonight, Lise. But thank you for trying." Molly's tone was so dry, it would've killed most of the creatures inhabiting the gym, back when they were alive.

They weren't alive anymore, as far as Karl could tell, but . . .

Holy shit, please let them not be alive.

Diab—a marine biology professor at Ladywright College— and his pals had clearly taken the "Under the Sea" theme and *run* with it.

Actually, no. Screw that. The word *run* was inadequate as hell.

Armed with their favorite theme, those overenthusiastic nerds had *sprinted* into the horizon like marathoners on fucking speed, directly into an aquatic nightmare of horror-movie proportions, then sprinted some more.

Shifting blue lights illuminated the large room. Instead of streamers, brownish-green kelp dangled along the walls, arranged in wide swoops. Hanging from the ceiling? Not a mirror ball. Not balloons. Horrifying blobby fish, who looked like the mutated offspring of a terrible nuclear accident. Pissed-off, powerfully built orcas ramming model yachts. Clawed, beady-eyed crustaceans. Sea snakes with beaky noses and fangs that glistened whenever spotlights passed their way. Other creatures with spiny protrusions and huge, sightless eyes—or no eyes at all—and way, *way* too many goddamn teeth.

Crooked teeth. Needle-sharp.

"Holy shit," Karl muttered. "Thought there'd be coral and frilly-ass fish, not the open-water equivalents of Charles fucking Manson."

"When she sat down to design deep-sea creatures, Mother Nature was clearly going through some stuff." Molly squeezed his arm, sounding amused. "Or so it seems."

Lise followed their gaze. "Completely accurate reproductions of the committee's chosen species, according to Janel."

Reproductions? Meant *never alive*. Thank fuck.

Although the gym did kind of smell like a day-old seafood platter. Probably the kelp. Hopefully the kelp.

"From what I know, everything is spot-on." Wide-eyed and grinning, Athena looked *enthralled*. "This whole freaking display is stupendous. I can't even imagine how much time the committee spent getting everything just right. Not to mention money."

Lise lifted a shoulder. "Victor won the lottery a few years back. Drives the same beat-up Honda. Lives in the same small house. I guess he needed to spend his cash on something?"

"And he chose lifelike nightmares of the deep." Molly thought about that for a moment. "Huh."

"Have you seen the cakes yet?" Karl asked Lise, his curiosity piqued to hell and back. "Got no idea what they look like, since I don't do sculpted illusion shit. Told Janel she'd have to go somewhere else for that."

Stationed next to those cakes—assuming Janel had found a baker to tackle them—and hidden behind crowds of former classmates, Charlotte, Bez, and Johnathan should have already set up the first round of refreshments. He'd check on 'em soon enough. No hurry.

During the last few days of working side by side, including at the picnic, they'd more than demonstrated their fundamental good sense and trustworthiness. Plus, they knew his cell number. Understood they could call if they needed him. Had urged him to forget about work and enjoy himself with Molly.

Normally, he'd help them anyway. But since Molly was maybe—possibly—leaving in two days? His catering team was on its own tonight, unless everything went to shit.

"There are two cakes on offer." Lise held up a finger. "One huge barracuda. Its razor-sharp teeth are apparently very convincing sugar work and have already required the procurement of a box of bandages." A second finger. "And one enormous eel. Complete with a mucus layer comprised of lime-flavored gelatinous slime. At least one alum has thrown up in a trash can after seeing the eel." She paused, and the faint sound of gagging drifted from the far corner of the gym. "Make that two alums."

Molly winced, while Athena gave a long, low whistle and Karl contemplated the possible flavors of the actual cake. If he'd baked it? White chocolate, maybe. Real cherry filling. Lime zest-vanilla frosting. Lime mucus on top, possibly made with either gelatin or sweetened, condensed milk, cornstarch, and food coloring.

Might have to make that next week's cake special. Minus the goo.

"I can't look away," Matthew whispered, eye-to-terrified-eye with the nearest toothy demon-fish. "Athena, save me."

Fuck. Karl had forgotten his best friend's utter lack of chill when it came to scary shit. Before he could do anything to help, though, Athena sprang into action.

"Did someone say my—oh!" Startled out of her dazed wonderment, she whirled to face her husband. "Babe, I'm so sorry. I wasn't thinking. Are you okay?"

He opened his mouth. Closed it again. Offered her a weak smile.

"We'll go." With a gentle hand on his arm, she began steering him back toward the door. "Say good night to everyone, Dr. Vine, because we're leaving. I'll send the limo back once we're home."

He gave their group a shaky wave but lodged a faint protest as he and Athena stepped out into the hall. "Sweetheart, we can stay. I know you wanted—"

"I know what I want right this second." Her rapid strides didn't falter, and her voice grew fainter as they moved farther away. "Namely, for my husband not to avoid every body of water larger than a toilet from now on. So we're done here."

"Well." Lise watched the couple depart. "I'd ask if it was something I said, but there's just no out-traumatizing unexpectedly bloodthirsty marine life."

"They're truly the GOATs when it comes to inflicting emotional damage." Molly's voice remained dead solemn. "Even though they're not mammals."

Lise giggled merrily, and Molly cracked a smile too before turning to Karl. "Remind me to text Athena later tonight to check on Matthew, okay?"

"Got it." Fishing his phone from an interior jacket pocket, he set his timer and sent his own quick message to Matthew: *Should've noticed your suffering sooner. Sorry, man.*

Matthew wrote back immediately. *No worries. Have fun tonight.:-*

) A brief pause. *Athena says to—and I quote—"Pull up your big boy underpants and use your words, Special K."* Karl was halfway through typing his response when Matthew texted again: *P.S. Please know that I will *not* tell my wife to go fuck herself, so don't bother writing it.*

Karl deleted his message-in-progress, grumbling all the while, and put away his phone. When he glanced up again, Lise was eyeing him.

"Why don't you go admire the cakes and check in with your staff while Molly and I visit Janel?" Reading his mutinous expression correctly, she held up a hand. "I know you don't want Molly too far away, but I was told to bring her by for a chat or suffer the consequences."

"I did promise to talk with her tonight." Molly patted his arm, looking faintly apologetic. "I'll meet you by the cakes. I promise not to be long. Okay?"

"Fine," he grumbled.

He hated crowds. Hated casual chitchat with near strangers even more. But Lise was right—he should go check on his crew and see if they needed help.

Lise's neck twisted as she scanned the room. "Also, I see Sylvia near the DJ, taking photos for next week's paper. In case you want to avoid her."

Occasional pictures didn't faze him. Getting grilled again about his nonexistent ties to organized crime and whether Sweeney Todd and Hannibal Lecter would've given Karl's baked goods two severed-and-ground-into-burger-meat-thumbs up? *That* shit got annoying.

"Thanks for the heads-up, Lise." He leaned over and pressed a kiss to the elegant shell of Molly's ear, where he couldn't mess up any makeup she might've applied. "See you by the cakes, Dearborn."

After Molly gave him one last smile, the two women left him alone in the aquatic horrorscape their high school gym had become. Grumpily, he edged his way around clumps of excitedly chattering people, a good chunk of them his customers, and headed for the refreshments setup in the back right corner of the room.

When he finally got there after two pointless conversations about the goddamn weather, Bez was describing the food offerings to a reunion attendee wearing an expensive-looking suit—was that chemistry-class Ned?—while Charlotte and Johnathan brought out more trays of Gruyère-packed gougères, bacon-topped deviled eggs, mini quiches with various fillings, raspberry-brie bites in puff pastry, crudités and dips, and cookies decorated like seaweed.

In retrospect, the latter should've been Karl's first clue things were gonna be odd tonight.

There was more food too, back in the school-cafeteria staging area and walk-in cooler. All of it was delicious. And for once, that wasn't solely due to him.

"How's it going?" He took a heavy tray from Charlotte and placed it on the long, cloth-covered table himself. "Problems?"

"Not even one." Pausing, she blew a stray strand of pale hair from her eyes. "Nothing damaged in transport. No complaints from partygoers and lots of compliments. We're a well-oiled machine with all our supplies in place, boss."

Her skin was a bit flushed from exertion, and tiredness had her looking her actual age for once. But she was . . . huh.

Sounded stupid, but she was *glowing*. Back straight, chin high, *brimming* with self-assurance in a way he'd never seen.

He examined her, curious about the transformation. "Anything you need from me?"

"We're great." A nudge of her finger straightened a display sign listing the quiche filling options, ingredients, and allergens. "But thanks, Karl."

Her sharp-eyed survey of the table had a proprietary air. That unmistakable mixture of bone-deep pride and dogged determination to catch and fix whatever might go wrong before anyone else spotted it.

Same thing he felt every time he walked into his damn bakery. *Ownership.*

"You *like* doing this shit," he said slowly, shocked by the realization. "Charlotte, I—"

"Karl?" A polished fingernail tapped his arm. "There you are."

He turned on his heel to find . . . Becky. In a slim-cut, champagne-colored dress and matching heels. No corsage, because yeah, this wasn't actually prom. Even though it kind of felt like it.

"Janel said you were here." She beamed up at him, her blond hair braided into a pretty crown atop her head. "I've been searching for you."

She looked almost exactly the same as twenty years ago. But when he studied her, he couldn't drum up any of the old longing. Not even any of the old affection. The last faint lick of attraction had faded over fifteen years ago, and it wasn't coming back.

Even the hurt had gone now. The embarrassment too. Something about confessing to Molly had sealed the edges of that particular wound, and seeing Becky didn't reopen it.

He had not one goddamn ounce of desire to talk to her. But since he tried to be a decent human being—"Hey, Becky. How are you?"

"Good. Still in Baltimore, still a mortgage broker." The tip of her fingernail brushed one of his shirt studs. "And at the moment, I'm having trouble believing my eyes. *Karl Dean* rocking a tuxedo? I wouldn't have predicted that. Not in a million years."

No way he was discussing his prom-redux plan with her. So he just grunted, because what the hell else could he actually say in response? *Yeah, turns out my body doesn't physically reject fancy clothing, even though I don't usually wear this shit?*

"I would've expected you to be fidgeting, but you seem incredibly comfortable." She was still marveling. Still talking as her fingertips smoothed over the deep blue lapel of the jacket, then traced the fragile petals of the rose in his boutonniere. "Confident, even. I'm impressed."

Was he supposed to thank her for acknowledging that he wasn't a total disaster in formal wear, despite her expectations?

"Yeah." He took a big step back, hoping that'd quash all her weird touchy-feely shit. "Rental place made sure everything fit well. Starch in the shirt collar's itchy, but otherwise? Comfortable enough."

She nodded but didn't seem like she was really listening. "I was hoping to talk to you, Karl. Do you have a minute?"

When he craned his neck, he was hoping to spot Molly's approach, or even a disaster-in-progress at the refreshments table. But . . . nope. No Molly. No issues to solve.

"I guess." Scowling, he followed her to a quiet spot along the far wall of the gym, near a pissed-looking anglerfish. "What's up?"

A flash blinded him, rapidly followed by another.

When he'd blinked the spots away, he saw Sylvia moving toward her next victim. Which meant Saturday's paper might feature a photo of him cozied up in a private spot with Becky, who was standing far too close. The last thing he wanted, for a million reasons.

The nosy-ass people of Harlot's Bay were one thousand god-damn percent going to start bugging him about whether he and Becky were together again. If Molly left, they'd figure she'd gone because he was reuniting with his ex and hassle him about *that* too.

Bad enough. But way fucking worse? If Molly saw the picture, she might think something she shouldn't. Especially given her personal history.

The next time Sylvia came by for a latte, he would be leaving his workroom, having a private conversation with her, and taking care of the problem. Even if it meant offering her the exclusive interview she'd been haranguing him about for weeks.

"—owe you a long-belated apology," Becky said, because apparently she'd begun talking at some point. "When I ended things way back when, I was cruel, and I'm ashamed of what I said to you. My only excuse is that I was a dumb kid who didn't know how to tell you 'I need to see more of the world before I settle down with anyone.' And to make the break feel easier, I convinced myself we should split up because you weren't enough for me. But the reality is that *no one* would've been enough for me, because *I* needed to become more than I was. I'm so sorry."

He blinked at her, stunned by the unexpected apology.

Sounded sincere. Not just nice, but also honest and . . . yeah, *kind*.

"Now here we are, twenty years later. I've finally wised up, and from everything I hear, you're still the same person you've always been: a hardworking, successful man who cares about his family and his community. A *good* man." Her mouth twisted into a sad smile. "I've found that if you hitch your star to someone who's *not* a good man . . . sooner or later, he won't be good to you either."

That was the voice of painful experience, and he wished like hell she hadn't learned her lessons the hard way. But—

"And we always had great chemistry, didn't we?" She sucked in a deep breath, hands trembling slightly, and moved in a step closer. "So I was wondering . . ."

At long last, there was Molly, only a half-dozen steps away, her eyes on them. Only—why was she turning around and angling toward the refreshments table instead?

"Molly!" he shouted. "Over here, woman!"

She swiveled on her heel and headed their way again, taking her damn time about it.

"Sorry to interrupt," he told Becky, whose soft, pink lips had formed a tight line. "Promised her we'd dance as soon as she got done talking to Janel."

Her shoulders rose and fell in a silent sigh. "You and Molly, huh?"

"Yeah." He certainly fucking hoped so. "First time she's been back in twenty years, but . . . yeah."

"Oh, wow." Becky snorted, shaking her head ruefully. "My timing is the freaking *worst*."

"I guess," he said, not really following the conversation. "Appreciate the apology, Becky. All the kind words too."

When she asked for forgiveness, apparently she liked to sweeten the pot with compliments. He'd have accepted the apology either way, though.

That sad smile returned. "I'm glad, Karl."

They both watched Dearborn's approach. When Molly finally arrived at the semi-private spot along the wall, Becky held out a hand in greeting before he could say anything.

Her voice was friendly, her chin tipped high. "Good to see you again, Molly."

"Likewise." Molly accepted the handshake, smiling pleasantly. "How are you, Becky?"

"I've been better, but I've certainly been worse too. Thank you for asking." Becky's arm dropped to her side, and she studied Molly's suit for a moment. "I hear Karl owes you a dance, so I'll get out of your hair."

Karl nodded. "See you around."

"That's not necessary," Molly told her at the exact same moment.

"It really is, Molly." Becky huffed out a soft laugh. "I'm going to grab a slice of eel cake out of sheer morbid curiosity. Take care, you two." She paused, already mid-turn, and spoke over her shoulder. "I always had a feeling you'd get together sooner or later, and I guess I was right. Didn't think it would take quite this long, but . . ."

Becky disappeared once more into the crowd.

"*Finally.*" He grabbed Molly's hand. "Let's dance, Dearborn."

When he tugged, though, she didn't move an inch. Her expression was that serene mask he hated, but he could read her eye crinkles now. She was upset, or at least worried.

"For fuck's sake, don't tell me you think—" he began.

She held up a hand. "I know you weren't flirting with her. You might not be the world's suavest man, but as I've seen for myself, even you have better game than *that*."

Good she at least trusted him not be her father. Still, *something* was clearly wrong. He watched her warily, waiting for the other shoe to drop.

Once he ran out of patience, he prompted, "But . . ."

"But I . . . I can . . ." Her jaw ticked, a faint tell. "I can bow out if you want."

For two heartbeats, he couldn't do anything but *gape* at her, unable to understand what the hell she was even talking about. Then he somehow managed to parse her bullshit, at which point he nearly lost his goddamn mind.

"*What?*" he shouted, throwing his hands in the air and ignoring another way-too-bright flash of light from the side.

Her voice lowered to a hushed whisper. "She's local, unlike me—"

"She lives in *Baltimore*," he snarled, incensed.

"—and pretty, and smart, and clearly into you again." Her shoulder hitched in a jerky shrug. "You could do way worse, Karl. That's all I'm saying."

In the white stillness of another blinding flash-burst, he envisioned it. A future without Molly. A life with Becky or one of the other women in this room, who were all—yeah, okay—pretty enough. Some of them were even beautiful. Smart too. Friendly. Funny. Kind.

But they weren't *Molly*. None of them made him feel like Molly did, and always had.

Even if one of them wanted him—doubtful, despite Molly's claim about Becky—he didn't want *them*, and he certainly didn't *need* them the way he needed Molly fucking Dearborn, who was slipping through his fingers with each moment that passed.

He had to say something. Had to fix this shitshow, ASAP.

"Come with me," he told her, and she didn't resist this time as he marched them away from the wall, hand in hand. Didn't question him as he forged a path through the crowds, to the gym's entry, then down one dimly lit hall after another, until he'd reached their old homeroom.

It was unlocked, which was a mistake on the school's part—chances of drunk people banging in here later tonight were damn near one hundred percent—but handy for his purposes. Which might or might not include some non-drunken banging of his own, depending on how the next few minutes went.

Moonlight illuminated the classroom, so he didn't flip the light switch before closing the door behind them. Did flip the deadbolt, because they needed privacy for this conversation.

Palm sweaty against hers, heart thudding against his rib cage like it was trying to escape, he gathered all his courage and forced the words from his reluctant throat, one by one.

"Stay," he told her. "*Stay* in Harlot's Bay, Molly. *Please.*"

26

*E*verything Molly wanted, so damn much it terrified her, was almost within her grasp. She and Karl were finally—*finally*—discussing what a future together might look like.

To be fair, it wasn't the first time he'd mentioned wanting her to stay in Harlot's Bay. Two weeks ago, after their steamy bakery encounter, he'd raised the topic. Back then, though, she hadn't been ready to throw her life into upheaval for him. Hadn't trusted either him or her own heart enough to make that leap.

Circumstances had changed. So had she.

At this moment, there was only one more thing she needed to know, needed to *hear*, before she let herself tumble heart-first into a commitment with a man she'd never forgotten, but had reunited with less than one month ago. And his near-trembling intensity, the pleading shine in his intent brown eyes, finally gave her the courage to address her last remaining uncertainty.

The single word took all her bravery. "Why?"

Before she dug out the fragile roots of her life in LA and transplanted herself into fresh soil a continent away, she needed to know she'd be safe. Sheltered from inevitable droughts by his love, not simply left to wither in the unforgiving sun on her own. Because she could do that in Los Angeles, quite easily, no move required.

"W—" He drew back a fraction of an inch. "*Why?*"

How in the world could he sound so startled, when it was the most obvious question in the world?

"Yes. *Why*." Her fingers felt numb against his, and her blood pressure was probably through the freaking roof. "Why should I stay?"

He shifted his weight. Started to say something. Hesitated. Then—after one last, convulsive squeeze—loosened his grip on her damp-palmed hand.

In that moment, the balance of her emotions tilted away from hope. So she was braced, fortunately enough, when the words he finally dredged up weren't anything like what she so desperately needed from him.

"You've been lonely in LA. Got friends here." His throat bobbed in a swallow. "Lise. Athena. Uh . . . Janel, maybe?"

Lise, her closest friend, did in fact live here. But— "Are you under the impression I don't have *any* casual friendships in Los Angeles? Not a single connection I could cultivate, if I wanted to?"

And what about Karl himself? Did she not have a friend in *him*?

For that matter, hadn't the two of them built something far beyond friendship? But if they had, why wasn't he telling her so, or listing their relationship as a reason for her to stay?

"Don't need to *cultivate* anything with Lise," he pointed out. "Work from home too. Nothing for your job keeping you out there."

Okay, yeah. Being an audiobook narrator didn't require a specific location, and she could transport and reassemble her studio with relative ease. Being physically near Lise, her most prolific author, might even make certain things less complicated, professionally speaking. In general, though, there were way more entertainment-industry opportunities in Los Angeles. He knew that, right?

She withdrew her hand completely. Let it drop to her side,

empty. "If I ever decided to pursue voice-over work, living in semi-rural Maryland wouldn't serve me well."

Voice-over work didn't particularly interest her at the moment, but whatever. That might change.

Besides, did he expect her to haul her entire life across an entire fucking continent just because her job *allowed* for that? Like she was a restless kid in her early twenties with a futon and a bean bag chair, rather than a nearly forty-year-old woman with a king-size bed and a freaking *dinette set*, whose stress levels already had her doctor worried?

His hand reached for hers again. Fell.

"Yeah, but—" He rocked back on his heels, deep lines carved across his forehead. "Housing's way damn cheaper in Harlot's Bay. Could buy something new. No renos needed."

Because she wouldn't be living with him, apparently.

Just what the hell did he think they were doing here?

Suddenly, her remaining store of patience vanished, and she laid it out for him as bluntly as she could. "So I'd have friends. Work. Cheap housing." She stared at him meaningfully, begging him with her eyes to give her what she needed. "What about *you?*"

"I'd—" He paused then, chest expanding, and a flicker of hope reignited in her own chest. Then he deflated again. His voice barely audible in the still, moonlit classroom, he muttered, "I'd be here too."

For once, he'd managed something quieter than a shout. Unfortunately, though, the content of his answer—the emotion it expressed—was as faded and threadbare as its sound.

She squeezed her eyes shut for a moment, gathering herself.

What he was offering? It wasn't enough.

Only an utter fool would move cross-country for a man who'd

never said he loved her or even that he wanted a future together. And she'd already been a fool for two men in her life.

How did the saying go? First time, shame on him. Second time, shame on her.

Her mental addendum?

Third time, not fucking happening.

"I—" Her heart wasn't literally at her feet, broken. But it sure felt like it. "I appreciate the invitation. But I can't say."

To her credit, her voice didn't shake. She wasn't crying. She even conjured up a slight smile of thanks. Gratitude for his kindness in asking her to stay, even though she hadn't wanted kindness from him in this moment. Only love.

The sort of love she could rely upon for a lifetime. The sort of love she'd never had from a man, and probably never would.

"Yeah. Okay." Karl's chin dropped, and he scowled at the floor like it owed him money. Hands clenched into fists, all jutting knuckles and bulging veins, he remained silent for a few seconds. "Figured. No big deal."

It was no big deal to him whether she stayed or left?

All the raging emotion she was seeing in him must only be damaged pride, then. Lovely.

"No big deal," she echoed, and turned for the door. "Shall we get back to the party?"

"Why the fuck not?" His voice was gravel-rough, and he rounded her to unlock the door and enter the hall first. "No goddamn reason to linger, right?"

She kept a careful distance as they walked. Held herself slightly too far away to touch. Studied the passing lockers and swallowed back the emotion blurring her gaze.

"Right," she said finally, her tone unperturbed, as they neared the gym.

And when the crowd swept them in two separate directions, she didn't fight the tide. She simply let herself be carried far, far away.

* * *

DUE TO MOLLY'S extraordinary efforts at avoidance, tracking her down took Lise an entire hour. At long last, however, Molly's best friend managed to find her in the bathroom farthest from the actual reunion, where she'd hoped to erase any sign of tears in absolute privacy.

Lise let the door swing shut behind her, propped her butt against a white porcelain sink, and passed Molly a clean tissue. "Want a hug?"

"Not right now." An embrace would break her, and she needed to get through the rest of the evening with believable aplomb. The acting job of a freaking lifetime. "Thanks, though."

Lise didn't look offended.

"What's going on, Mol?" When her head tipped in inquiry, strands of her wavy brown hair brushed her half-bared shoulder. "Karl's slapping hors d'oeuvres down on plates like they personally insulted his mother's virtue, and his vocabulary currently contains two—and only two—categories: various forms of the word *fuck* and curt descriptions of quiches. And here you are, putting on your brave face in your sexy suit all by yourself, on the other side of the damn school, even though you're leaving that man's very fine ass in two days. Something's clearly amiss, so you might as well tell me about it."

Molly couldn't remember the last time she'd worked through a problem by talking it over with someone. But her old way of doing things had only given her insomnia and high blood pressure, so maybe it was time to proceed a little differently.

"I, uh . . ." Using the side of a knuckle, she brushed away another disobedient tear. "I'm going to warn you now: This is the most late-nineties-teen-movie crap ever, which serves me right. I should've never agreed to Karl's cockamamie plan."

"I've hereby been warned. Bring it on." Lise waggled her brows and held up her hand for a high-five. "Get it? *Bring It On?*"

"That came out in 2000," Molly told her, reluctantly amused, but high-fived her friend anyway. "Okay. So . . ."

Over the course of the next ten minutes, she spilled everything in a way she hadn't done since before her dad left. About halfway through, Lise ushered them both into a dark classroom so they could sit, but she brought a bundle of paper towels with her, because she was a very forward-thinking individual. And once the tale had been told, Molly blew her nose on one of the paper towels while she mopped her eyes with another.

Single-ply. Way too rough for these purposes. There'd be no hiding her distress after this, unless she fled from the classroom directly into the dark night. Which would also be very teen movie of her, but more the horror iterations than the romcom ones. Because, come on: a fat, haughty female character crying and running from a school dance after having engaged in recent sexual escapades? She'd be freaking *doomed*.

Kind of how she felt already, to be honest.

"This is purely a pragmatic question." Lise stacked her forearms on the back of the orange plastic chair she was straddling, then plonked her chin on top. "Why haven't you just . . . left the party? Taken the limo and gone home to the Spite House, then sent the driver back for Karl?"

The question sounded casual. Lise's eyes on Molly, though, were as sharp as the tacks securing various announcements to the classroom bulletin board.

"I guess . . ." With a sigh, Molly mirrored her friend's pose. "I guess I thought maybe he'd come after me, and we'd talk more. Fix things. Which probably isn't going to happen, but the idea of leaving without him feels *wrong* somehow."

Lise didn't mince words. "Because you love him and want to stay with him."

There was no point pretending, was there? Not when Lise already knew her far too well and wouldn't hurt her with the truth anyway.

"Yes. I love him." Unfortunately for her. "Too bad he doesn't love *me*. At least, not enough to tell me so in words."

"So you and Karl are spending the evening within easy distance of each other but functionally apart, even though you're leaving on Monday," Lise summarized. "The two of you haven't officially broken up, but you're not officially together either, and you never were. Thus, both of you are miserable at reunion-prom, neither of you appears to have any clue how to rectify said misery, and now I'm the fat, funny bestie swooping in to give you the sage advice that'll fix everything."

Lise's headshake was rueful. "You're right. This *is* the most late-nineties-teen-movie crap ever. So much"——she did a creditable set of jazz hands——"*drama.*"

"Thank for you for saying I'm right. You know I live for that." Molly's nose was still running, and she dabbed at it with a fresh paper towel. "I'm fat too, though. I mean, *legitimately* fat. Not what the media back then tried to make us *believe* was fat, like Kate Winslet or whoever. Anyway, my own genuine fatness isn't very nineties-teen-movie-main-character of me, and I apologize for the discrepancy."

Lise waved a dismissive hand. "Kate and I hereby accept your apology."

"Very gracious of you both." Sighing, Molly laid her cheek on her forearm. "Here's the thing, Lise. I'm sure your counsel will be wise beyond your teenage years, but I doubt even the sagest advice could fix everything that's wrong at this point."

"Maybe not." Lise smiled sympathetically at her. "How about I give it my best shot anyway?"

"Go . . ." Molly's nose was stuffed up from crying, and she twisted away to blow it on a paper towel before turning back to Lise. "Go right ahead."

Lise raised a finger. "My turn to issue a warning: I'm about to go Socratic on your stubborn ass."

"Not the worst thing that's ever been done to it." Molly shrugged tiredly. "My first—and last—foray into kink with Rob featured the least sexy spanking of a consenting adult woman in human history."

"I don't want to know." Lise paused. "Actually, that's a lie. I do want to know, but we have other matters to address beforehand. Namely, my first question: What's more valuable to you, what Karl says or what he actually does?"

Molly knew where that line of argument was going, but whatever. She'd follow the path regardless, because she couldn't currently see any other way forward. "I've loved two men who said all the right things and left me anyway, so actions are definitely more important to me than words. And Karl does in fact behave like a man who loves me, no matter what he does or doesn't say. I've never had anyone work so hard to meet my needs and make me happy."

"I know there's a *but* coming." Lise's lips suddenly quivered, and she bit back a smile. "Much like when I'm writing the final sex scene in one of my books."

Molly had to laugh. "There is, in fact, a *but* coming. No lube required." Sobering, she told her friend, "Actions are more important to me, like I said, but they aren't enough to make me fundamentally alter my life for someone again, much less trust them with my heart. Not by themselves."

"Why not?"

"I'm a woman of words, Lise." She had no better explanation to offer than that. "I need them."

"Huh." Lise mulled that over for a moment. "So you, Molly Dearborn, are a woman of words. Interesting. How often would you say you speak about your own emotions, then?"

Stupid Socrates. Squirming uncomfortably in her seat, Molly directed a heartfelt scowl her best friend's way and struggled in vain to find a non-damning answer.

When Molly didn't respond, Lise offered prompts. "Do you speak about your emotions all the time? Frequently? Some of the time? Never, except on this very singular occasion, when I actually caught you crying in a high school bathroom, and even then, I could tell you were tempted to say you'd been yanking out nose hairs in the mirror instead of wallowing in Febreze-scented heartbreak?"

Molly's middle finger rose without her conscious permission. "You know the answer."

"I sure do." Lise shook her head. "You and Karl are two of a kind, babe."

Socratic method be damned, *that* couldn't be true. "I issue far fewer threats of violence."

"Sure," Lise acknowledged. "But between the two of you, who's more likely to actually murder someone?"

"Fair point." Molly sat up straighter. "In my defense, whomever I offed would deserve it."

"Naturally." Idly, Lise drummed her fingers on the chair back. "Here's what I'm wondering, Mol. You're a self-proclaimed woman of words. How sure are you that Karl isn't a *man* of words?"

Molly started laughing so hard she almost cried again.

"Karl?" she finally managed to choke out. "You think Karl 'Pronouns and Complete Sentences Are Like Unto Death for Me' Dean is a *man of words?*"

"From what I gather, he listens to your audiobooks every morning in the bakery, for hours at a time. Just to hear your voice. Endless words and sentences and pages, one after another." There was no levity in Lise's gaze anymore. No indication she didn't mean every word she was saying. "Maybe he's not an all-occasion man of words. But he might be a man of *your* words, Molly."

At that, all of Molly's amusement vanished too. Because her best friend's endgame was now becoming clear, and—

Lise rolled on, relentless. "Maybe he needs three words from *you* before he can bring himself to ask for a commitment or declare his own love."

And there it was. The suggestion that Molly reveal her feelings first. Lay her heart on the line once again, despite the battering it'd taken only two short years ago, without any verbal assurance of her devotion being returned.

"I don't know . . ." Her throat hurt. From swallowed tears. From fear. "I don't know if I can give him those three words."

"I think you can give—and *do* give—far more than you realize,

Molly." Lise graced her with a down duvet of a smile, the expression so warm Molly couldn't help relaxing under its comforting weight. "And one thing *I* know for sure? That man is freaking oblivious when it comes to spotting women's feelings for him."

Lise's chair screeched on the smooth tile floor as she scooted it slightly closer. And even though the two women were utterly alone in a dark classroom, she lowered her voice to a whisper, as if sharing a deep, dark secret. "I mean, did you watch Becky make her move? Short of borrowing the DJ's microphone and declaring to our entire graduating class that she wanted the local baker to thrust his spotted dick inside her cream horn—"

Molly wrinkled her nose. "Ugh."

"—while she got her ladyfingers on those hot, round buns of his, she couldn't have made her interest much more obvious. But I don't think he even realized she was taking her shot at him."

That was the sense Molly had gotten too, although she hadn't been certain—and she hadn't wanted to presume a lack of interest on his part. Because how could she know what he might want, when he wouldn't freaking *tell* her?

Of course, he could say the same thing about her. Which she wished Lise hadn't pointed out with such persuasive conviction.

"Like I said: That. Man. Is. Oblivious." Lise's voice returned to its normal volume. "So if you don't express your love—preferably in words of a single syllable—he'll never know, babe. This isn't a situation where he suspects how you feel and can't match those feelings, so he's avoiding the topic. This is a situation where a man terrified of his emotions is fumbling to show them the only way he knows how, without a single solitary clue as to what emotions you might be experiencing in return or what you want from him."

That sounded . . . plausible. Much to Molly's consternation. Because if Lise's explanation was correct, that meant Molly could not, in fact, wait for him to meet her more than halfway.

She'd have to step across the center line herself, with zero guarantee of what might happen next.

"I suspect the only reason he got up the courage to ask you to stay again is some intensive coaching from Athena and Matthew. Maybe Charlotte too. And then, when you didn't agree right away, he simply lost his nerve." Lise's hands spread wide. "I could be wrong, however."

Molly's tired eyes stung, so she rubbed them with her knuckles and hoped her waterproof mascara held strong. Unlike—for example—her resolve not to make herself completely vulnerable to another man, ever.

Before she surrendered to the inevitable, though, she needed to make one last attempt at avoidance. "If he truly loves me, shouldn't that make him brave enough to take a chance and declare his love?"

"You tell me." Lise raised a single, damning brow. "Has your love for him made *you* brave enough, Molly?"

In response, Molly's middle finger made a return appearance, because Karl had clearly been a bad influence on her.

"No? Then let me help you." Lise's words were quiet, sympathetic, and entirely relentless. "I want you to imagine cutting things off with Karl now, without ever telling him you love him. Going back to LA and never returning. And then—five, ten, fifteen years down the line—getting another message from me."

Molly cringed, already knowing what came next.

"A text telling you he's married to someone else." Lise waited for that prospect to bloom in Molly's imagination, like a growing blot of midnight-black ink. "Or, heaven forbid, an email sharing the nonfictional, entirely correct obituary for him in the *Harlot's*

Herald. How would that feel?"

Like someone grabbing her by the throat and squeezing. Like reading her own obituary.

Her face crumbled, and her fist against her mouth couldn't quite stifle a sob.

Immediately, Lise's chair gave another ear-splitting shriek as she scooched closer again. She took Molly's hand, her round brown eyes solemn and sincere and tear-glazed too.

"I only have one more thing I need to say, and then I'm done. I promise." She held Molly's blurry stare, her own expression pained. "For the last two years, you've clearly been beating yourself up for trusting Rob. Enough to marry him and give him seventeen precious years of your life."

Her hand squeezed Molly's, demanding her friend's full attention. "But babe, I'm not sure you ever *did* trust him. You told me once that your insomnia only got bad after your wedding, and that's what people in the book biz call *a telling detail*. Part of you *knew*, Molly. Always. Your instincts were good. You simply didn't follow them, for completely human reasons. The sunk-cost fallacy is some powerful shit, am I right?"

"Karl . . ." Molly had to clear her throat and blow her nose with the paper towel in her free hand before she kept speaking. "Karl said pretty much the exact same thing. Minus the sunk-cost fallacy bit, because he's not nearly as nerdy as either of us."

"Then Karl and I are both right." Another fierce squeeze. "Forgive yourself, Molly. Trust yourself and your own instincts, if you can't bring yourself to trust him. Even though I think you *should* trust him, because that man's freaking *gone* for you."

Her instincts were screaming at her right now. Shouting that Karl wasn't the sort of man who'd casually fuck *anyone* and toss

her aside, much less an old friend whose voice he'd recognized after almost two decades apart and listened to every . . . single . . .
morning.

He'd worked incredibly hard to convince her to stay for the entire month. Given up sleep to ensure they'd have plenty of time together. Tried to earn her trust through bizarre corporate activities.
Shared his secrets and listened attentively to hers. Made love to her
like she was a miracle in human form, dispatched directly from the
heavens in the exact shape of his desires.

Why would he have done any of that if he didn't love her?

Why would he have asked her to stay if he didn't intend to pursue a future with her?

Molly's loud sniff echoed in the dark classroom. "Thank you for
the sage advice, Lise. As mandated by the Motion Picture Associa-
tion, circa 1998, it was very helpful."

"As your fat, funny bestie, it was my pleasure. Also my contrac-
tual obligation." Lise's small smile faded. "But like you said, even
my wisest counsel can't fix everything. Only you can do that." Her
eyebrows rose in inquiry. "So what are your instincts telling you?"

With a heavy sigh, Molly let go of Lise's hand and stood. "Unfortunately, I need to talk to Karl."

"Good plan." Lise pushed up from her own chair. "Let's go find
him."

Molly lingered, hesitant, then swallowed her pride. "But first, I
need a hug. A long one."

"Yeah, you do," Lise agreed, then wrapped her best friend tight
in her arms and gave Molly exactly what she wanted. Exactly what
she'd finally admitted to needing.

Exactly—*exactly*—what she'd had the courage to ask for.

In the end, it didn't matter whether Karl liked how it'd happened. Regardless, Charlotte had grown up. Become smart and strong and beautiful, in every way possible. Maybe because of her parents' steadfast support. Maybe because she simply *was* a smart, strong, beautiful person and always had been.

Most of the newest, most popular items on Karl's menu?

Her ideas. Because she'd researched and taught herself a crap ton about food and creative flavor combinations in her nonexistent spare time.

Most of the items on this very table?

Her work had helped create 'em. She'd arranged the child care she'd needed and labored capably by his side without a single complaint, after paying close attention to his instructions and soaking in anything he taught her like a damn dish sponge.

Despite his fatigue-blurred eyes, he felt like he was seeing her clearly for the first time in years. Not as a kid, not even as a protégé or surrogate daughter, but as a colleague. As a friend, whose good will and strength he could rely upon, even as he offered his in return.

And if he was with a reliable friend?

He could let down his damn guard. "You really want to know what happened with Molly?"

"I really want to know," she said without a moment's hesitation.

So he told her everything. Except the sexual shit, because she might be his friend, but he was still her boss, and he wasn't going to *harass* her. She listened silently the whole time, nodding on occasion to show she understood what he was saying.

And when he finally finished yammering, Charlotte looked straight at him and asked a simple, quiet question. "You didn't tell her how much you want her here?"

He fidgeted. Got blustery and defensive, because he knew where this was damn well going: the same place it'd gone with Matthew and Athena. But Charlotte just waited patiently until he was ready to admit the plain truth.

"Said *please* when I asked, but . . ." After scrubbing his hands over his face, he dropped them. "No. Guess I didn't."

"And you haven't told her you love her?"

"She hasn't said she loves *me* either," he pointed out immediately.

Other than his mom and sisters, no woman had ever told him that. And for the longest time, that absence—the lack of those words—had hurt him more than actual insults. More than most of his breakups ever had. At least until Molly had returned and showed him what actual love looked and felt like, and he'd finally understood.

His exes hadn't declared their love because those relationships *weren't* love.

Molly didn't have that excuse. Although . . . she might have others.

"Hmmm." Stretching her back with a faint hiss, Charlotte waited while he helped a partygoer. Once they were alone again, she asked, "Does Molly have any reason to be skittish with men?"

Apparently he and Charlotte were thinking along the same lines.

"Yeah." Her father's second life wasn't his secret to share. Her divorce wasn't particularly privileged information, though, from what he could tell. "Together with an asshole seventeen fucking years. Marriage ended badly. Got divorced two years ago."

Charlotte winced. "So she's understandably wary."

"Yeah," he repeated, and braced for the inevitable.

"I . . ." She spoke cautiously at first, testing out each syllable before she continued. "I know you're a sensitive soul, Karl, but—"

"Holy fuck, not this shit again." With a heartfelt groan, he stabbed a finger in her direction. "If you compare me to a chocolate egg, Charlotte, swear to Christ—"

"—maybe you need to be the one who leaps first, even though it's scary," she added more hurriedly, ignoring his interruption. "Because you love her, and if you let her leave without telling her, we both know you'll regret it. Maybe forever." She laid an encouraging hand on his shoulder. "You still have one more full day together. You've got time to gather your words and your courage, then make your declaration."

Woman wasn't wrong. Which blew.

"Hmmph." Tugging irritably at his bow tie, he glowered into the far distance. "I'll think about it."

Silence. Lips pursed into a skeptical line, Charlotte raised her brows at him.

"Wasn't lying. Thinking about it now, actually." His main conclusion, after a quick glance at his phone display? It was way too late to have such an important conversation tonight. Such a goddamn shame. And now: time for a distraction. "Also thinking I'm pretty sure Johnathan fell asleep on the toilet again."

That kid could nod off anywhere. A real talent, assuming he didn't have sleep apnea. Should Karl open a browser window and check on that? As opposed to planning a terrifying heart-to-heart with Molly?

"Probably. If he's not back in five minutes, we'll check on him." Charlotte let her hand drop from his shoulder. Didn't step away, though. "Hey, Karl?"

Midway through a Mayo Clinic rundown of sleep apnea symptoms, he paused. Looked up at Charlotte again. "Yeah?"

"Thank you," she said softly.

His brows drew together. "For what?"

"You've never shared something so personal with me before. I didn't . . ." Biting her lip, she took a moment before continuing. "I didn't realize you trusted me that much. So . . . thank you for telling me what happened with Molly, and thank you for listening to what I said in response."

What the hell?

"I've *always* trusted you. Just knew you had a full plate for someone so young. Didn't want to burden you with my shit too."

She looked shocked. "Really?"

"*Yes*, really." He glared at her. "Jesus H. Christ."

Still wide-eyed with disbelief, she spread her hands helplessly. "I know you care about me and my kids, obviously. But I guess I assumed you thought of me as kind of a dumb kid too. Your personal albatross, until some other workplace took me off your hands."

Jaw dropped in absolute bewilderment, he couldn't do anything but gape at her.

Her lips curved into a wry, faintly bitter smile. "I mean, I was a teenage mom two times over. Then I kept quitting a good job to try to work things out with someone who clearly wasn't ready for a family. I'm not exactly . . ." She paused for a moment. "How would Athena put it? I'm not exactly an *exemplar* of great decision-making."

How could she have possibly believed he felt that way about her?

"Charlotte." Reaching out, he grabbed her hand. Held tight. "I never—*never*—thought that. Of *course* I never thought any of that bullshit."

"But . . ." Lines scored her brow. "But isn't that why you don't want me to apprentice under you?"

"*What?*" They hadn't discussed an apprenticeship. That much, he knew for damn sure. "We didn't . . ."

Then he remembered the conversation they'd had weeks ago, in his workroom. The day he'd been agonizing over Molly's unwillingness to stay in Harlot's Bay any longer than necessary, and Charlotte had recognized their visitor's voice from the Sadie Brazen audiobooks.

Maybe I could help you back here sometimes? she'd tentatively suggested. *You work such long hours, and I'd really like to—*

And then he'd cut her off.

He'd told her he was fine. Dismissed her, unwilling to add more stress to her life. Assumed she'd made the offer out of pity, not a genuine desire to learn from him.

But had he explained his reasoning? Or asked her what she truly wanted and why she wanted it?

No. He sure as fuck hadn't. And now, here they were, just figuring this shit out, when she could've been helping him weeks ago. Could've been learning valuable skills at his elbow. Could've allowed him more time off to spend with Molly.

Molly, who'd tried to talk to him about Charlotte. He hadn't listened to her either.

And because he hadn't told Charlotte how he felt about her, hadn't expressed himself in even the most inadequate goddamn way, his daughter—in his heart, if not by law or blood—thought he considered her stupid and untrustworthy. A burden. That he put up with her, rather than considering her one of the great joys of his fucking life.

The shame of it curdled his stomach.

Swallowing down nausea, he finally asked the right questions. "You really want to be my apprentice? Even though I'm a surly asshole and the work hours completely blow?"

"Yes." There was no doubt in her tone. "I want to be a baker, and I want to train under you. I already told my parents months ago, and we figured out ways to make the logistics work, if you were willing."

When he spoke again, he was careful to make things crystal-fucking-clear. All pronouns in place, with no room for any more confusion.

"When we talked last month, Charlotte, I didn't understand what you were asking or why, and I didn't make any effort to clarify things. I'm so damn sorry. But I understand now, so here's my updated answer." He met her wondering gaze directly. "You're smart when it comes to flavors, you listen well, and you pick things up quickly. You work hard. You're friendly, kind, and a great colleague. A great mom too, although that's less relevant to your apprenticeship. And above all else, I actually enjoy your company, which isn't something I can say about too many damn people."

With each compliment, her eyes grew brighter. Wetter.

By the time he finished, she was outright crying. She was also beaming.

"Charlotte, will you please be my apprentice?" He squeezed her trembling fingers. "My stupid back and I could both use a little more time away from the bakery."

When she opened her mouth to answer, he held up a staying hand.

"I want to say one more thing: No matter what you decide, you'll always have a place in my bakery and my heart. Not because

I feel obligated. Because I want you in my life. And no matter what you do or where you go, I'll always be proud of you and everything you've accomplished. I admire the hell out of you, Charlotte."

He'd never seen her stand straighter or look more confident, even as she blotted away her tears with a spare napkin.

"Yes, I'll be your apprentice." She wrinkled her nose at him. "And brace yourself, Karl, because once Bez hears the news, she'll definitely ask next."

He rolled his eyes. "Fine."

"And as soon as Johnathan's out of college . . ."

"We'll deal with that shit when the time comes." He paused. Worked up the courage to say what he now knew was damn well *necessary*. "You know I love you, right? Like my own daughter?"

His ears were burning, his hands shaking.

"I hoped you did." More napkin dabs. "But I didn't know. Not before tonight. It feels . . ." She paused. Choked a little. "It feels really good to hear it."

Without warning, her slight frame barreled into his chest, and she wrapped her arms around his waist. He held her tight, rocking her back and forth a little.

"All these years, you've been my anchor, Karl. The one person I could always rely on, other than my parents," she whispered into his tuxedo jacket. "You know I love you too, right?"

After hearing her breath hitch, he rocked her some more. "Figured you might."

But . . . yeah. She was right. It felt *really* fucking good to hear it.

The words sank into his bones. Braced and warmed him from the inside out.

And at long last, he finally, fully got it. What Athena and Matthew had been trying to tell him, again and again, for a while now.

What Charlotte had just tried to tell him too. What his defensiveness, his fear, had stopped him from recognizing and acknowledging.

Honesty and protectiveness, acts of service to everyone he cared about—they came naturally to him, and they were important. Crucial, even. But not sufficient. Because if he didn't tell people how he felt, they might not ever understand. Even Charlotte—a bright, perceptive woman he'd known and seen almost daily for years—hadn't been confident of his love.

After less than a single month together, then, how was *Molly* supposed to read the contents of his goddamn soul?

And after all his endless talk of earning her trust, had he actually trusted *her*?

Nope. Not enough to openly express his emotions. Not enough to share his heart.

How the fuck had he expected her to haul all her shit across the country, remove herself from almost everything familiar to her, and risk more heartbreak and disappointment for a man who hadn't even said he loved her?

Hell, had he even told her how much he *liked* her? Using comprehensible human words?

She might know that much already. But she might not.

Had he imagined she'd make fun of him for how he felt? Had he thought she'd find him pathetic? Cringe? Laugh?

Even twenty years ago, he'd understood one thing well enough: Molly Dearborn wasn't nice. But she was kind. She wouldn't meet his vulnerability with scorn. Even if she didn't love him the way he loved her.

But what if she *did*? What if she simply needed those three words from him before she could muster the nerve to offer them back?

He'd never know if he didn't damn well try.

Screw appropriate bedtimes. He was talking with Molly tonight. Which meant Charlotte and Johnathan would need to be in charge of cleanup.

After one last squeeze, he let Charlotte go. Handed her another napkin to blow her nose and appreciated the joyful smile on her tired, red-eyed, red-nosed face.

"Listen, Charlotte, you and—" he began.

"Hey, Karl, you need to—" Johnathan arrived out of nowhere at a run, then skidded to a halt and eyed them in hard-breathing confusion. "Everything okay here?"

"Everything's great," Charlotte said, still sniffling happily.

"Yep. We're good." Karl eyed him assessingly. "You fall asleep on the damn john again? Because I read an article just now, and maybe you should go see a—"

"Not the time." The younger man looked frantic. "If you're fine, then you need to get to the hall outside the gym, Karl. *Now*."

Karl frowned in confusion but followed his employee toward the exit, with Charlotte trailing close behind. "Why?"

"There some sort of confrontation happening." After glancing over his shoulder to make sure Karl was keeping up, Johnathan hustled faster. "Molly's facing off against a random blond dude. He kind of seems like a dick?"

At that news, Karl broke into an outright *run*.

Molly was still here? And publicly arguing with someone, when she was the most private person he knew? Jesus H. Christ, what the—

"She hurt?" he shouted to Johnathan. "In danger?"

"Not that I can tell," his employee yelled back, still jogging.

Staccato flashes lit the hallway outside the gym, as Sylvia took photos of whatever the hell was transpiring. And as Karl drew closer, the unmistakable cacophony of a three-way argument became way too audible.

Molly was much louder than normal, her tone livid. Lise, her own volume cranked to eleven, was backing up her best friend. And some smarmy-voiced asshole was telling them to *calm down*, which meant at least one of the women would shortly gut the fucker with whatever sharp implement was within reach.

Karl neared the entrance at last. Identified all three combatants in the hallway. Molly, flushed and angry but not obviously harmed, standing next to Lise, both women squaring off against a tall blond asshole. Who was—was he reaching for Molly's goddamn arm?

At the absolute end of his rope, still running, Karl roared, "What the *actual fuck* is going on here?"

Molly, Lise, and Blond Asshole turned his way.

The blond man's nose wrinkled, like he'd smelled dog crap on his shoe. "Who's *that*, Mol?"

"That's my new boyfriend. His name is Karl." Molly offered her adversary an evil smile. "He's apparently very eager to meet you."

Wisely, Blond Asshole stopped trying to grab her arm.

Somewhere behind Karl, Johnathan asked Charlotte, "Is it just me, or is this, like, peak teen- movie shit happening right now?"

"Rest assured, Johnathan," Charlotte managed to pant out as she caught up with Karl and elbowed aside a gawker in the doorway, "it's definitely not just you."

28

After repairing her minimal, tear-ravaged makeup as much as possible in the high school bathroom, Molly had headed back toward the reunion with Lise at her side. Only to find her ex-husband in the hallway outside the event, scrutinizing its participants through the open gym door. Searching for her, she presumed.

Stunned, she abruptly halted. Stared uncomprehendingly.

Why wasn't Rob in California? And even if he'd followed her to Harlot's Bay for some unknown, utterly bizarre reason, how the hell could he have possibly known she was here, at the school?

"Lise . . ." Had all the drama of the evening caused hallucinations? "You see the tall blond guy in the boring gray suit, right? I'm not just imagining him? Or having a nightmare?"

Stumbling to a stop alongside her, Lise looked around. "Yeah, I see him. But . . . Molly, who—"

At the sound of his ex-wife's name, he swung around. Spotted her.

"Molly. There you are." With a charming smile and a smooth stride, he approached her. "I was beginning to think you'd left already, and I'd have to drive to the . . ." His brow crinkled attractively, and he checked the note-taking app on his phone. "The local . . . Spite House? Is that correct?"

Because politeness had been drummed into Molly's core being since she was a child, she turned to her companion. "Lise, this is my ex-husband, Rob Brandt. Rob, please meet Lise Utendorf."

Molly's best friend didn't say a word. Just stared at him stonily, arms folded across her substantial chest.

"Lise . . ." He thought for a minute. "Oh, right. She's the one who wri—"

"Do *not* finish that sentence," Molly warned. "Rob, why are you here? And how on earth did you even find me?"

A flash bulb went off at close range, and she screwed her eyes shut for a moment.

"Because of . . . that woman, I believe," Rob said, his voice amused.

Once Molly could see past the sparkling dots in her vision, she followed Rob's pointing finger to . . . Sylvia, whose huge camera hung on a strap around her neck. The older woman waved, then took another photo.

"I don't understand." Which was the understatement of the century, as far as Molly was concerned. "What does Sylvia have to do with anything?"

Rob looked pleased with himself. "When I asked people in town where you might be, someone said he knew you were here, because he follows the local newspaper's Instagram account."

"Some dude in Harlot's Bay needs to mind his own freaking business," Lise muttered. "Or at least keep his damn mouth shut."

Molly waved that off, too tired to care. "Fine. That's how you found me. But why are you *here?*"

"I could ask the same question." A graceful flick of his fingers smoothed his rumpled hair. "Molly, why in the world have you stayed an entire month in the middle of nowhere?"

At that, Sylvia stopped taking photos and started glowering at him.

"This is so unlike you." Rob peered closely at her, as if looking for evidence of trauma, or maybe a mental break of some sort. "You've lived in a dozen places, and we both know you never cared much about the people you left behind. So why come back here?"

He made her sound utterly heartless, but . . . at a certain point, once she'd moved often enough, she'd gotten so freaking tired of making connections, then having them ripped away without warning. So, yes, she'd stopped getting attached.

Harlot's Bay had always been her one exception, though. Not that she'd ever told Rob. Something inside her hadn't trusted him with that bit of her heart, and she'd kept it to herself.

Just another sign that Karl and Lise were right: Her instincts were fine. She simply hadn't listened to them. But now was a great time to start, and those instincts were clear on one thing: Her past was none of Rob's business, and she shouldn't let him goad her into discussing it.

She kept her voice even. "I repeat: Why are *you* here?"

"Let's go somewhere more private to talk." Rob side-eyed the growing crowd of people either discreetly or openly staring at the three of them. "I know how you value your privacy."

Something about that confident, knowing statement sparked her temper.

"Sure. You care *so much* about my privacy and my preferences. Which is why, after I blocked your number, you chose to track me down in a high school gym during a reunion." Molly shook her head, face heating in anger. "That's borderline stalker behavior, Rob. I'm not going anywhere with you. Especially since I haven't heard from my lawyer, which means you and I have nothing important to discuss."

He actually laughed. *Laughed.*

"I'm not *stalking* you, Molly. I was simply in the area because of a conference in DC this weekend, and Alexis said the workers must finally be done with our . . ." He paused. "With *your* house, because all their tools and supplies are gone. So I figured now was the perfect time to chat about the next steps."

Too incensed to pay much attention, Molly let Lise nudge her toward the nearest wall, so they weren't blocking traffic out of the gym as their former classmates either called it quits for the night or gathered to watch the show.

"So you're not stalking me, but you're here in Harlot's Bay without my invitation, and your wife has driven past my house to check on the status of my renovations?" Multiple times, it sounded like. Aggravated and incredulous, she threw her hands in the air. "There are no *next steps*, Rob. It's none of your concern whether my renovations are done or not. My home *is not for sale*. And even if it were—"

"I'd make a better offer than before. I heard what you said during our last conversation, and I want to respect your position. You're smart to hold out for more." Rob smiled at her. "Alexis and I talked about it, and we're willing to go as high as . . ."

He named a genuinely generous price, and it only infuriated her more. Why the hell was he acting like she'd balked at his specific offer, rather than the entire idea of selling her home? Why, after all this time, wasn't the word *no* getting through to him?

He didn't *respect her position*. He didn't respect *her*. Not even a little.

What she was witnessing outside her high school gymnasium was evidently his main takeaway from their relationship: total confidence that he could bend her to his will if he refused to listen, wore her down, and convinced her that his position was the only just and rational one.

For far too long, his confidence had been well founded. During their marriage, she'd striven to make *reasonable* decisions, according to his definition of the term. She'd spent nearly two decades questioning her feelings, ignoring her instincts, because she wanted to be fair—to him and in general.

That period of her life was over now. From this point on, she intended to care less about what was rational and more about being true to herself. He needed to understand that.

Maybe once he did, he'd give up and leave her the fuck alone, at long last.

"Let me put this as clearly as possible." She articulated each word crisply, in distinct syllables, like a linguist reading the dictionary aloud. "My home is not for sale. Even if it were, I would *not* sell it to you."

It was the first time she'd admitted as much, even to herself, because she'd known her disinclination was pure pettiness. She no longer minded being petty, though, so her ex-husband was about to finally discover one of life's great truths.

Finding out was much less fun than fucking around.

"Wow. Molly." His slow headshake radiated disapproval. "I never thought you'd take advantage of our relationship to squeeze even *more* money out of me, but I suppose I could go . . ." His lips pursed as he thought for a moment. "I could go ten percent above the price I just quoted you."

Was he . . . was he *haggling* with her?

Fucking hell, was he even *listening* to her? To *himself*?

"Holy crap, dude." Lise glowered at him. "Do you have a head injury? Too much ear wax? A curse on your bloodline that doesn't allow you to hear anything that you find inconvenient? Because *something* is clearly stopping you from getting the point."

Any remaining semblance of civility shredded by his condescension and obstinate refusal to understand her position, Molly planted her feet on the tile floor and her fists on her hips, and she made absolutely freaking sure he *heard her* this time, with no confusion possible.

"You could offer me ten times the house's value. A *thousand* times. It wouldn't matter, because after everything you've said and done to me, I. Will. *Never*. Sell. It. To. You. I'd rather burn it to the damn ground than let you have it." She bared her teeth at him, in what might technically be considered a smile. "And don't bother looking shocked and disappointed that I'd refuse a tidy profit. We both know that between the two of us, you're the one who cares about his money more than his heart."

His face creased in a wince when she raised her voice, and he aimed a speaking glance at their surroundings. He'd always hated loud confrontations, especially in public. Considered them *common*. And sure enough—

"Pipe down, you two," he hissed, leaning closer. "There's no need to make this some kind of juvenile confrontation. Even though you're . . ." He shook his head again, as if in helpless disbelief. "You're refusing to sell me your home out of childish *spite*? Truly?"

"You've got *some* nerve, jackass, to come in here and pretend Molly's the one at fault." In direct contradiction to Rob's order, Lise's voice had risen in volume. "She only told me the bare minimum about her divorce, and you *already* sounded like a total dick. And now that I've met you, it's clear that she didn't give me even the faintest, most infinitesimal *idea*—"

For all that Lise was shouting, Molly could barely hear anything over the insistent buzz in her ears and the rapid thud of her heartbeat in her skull.

She'd married this man. *Married* him.

Let him shove cake *in her face* and *stayed with him*.

"If I'm being spiteful, I have damn good reason." She stepped into his space. Thrust an accusing finger at his chest, stopping a bare inch away. "You *used* me, Rob. Wrung me dry, then left in the cruelest way possible, like the absolute *asshole—*"

"Calm down, both of you." Rob reached for Molly's arm, sighing when she jerked it out of reach. "Listen, Molly, why don't you and I go someplace more private, where you can cool off, and then we can—"

"What the *actual fuck* is going on here?"

Oh, thank god. At the sound of Karl's infuriated roar, Molly could literally *feel* her blood pressure drop back to non-dangerous levels.

When the three hallway combatants—along with dozens of onlookers—swiveled in Karl's direction, he and his employees still remained inside the gym, but they were racing toward Molly and closing in fast.

He was red-faced with both anger and effort, his tux rumpled. Not the world's most natural sprinter. Mutter-shouting breathless obscenities with each step.

Not once in her entire life had she been more relieved to see someone.

Whatever was wrong between the two of them, she didn't doubt for a moment that he—like Lise—would have her back and protect her however he could. Down to the marrow of her bones, she *knew* he'd comfort her in the aftermath of whatever happened next. Hell, he'd turn himself inside freaking out if that was what it took to make her feel good in her own skin again.

And she knew that because she trusted him. Wholeheartedly. Without reservations.

Lise was right: He didn't need to declare his love aloud. Not when everything he did figuratively shouted his absolute devotion. Molly had simply been too busy wallowing in past hurts to understand that before now.

Rob's nose crinkled. "Who's *that*, Mol?"

"That's my new boyfriend, Karl. The one you heard on the phone." Molly grinned, suddenly calm again. "He's apparently very eager to meet you."

Karl ran until the last possible moment, nearly hitting the hallway wall with all the momentum he'd achieved trying to reach them as quickly as possible.

"Baby—" He planted himself between her and Rob and gently clasped her shoulders, presenting the other man with his back. "You okay?"

"Yeah." She sucked in a huge breath. Counted to five. Exhaled. Felt her blood pressure lower even further. "Yeah, I'm okay. It's just . . . Rob showed up without warning, and . . ."

"Got it." His blunt finger tucked a piece of hair behind her ear. "You want to have it out with the asshole here, or would you like more privacy?"

Unlike Rob, he was asking what she preferred. Not telling her who she was. Not proposing something for his own benefit and pretending it was for her.

"I don't . . ." She mouthed the words more than spoke them, keeping her voice too quiet for anyone else to hear. "I don't want to spend even an extra minute of time with that man or go anywhere with him, especially not to an enclosed space. I don't want to be reminded of him anywhere else in Harlot's Bay. And I don't want to be alone with him."

"Molly, what in heaven's name——" Rob began, somewhere behind Karl.

"Lise and I would never leave you alone with him, unless you specifically told us to go." Glancing over his shoulder, still ignoring Rob, Karl surveyed the visible portion of the gym. "Could head back to the refreshments table. Use it as a physical barrier between you two while you talk. Have Lise, Charlotte, and Johnathan keep people away. It'd be public, but with some privacy. What do you think?"

She inclined her head. "That works for me. Thank you."

"No need for thanks. Don't want you alone with that bastard either." His jaw ticked. "Fair warning: Can't promise to stay out of things if I hear him dicking you around. You want me to try to keep quiet, though, I will."

"*Molly*." Rob poked his head around Karl's broad shoulder. "Can't we simply——"

"As long as you don't talk over me, Karl, I honestly don't care. Just make sure to keep your contributions to the discussion verbal only." She held up her midnight-blue clutch. "I didn't bring bail money tonight."

He looked genuinely disappointed that she hadn't okayed violence against her ex-husband. "Goddamn shame."

The deepest, angriest recesses of her id kind of agreed. But as their new group of six made its way back to the back of the gym, she certainly didn't tell Karl that.

She didn't need him to physically fight for her. Just love her.

Good thing he clearly already did.

29

*F*ive minutes later, Molly's ex-husband had finally accepted the obvious: She wasn't going to sell him the house, no matter what. At which point, Rob began a bitter litany of accusations, because apparently no one had ever flat-out refused the man before when he really, *really* wanted something.

She was the reason their marriage had failed, he informed her.

She was hard and unforgiving.

She was irrational.

She was selfish.

With each charge laid against her, she simply blinked at him, unimpressed by his lack of creativity. Honestly, she still recalled his I-want-a-divorce monologue just fine. If she'd wanted an encore, she could've simply consulted her own memories.

This delightful encounter wasn't going to last much longer, though. She'd decided five minutes was more than enough time for him to purge the vitriol from his system once and for all. After that, she'd put an end to their unexpected rendezvous—and tell him any further contact would either happen through their lawyers or end in a restraining order.

Her hands were steady. Her cheeks had cooled. She'd even transcribed a few key chunks of his soliloquy in her phone's note-taking app, then discreetly posted brief updates to her social media accounts while he was still droning on and on about how terrible a wife she'd been, because when Rob got in the lecture zone, her participation was entirely unnecessary.

She was back in control.

His words stung. Of course they stung. But they didn't *wound* the same way they had before Karl showed up. They didn't threaten her composure or make her doubt herself in the way Rob obviously intended.

The man glued to her side was having a harder time maintaining his equanimity, however. And after Rob's ridiculously hypocritical accusation of selfishness, Karl gave up even the unconvincing pretense of putting food away. Propping his white-knuckled fists on the catering table, wearing an expression generally reserved for bloodthirsty serial killers finally taking their knife-wielding revenge upon their lifelong enemy, he leaned in dangerously close to her ex-husband and unleashed his tongue.

"If Molly's *hard* sometimes?" A furious, rumbling sound rattled in his chest. "It's because she's had to be. Because motherfuckers like you would've taken advantage otherwise. Part of her damn well *knew* she couldn't trust you with anything soft."

She took a sip from her water bottle. Smiled at him.

"If she's *unforgiving*, it's because you don't *deserve* her goddamn forgiveness." When his fists thumped against the table, it shuddered. "And it's not irrational or *selfish* to say no to you. It's *her* house, you shit stain of a man. She can do whatever she fucking *wants* with it."

It was genuinely startling, the extent to which seeing—and hearing, obviously; everyone in Harlot's Bay could probably transcribe his profanity-laden screed at this point, word for word— Karl's anger eased hers. Like he'd lifted its weight directly from her heart and heaved it onto his own broad shoulders, carrying it like he had so many other burdens during the course of his overworked life.

And he was only gaining momentum as he spoke. Maybe a bit *too* much momentum. Again: If Karl utterly lost his cool, she didn't know whether the Harlot's Bay jail took credit cards, and she didn't want to find out.

"—go fuck yourself, you prick," he was ranting. "I'll tear down every brick of that house with my bare hands and sledgehammer the foundation into motherfucking *atoms* before I let you get your cruel—"

A single light tug on his jacket's sleeve, and he cut himself off and looked over at her.

"You have extremely strong hands, but I doubt they're strong enough to tear apart mortared bricks." She covered one of those hands with hers. Squeezed consolingly. "Even if they were, you should wear gloves to protect them. Also, a quick note: While I have, on occasion, been referred to as a *brick house*—"

"She's mighty-mighty," Lise murmured from a few feet away.

"—my actual house is not, in fact, brick." She raised her free forefinger. "And finally, I'm relatively certain a sledgehammer can't apply the necessary force to break elements down to their constituent atoms."

His lips twitched, if only faintly. "Nitpicker."

"Guilty as charged."

"Molly." In the put-upon tone of a reasonable person ill-used by circumstance—oh, yes, her ex-husband been an excellent narrator before his decision to attend medical school—Rob addressed her directly. "Why are you letting this man speak for you?"

"Because I've said what I needed to say, over and over again," she answered plainly. "You didn't listen, and there's no point wasting more of my time or my energy. Right now, I'm simply letting you run out of steam. And for your information, I've already transcribed the most problematic things you told me tonight. Just in case I need to file a restraining order."

While her ex-husband spluttered and postured and informed her she was overreacting—*hysterical*, even—Karl leaned over to plant a hard kiss on her head.

"Be right back." He began edging around the table. "Getting us both some eel cake before it's all gone."

Apparently he considered the matter settled. And to be fair, the threat of legal intervention had seemingly taken most of the wind out of Rob's sails.

Most, but not all.

"We both know you're not cut out for relationships, Molly." Rob watched Karl walk over to the nearby cake display, then turned back to Molly. "He might play the big man and beat his chest in front of your ex, but he'll never love you."

Over at the cake table, Karl's shoulders bunched into hard knots of muscle, and he rumbled ominously. The word *motherfucker* was clearly audible, although he probably thought he was speaking under his breath.

She had to smile. "Oh, he definitely loves me. No doubt about that."

Karl jerked and swung around to face her, a plate with an enormous, uncomfortably lifelike slab of eel cake clutched tight in one large hand. His eyes were wide, his lips parted in shock at her announcement.

"That . . ." Rob snorted. "That apparently comes as surprise to *him*, Molly."

She lifted a shoulder, unconcerned. "He hasn't told me yet."

Rob's smirk spread. "I'm sure he hasn't. Let's find out for certain." He turned his attention to Karl. "Do you love her? Be honest, man."

Clearly, her ex-husband considered this a *gotcha* moment of the highest order. The perfect opportunity to soothe his own injured pride by watching hers get savaged.

It wasn't going to work out the way he imagined. No matter what Karl did or didn't say.

"Karl's always honest," Molly felt obligated to point out. "But he doesn't have to share anything he doesn't want to. If you'd rather not respond to this jackass, Karl, feel free to ignore him."

Karl was nearly hyperventilating. But he stepped closer anyway, plate shaking in his hand, and stopped right next to her ex-husband.

"Dearborn." His throat bobbed with his audible gulp. "You really want me to tell you for the first time in front of *this* asshole?"

She huffed out an amused breath. "I might as well have *one* good memory associated with him. But again, it's up to you."

Karl closed his eyes for a moment, mouth working as he gathered the courage to bare his heart. And despite what she'd just said, her ex-husband might as well have disappeared from the face of the Earth, along with everyone else in the gym.

All she could see was the man she loved, struggling with his fears, and she had no desire to make anything in his life harder than it already was. Even this.

"It's okay. Really." She reached across the table to him. "You don't have to—"

"Love you like oxygen, Molly," he told her plainly, then met her stare directly. "Like fucking daylight. Good-sized part of me? Loved you for over twenty-two goddamn years now. Even when I thought I'd never fucking see you again."

Raw honesty vibrated through each choked word, and his eyes were bright as the sun, shining with tears and gut-deep emotion. With naked vulnerability, left unguarded and exposed.

"Oh," she murmured through numb lips. "I . . ."

Somehow, even though she'd known, hearing the words . . . it overwhelmed her. Left her wet-eyed and thick-throated and dazed.

Gathering herself, she shook off the haze of shocked joy. "Oh, god, Karl, I l—"

"Been thinking about logistics." He barreled right over her attempt at returning his declaration, his face taut with determination. "We do a few renos, your recording studio can fit in my house."

The way he looked at her—intense, searching, like she was the answer to every question he'd posed over an entire lifetime—stole her breath again.

"But if you'd rather stay in California, fine. Pack up my shit and join you there," he added, to her shock. "Wouldn't be able to sell the bakery and move until I got Charlotte and Bez trained up right, but—"

"You don't need to uproot yourself or leave your business, Karl. I'm willing to sell my house"—she cast a derisive glance at her ex, who appeared frozen in utter bewilderment—"to almost anyone but him."

The offer, though—the way Karl hadn't assumed she would be the one to move; his willingness to abandon his lifelong hometown and the business he'd served for decades, if that was what she needed—meant the absolute world to her.

His lips curved slightly. "Yeah?"

"Yeah." She smiled back at him. "Although . . . your taking on an apprentice or two would be great, Karl. If I'm going to move across the country to be with you, I want to actually spend some time together. *Without* you working ridiculous hours or giving up sleep to make that happen. And when was your last vacation?"

He considered the question. "Technically?"

"Technical correctness is the most satisfying correctness of all."

Somewhere off to the side, her ex-husband groaned and muttered something derogatory. In response, a woman who sounded very much like sweet, gentle Charlotte told him to shut the hell up and stop ruining the moment.

Karl snorted. "Then my last vacation? Not long ago. When I had the flu."

"And Sylvia thought you'd died." As if on cue, the journalist's flash left Molly blinking away more spots. "I think we can do better than that."

His small smile got bigger and bigger, until his joy was as brilliant and blinding as Sylvia's flash. "Sure as hell can."

Rob ostentatiously cleared his throat, and they reluctantly looked over at him. "If and when you come to your senses, Molly, I'll accept your apology, and we can talk about——"

Karl groaned so loudly, her ex-husband jumped.

"Quit dicking around, fuckface," he told Rob, "and just *go*."

"Please do." Sylvia held up her camera. "You're blocking my view, young man."

"Make like Walt Whitman's grass," Lise said, "and *leave*."

"Do what the lit nerd says, asshat!" a random spectator—was that Ned?—called out.

After a final long-suffering sigh, Rob did in fact turn to go. Only to get tangled with Karl's foot somehow. Her ex-husband staggered, half falling to the floor. And as Karl reached out to assist—

After a collective gasp, utter silence blanketed the gym.

Then Rob raised his cake-covered face, and a dollop of eel slime dripped from his nose. At which point Molly had to look away before she totally lost her shit, like the rest of the crowd.

"Oh, no." Karl wiped his hands on a napkin, sounding unutterably bored. "Such a fucking shame. My apologies, dude."

From the corner of her eye, she saw Rob puff up like a rooster and snatch at the pile of neatly folded napkins too. "You did that on purpose, you dick."

"Don't know what you're talking about." Karl patted at the most unconvincing yawn in the history of theater, all while eyeing the other man like a cockroach. "Must suck to get a cake in the goddamn face when you didn't want that, though."

They both knew she'd never have done it herself, because— even now, in her petty era—she'd be too concerned about reasonableness and maturity. So he'd done it for her, where she could watch and appreciate every frosting-caked bit of glory.

Truly, Molly had never loved anyone more. Which he didn't yet know, because he'd interrupted her declaration of affections several minutes ago.

She should probably get back on that.

Ignoring Rob's various complaints and inadequate attempts to clean himself, she stretched out her hand to Karl. "Hey, Dean? I have something you should probably look at."

"Jesus H. Christ." Without even a flicker of hesitation, he put down the cake plate, dismissed her ex-husband from his attention, and rounded the table to claim her hand and intertwine their fingers. "What *now*?"

"Nothing bad." With her free hand, she showed him her phone display. "See?"

He squinted down at the screen. "The hell am I looking at, Dearborn?"

"A social media update. Which, as you'll notice, I posted at least five or ten minutes before you said you loved me." A tap of her fingernail against the phone's screen directed him where to look. "While Rob was still lecturing me, I shared my upcoming move with my Facebook fan group. Announced I was pulling up stakes and heading to Maryland sooner rather than later."

"Really?" He bent closer to the text. "You did that *before* I told you how I felt?"

"As my post's timestamp clearly indicates."

"I don't get it." His back made a cracking noise as he straightened, and he stared at her with a creased brow. "Why would you—"

"Because you said you wanted me to move here. That's not something you'd ask a casual lover to do, or anyone you weren't absolutely sure about." She tucked the phone back into her clutch. "And I've never met a more steadfast person in my life. When it comes to loyalty, you're basically the Rock of Gibraltar—"

"Home to a shit-ton of macaques?"

"—which means you won't change your mind or find someone you want more than me. Not soon. Not ever." She stepped into him, close enough to bask in his unfaltering heat. "Your declaration of undying love was merely the icing on a delicious eel-shaped cake. I'd already made my call."

His hands lifted to cradle her face. "You know I won't be an asshole and take advantage of you, right?"

"Yep." When he swept his work-roughened thumbs over her cheekbones, the slight friction set her nerves alight. "I know."

"Good." His lips brushed her temple. "And you know I'd rather rip off my own dick than leave you?"

"That's . . ." She eased back and blinked at him for a moment.

"That's very graphic, Dean. But yes. I know that too."

His entire body stilled. Tensed.

He sucked in a harsh breath, then found the courage to ask. "You trust me?"

"Yes." No hesitation. Not a flicker of doubt. "Completely."

His eyes searched hers. "You love me?"

"With every un-sledgehammered atom in my body."

Exhaling slowly, he grinned down at her. "We gonna fuck in that limo outside?"

"Like those aforementioned macaques."

He laughed, the sound earsplittingly loud and incandescently happy, then gathered her in his arms and bowed his head to kiss her with insistent passion and the sort of heedless devotion she'd never imagined could be hers.

Even behind her closed lids, rapid flash-bursts created fireworks in her vision. They were clearly the work of Harlot's Bay's finest journalist and Sylvia's trusty Nikon, or maybe even the crowd of nosy spectators and their cell-phone cameras, but . . .

Nitpicky pedantry be damned.

Molly would have sworn those joyful pinwheels of light came straight from her heart.

* * *

ROUGHLY AN HOUR later, Molly tugged her pants back in place and tipped her head toward a discreet package of wet wipes. "Should we . . ."

"Yeah." Karl sighed, then buttoned his own pants and heaved himself up from the back seat. "Be assholes if we didn't."

In theory—and in movies—banging in a limo was hot.

In reality . . .

Actually, yeah, it was still really damn hot. But also kind of painful to middle-aged joints. Not to mention questionable in terms of hygiene, for both them *and* the limo driver.

For the poor man's sake, the least they could do was clean up after themselves.

As she hummed a few bars from "The Wreck of the *Edmund Fitzgerald*," they both went to town on the wet wipes and made absolutely sure they hit every relevant interior surface in the limo.

After a minute, she glanced over to where he was scrubbing at her footprint on a window. "Anyone in sight out there?"

By the time they'd finished making out in the gym, Rob had already left the premises, and so had most other reunion attendees, including Sylvia. Even so, Molly and Karl had hustled to the limo and instructed the driver to take them to Karl's home using both a circuitous route and the maximum legal speed limit, in hopes no one would follow them and take candid photos—or worse, videos—of what they intended to do next.

The windows might be tinted, but the limo's shocks would never be the same.

"Nope. All clear." Grumbling to himself, Karl stretched his back, then grabbed another wipe. "Y'know, teen movies never show this sort of shit."

"To be fair, most teen movies don't contain the sort of explicit sex we just had, and neither one of us has been a teenager for a very, very long time." Flopping down on the newly cleaned seat, she took a moment's break. "Also, teenagers typically have curfews and very little money. We, on the other hand, had all the cash necessary to pay off the limo driver and keep him away for an hour, even though it's almost two in the morning."

"Can't argue with that." He flashed her a grin and flopped beside her. "Our forties? Gonna fucking *rule*, Dearborn."

Just the thought of it—ten entire years spent side by side—had her almost giddy with joy. And that was just the beginning.

She laced their fingers together on the damp leather upholstery. "Also our fifties. And sixties. And every other decade we get to spend together."

He leaned over to give her a brief, hard, very enthusiastic kiss. "Fuckin' *A*."

"Fuckin' A," she agreed.

Epilogue

Ten years later

*E*very year, the orders got more ridiculous.

Yeah, Karl appreciated the couple's business—both in terms of the money they paid for their annual wedding-anniversary celebration cakes and all the vibrating shit they stocked in their now jointly owned sex shop—but come the hell *on*.

Piping out this much text? A real bitch, especially given his irritable back and wrists. But he persevered, because he was a damn *professional*.

Letter by careful letter, he wrote the first cake's message:

"Go fuck yourself—and not in a fun way, woman."

"PS. Okay, maybe in a fun way."

"PPS. Can I watch???"

Then, with a heartfelt groan, he moved on to the second cake and its way-too-long, overly informative message: "You're a dick, and while I generally really like those, said liking doesn't apply to YOU. (JK, I ♥ you and your dick SM.)"

Thank fuck for social media abbreviations. That cake was smaller, and he'd almost run out of room to fit everything.

Now, of course, he had to pipe out another year's supply of decorative wangs and vulva, because those two weirdos were nothing if not predictable.

"Why don't I finish that?" Charlotte appeared at his shoulder, pastry bag in hand. "Molly should be here any minute, and you need time to clean up."

With heartfelt gratitude, he straightened and surrendered the cakes to his co-head baker. "Thanks. Text is done, but I haven't started on the schlongs."

These days, thanks to Charlotte—as well as Bez and Johnathan, who'd jointly taken charge of the ever-growing catering branch of his bakery a few years back—he could sleep way later in the morning, work shorter hours, and take weekends completely off. And since Molly had adjusted her in-studio time to suit his less flexible schedule, that meant they could take a walk around Historic Harlot's Bay almost every afternoon.

Her blood pressure might be okay now, and her insomnia might've disappeared almost a decade ago, but he wouldn't give up his walks with her for anything in the entire goddamn world. Best time of his day, other than when they climbed into bed together.

Charlotte retrieved a stack of wax paper squares and began crafting very convincing cocks, every gesture deft and confident. "Got it. A cavalcade of penises, coming right up."

Seriously? *Penises, coming right up?* "You do that on purpose?"

Her dimple peeked out. "I have no idea what you mean."

"Bullshit," he told her, grinning as he peeled off his gloves.

Charlotte giggled, then added a squiggly vein to the side of a cock. "We're still on for tonight? My parents said they'd watch the kids, so Hector and I can definitely make it."

He threw out his beard net and gloves, then tossed his apron onto the laundry pile. "Yep."

Later that evening, everyone in their friend group had committed to hanging out together. After he and Molly had their daily walk and grabbed dinner at Doxy Diner with Lise and her husband, they'd all meet Charlotte, Hector, Matthew, Athena, Bez, Johnathan, and various Nasty Wenches at the Historic Harlot's Bay ticket office. Sylvia would no doubt be there as well, camera tucked safely in the pocket of her motorized wheelchair, for the paper's coverage of the historic area's brand-new, Lise-scripted, after-hours tour.

Janel would probably stroll over during one of her breaks too and hassle them about attending the upcoming thirty-year reunion, but whatever. Woman was a good friend to Molly and paid through the nose for the bakery's catering services, so he could deal.

Plus, he had some damn fond memories of the twenty-year reunion. Couldn't begrudge Janel's desire to stage a repeat banger of an event. And at least Molly's asshole ex wouldn't show up this go-round. Once she'd sold her old home to one of her LA friends, the prick had stopped yapping and started leaving her the hell alone, at long fucking last.

Truth be told? Janel didn't even need to convince Karl. He already knew he'd stuff himself into a rental tux, help Molly shop for another shit-hot suit of her own, and drag them both to that stupid gym again. Kind of a tradition at this point. Also: slow-dancing together to the *Titanic* soundtrack?

Everything he'd dreamed it'd be as a teenager.

No, *better*. Because Molly wasn't leaving town for college in a few weeks. Their fears and insecurities about each other were long gone. They had no curfews, no separate houses. They were going home together, just the two of them, that night and every damn night.

And she *loved* him. Told him so all the time.

He was the luckiest motherfucker on this goddamn planet.

"Won't Matthew absolutely hate Lise's ghost tour?" Charlotte glanced up from a particularly turgid dick. "I thought scary stuff bothered him."

Karl shook his head and arrowed toward the bathroom. "He'll wear headphones and stay outside."

Cling to his wife too, but Athena didn't mind that. Karl had caught her copping a feel of his best friend more times than he cared to remember.

"If it bothers him, why doesn't he stay home?"

"Super-glued to Athena." It'd be nauseating, if Karl weren't the same way with Molly. "Be right back. If Molly gets here early, tell her to sit her ass down and stop trying to help out front."

Charlotte saluted him as he shut the bathroom door.

By the time he finished washing up and changing into cleaner clothes, Molly was waiting on a stool in the back, admiring buttercream dicks and telling Charlotte all about the latest work project with Sadie-slash-Lise.

"In the book I'm narrating now, *Honk of Desire*, the guy's a duck shifter." When Charlotte's eyebrows rose, Molly lifted a hand. "I know, I know. Technically, I'm not sure a corkscrew-shaped penis would actually work that well in a human woman's vagina, but Sadie's fictional dick is *prehensile*, and it *vibrates*. Also, you would not *believe* what that duck-man can do with his bill and a few stray feathers. When he says he's *going down* on her, he means that in at least two different ways."

Charlotte's piping paused. "Wow. That's . . . *wow*."

"Exactly." Molly nodded and leaned in closer, lowering her voice. "By the way, try saying the word *beak-gasm* without laughing. Go ahead. I'll wait while you experience my professional travails for yourself."

While Charlotte was still giggling helplessly, Karl glared at his inattentive wife. "Stop corrupting Charlotte and start corrupting *me*, woman."

She promptly hopped off her stool and headed in his direction. "Don't mind if I do."

"Fucking *finally*," he muttered, and wrapped his arms around her.

Despite all her strength, her body was softer than ever—as was his—and he couldn't get enough. Even after their brief kiss, he didn't let go. Just buried his face in her neck and breathed in her familiar scent. Lavender—because he did all the laundry, and he enjoyed Provençal shit—and that woodsy body wash she preferred. The combination settled something inside him. Made him feel warm and *loved*, every time he smelled it.

Her hands gently rubbed his lower back, where he was aching most. Probably needed to make an appointment with his doctor about that, like she kept insisting. Not now, though.

It was time for his second-favorite part of the day.

He raised his head, content. "You good to go, Charlotte?"

"I'm good." She was smiling sweetly at them both, pastry bag at the ready. "Hector and I will meet you at the ticket booth later tonight. Have fun in the meantime, you two. But not so much fun that Sylvia catches you rounding second base again, okay?"

"No promises." After lifting a hand in farewell, he steered Molly toward the rear exit. "Ready for our walk?"

Her hip bumped his, a playful nudge. "Definitely."

Once she'd waved goodbye to Charlotte too, they stepped outside into the dazzling late-September afternoon. As usual, Molly paused to dig through her messenger bag, then handed over his set of shades and donned her own. When he checked her feet, she was wearing her comfy sneakers with the decent traction. His Crocs were bright pink—Brooklyn had picked them out the last time he and Molly babysat Charlotte's kids—and supportive as hell.

They were set.

Bending down, he rested his lips against the sun-heated crown of her head. "Wanna visit the snapdragons in the Mayor's Mansion garden today?"

"The foxgloves should be in bloom too." She tipped her face upward, a silent request they both understood. He promptly, gladly gave her another kiss—this one slower and with more tongue, since they were alone. "Let's do it."

As they walked in comfortable silence down the town's cobblestone streets, she swung their hands slightly. Peered through her sunglasses at all the businesses and homes surrounding them on both sides. Greeted friends and acquaintances.

And once the street had mostly emptied, she quietly told Karl, "I got another email from my dad today."

He kept his expression as blank as possible. "Okay."

Whatever she did in response, he'd support her. Didn't mean he liked her father. The asshole had recently started contacting her again, yeah, but hadn't ever apologized for lying or leaving his first wife and daughter in the dust.

Molly's perspective? Hard to forgive someone who didn't acknowledge he'd done wrong.

Karl's perspective? Even harder to forgive anyone—literally any fucker on this planet—who'd hurt Molly.

"Gonna write back?" he asked neutrally.

She hesitated. "I'm not sure yet."

"You do, great." He lifted a shoulder. "You don't, it's his loss. Not yours."

She nodded in acknowledgment. "I agree. Either way, it'll be fine."

When she didn't say more, he let the topic drop. Hand in hand, they kept walking until they'd reached the outskirts of Historic Harlot's Bay. Near the living museum's main ticket office, though, she slowed almost to a stop.

"Molly?" He studied her round, pretty face. "Everything okay?"

"I just realized . . ." She swept her left arm. "I know almost everyone on these streets. I know who lives in these houses. I've bought things at all these local stores. I've never, ever been this familiar with any place I've ever lived. Even Los Angeles."

Since she didn't sound upset about that, he relaxed. "Smaller town. Three years here as a kid, ten years as an adult. Makes sense."

"Yeah. It does. But . . ." When she halted entirely, he did too. "Here's the thing, Karl. I know this place inside and out, and I love it here. I truly do. And I love our circle of friends. But without you, even that wouldn't be enough to make Harlot's Bay my home."

Her lips trembled slightly. Which was alarming as hell, because Molly didn't cry. Not if he could damn well help it.

"Hold up, baby." He cupped her cheek with his free hand. "What—"

"Without you . . ." Her fingers tightened on his, even as she talked over him. "Without you, I wouldn't have a home, no matter where I went or how long I stayed. Without you, I *didn't* have a home. Even when I was living in my grandparents' house. Even after twenty years in Los Angeles. You gave that to me, Karl. You're *giving* it to me, every day we're together."

Shit, now he was getting blurry-eyed too. "Every day for the rest of our lives, Molly. Swear it on my fucking grave."

"Not necessary." She shook her head. "I believe you. What you tell me, I always believe."

That simple statement somehow made him feel like an all-powerful god, even as it weakened his stupid aging knees. In fervent gratitude for everything she was, he pressed a kiss to her temple, where she'd gotten a few silver hairs lately.

"Anyway, my point is that you're my home, Karl. Just you. I should have thanked you for that before, but at least I'm doing it now." Her mouth quirked. "And I know it's not what you meant, but—knowing you, yes, you will *definitely* swear on your grave. At least one *fuck*, and maybe a *shit* or two. Your headstone will need to be freaking *redacted*."

He laughed. Knuckled away the wetness escaping under his sunglasses' frames.

"I love you." She got up on tiptoe to claim one more quick kiss. "So much."

His wife calmly started walking again. As if she hadn't just knocked his world out from under him in the most gorgeous way possible, for the billionth time in the last decade.

Her hair gleamed copper and silver. Her lips were soft with her smile and his kisses.

Looking at her was like staring at a goddamn supernova. Even with his shades on.

Using their entwined hands to hitch her closer, he told her, "Love you more."

Then, hip to hip, they walked to see the flowers waiting for them in the autumn sun.

Acknowledgments

Some stories spring from my brain and my keyboard almost fully formed, demanding time and effort but not much struggle in their writing. Others . . . well, they're more like this one, which required a *lot* of extra care and support to gel into a final, satisfying shape. Luckily, I couldn't have asked for more or better support while I was grappling with my draft of *Second Chance Romance*, and I want to make sure I acknowledge everyone who assisted me along the way and helped make my book shine.

As always, my family offered me unending love as I worked, and their patience and pride in me bring joy to every day of my life. I love you right back, more than I can say.

I also owe enormous gratitude to my dear friend Emma Barry, who read at least two iterations of this story and gave her usual brilliant feedback in response. Liza Street, another wonderful friend, read my draft too and couldn't have been more helpful or kind in her commentary. Thank you to both of you—and thank you to everyone who kept me company during the many months I wrote this book!

Sarah Younger, my stalwart, indefatigable agent, encouraged me the whole way and made sure I had the time and space I needed to write this story. I appreciate and adore her so very much.

I am very grateful to have Joy Nash as my uber-talented audio-book narrator once more. And yet again, Leni Kauffman created the most tender, lovely cover illustration imaginable for my story. I am incredibly lucky to work with her, and I know it. She's *amazing*.

At Avon, Shannon Plackis and Tessa Woodward simply couldn't have been more patient with my slow, halting progress on the manuscript. And once I finally got the story to her, Shannon gave me such thoughtful, incisive feedback! I'm so very grateful for her guidance and support.

I also want to acknowledge and express my gratitude to everyone else at Avon who shepherded my book from its inception to its final printing, and this is my best attempt at doing so:

Shannon Plackis **Editor**
Yeon Kim **Art Director**
Diahann Sturge-Campbell **Designer**
TK **Senior Marketer**
Beatrice Jason **Marketing Director**
Hannah Dirgins **Publicist**
Rachel Weinick **Production Editor**
Brittani DiMare **Production Editorial Manager**
Marie Rossi **Production Manager**
Hope Ellis **Managing Editor**
Kim Lewis **Copyeditor**
TK **Audio Producer**
Liate Stehlik **Publisher**
TK **Associate Publisher**
TK **Proofreader**

Thank you, thank you, *thank you* to all of you!

And finally, to my readers: I owe you the world. Thank you for trusting me with your time and letting me share a small corner of my heart with you. ♥

About the Author

Olivia Dade grew up an undeniable nerd, prone to ignoring the world around her as she read any book she could find. Her favorites, though, were always, always romances. As an adult, she earned an MA in American history and worked in a variety of jobs that required the donning of actual pants: Colonial Williamsburg interpreter, high school teacher, academic tutor, and (of course) librarian. Now, however, she has finally achieved her lifelong goal of wearing pajamas all day as a hermit-like writer and enthusiastic hag. She currently lives outside Stockholm with her delightful family and their ever-burgeoning collection of books.